Lerje

THE KILLING
OF RICHARD THE THIRD

THE KILLING OF
RICHARD THE THIRD

Robert Farrington

Charles Scribner's Sons,
New York

FOR
ROSALIND JUNE

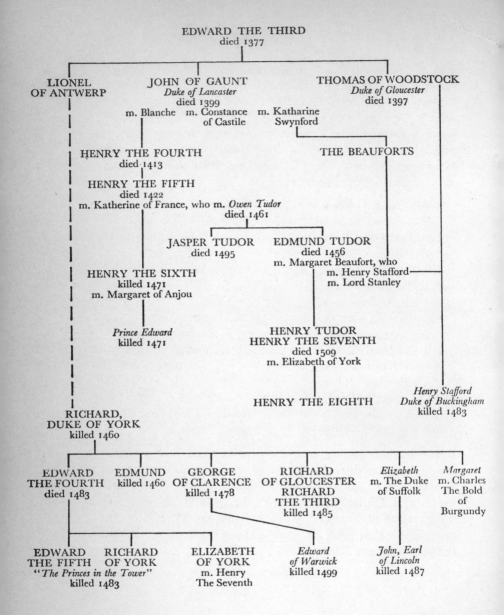

EDWARD THE THIRD
died 1377

LIONEL
OF ANTWERP

JOHN OF GAUNT
Duke of Lancaster
died 1399
m. Blanche m. Constance m. Katharine
of Castile Swynford

THOMAS OF WOODSTOCK
Duke of Gloucester
died 1397

HENRY THE FOURTH
died 1413

THE BEAUFORTS

HENRY THE FIFTH
died 1422
m. Katherine of France, who m. *Owen Tudor*
died 1461

JASPER TUDOR
died 1495

EDMUND TUDOR
died 1456
m. Margaret Beaufort, who
m. Henry Stafford
m. Lord Stanley

HENRY THE SIXTH
killed 1471
m. Margaret of Anjou

Prince Edward
killed 1471

HENRY TUDOR
HENRY THE SEVENTH
died 1509
m. Elizabeth of York

HENRY THE EIGHTH

*Henry Stafford
Duke of Buckingham*
killed 1483

RICHARD,
DUKE OF YORK
killed 1460

EDWARD
THE FOURTH
died 1483

EDMUND
killed 1460

GEORGE
OF CLARENCE
killed 1478

RICHARD
OF GLOUCESTER
RICHARD
THE THIRD
killed 1485

Elizabeth
m. The Duke
of Suffolk

Margaret
m. Charles
The Bold
of
Burgundy

EDWARD
THE FIFTH
"The Princes in the Tower"
killed 1483

RICHARD
OF YORK

ELIZABETH
OF YORK
m. Henry
The Seventh

*Edward
of Warwick*
killed 1499

*John, Earl
of Lincoln*
killed 1487

NOTE TO THE READER

Henry Morane is not mentioned in any of the histories of
King Richard's reign, but the accuracy of his story may
be judged by his description of the more important events
which are known to have taken place, and of the more
notable personalities who were involved in them. There
are other characters in the story whose names have not
been recorded before, and it may be helpful to list them as
they appear in the narrative:

John Osgood—clerk to the Bishop of Bath and Wells.
Alice—mistress of Sir William Stanley.
Lambskin & Rougemain—retainers of Sir William
    Stanley.
Matilda—who lived not far from the Wall Brook.
Ned Bennett—shipmaster of Lyme.
Joseph Anderson—Captain of Archers.
Geoffrey de Vannes—knight of Brittany.
Jean Toussaint—Seneschal to the Duke of Brittany.
Ali—nephew of a horse-trader near London Bridge.
Alan—retainer of Lord Lovell.
Nick Benson—Thames boatman.
Agnes—wife of John Kendall.
The Coombe family—of Kingston-upon-Thames.
John Tanner—clerk to Christopher Urswick.

But even these people, whose existence cannot be proved,
should not be disregarded by students of history. It is
known, for example, that both the Bishop of Bath and
Wells and Christopher Urswick had clerks, indeed the
functions of their offices necessitated them. And it is not
improbable that John Kendall had a wife, and even less so
that Sir William Stanley had a mistress.

WITH A lighted taper in one hand and a knob of warm sealing-wax in the other I was having difficulty in crossing the room. John Kendall was waiting to seal his correspondence, and that gave me an additional reason for speed. I saw that there were fewer people by the window, where Queen Elizabeth Woodville was talking to Jane Shore.

They were on good terms, those two, the Queen and the royal mistress, although they rarely lost the opportunity of sinking their barbs into each other. This time, as I approached, I heard the Queen telling Jane that she looked pale and drawn, and to take care, for her husband liked his women lusty and well-found. Jane, not to be outdone, replied that it was due to King Edward's attentions, and his lack of consideration for her small frame under his huge and increasing weight.

"Ah! Master Morane!" she called. "Do you not agree that the King is running to fat?"

It was a troublesome question, for she had not been fond of me since the day I had refused her blandishments. My reluctance had been due to no more than prudence, for the wise man does not meddle with the mistress of one of higher station, and only a fool when she is the King's.

I stopped, bowed slightly to Elizabeth Woodville, and cursed Jane Shore under my breath.

"He is a giant, as we all know," I agreed. "But I have not yet heard his horse complain of carrying him when he wears eighty pounds of plate. Now, if he were to mount you in full armour . . ."

A great bellow of laughter came from behind me, and a heavy hand lay down on my shoulder, spinning me round. It was King Edward himself.

"By God!" he guffawed. "The clatter would be deafening!"

He looked down at me, frantically trying to keep the taper aloft, and laughed again. "Morane," he said, "for a scrivener you have a ready wit. I will hear more of it. Meanwhile take your taper to my Secretary before it melts away, and he melts with impatience." As I turned to go, he added,

"And tell him to raise your salary by eight pence every Friday."

It was my turn to wink at Jane Shore. But she was biting her lip, for even the Queen was smiling.

John Kendall shifted his fat buttocks on the wooden seat and glared at me. "You were fortunate," he said. "If the King had not overheard you there would have been no joke of it. If I know the Shore woman she would certainly have struck you." He pointed a stubby forefinger at me. "And then you would have been in trouble, my friend."

"The Queen was there. She . . ."

"The Queen!" he snorted. "Do you think she would have taken your part if they had been alone? She and Jane Shore are closer than thieves. Why, she would have laughed to see you taken away by the guards, and have come to see you strapped and beaten, and probably your tongue cut out . . ." He stopped, eyeing me reproachfully. He had no liking for the Queen. In fact there were very few in whom she inspired any affection at all.

Yet Queen Elizabeth Woodville was a beautiful woman. Tall, dark haired, and pale as a winter dawn, I would not have been loth to bed her myself if the King had not seen her first. But she had a large family, sisters, brothers, uncles and the rest, who had swarmed into Court like locusts over a tree, eating up titles like the leaves upon it. Six of the girls had been married into noble houses, and even a hardened, cynical Court had been appalled when John Woodville, barely eighteen years of age, had married the wealthy dowager Duchess of Norfolk, who was past eighty. Elizabeth herself had been no virgin either, having children by a previous husband. But her price for being bedded by Edward had been marriage, no less, and the monarch, bemused with lust, had paid it, the nuptials being carried out secretly with the connivance of his bosom friend and whoring companion, Lord Hastings.

Richard of Gloucester, when he heard of the marriage, had exploded with fury, but in the end his loyalty had overcome his rage against the Woodvilles, and what might have been a royal quarrel came to nothing. It was as well, for Edward, in spite of his affability, had steel inside, and would not have tolerated opposition from anyone, not even from his favourite brother. The outburst had not endeared Richard to Elizabeth Woodville, of course, but she was able to do little because of Edward's affection for him, and in any case he was away much of the time at his northern fastness of Middleham, or fighting the Scots.

With the other brother, George of Clarence, it had been a different story. Where Richard was outspoken and unsubtle Clarence had been sly-tongued and devious, and his earlier attempts at treachery, while forgiven by Edward, had not been overlooked by the Woodvilles. He had been their first target.

"Aye," I said to John Kendall. "I do not forget what happened to Clarence. Condemned for slander against the King's person. Against his own brother! And no one ever knew what the slander was. The Queen and the rest of them arranged that . . ."

"Yes, yes," he said quickly. "But the slander was a lesser charge."

"It is in fact what killed him. He had committed acts of treason before and had always been forgiven. But this time the slander was added and . . ."

"I know," John Kendall agreed. "But it is a matter best not re-opened, for whatever the slander was it must have been grave enough to send him to the block."

"Which he never reached."

"Only because, as you know as well as everyone else, he was so drunk with Malmsey that he fell into the Tower vat."

"Fell? Or was pushed? And on the very night before his execution?"

"Perhaps so. Perhaps to save him, the King's brother, from the ignominy of the block."

"Or to prevent him from repeating the slander publicly from the scaffold? And before a priest could shrive him?"

John Kendall waved an impatient hand. "What does it matter today?" He looked up at me. "But there was a priest. Two of them, in fact. Condemned for the same slander. If Clarence was murdered, as you assert, then he could have been shrived by his fellow prisoners. And one of them was the Bishop of Bath and Wells, no less. He was imprisoned for six months, if I remember, and then released on payment of an enormous fine, ten thousand marks or so . . ." he smiled "which he complained he could ill-afford and would have to borrow from the Florentines."

"Ten thousand marks!" I whistled. "Even a bishop would be hard put to it to find so much money."

"Not that one! The old skinflint has untold wealth stored away. I heard that he was in two minds whether to part with his money or his freedom. Even now they say he is not sure if he made the right decision." He chuckled. "He worships angels, but those of golden coin more than those that are holy."

I smiled. I knew that John Kendall had little liking for the priesthood. "And the other one?" I asked him.

"The other one? Oh, the other cleric. Merely the bishop's clerk." He shrugged. "I never heard of his release, so he probably lies in a dungeon somewhere. King Edward is not one for cutting off the head of a priest."

"The Bishop of Bath and Wells? That is Robert Stillington?"

"The same. The old man who fingers the inside of his nose during the meetings of the Council."

"Then he could tell us what the slander was."

"Great God!" John Kendall sat up suddenly. "You would not be so mad as to think of questioning him? If he has not spoken of it these five years it is because he does not dare. In any case he would not have been released without taking an oath to keep silent. What do you think would happen to you if you questioned him?" He stopped and eyed me. "And what interests you in this all of a sudden?"

"No more than a curious mind," I said airily. "Since the subject has been raised."

"And who raised it, eh?" The finger pointed at me again. "I will hear no more of this, you understand? The curiosity of your mind is of great use to me, Henry Morane, but not when it lies in a head that is skewered to a stake."

"Injustice may have been done him by the Woodvilles. And even if he does tear at his nose he is a likeable old man." I grinned at him. "Which I hope to be one day."

"If you live so long!" John Kendall snorted. "And one way to ensure against that is to meddle in this old affair." He muttered something to himself, picked up his pen, put the end of the feather inside his nostril, saw me watching and took it away quickly. "Ah!" he murmured. "God knows what trouble would ensue!"

"Trouble?" I said. "How can we be sure, if we don't know what the slander was?"

He gave a long and exasperated sigh. "A slander that led to the King's own brother being condemned could even lead to the wars beginning all over again. Clarence flirted with Lancaster, as you well know, and there may be some connexion. And in spite of twelve years of peace and good government people still remember the twenty years of war and lawlessness that preceded them. You may not remember it, my friend, but older people do. Ah, no!" he cried. "God forbid another civil war."

"There is little chance of that now, with two sons fathered by King Edward. And maybe more, if Jane Shore does not sap all his strength. But at least the Yorkist succession is assured . . ." I stopped. "Ah! You mean that the Lancastrians may rally to the Welsh lad in Brittany?"

"Henry Tudor?" He made a noise that sounded like "Pifft!" and added, "He is of no account. Although not a lad any more." He counted on his fingers. "He will be twenty-six by now. A man of twenty-six who has never seen a battle, nor even been seen in England since he was a little boy, living in miserable state in Brittany on the bounty of Duke Francis! You think they would rally to him?" He saw my expression. "Henry Morane, you are pulling my legs!"

"Pulling your legs? God forbid," I said devoutly. "Since legs are only pulled to help strangle a poor wretch on the gallows to end his misery."

John Kendall put his pen down on the table and began to laugh quietly. "Well, well!" he said after a few moments. "There you stand, Henry Morane, my privy clerk, with one ear always in the Court, and yet you have not heard that expression!" He went on chuckling, the fatness of his face billowing round his chin. "I would not have thought it possible! And even the King used it the other day." When he had finished enjoying himself at my expense, he added, "It means to make jest of someone."

"It does, does it? Then in view of what we have been discussing it is not an expression I care to use. It would be as if I were asking the Devil to intervene."

John Kendall crossed himself quickly. "Yes, Master Morane," he agreed, "it might be. And now I will have your assurance that you will not meddle in this long-dead affair of Clarence."

It was the voice of authority. I held up my hand. "You

13

have it, sir. For as long as Queen Elizabeth sits the throne."

He gave me a sharp look at that, then nodded, apparently satisfied.

Three weeks later, on the ninth of April 1483, King Edward the Fourth died unexpectedly after a fit.

THE whole country was stunned. It was as if a banquet table, loaded with meats and confections, had suddenly been overset, and everyone stood undecided as to how to go about picking up the pieces. The new king would be a mere boy of twelve. It would be the third royal minority within a hundred years. The first two had brought civil war and the collapse of government. Was the same to happen all over again?

Richard of Gloucester was far away in the north country. His nephew, the new King, was at Ludlow in the care of another uncle, Lord Rivers, detested brother of the Queen. Hastings, who had been at Edward's bedside, swore that his last wish had been that his brother, Richard, should be Lord Protector until the boy came of age. Last wish or no, we all knew it was the dead King's desire, and John Kendall wasted no time in sending a message to Richard to that effect. The letter was carried by the new system of posts which Richard himself had instituted, and reached him within the astonishing time of four days.

Soon afterwards the Duke of Buckingham sent Richard another, more ominous message from Wales: Lord Rivers was on his way to London with the boy, escorted by two thousand men. The Woodvilles were out to set up a regency of their own.

Richard marched south straightaway, summoning Buckingham to join him. They met at Northampton, the latter being dismayed to find Richard with only six hundred men, all unarmed, and all in mourning black. Yet when they caught up with Lord Rivers and his friends Richard, dark-browed with fury, strode right through the armed escort and arrested them on the spot. It was all done before the surprised Woodvilles could find time to think of offering resistance, and within the hour Richard and Buckingham were themselves taking the young King to London, where he was lodged in the style that befitted him in the Royal Apartments of the Tower to await his coronation. The boldness of Richard's action had prevented bloodshed, at any rate among the soldiery. For that which subsequently came from the heads of Lord Rivers and his associates was regretted by no one.

Elizabeth, now dowager Queen, seeing the loss of the Woodville cause and fearing for her own safety, gathered up her other son and her daughters and fled for sanctuary in West Minster. No entreaties nor promises by anyone could induce her to come out, and she set up house there, even having part of the abbey wall knocked down to let in her furniture.

Jane Shore must have been privy to the Woodville plot too, for she was not seen for several weeks. Then I heard that she had taken up with the Marquess of Dorset, one of Elizabeth Woodville's earlier sons, but on that flat-faced worthy's flight to Brittany she had stayed in England. Soon afterwards she appeared again in the care of Lord Hastings, a new Hastings, more serious of mien and better groomed, his unaccustomed black clothes accentuating the taut lines of lechery on his face.

These events had been of direct concern to me, for I wondered if I should retain my appointment under the new regime. But John Kendall continued as Secretary to the Lord Protector, and so I remained with him as his privy clerk. All was well. At least we thought it so until secret correspondence was intercepted between Hastings and the Woodvilles who had fled to Brittany.

Hastings of all people, one would have thought, as the best friend of the late king, would have remained faithful to his brother and to his sons, but once the Woodville influence had been removed the troubles attendant upon a royal minority began again. Ambition and greed gripped the nobility, and Hastings was the first to feel their bite. He used as courier one Sir William Catesby, which was unfortunate for him, as Catesby was our man.

The correspondence disclosed that Hastings was passing messages to and from the Queen Dowager in sanctuary, but what perplexed John Kendall was that the liaison was taking place at all as Hastings was known to be an enemy of the Woodvilles.

"Treason makes strange bedfellows," I told him. "It must be due to Buckingham."

"Buckingham?"

"Aye. The Duke has taken the place of chief counsellor to

the Lord Protector, which Hastings would expect as of right. He is, after all, Lord Chamberlain, and was closest companion of the dead King, yet Buckingham has more call on Dickon's loyalty after the affair at Northampton."

John Kendall eyed me and then nodded. "It could be so," he agreed. "It could be so. Yet if Hastings is sending letters to and from the Dowager Queen in Westminster, who is carrying them?"

He saw my face, and smiled. "Ah, yes! Of course!"

It happened, then, that on the next day on one of her visits to West Minster Jane Shore was waylaid by thieves. She laid a complaint to the Justices, but the miscreants were never discovered. One of them told me afterwards that her main cause of grievance was that they had not raped her. This was true, without a doubt, for very soon afterwards she visited an astrologer to discover whether her charms were about to fade. I had no need to threaten the man to divulge this information as he admitted it freely, adding with a knowing smile that he had been able to assure her that her fears were groundless, and proving it to his satisfaction, and hers, during the ensuing half hour.

No letters had been discovered on Jane Shore, however, but John Kendall suggested that she might also be visiting sanctuary secretly after dark. He was right, for she was arrested one evening and a letter from Elizabeth Woodville was found on her.

Hastings went to the block right quickly, almost too quickly, for he went without trial. But then Dickon had always been impetuous. The other three implicated in the plot were dealt with more leniently, though. John Morton, the silver-tongued Bishop of Ely, was sent for imprisonment in Buckingham's castle at Brecon; Rotherham, Archbishop of York and Lord Chancellor, was only removed from the latter office, and Lord Stanley was locked up for less than a week. His case was no more than one of suspicion, however, as he had recently married the widowed mother of Henry Tudor.

It was with Jane Shore that Richard was most incensed. When King Edward had been alive she had been foolish enough to bait him on his few appearances at Court. The baiting had taken the form of teasing him as being the country bumpkin, and Dickon had not forgotten it. Edward had laughed, thinking the banter good-humoured, for both

17

of them were close to him, but there had been spite in Jane's talk, and it seemed to me that Dickon was another on whom her charms had not prevailed. But then she should have known that Dickon's loyalty to his brother was absolute, even to his whores. And now Jane would have to suffer.

She was not charged with treason, Dickon would baulk at the execution of such a sentence upon a woman, but with being a whore. For that she was condemned to do penance as a harlot and then be confined in Ludgate prison.

The penance was carried out by the Cross in Saint Paul's churchyard, and most of London turned out to watch. It was not often that a royal strumpet was part of the show.

With a long procession of priests and holy clerks chanting monotonously, Jane Shore led the single line of whores who came next. Bareheaded, with her brown hair now falling lank upon the kirtle over her shoulders, and carrying a lighted taper in one hand, she picked her way carefully over the rough cobbles. Unlike the others, who were used to being unshod, her feet were already bloodied. As the kirtle was the only garment she wore her allurements were displayed for all to see, and many a cheer was raised. Ribald comments were flung at her, and one bold fellow broke past the City Archers that posted the route and was arrested for his pains. That set the crowd laughing even more and wishing him the good fortune of sharing the same cell with her in Ludgate. But a groan went up when the archers clubbed him senseless, followed by howls of execration as he was dragged away.

Jane Shore ignored it all, or seemed to. With her head down, inspecting the stones she walked on, she moved forward slowly, a deep blush spreading over her face and stomach. She was indeed a beauty, and when she had passed I turned away with a slight pang of regret for the charms I had forgone.

Two mornings afterwards Richard of Gloucester himself came into our office. His normally pale and serious face was eased into a thin smile as he handed his Secretary a letter. John Kendall, his portly form nearly knocking over the trestle as he struggled to his feet, came round to take the parchment. He read it, glanced at Dickon, and then beckoned me over. It was a formal request from the Solicitor-General to marry Jane Shore. I nearly burst into laughter, but John Kendall was outraged.

"My Lord!" he protested. "Mistress Shore! Why, the woman was plotting with Lord Hastings! Surely Thomas Lynom knows that?"

Richard nodded a little. "Of course he knows it, Master Kendall. And he will soon learn that I disapprove of my Solicitor marrying a whore . . . ." He paused and took a few thoughtful paces across the tiles. "Yet, upon consideration, it may be no bad thing. I do not have any great desire to keep Mistress Shore under restraint now that her penance has been so successful . . . ." His dark eyes turned and rested on me for a moment. "And, although Lynom was Solicitor to my late brother too, his aversion to the Queen Dowager is well known. Mistress Shore can pay for her security in marriage by keeping away from trouble in that direction."

"She has a nose for it," John Kendall muttered.

"Aye," Dickon laughed a little. "Even in Ludgate Prison. And now that Lord Hastings has departed the Marquess of Dorset may have thoughts of her again." He sighed. "Write to Tom Lynom," he directed, "and say that I disapprove of the contract, but, in view of the high office which he holds, and of my certainty that he will adhere to it for the good of the realm, I will agree in spite of my reluctance."

I smiled as I wrote it down. Dickon was astute. For Tom Lynom was not wealthy enough to risk the office he held. Neither was he of the stuff from which Hastings had been made. Once his first ardour had thinned he would see to it that his wife's nose remained unsmirched.

John Kendall said something under his breath, bowed, and looked at me to see if I had noted it. But the Lord Protector was not done.

"There is another matter," he said, and John Kendall turned back quickly, coughing to hide his confusion.

"It is not of immediate importance," Richard said, "but a representation has been made to me by Robert Stillington, Bishop of Bath and Wells, for the release of one of his clerks imprisoned these six years without a charge being proved against him . . . ."

I drew in my breath quickly, and Richard's eyes swung to me again. This time they remained there for several moments. "I will have no man, especially a priest," he went on, "imprisoned without proper cause. Therefore," he turned back to John Kendall, "write an order for the release of one

John Osgood, former vicar of Greve in the county of Warwick."

He nodded at us and strode off through the doorway. I heard the sentry outside come clattering to attention.

John Kendall sat down and put a hand across his forehead. From under it two small eyes glared up at me. "John Osgood, eh? So that is his name?" The hand came down again and banged on the table. "And what devilry have you been at, Henry Morane? So that a bishop of the Holy Church can be persuaded to press for the release of a mere clerk?"

"Why," I said, "surely it is a Christian thing to do?"

"Not where you are concerned!" he roared. "What have you been up to?"

"Me, sir? Why, nothing. But I remember that you yourself told me that Robert Stillington has an over-fondness for money. Could it be that he is under the impression that if his clerk is released his own case might be heard again, and possibly the fine, or part of it, remitted?"

John Kendall sat back. "Oh? And how would he have gained that impression, I wonder?"

I shook my head. "I cannot think," I said.

"I can!" he snapped. "And don't try to persuade me that it was due to injustice being done, Henry Morane, or to your curious mind. I know you better than that!"

"I would not presume to," I told him.

He got up slowly and came towards me. "So it was for money? And what unholy bargain have you made?"

"Not unholy," I grinned. "It was, after all, with a bishop. I merely suggested a way to him in which his case might be heard again, and the fine possibly remitted."

"I see! And of course you would be recompensed?"

"Of course."

"How much?"

"It depends on the amount remitted."

"How much?" he roared.

I shrugged. "A small part, that is all. A tenth."

"A tenth part? Great God!" he exploded. "A tenth of ten thousand marks? And you call that a small part?"

I went out quickly, giving the sentry a huge wink as I passed.

THE release of John Osgood passed unnoticed. No one, not even John Kendall, seemed to have heard of him previously, and his case had long been forgotten. And when, hearing of his reinstatement as priest of his parish, he demanded an audience of the Lord Protector it was assumed he wanted no more than to express his gratitude in person. Thus it was that only Buckingham, Lord Lovell and Sir Richard Ratcliffe were present, apart from John Kendall and myself.

It had been raining all the morning and, as the wretched man had been brought by open boat from the Tower, he left a trail of water all along the corridor stones. Even by the time he reached the audience room it seemed not to have all drained off him, for little pools filled the indentures in the floor-tiles, sending a colony of tiny ants scurrying for safety.

I took him from the guards and, when they had closed the doorway, he ran suddenly forward shouting and insisting that he take an oath. I caught him and drew him back gently, putting an arm round him, and felt his prison-shrivelled shoulders under the filthy gown. The very stink of him foamed at my nostrils.

"An oath, reverend sir?" Richard said, his expression showing that the smell had reached him too. "What oath would you swear?"

"Sire!" I spoke up. "Let him first have food and wine to gather his strength."

"Aye," Richard agreed, his eyes twinkling, "and be bathed too."

I had him washed, gowned in a new robe, and poured enough wine into him to make his bladder begin to smart right soon. The Lord Protector would not want a long audience of this distraught creature. And when I took him back he rushed from me and stood in front of Dickon's chair with his arms across his chest.

"My Lord!" he shouted. "I demand to take an oath!"

"Concerning what?" Richard inquired mildly.

"It is ancient law that what is alleged to be slander is not so if it is true!"

"We are aware of that, my friend."

"Therefore I wish to swear an oath to that effect."

"You do?" Dark eyebrows went upwards. "But why? Do we have to disbelieve the word of a priest unless it is attended by an oath?"

John Osgood was taken aback. He stood and looked at the Lord Protector for several moments. In the end he spoke more quietly. "It was not believed before, my Lord. I was condemned as a liar. Without trial and without chance of attesting to the truth. I was . . ."

Dickon waved him to silence. "You may take an oath if you wish. But later. First tell us of your so-called slander . . ." he looked round at the others, who shook their heads ". . . because no one here knows of it."

"No one?" Osgood stood amazed. He stared at each of us in turn. "No one?" he repeated. Then, to Richard, "Not even you, my Lord?"

"Not even I." His tone was impatient. "Say on, man, and let us not waste time bringing holy relics to support oaths."

John Osgood took a deep breath. I heard his ribs creak with the unaccustomed effort.

"My Lord of Gloucester," he said after a moment, "your brother's marriage to the Lady Elizabeth Woodville, who calls herself Queen, was bigamous!"

"Jesu!" Richard exclaimed involuntarily, and the rest of us gasped. The priest drew his head back and thrust out his bony chin.

It was a long time before anyone spoke. Then Richard, his voice very quiet, said, "It is no wonder you were imprisoned, Master Osgood. It is a most grievous slander." His black eyes studied the man in front of him. "Unless you have proof."

"That I have, Sire. Upon my oath."

"Then let us hear it."

"The late King was already married to the Lady Eleanor Butler. This I know, my Lord. Because I married them."

No wonder he had been imprisoned! No oath of silence would have earned him freedom as it had Bishop Stillington. And no wonder the Woodvilles had used every means to keep the matter quiet. We stood there, watching the man, and a miasma of tenseness filled the room.

Then Richard spoke again. "And when was this?"

"Eighteen years ago, my Lord. It was on . . ."

"Eighteen years!" Richard exclaimed. He turned to John Kendal, but the latter shook his head.

"I was not in attendance upon your late brother then," he said. "At that time he would have been no more than twenty-two years old."

"Aye," Dickon reflected, "and I but twelve."

"In that case I would have been ten," Buckingham observed. He glanced at Lovell and Ratcliffe, and nodded. "We were all children."

Dickon was eyeing the priest suspiciously. "And who were the witnesses to this ceremony?"

"The lady's serving woman, my Lord. She was very old . . ." Richard grunted. "And also the Lord Hastings, as well as the King's own brother, George of Clarence."

And they were both dead. I shook my head as I considered it. Clarence would have been sixteen at the time, too young to have taken the matter seriously. To him it could only have been a jest, a frivolity to enable his brother to bed the lady. A short ceremony conducted in secrecy and great haste, and later forgotten—for a time, at least. Certainly Clarence had not mentioned it at the time of his first treachery, when he had temporarily defected to Warwick and the Lancastrians.

Yet Clarence had been sly. The story would not have had much importance after Warwick had deposed Edward. It would be better kept in case the business went wrong and Edward regained the throne. If he did, and the Woodvilles were restored to power, then Clarence would have a curb on their ambitions. That is what happened, of course, but Clarence found that the Queen was made of sterner stuff. His blackmail had failed. He had tried to publish the story and had been condemned for slander, the priest, his essential witness, being condemned too, although the latter, because of his holy office, had escaped the extreme penalty.

And then there was Robert Stillington, who also had been imprisoned. As Bishop of Bath and Wells, he must have tried to lend his weight to the tale. His friendship with Clarence, and their joint distaste for the Woodvilles, had been well known. He had connived in Clarence's treachery, of which the story of the previous marriage had been part. But, not being a direct witness, Edward had let him off with a fine and an oath never to speak of it.

Richard got up from his chair and stalked across to John Osgood. "Clarence and Hastings?" he repeated. "And the Lady Eleanor Butler? What does she have to say of this?"

The priest recoiled a step. "She took to Holy Orders, my Lord. At the Carmelite Convent at Norwich, where . . . where she lies buried."

"God and All the Saints!" Richard threw his hands in the air. "And no doubt the old serving-woman lies buried too?" Osgood nodded mutely. "And so all those who know of this marriage contract are dead?" The dark eyes glittered at the priest. "Except you, eh?"

"What of the Bishop of Bath and Wells?" It was Sir Richard Ratcliffe's thick Yorkshire voice. "He was condemned for slander too."

"Aye," Richard muttered, "we might hear what he has got to say." To John Kendall he said, "Where is he?"

The latter shook his head. "Until your Council meets again, Sire, I expect he will be . . ."

"My Lord!" I spoke up. "He is in West Minster, I am sure. At least if it was he I saw this morning stepping off a boat." I turned slowly to meet John Kendall's stare with a look of bland unconcern.

"Then have him brought here." Richard swung round to stalk back to his chair. "And have that crazy priest taken away."

As I took John Osgood by the arm Buckingham cleared his throat and stepped towards him. "You are prepared to swear to this?" he asked him.

"I am, my Lord!" The chin went up again. "I have already said so."

"Then I think he should," Buckingham said to Richard. "And before parliament too."

"What?" Richard exclaimed. "An oath to the event of which all the witnesses are dead? Sworn by a priest half-crazed after being six years in a dungeon?" He eyed Buckingham. "I will not have it! It is patently untrue. My brother would never have gone through such a contract."

"He did," Buckingham pointed out, "in the case of the Lady Elizabeth Woodville."

There was a long silence while they stared at each other. Henry Stafford, Duke of Buckingham, tall, with curling brown hair, thumbs tucked into his belt, stood looking down at Richard of Gloucester. He was the only one of us who would have dared to hold Richard's gaze like that, but then he, too, was of royal descent, being another sprig in the line of Edward the Third, said to have fathered more children than the French he killed at Crecy. Apart from that, though, Buckingham and Dickon were close friends.

"The story smacks of truth," Ratcliffe said in his forthright way, and Lovell nodded assent. "Otherwise your brother would have denied it right quickly, and Clarence . . ."

"Would have been condemned for slander, as in fact he was."

"But do we know whether he denied it or not?" Buckingham inquired airily. "Or do we care? Whether the tale was true or not—at that time—Clarence's mouth had to be stopped. At that time," he repeated significantly. "But today we know it to be true."

"Do we?" Richard said. "By the word of one man?" He pointed at John Osgood. "A prison-ridden priest!"

"Then let us hear what Bishop Stillington has to say."

Richard shrugged. "As you wish. We might as well have it all."

Robert Stillington, Bishop of Bath and Wells, came in slowly, his feet unsure of themselves under his long gown, his breath whistling through his rotten teeth like a kettle with a broken lid.

"Now, my Lord Bishop," Richard said without preamble, "what is this old wives' gossip of my brother's premarriage to the Lady Eleanor Butler?"

Stillington halted abruptly, swaying. He was well fortified for the interview, the Malmsey on his breath preceding him like a noxious cloud.

"Ah, yes, Sire!" he replied, shaking his head carefully. "The daughter of the Earl of Shrewsbury. He will not like it."

"Whether he likes it or not I will hear it," Richard said, controlling his temper.

"That was the oath I took for your brother," the Bishop said, keeping his eyes away from me. "Not to disclose it." He took a deep breath, and then did glance at me. "But as it seems to have been disclosed already I am no doubt free of my oath."

"I am glad to hear it," Richard said ironically. "Then

perhaps you will, in your own good time, tell us whether it is true that my brother was already wed when he contracted marriage with the Lady Elizabeth Woodville."

The Bishop hesitated. "That is what I was told," he admitted after a while.

"Told? Great God!" Richard exclaimed. "Only told! And who by?"

"Your lamented brother, my Lord. The Duke of Clarence. He was present at the ceremony, he said."

"You would swear to this?" Buckingham asked Stillington.

"He is so drunk he would swear to anything," Richard muttered.

"Then we'll keep him that way," Ratcliffe chuckled, and Richard glared at him.

"You would swear to this before parliament?" Buckingham persisted.

Stillington wiped the back of his hand across his face. He was an old man, sixty years or more and, like those who have never enjoyed the fullness of life, wished to cling to it for ever. He mumbled, "I could only swear to what Clarence told me."

"You could . . ." Lovell spoke slowly ". . . also swear that you took an oath not to discuss the matter during King Edward's lifetime." He turned to Richard. "That in itself would show how it weighed on the King's mind. If it had not been true he would have laughed it away." To Stillington he said, "It is well known that you took an oath as the condition of your release."

"And a fine too . . ." Stillington started to say when Dickon cut him short.

"Bah!" he said. "I have heard enough of this nonsense. Take them both away and let me hear no more of it. Give the priest clothes and money and let him go."

Lovell shook his head. "The priest cannot go free, Dickon. He is crazed enough to go on talking about it. He must go back to prison."

Richard hesitated. "I will not have him locked away again," he said. "Let him swear his oath not to speak of it."

"I would prefer to hear him swear otherwise," Buckingham said. "And before parliament." He eyed Richard. "And as one of your Council I have a mind to demand it."

"Demand it?" Richard got up. "Demand it, you say?"

26

"As Lord Protector of the Realm," Buckingham replied evenly, "it is proper that you should disclose everything that pertains to its good."

"Pertains to its good?" Richard snarled. "And what good would it do to assert that my brother's marriage to the Lady Elizabeth Woodville was bigamous, so that their children—my nephews—are bastards? Am I not their protector too?"

John Kendall gave a loud sigh. "Exactly, my Lord! Exactly! And the boy King . . ."

"God in Heaven, master Secretary!" Richard shouted. "What does that mean? I will not listen . . . !"

"Neither will I, my Lord of Gloucester," the priest beside me said suddenly, taking Richard quite aback, so that he stopped, his face showing red at the interruption.

But the priest was unperturbed. "I will not stay out of prison," he went on, "if it means taking an oath to keep their bastardy secret."

"You will not, eh?" Richard said menacingly. "Or perhaps you would rather hang?"

"Even that," John Osgood replied with dignity.

Richard studied him carefully, then gave a wintry smile. "You are a brave man, sir," he said, "for a priest . . ." And I heard John Kendall chuckle. "And so you shall have your chance. You may swear your oath before parliament." He swung away. "And God help you if you are not believed."

The silence that followed was only relieved by Buckingham letting out his breath in a long sigh.

The oath was believed. Perhaps it was because of the added weight attached to it by the declaration of the Bishop of Bath and Wells, which the old man in the end decided to make. Perhaps he was encouraged by the example of his clerk, or perhaps there may have been other persuasions. Whatever the reasons, the oath was solemnly recorded as being accepted and the children of Edward the Fourth were proclaimed bastards. The royal minority was ended. But there was no king.

Buckingham and the Council, fearful lest the Lancastrians might use the occasion to further the claim of Henry Tudor from Brittany, passed a resolution that, as Richard was next in succession, he should be called upon to take the crown. He, Lovell and others went to Richard with the offer. John

Kendall told me that Dickon accepted with an expression far removed from that which might be expected on a man about to take the highest office in the land. The coronation duly took place, although two months later than originally planned, with Richard kneeling in the place of his nephew, and the two sons of Edward the Fourth ceased to have any further importance. At least that is what we all thought until they disappeared.

But it did not seem a great matter. John Kendall and I both thought that King Richard, now the Third of that name, had sent them away for safe-keeping, but then we heard rumours that they had been murdered. One said that Buckingham had seen to it, others accused Richard himself. As the latter emanated from Brittany I did not think such Lancastrian calumny would carry much weight, for all that Richard needed to do was to parade the boys for all to see. Yet he did not do that, perhaps because the denial of such a false rumour was beneath contempt, or because the boys were being cared for at his favourite castle of Middleham and it was too burdensome to bring them all the way from Yorkshire for such a temporary purpose, which might have to be repeated on each occasion of a similar rumour. Besides, they had no importance, being commoners now. Yet in spite of that there were times when I wondered where they were.

AS CHIEF clerk to the King's Secretary my duties were varied. One day I might be hiring—haggling is a better word—a team of Flemish acrobats to perform at a royal banquet, trying to make them understand that while some of their cruder antics might make me laugh the new King was different from the last and would not approve. Another day I would be in sombre clothes attending John Kendall at a meeting of the Council, and endeavouring not to yawn while I wrote down monotonous dissertations on trivial subjects which would have flowed on interminably had not the King's arrival brought them to an end. Once Dickon took his place trivialities were brushed aside and the real business commenced.

There were some fifteen members of the Council, most of whom have banished themselves from my memory by their tedious pomposity. One of the three lawyers was Thomas Lynom, who had decided not to marry Jane Shore after all, and of the four bishops Robert Stillington still held his bumbling place. The three commoners I knew well: John Kendall, Sir Richard Ratcliffe, and Sir William Catesby, whom Hastings had unwisely attempted to suborn. The remainder were Lords; Buckingham, Lovell, Stanley and so on.

Ratcliffe and Catesby were knights of the body who, with Lord Lovell were the closest associates of the King. They disliked each other, as familiars often do, but they hated Buckingham more. But then it is often necessary in human affairs to have someone to hate. It channels any incipient revolt into other directions, as witness the recurring aggressions against the French, the Saracens and the Jews. Buckingham, who had helped Richard to the throne, bore the greatest power and influence under him. And then of course there was the Stanley family.

Thomas, Lord Stanley, was the senior member, a man of substance—in wealth as well as body. Forty-eight years of age, and showing it (his armourer had once complained to me that each summer he had to forge a complete new cuirass as the speed of his growth round the stomach was too fast to be met by fillets), his influence, stemming from his great estates in the north-west, had been brought to bear alternately on the side of the Lancastrians and the Yorkists during the civil wars as it suited his purpose.

In spite of these tergiversations he must have convinced Edward the Fourth of his loyalty, for that affable giant had appointed him Privy Councillor and Lord Steward of the Household. Perhaps the fact that the Stanleys could put three thousand men into the field at short notice had influenced his appointment, as it is better to have such a force as an ally than an enemy, and Edward was no fool. Whatever the reason, Lord Stanley's fortunes had not suffered. Only a year previously he had been supporting Richard of Gloucester's campaign against the Scots and now, as King, Dickon had made him Knight of the Garter and Constable of England. It could be said that his loyalty had been to the throne rather than to its occupant, but a dispassionate observer might have added that Lord Stanley also knew which side of his venison was the better turned.

It is true that, with the discovery of the Hastings plot, he was put into prison, but in the excitement of that moment nearly everyone came under suspicion. And as he had recently become the third husband of the mother of Henry Tudor it is not surprising that some attached to him at first.

Yet he was likeable, with a quiet and courteous manner to all, whatever their station. His younger brother was a horse of a different colour.

Sir William Stanley would have been similar in looks if he had been better covered with flesh. Unclothed, and I only saw him that way once, he was an exercise in the ancient art of geometry, of which his face was another example. Narrow, with pale, slightly hooded grey eyes protruding each side of an arrowhead nose, he had the expression of an unsatisfied hawk. Neither was his manner endearing, especially to his inferiors. I was glad not to be an inhabitant of Chester, where he was Chamberlain, and have to seek justice at his court. But as no one in his right senses would exchange the delights of civilized London for a place as far away as Chester the situation was not likely to arise.

Like his brother, he too knew the right side of his venison. When Edward the Fourth and Richard had returned from Flanders to try conclusions with Warwick one of the first to join them had been Sir William Stanley. It was as if he already knew which side was going to win. In fact all through his career Sir William Stanley seemed to possess an uncanny prescience of the way events were about to shape, like some ghostly weathercock that would swing silently round to a new direction long before the wind changed.

Although his official duties did not often call for his presence in London he and his brother, like most of the barons, had large establishments there. Buckingham, as befitted the man next after the King, owned the most magnificent, a landmark in splendour to be pointed out to the visitor, but in opulence the Stanley's households were not far behind. Buckingham's amours were public property, topics for enthusiastic discussion and fervid wagers in tavern and market place, but those of the Stanleys were more discreet. And so it came as a shock when one morning Alice let fall that she was also the mistress of Sir William Stanley.

ALICE was tall and blue-eyed, with the corn-coloured hair that bespoke a Saxon ancestry. Her clothing she carried with the regal dignity that attaches to height, while under it was the body of a ripe goddess. She also had a prattling tongue.

When I suggested that she would be wise not to let fall in turn to Sir William Stanley that I was her lover the blue eyes had opened very wide and she told me that it was more than her life was worth, as he would surely kill her if he found out. But I would always know, she added anxiously, through my official duties when Sir William was likely to be in London, would I not? And when I agreed somewhat doubtfully she threw her arms round me and assured me that our romps together were something that she could not bear to forgo, when all that would remain for her would be the austere love-making of Sir William Stanley. It was only a pity that a mere clerk in the King's service could not provide the comforts to which she had grown accustomed, but I could be sure that those provided by Sir William were more than well-earned.

At least there was nothing of the hypocrite about her, and I decided that the danger of continuing our liaison was not too great. She was a pleasing companion and cost me little. It was her careless tongue that I should have to guard against. And then, only a few weeks afterwards, she prattled that Dickon would not be King for much longer.

That brought me up short. When I asked her what she meant she put her cheek against mine and murmured that it was nothing. Men talked that way at times, didn't they?

I agreed that they might, but added that if there was to be a new king I should like some warning as my employment might be affected.

She pouted at that and replied that my employment made no difference to her. Whatever I did I would always be welcome in her house, as I ought to know.

I did not persist, because if I appeared to be too anxious she might take it upon herself to question Sir William further, for the sentiment could only have come from him. She had said, "Men talk that way at times," not "It is common gossip" or some other expression. It seemed to me to be significant enough to report to John Kendall.

He put down his pen and eyed me with mild surprise. "It is unlikely that Sir William would have been so indiscreet," he observed.

"Who knows, John, what a man will say when he is with a woman?" I replied. "Not everyone is as discreet as you are."

He coughed, and I found it hard not to smile. John Kendall's discretion in matters of the heart was absolute. It had to be, for his wife Agnes had the disposition of a wild boar. I would not put it beyond her to come storming into West Minster and root him out from the Chamber even while the Council was sitting if she thought she had cause.

"It could have come from no one else," I told him. "Alice does not have any other lovers."

"If she deceives Sir William then she could as easily deceive you."

"She could," I admitted. "But as I take up all of her time when he is away it is unlikely."

He looked at me and a slow smile spread across his face. "Yes," he said. "Knowing you, Henry, it is unlikely."

I grinned back at him. "Nevertheless it might be safer not to continue the affair."

"Would it?" He shook his head. "Perhaps it would. But if you suddenly cease seeing her she will be curious. And she appears to be the kind of person whose curiosity might become active. She could make trouble. And if you continue with her you might learn more." The smile became broader. "And that might suit you, eh, Henry Morane?"

"If it is your order, Master Secretary," I said solemnly, "then I will consider it as part of my official duties henceforth."

I heard him chuckling as I went through the arras.

From time to time I made allusions to the matter, ostensibly in fun, but Alice had no more to offer on the subject, which meant that Sir William Stanley had not said any more, or she would surely have told me. No doubt the Chamberlain of Chester was well aware of her slipshod tongue, but in one respect she seemed to have kept it stilled. For she and I remained alive.

As time went on she tired of me a little, and I of her, but since she was too lazy to seek another lover and I still gave her satisfaction, our affair continued. For my part I thought there might be more to be learned from the Stanleys, although I did not deceive myself into thinking that she did not continue to excite me. But it was a liaison that would come to an end in due course, and that end was hastened when Sir William Stanley arrived one evening and surprised us together.

He was surprised too. He stood with one hand on the doorway, more than ever appearing like a bird of prey as the cloak swung round his shoulders. Then he threw it back and stepped inside. The light from the candle glinted on his sword-blade, and Alice gasped.

"I know you!" he said in a voice that was hoarse with rage. The point of his weapon was thrust towards my chest. I felt a sharp, sudden pain, and the wetness of blood coursing down my skin. "You are Henry Morane!" he mouthed ."A menial in the King's household."

There was no reply to that. I backed away instinctively. The sword-point followed me. Then I held my ground and turned to look at Alice. Her eyes were very wide and she was shivering under a robe she had pulled over her. I was even colder. I had nothing on at all.

Sir William Stanley held me with his weapon while he looked me up and down. I watched him helplessly, waiting for his eyes to narrow as the final thrust came. But the point drew away a little as he opened his mouth to call out, "Lambskin! Rougemain!"

A few moments later there followed the thumping of wooden shoes up the stairway and two men came in. They were of a height, one red-bearded and bringing with him the smell of months of unwashed sweat, the other shaven and clean, but distinguished by a notch in one ear and a scar that extended his mouth-line across his cheek. But at that moment I was not so much concerned with their aroma or appearance as what their orders were going to be.

"Take him away, Rougemain," Stanley said to the bearded one. "And dispose of him . . ."

"Where, Sir William? The river?"

"Anywhere, you fool!" Stanley snapped, not taking his eyes off me. "Just so that his offal is not smeared around here." He moved back a little to let them come round him.

Rougemain grunted, nodded at his companion, and they

started towards me. I could see that they had carried out orders like this before.

My only chance lay in attack. And the target would have to be Sir William Stanley. He had the quicker intelligence. The two oafs might be momentarily dumbfounded by a sudden assault, but he would not. Yet there was that long, sharp steel blade between us. And when his men came abreast of him I began to think there would be no chance at all. It was at that moment that Alice screamed out loud.

Sir William swore and turned involuntarily. The sword-point moved away a little. I leaped forward and kicked him in the groin. I hurt my toe severely, but I hurt him more. He bent forward, shrieking, and lunged at me. I dodged the wild thrust, but there was no time to grab for the weapon. While Rougemain was standing, gaping stupidly at his master, Lambskin had hardly paused. He merely glanced at Sir William before continuing his advance on me.

I swung round towards the window. Bursting through the shutter with a crash I fell to the ground outside. A moment later I was up and limping as fast as I could along the street, barefoot through the filth.

6

THE streets of London, so full of vitality, colour and unceasing din, belong at night to a different city, a city abandoned by its inhabitants, like a silent monument to a past civilization. Yet when once again daylight probes its grey fingers through the narrow and often noisome alleys, the first doors open, shopkeepers drop their shutters and spread their wares, and early urchins begin their raucous day. Their elders, thankful that another night has passed without violence, look out cautiously at the weather and turn back to discuss its prospects with those inside. The weather of London has been a topic for discussion since before Caesar came.

Yet at night, in certain parts where wealth abounds, there are people to be seen. The Watch beats its rounds, there are groups of retainers bearing lanterns and armed to the teeth, escorting their betters on their business, which at that time is often one of seeking pleasure. Elsewhere the streets of London are places to avoid. No honest citizen ventures out alone. Thieves and cut-throats wait for him, tall in the shadows, while at his feet dark shapes with shining, beady eyes scuttle across his path with shrill squeals. They will not harm him— unless he has been beaten and stripped and left for dead. Then they close in, hairy little bodies trembling with anticipation, fighting among themselves for the first tentative bite. Sometimes the prowling skeleton of a cat, trailing clusters of mangy fur, will waylay a laggard and carry off its prize with astonishing speed over the nearest wall before its rodent brothers can come to the rescue. Dogs too, ferocious and cunning as only a London dog can be, with generations of experience in the unceasing search for garbage, follow their trails, sometimes meeting another of their kind, when the encounter ends in either the shriek of mangled hide or silent, shuffling copulation.

The fall itself had not been great. The living floor of Alice's house was built above a store-room in which only a short man could stand upright. But I had come down into a street at the side of her house which I did not know. It was narrow, and the balconies of the houses on both sides leaned out almost to touch each other, making more darkness than the night above. Along the middle I could hear the gushing of water in an open sewer. It had overflowed with the rain and the ordure was cold on my feet. But it was not the smell that worried me. Neither was it the fear of Stanley's men catching me so much as the fear of slipping into that open ditch and drowning in the dark.

I could hear them behind me, splashing through the muck. Then they slowed. They knew those back streets of London as well as I. They could afford to slacken their pace. If they heard me slip they would have me.

I tried the doors of the houses as I went along, but I knew that none would open. All good citizens barred their doors after dark. Then there was a side alley, paved with large stones, and dry. I turned along it gratefully to find that it ended at a high wall surrounding a heavy wooden door, which was securely bolted against me. And when Stanley's men turned into the alley there was nothing else to do but climb the wall. By the time they reached it I was lying flat on the top, praying that they wouldn't hear my teeth chattering like an old coat of chain-mail being pulled on.

They stopped below me and tried the gate. Rougemain's sour odour came up in the damp air and I had to stifle a cough.

"He couldn't have come this way," Lambskin said.

The other grunted agreement and then swore. "We'll have to go back and try farther along that sewer."

Lambskin chuckled. "At least you won't notice the smell. Unless the water frightens you." He paused, then added slowly, "But we don't have to. We can go back."

Rougemain called on the Devil to tell him what the other man was talking about.

"You stinking Flemish half-wit," Lambskin said viciously. "Use your nab. All we need is to tell Sir William that we caught him and did with him like he said. That man won't never come back. He won't dare." There was a loud gasp as if the other had been prodded in the stomach, then he went on, "And if you so much as breathe to anyone that he's still alive, by the Buttocks of God I'll twist out every red hair from that beard of yours and stuff them up your arse so that you'll never whid again. See?"

I waited until they had left the alley before I began to climb down the inside of the wall.

37

The courtyard was not very wide, but it was paved, with the backs of three houses at the other side. I came down on to a stone hut, which seemed to be their bakehouse. Inside, I found some tow and cleaned my feet in a puddle on the floor. Then I crossed the yard past a tree that seemed to grow out of a great pile of dead leaves, its gaunt branches parting upwards to the stars. I chose the house in the middle, behind the tree, where a gleam of light showed through an ill-fitting shutter. I ripped it off and went in through the window.

Brittle rushes scored my feet as I trod across the floor. I was in a small, sparsely furnished room, with a bed against the opposite wall. There was a taper burning in a stand beside it, its yellowish flame making the woman's skin as smooth as ancient ivory, while her eyes were wide and very dark.

I held up a placating hand. "Don't be afraid," I told her. "I am not a thief in the night. I am in trouble and need help."

She looked at me steadily and said, "I am not afraid, sir. By some miracle you must be Saint Michael himself." She was not as young as Alice, but quite as beautiful, with dark hair over her shoulders and a tarnished crucifix swinging between her breasts.

"I am not Saint Michael," I assured her. "I am an ordinary man and . . ."

"Indeed you appear to be," she said, looking me up and down with a faint smile. "But it is not usual for ordinary men to call upon me in your state."

I went across and sat down at the end of the bed. There was nowhere else to sit except upon a wooden chest, and the carvings on its top seemed like to etch their patterns into my buttocks. She moved the taper stand and held out her arms. "Saint Michael!" she said.

"No, no!" I exclaimed. "I am in trouble!"

She laughed then, gently. "Yes? And you are without clothes. That way I cannot tell if you are saint or scullion . . ." A soft arm went about my shoulder. "But meanwhile I will dream that you are at least an earl, or perhaps even the Lord High Admiral himself."

"Or perhaps the Master of the Wardrobe," I grinned, returning her embrace.

". . . and this Alice?" she said some time afterwards. "She is the whore of someone at Court?"

38

"Mistress," I corrected.

She shrugged her ivory shoulders. "Mistress? Whore? What is a word? Are not we women all the same? I too, was once the . . . mistress of a man at Court, but he was killed at Tewkesbury, as were so many other gentlemen of noble blood."

I stirred. "At Tewkesbury? Who was he? And on which side?"

"Who he was is of no importance any more," she said without emotion. "And as to which side he fought on I really cannot remember. He fought in so many battles on different sides that after a time I did not even try to remember. And if one fights in enough battles one will surely be killed in the end." She stopped and looked at me. "But you? If you are not Saint Michael then what is your name? No," she added, getting off the bed. "Do not tell me. I will find out for myself." She reached for some garments and drew them over her head. When she was tying the waist of her dress I asked her what she was doing.

"The house of this Alice of yours . . . you said it was at the end of this street . . . then it will be one of three . . . which one?"

"On the corner, but . . ."

"Sir William Stanley's? Yes. I know it. The one where he keeps his . . ." she laughed ". . . mistresses!"

I sat up quickly. "You're going there? What for? You can't . . ."

"I am going to see if your clothes are there. If I find them I will know you are telling the truth. And they, by their quality, will tell me what sort of man you are, your station."

"I am telling you the truth," I assured her. "You must not go out. I will get them for myself."

Her dark eyebrows rose. Her face, framed by her long hair with its widow's peak in the forehead, reminded me of Elizabeth Woodville's, but without the look of calculation that had narrowed them over the years. This one's eyes were even a deeper, darker blue, and gazed out at the world more honestly. They had suffered defeat, and pain, but would not give up easily.

"You will fetch them yourself?" she said. "Naked as you are? You would be killed by the first Watch that encountered you. And if you did reach the house do you think Sir

William Stanley will be pleased to find you still alive?" She shook her head. "No, my friend. I will get them for you. Your buxom Alice will give them to me when I tell her I know where you are."

"And if Sir William Stanley is still in the house?"

"Then he will be too busy with Alice to notice me take them away."

I nodded reluctantly. She had the argument. But I got off the bed and went over to her. "No," I said. "The streets at night are dangerous, especially for a woman."

She laughed at that and went back to the bed. Stooping, she drew out a long dagger from under the palliasse and showed it to me. It was three-sided, the kind used in Italy. "Do you think I have never been out at night before? Have you not thought I might have had my hand on the hilt when you came in through the window?" When she saw my face she laughed again and kissed me. "But I had no need to use it, did I?"

"I will at least come with you."

"And have me arrested as a witch?"

"A witch?"

"Yes. A witch. To be seen outside after dark with a naked man would mean death for any woman. How little you men know the risks we have to suffer!" She paused. "Besides," she added, pulling the hood over her head, "there is a yard at the back of the house, I know. Like this one. And a door. And if Sir William Stanley is still inside his men will be there." A smile crossed her face. "They will let me in."

"And if my clothes are gone?"

"Then I will know that you have not told me the truth. That you are not Saint Michael after all." She smiled and kissed me. Then she pointed through a low arch at the side of the room. "That leads to the door into the street if you need it . . ." I gave her a puzzled look ". . . but I shall go the way you came. There is a narrow passage from this yard behind the houses. So you see, my precious Saint, I do not need to use the streets after all."

I started after her, but she was gone through a narrow door by the window which I had not noticed. I would have followed her, but I saw it was raining again, and shivered.

Pulling the thin coverings over me, I lay back on the bed. What a wonderful place London was! No man in trouble need be without a friend. Unless he was high-born, when he would have no real friends at all, only companions who smiled to cover the jealousy in their hearts. I was glad to be an ordinary man, a common man who need not fear the treachery of his comrades. I thought about the woman who had gone to fetch my clothes. She had told me, almost shyly, that her name was Matilda. Perhaps because it was an old-fashioned name. I thought about fashions and decided that I would buy her one of the new-fangled nightshifts, for it was the mode to wear clothes at night again, although as far as she was concerned . . .

The door opened and she came into the room quickly. I saw that she had a bundle over one arm. "Good!" I said, and started to get up.

Her dark eyes were wide in the light from the taper. She threw the clothes down beside me and stood back. "Put them on and go," she said in a flat voice.

I looked at her and said, "What . . . ?"

"Your Alice is dead," she said tonelessly, as if repeating a rhyme. "Get dressed and go."

I stood up and seized her by the shoulders. "Alice dead?" I shouted. "Is that what you said?"

She winced and struggled free, backing over to the other side of the room. "She had been killed." A hand went over her eyes and she started to sob. "It was horrible! Sword thrusts . . . several . . . through her!"

"Sir William Stanley!" I exclaimed. "He had the sword!" I moved towards her.

"No, no!" Her voice rose. "I don't care who it was! Keep away from me! Put your clothes on and go! Don't ever come near me again!"

"Matilda," I said patiently, "this is not . . ."

But she wouldn't listen. She started to cry. I dressed myself in the damp clothes, giving her time to collect herself, and then went up to her again.

"Matilda," I said, "listen . . ."

She screamed suddenly and pointed a finger at me. "Not Saint Michael, but the Angel of Death! That's what you are! That's what you were all the time! I don't want to die like your Alice," she sobbed.

I turned slowly and went to the door that led into the street. It was still raining.

7

THERE were many questions I had wanted to ask Matilda. How had she been able to collect my clothes? Had the house been open? Was it empty, apart from Alice? Or had she seen anyone there? I shrugged to myself. I would find out soon enough. At least she hadn't forgotten to bring my belt with the dagger in it, so that I was not unarmed any longer. If Sir William Stanley were still there he would have to answer to me for Alice, whatever his wealth and position. And if I were caught afterwards at least I should have the chance to appeal to the King's mercy. Before he had become King, or even Protector, as Lord of the North he had been famed for his justice. . . . up there they swore by him . . . but perhaps justice might not appeal to him any longer, especially as far as the Stanleys were concerned . . . they were more important than I was . . . the best I could hope for was a quick hanging. The worst? I had seen often enough the bloody shambles caused by an inept executioner. My thoughts went round and round. Then I put them away. One fact was certain, even though I meant little to Alice, and was but a passing pleasure, the least she deserved was vengeance.

The clouds racing low across the sky parted suddenly and a thin moon peered between the gaps in the houses above me. A shadow moved in the hollow of the wall opposite and I put my hand on the hilt of my dagger. But I trudged on. A cut-throat would have to splash his way across the street to attack me and there would be warning enough. Nothing came. My clothes were soiled and clung damply to me. Even in that dim light I could not have seemed worth looting.

A few yards farther on the road curved to the left, taking me away from the road that fronted Alice's house, but then it swung back and I was at the corner of a cobbled street, cobbles which I had crossed often enough to see her. And then I saw a gleam of light and ducked back quickly.

The light came from a torch held by Rougemain, the flames making his beard redder than before. He was standing in the street by a handcart, while two other men carried a long bundle towards it. It was easy to guess what the bundle contained.

The rest of the street was in darkness. No citizen would open his shutters to see what the light was. It was safer not to be curious about lights and voices outside after darkness.

They were intent on what they were doing. I drew my dagger and crept along the wall towards them. I had reached the edge of Alice's house when a voice spoke from the shadow of its doorway.

"Are you oafs going to take all night about it?" It was Sir William Stanley.

The two men tumbled their burden into the cart and seized the shafts. I waited for them to move off. Then there would only be Rougemain.

"You stay here," Stanley said to him. "I want you and Lambskin to find that fellow's clothes."

"Who is he?" Lambskin asked, and I swore quietly. He was only a few feet away, and I hadn't even noticed him. "I mean," he went on, "who was he? And why do we need his clothes?"

Stanley gave a loud, impatient sigh. "He was one of the King's spies."

"A spy?" Rougemain lowered the torch nervously. "What was he doing here?"

"Working with that woman of mine. Trying to worm secrets out of her."

"Did she know any?" Lambskin asked.

"No," Stanley said impatiently, "but he must have thought she did."

Lambskin hesitated, letting air out through his nose. He was a fellow of some intelligence, curious, and yet reluctant to question his master too far.

"How did you find out, Sir William?" he asked after a pause. The question contained the right blend of deference with admiration for his superior's cleverness. The answer, if he got one, might satisfy some of his curiosity. It might satisfy some of mine, too.

"Oh, I have known for some time," Stanley said airily, but I didn't believe it. "And then, only yesterday, she repeated a remark that she said I had once made."

I believed that, though. Poor Alice had signed her own death warrant.

"As it was a treasonous remark," Stanley went on, "it couldn't have been made by me." He gave a short laugh.

"So she must have confused me with someone else. I therefore laid a trap to catch that someone."

That didn't quite meet with his earlier statement that he had known of me for a long time, but Rougemain sucked his breath in through his teeth.

"Jesu!" he said admiringly. "And we caught him!" He stopped quickly and glanced at Lambskin, and then looked away and started to scratch his beard with his free hand.

Stanley noticed the movement. He began to say something, but Lambskin cut in abruptly. "But I cannot see why we need to find his clothes."

Sir William Stanley gave another impatient sigh. "Because they must not be found by anyone else and identified as his, or it will be guessed that he has been killed." He shot a glance at Rougemain, and went on, "If he and his clothes are destroyed then it will be thought that he has run away, and if I am consulted then I can say that he has gone off with my woman to join the Tudors in Brittany."

Lambskin gave a long, low whistle of appreciation.

I had heard enough now, but I waited. The squeaks from the cart showed it to be near enough for the other two men still to be within call. The others stood and watched it for a little while, then, as it trundled away into the darkness Stanley held out his hand for Rougemain's torch. It was my opportunity.

I jumped out from the shadows and buried my dagger in Lambskin's side. The wind went out of him with a hollow groan and he doubled up. Stanley, his hand out reaching for the torch, turned, astonishment over his face at the sight of me. I gave him a violent shove backwards through the doorway and seized the torch from Rougemain's slackening grip. I swung round with it quickly, but Stanley had disappeared. Behind me, Rougemain was recovering himself. I turned back to see him with a dagger in his hand. Mine was still in Lambskin. He had fallen forward, forcing my hand from the hilt. There was only one course left. As Rougemain leaped towards me I thrust the flaming torch straight into his face.

He stopped short, eyes widening with shock, and then gave a terrible scream. He put his hands over his face and went on screaming as he tried to beat out the burning mass of pitch and hair where his beard had been.

44

I charged into the house and up the stairs. It was a mistake. I should have dodged Rougemain and thrown the burning torch into the store-room, setting the place afire and waiting for Stanley to come out. But on occasions like that, when events move so fast that there is little time to think, one has the wisdom afterwards.

The room was a fearful sight. There was blood on the bed and over the walls. No wonder Matilda had been crazed with the shock. But it was empty now. Sir William had waited below while I had charged past, and now he was in the doorway behind me.

We stood there, breathing hard and glaring at each other, while outside Rougemain's screams grew louder. Then a sneer crossed his thin face when he saw that I was unarmed.

"The second time, Henry Morane!" he said, the point of his sword making a small circle in the air.

There is little a man can do against three feet of steel held by someone who knows how to use it. The bed-cover, damp with great spots of red on it, was rolled in a bundle on the floor. If I could seize it and throw it at him I might have a chance. At least the window was open this time. But he saw my eyes move towards the bundle and was ready. Then there were boots on the stairs. The cart-men had heard Rougemain's screams and were coming back. All I could do now was to try the window again, if I could reach it.

Stanley heard them coming too and dropped his point. I ducked round and made for the sill. I was astride it and looking down into the moonlit sewer when I felt a violent blow in the back. I tried to squirm aside but something held me up. A searing pain spread across my body. I looked down and saw moonlight gleaming on steel. Six inches of it was protruding out of the front of my chest. It was as sharp and clear as a winter icicle, and there was no blood on it at all. I looked at it stupidly, trying to think what had happened. Then behind me I heard Sir William Stanley chuckle and a sudden agony brought lights flashing across my eyes. The steel disappeared back into my clothes. And then at last it dawned upon me that it was his sword he had thrust right through my body. As I fell into the street I heard him chuckling again.

Supporting myself against the walls of the houses I staggered blindly along the narrow way. They would be coming

45

out of the house to finish me off. But perhaps they might leave me until they had attended to Rougemain and Lambskin. How badly was Lambskin hurt? Gasping and sweating, I stumbled faster, and the last I remember was the stinking water rising in the moonglow as it came up to meet my face.

8

IT COULD have been a week, a month, or even a year that I lay in a welter of half-conscious impressions, frenzied dreams and unreal fantasies. There were periods of agony that lasted an age, while I fought desperately to stay alive, time after time seeming to die in a world of dread, the very pit of Hell. It was then that grinning creatures, sometimes bat-faced, sometimes with the cold, cruel countenance of a stone image, pushed arrows right through my chest, steel arrows of triangular shape, each edge serrated with sharp teeth. At other times I lay inert, helpless in my sweat and caked with blood, yet conscious enough to know that I lay on something less hard than the packed earth of the street, and wondering vaguely whether this was Purgatory. At those times the fantasies followed, fantasies in which Alice's staring eyes narrowed into vitality and beckoned me again, and others when I heard Matilda sobbing that the Angel of Death himself lay dying.

At one time the impression of a priest, or perhaps a wandering friar, came to me. I heard him giving me shrift and myself muttering to him that I would not die. Then rotting teeth became exposed in a smile as I felt his hand exploring my body. But it had been too late. All my money had been taken long before.

And then the day came when the mist across my eyes was not so thick, and there were roof beams above me with tiny black shapes moving under the wooden tiles. I lifted an arm, and found that I could do it with only a short gust of pain inside my chest. The deep agony was gone. And I could see! The black shapes under the tiles were spiders, dancing in the warmth. I could see! I could collect my senses and think! I could find out what had happened to me. I could find out where I was. I moved my head slowly to one side and opened my eyes again. I was on Matilda's bed.

It was the same room. But now there was a rough table along one wall, and a bench beside it. There were platters on the table. One held what was left of a loaf, another some pastries. An iron brazier stood on the floor, glowing with wood and sea-coal. Thin white smoke rose from it to the ceiling, while a tray beneath it sparkled with hot ashes. At least it seemed to be the same room, but perhaps Matilda had moved away and someone else now lived here. I was wondering about it when I fell asleep again.

Darkness had fallen when I woke, but a tallow and the stove gave enough light to throw jerky shadows across the room. One of them moved with more purpose than the guttering lights could give it. I raised myself a little to see who it was. The effort made the pain come back and I groaned.

There was a quiet exclamation and the shadow moved towards me. A moment later Matilda's face was peering down into mine. A face that had grown thinner since I had last seen it. I tried to smile, but it must have looked like a leer from the Old Man of the Woods through the unkempt beard that surrounded it.

Soft hands stroked my forehead and her face moved away a little. I saw her eyes close. "Thanks be to God!" she breathed.

"Amen!" I murmured. "And thanks to you, too. How am I here?"

"How are you here?" Her eyes opened again, and they were very bright. "How are you here?" They travelled over my face. "Because the Angel of Death left my house and I followed him."

"Why?" I asked her. "Why did you do that?"

"To see where he would go. I waited in the shadows, and then he fell from a window, and was dying. So I knew he was a man after all." She smiled a little. "A man who came to me for help, and who I sent away to be killed. A man who I had first called Saint Michael."

"My name isn't Michael." I told her. "It's Henry . . ."

"I know," she said. "As he lay between life and death he said often that he was called Henry. Henry Morane, scrivener at the King's Court. But there is no saint of that name."

"I am not a saint . . ."

She put her finger on my lips and shook her head slowly. "Maybe you are not, Henry Morane. But I need a saint. I have needed one for a long time." She leaned closer and kissed me. I closed my eyes momentarily, and in that moment I was asleep.

"How long have I been here?" I said what I thought was a few minutes later. And then I saw it was daylight again.

Matilda was at the trestle. She turned when she heard me and brought a mug of wine. Putting it to my lips, she said, "How long? Only the Lord himself knows. For me it has been a year waiting for you to come alive again. To others outside it is springtime."

"Springtime!" I tried to sit up, but the effort was too great. "But it was November when . . . when . . ." I gazed at her unbelievingly.

"It was before Christmas when I brought the priest. And when he came he asked for a fee. But I would not give it to him. Then he made to go away, and I cursed him. I cursed him and his hypocritical tribe with all the foul things I know. In the end he gave you Unction and sent for a cart. But when it came I would not let them take you away."

I reached for a hand and found it. Pressing it gently, I said, "You would not let them take me away?"

She nodded. "At first the priest thought it was the plague until I showed him your wounds. When he saw them he said it was the same thing in the end, and you would die anyway. It was then that he wanted money." She looked upwards and narrowed her eyes at the memory. "He said he was a physician too, and your wound was poisoned, but, as a priest may not shed blood he would have to call for his assistants. Hah!" she exclaimed, turning back to me. "Assistants! Have you ever seen physicians' assistants? Horse-gelders and spittle-house men, all of them!"

I grinned weakly. "I know. I have seen them. What did you do?"

"He said your wound was poisoned. As for me I would not have known. But I believed that he was right. So I bought oil . . ."

"That was right," I told her. "You poured boiling oil and honey on it?"

She nodded. "It seems to have made them heal. But perhaps they would have healed anyway, if my prayers were answered by the Virgin."

"She did," I said. "She told you what to do. And all winter I lay in your bed? You washed me and gave me wine, and what food I could swallow? You kept me warm . . ."

"I kept myself warm too," she smiled. "I lay beside you. And as for food and wine there was money in your purse." She fumbled at her waist and brought out a golden ryal.

49

"This is what I kept. It is an old coin but I kept it." She held it up. "See! On it is the head of King Henry. Another Henry . . ."

"No," I told her. "That is King Edward. But no matter. What would you have done when the ryal was gone?"

"Who knows?" she replied, and the devil came into her eyes. "I should have to steal, for there is not enough room on that bed for another man."

"There had better not be," I smiled. "Not any more."

She got up quickly. "Not any more? Is that what you think of me? If you were not sick you would leave this house forthwith!"

"It is not what I think," I said. "It was you who put the thought into my words."

"It was not! You were hinting that . . . that because you came in my window and . . . and . . ."

"You told me yourself that there was a man."

"And he was killed. Poor William! In spite of his wealth I had an affection for him. He was very gentle . . ." She looked down at me and smiled. "Not like wild scriveners who come bursting through windows in the dark."

"And you with a dagger under the mattress," I grinned. "Who was William?"

"William Bourchier, son of the Earl of Essex. Married against his will to Ann, one of the Woodville sisters, a hateful creature like all the others. William was happier with me, he said, and . . ." She saw the expression on my face and stopped. "Ah! So you think he told me that as any other husband might?"

"I don't know," I smiled. "But you would be worthy of such a tale. I must remember to tell you the same when I am well again. Then perhaps when I die you will call me 'Poor Henry'. Pity is love's kinsman, as the old saying goes."

"I do not think you are the kind of person anyone will ever call 'Poor Henry'," she replied. "But if you ever dare tell me you are happier with me than . . ."

"Never," I said, equally seriously. "Because it would not be true."

Her face froze.

"Because," I chuckled, "I do not have a wife to hate. Being only a clerk I was never given a Woodville woman and the large estates that go with them. As so far I have not encountered anyone rich enough . . ." I paused and eyed her speculatively. "But perhaps you, with all that William Bourchier gave you . . ."

Before she could collect herself for a reply I had fallen asleep again.

A week later I could walk across the room with Matilda at my arm, and two weeks after that she no longer came to the bed only to keep warm. It was then that I told her I must send a message to John Kendall. By now he might have given me up for lost, or dead, and I must tell him where I was. Besides, I added, there was some money due to me.

At that Matilda laughed and brought me a mug of wine to drink. She said that if I wrote him a letter she would take it.

"A letter?" I said. "What with?"

"Oh," she said casually. "I have paper of a sort, and materials for writing."

"It would be easier to go and see him and tell him what I say."

"Do you think I . . ." she pointed a finger at herself ". . . would be allowed to see the King's Secretary? His men would drive me away."

There was sense in that. Especially if Agnes heard of a woman visiting him.

"And even if he did see me he might not believe me. Whereas on a letter he would know your writing. Are you not his clerk?"

When the letter was finished and sanded she took the paper and folded it. "There is wax too," she added.

"I am not afraid of you reading it," I said.

That brought a frown across her face. "Because you think I cannot read? So!" She unfolded the paper and read out what I had written. "There! My time with William Bourchier was not wasted, you see? I made him teach me letters."

"I'm sure you did!" I laughed. "But perhaps it would be better to seal it and for me to address it to Master John Kendall. Otherwise someone might take it from you and read it. Someone like Sir William Stanley."

She spilled wax clumsily over the taper, filling the room with black smoke. When I had finished coughing, I said, "You must not take it tonight. It will be dark soon, and it is a long way to West Minster."

51

"I have been there before. It is not far. But I will go as soon as daylight comes and the boatmen wake. I will use the ryal."

I sat up. "But it won't cost as much as that! Two pence, no more."

"I know. I know."

"But a ryal is ten shillings, and . . ."

"Of course it is, Henry!" She held out her arms and pirouetted round. "But I shall need a new dress! Would you have me present myself at the office of the King's Secretary in these?"

She laughed and ran out of the room before I could catch her.

9

I T WAS some time after noon that a banging on the door
woke me. I groaned and cursed and shouted at the idiot
to stop making that din. Then I regained my senses and
staggered through to the door to open it. John Kendall
stood there, frowning down with distaste at his muddy boots.
He looked up and saw me, and came inside with his arms
outstretched.

"Henry Morane!" he said. "So you really are still alive!
When the woman brought the message I scarcely believed
it."

I took his hand, and saw that he was by himself. "Where is
she?" I asked him. "How did you find this house without
her?"

"She gave me good directions," he smiled, pointing down
at the sill. There were several blobs of sealing wax stuck to it.
As I brought him in and removed his cloak he said, "And as
to where she is, why, I should say that she is probably
somewhere along the Strand buying clothes."

"Buying clothes after she had seen you?"

"She said she would not return at once as you and I would
have much to talk about." He nodded with approval. "A
woman of perception, that."

I grunted. I wondered how much would be left of my ryal.

He sat down at the bench while I found him some wine.
"Well, Henry," he said. "I am alone. I came in my boat and
left my men with it. So you may speak freely to me."

"Speak freely?" I said, puzzled.

"Tell me what happened. I may be able to help you."

I inspected him curiously, but he waved me on, so I told
him my story. When I had finished he gave a loud sigh.

"So that was it?" he said. "Well, I, at least, knew that it
wasn't because you had defected to Buckingham."

"Buckingham?" I said with amazement. "Why should
anyone defect to him?"

It was his turn to look surprised. "But have you not heard
about the rebellion?"

I sat down. "Rebellion? Buckingham? You're pulling my
legs now."

"Quite incredible!" he exclaimed. "All England has been humming with it. And you hadn't heard?"

I shook my head. Then I remembered. "So Alice was right after all? There has been a plot to unseat the King. But Buckingham?" I shook my head again. "No. It must have been the Stanleys."

"The Stanleys had no part in it," he said evenly. "At least as far as we know. Your Alice, God rest her soul, was mistaken."

"Buckingham," he went on, "was in correspondence with Henry Tudor in Brittany. It was the same as the Hastings affair all over again, only this time it was much more serious, for Buckingham commanded a large following in the west country, as you should know . . ."

I went on shaking my head. It was unbelieveable. Buckingham had put Dickon on the throne. He was his closest adviser, and friend.

". . . and when the standards of revolt were raised in Wales and the west country the Tudors were to land their forces on the south coast. But God in His Mercy intervened. There were great floods along the Severn, the greatest, they say, in living memory. The Duke's army was cut off from England. It became dispirited, you know what the Welsh are, and in a short time it dispersed. Buckingham himself was betrayed to a sheriff, and after that it was all over for him. He asked for a last interview with the King for the sake of their old friendship, but it was refused." John Kendall gave a grim smile. "Dickon was wise. They found a dagger under the Duke's cloak afterwards. Although the Devil alone . . ." he crossed himself ". . . knows how it got there."

"And the fleet from Brittany?"

"It came to land, and those waiting ashore gave it shouts of welcome and encouragement. But Henry Tudor was suspicious." The smile crossed his face again. "Which was a pity, because he sailed away again. The men waiting ashore were ours."

"The rebellion is over, then?"

"Yes. Henry Tudor is back in Brittany. Buckingham's head has been taken off, but Bishop Morton has escaped to France, no doubt to sharpen his serpentine tongue again."

"John Morton? But he was imprisoned . . . ?"

"He was. At Brecon Castle. In the Duke's care. There is

little doubt that his evil words turned Buckingham from his allegiance. Even before the Hastings plot his foul tongue was poisoning Dickon."

I ran a hand over my hair. "Even so, I cannot see why Buckingham should try to unseat the King. There would be no advantage for him in having a Tudor on the throne instead. He would still be no more than the first man after the king."

"Ah!" John Kendall said, wagging a finger at me. "Remember that Buckingham was of royal descent too. In fact his claim is near the same as Richard's, and certainly greater than that of the Tudor. While by himself he could never have unseated Dickon, with Lancastrian help he appeared to think he could. Then, once Dickon was removed, who knows, he was popular, and had the power. He might have had the strength to remove Henry Tudor."

"God in Heaven!" I said. "It is more than a hundred years since old Edward the Third died, and still his descendants plot for the crown."

"There are not so many left now," John Kendall muttered sombrely. "And Henry Tudor will be dealt with if he makes more trouble."

"But the Stanleys were not implicated? Are you sure?"

"Sir William was not, as far as is known. Certainly he took no overt action of any kind. Although the Lady Margaret Beaufort, or the Countess of Richmond, as she likes to call herself, connived with Morton. But that was expected, of course, as she is Henry Tudor's mother."

"She is also the wife of Lord Stanley. And he was under suspicion at the time of the Hastings plot. How did he come out of it?"

"Unspoilt. In fact he declared his loyalty to the King."

I grunted, unconvinced. "And the Lady Margaret Beaufort? What was done about her?"

"All her estates were confiscated."

"A welcome addition to the royal treasury!" I laughed.

"Not at all. Dickon was very astute. He also had some sympathy for her as, being a mother, she would try to help her son. Her estates were put in charge of her husband, Lord Stanley."

"In charge of her husband?" Then I saw the smile on John Kendall's face. "So your devious hand was in it, was it?

If she plots to raise another rebellion she will have to ask her husband for the money first, eh? And then the King will know on which side Lord Stanley's loyalties lie, is that it?"

He said nothing, but went on smiling.

"And so the King does not really trust the Stanleys after all?"

"It could be inferred," he admitted after a moment. "But remember that no suspicion attaches to them. No slander must be made."

I sat and thought about it while he watched me. Then I said, "Did you trace the information that led you to suspect Buckingham?"

"When we found it was correct the source was unimportant."

"No one claimed a reward?"

He shook his head. "Not yet, at least."

"Then it could have come from Sir William Stanley."

That surprised him. "Sir William Stanley? Are you suggesting that he betrayed Buckingham? That makes no sense!"

"I am remembering what Alice said to me," I told him. "And that she was killed because of it."

John Kendall was staring at me. "Go on," he urged.

"Stanley is known to be jealous of Buckingham. He, like many others, did not relish his sudden rise to power. It would not suit him for any rebellion to succeed, a rebellion that still left Buckingham in power next to the new king. What better way of disposing of him than by giving you information of the plot in an indirect manner? It would of course have had to have been indirect, otherwise his part in it would have been exposed. I think he must have had a share in it with Buckingham at first, later to betray him."

"Ah!" John Kendall said, scratching his chin. "You make it specious indeed. But what if the Tudor army had landed successfully?"

"But it did not land, did it? Because, as you have just told me, the Tudors were suspicious. But why should they have been suspicious? Could they also have been warned? Warned by Sir William Stanley?"

"They could have been. But I cannot see why."

"Because it left Buckingham on his own, without an ally, and more readily destroyed." John Kendall started to say something, but I went on, "And, by warning Henry Tudor, Stanley would be building up credit for himself for a later occasion."

"By God!" John Kendall exclaimed, laughing. "It is a specious story, Henry Morane, but it is too far-fetched to be true. Consider the risks that Stanley would have run!" He patted me on the shoulder. "You have let your spleen against him cloud your reason, my friend, and have built up a tortuous conspiracy out of a woman's chance remark. Glory be! From the murmurings of a whore in bed you would conjure up a conspiracy against the Pope himself!" He went on chuckling, and then his face became serious.

"More important is to decide what it is be done about you."

"Me? Why, I will return to West Minster. Now, if you wish."

"Your absence needs explanation. It would be of little use to say it was because Sir William Stanley ran his sword through your back. Dickon would not believe it. He cannot afford to."

"I will deal with Stanley myself when the time comes," I told him. "I need not mention names when I tell what happened."

He nodded slowly. "Dickon himself will want to hear it. If he asks, how can you avoid telling the name?"

"How could I be expected to see a man who runs me through the back?"

"I hope the King will believe that," he said doubtfully. "You could have . . ."

The parting of the drapes across the arch made him swing round. Neither of us had heard the door open. But it was Matilda, and I looked at her with amazement.

She was wearing a long, green gown, caught at the waist with a plain leather girdle, and her dark curling hair was pushed up under a small cap with a loop of pearls falling over one side. The sleeves were long and loose-fitting, and each hem was embroidered with gold lace. She saw the expression on my face, and laughed.

"I have been at the Strand, shopping," she said gaily.

10

"SO I see," I replied, looking her up and down. "And it appears as if you have been all the way to Venice to do it."

"Ah, but styles have changed since the winter, Henry." She held out an arm, letting the sleeve fall. "See! Tight sleeves have gone! These are much prettier, are they not?" She turned to John Kendall to include him in her question.

He grunted. "It seems to me that they need much more material. I hope my wife doesn't find out about them too soon."

"She will," Matilda said cheerfully. "It is at Court where they began."

"They always do," he muttered. Then he smiled at her. "But at least we have you to thank for keeping Henry alive."

"More than that," I told him. "She saved my life in the first place. If she hadn't dragged me in here I should have died in the filth of the street." I was surprised to see a blush cross her face. I told her how it suited her.

"It is a long time since I have had a compliment paid me," she replied quietly. "Many things have been paid me, but not a true compliment." She came over and kissed me lightly. John Kendall cleared his throat. She laughed and went to kiss him too. "And now," she added, "I will go out and buy more food and wine."

"If you go out in those clothes," I said, "the shopkeepers will charge you double price. They will think that you are at least a countess."

"But I am!" she exclaimed, spinning round to bell out her skirt. "I am! To feel like a countess is to be one!" She went to the door and said over her shoulder, "Even the boatmen didn't know me at first. Then they cheered and sat me up high all the way from Fleet. So I paid them four pence."

"Four pence!" John Kendall was aghast. But Matilda was gone.

He muttered something about women's fashions being an invention of the Devil, crossed himself quickly, and added that Agnes was probably already running up a big account at the milliners. That made me laugh.

58

"It is no laughing matter, Henry," he said sternly. "Your woman's visit has caused me much embarrassment. She brazened her way past the sentries, saw the King at the other end of the hall, and would even have approached him if Sir William Catesby hadn't steered her aside. He brought her to me with a leer on his face, and is likely at this very moment spreading malicious gossip . . . and if it should reach Agnes . . ."

He paused and eyed me. "But we still have to decide about you."

"As I said, I will see the King and tell him the truth."

"He might be hard to convince. It could be said that you gained your wounds in the rebellion."

I gave a scornful laugh. "In the west country? And crawled all the way back here?"

"You could have recovered there. But that is not the point. As my clerk you held a position of trust."

"Has he noticed my absence?"

"Of course he has! More than once he asked me where you were." He made a gesture of helplessness. "And what could I say but that I didn't know? Fortunately on each occasion we have been alone, or there might have been comments from some of the others, Lovell, for instance."

"But they have said nothing?"

"Not to me. Perhaps to the King."

I shrugged. "Well, at least I am not important enough for my disappearance to carry any weight."

"If you were you would have been attainted of treason by now."

"What?" I exclaimed. "Dickon would never do that, to anyone, unless there was proof!"

"There is no telling what he might do after the Buckingham affair," John Kendall said soberly. "He is a man dazed with shock. Buckingham was, after all, one of the closest to him. To have such a friend turn on you without warning, why . . ." He hesitated, searching for a comparison. "Why, it would be as if you, Henry Morane, were to stab me in the back!"

"And now," he added, "the young Prince Edward has just died."

"The Prince of Wales? Great God!"

"Aye. And their son's death has affected the Queen

59

greatly. Even more than Dickon. She was never well, as you know, and now she ails more than ever. It is another burden for him to bear."

"Then what do you suggest? That I remain absent?"

"It might be best. At least until the Tudor question is settled."

"But you said the rebellion has been put down?"

"It has been. But the Lancastrians will try again, that is certain. And not too long in the future, either. They have the Duke of Brittany behind them, and may get help from France. And Bishop Morton is spreading the story again that the boys in the Tower have been murdered."

"But that is nonsense!" I protested. "Now that they have been proclaimed bastards there is no reason to have them killed. Or has some more come to light?"

He shook his head. "No one has seen them, that's all. And Dickon has said nothing. Although he has persuaded Elizabeth Woodville to come out from sanctuary . . ."

"What?" I exclaimed. "You didn't tell me that!"

"I've had little chance," he smiled. "It was a month ago. She accepted his offer of protection and came out with her five daughters, furniture, and all her belongings." He chuckled. "It was like moving house."

"In that case," I said thoughtfully, "something must have occurred suddenly to make her trust him. For she has had more cause to fear Dickon than any other man. After all, he has bastardized her two sons by Edward, executed one of her first two and driven the other into exile in Brittany. He has lopped off the head of her brother, Lord Rivers . . ."

"Yes, yes," he replied testily. "That is well known. Otherwise nothing has occurred apart from Henry Tudor announcing publicly that he will marry her eldest daughter, Elizabeth of York. But that was not 'suddenly', as you call it, for it was on Christmas Day in Brittany."

"Elizabeth of York? But she is sister of the boys in the Tower."

"Even so," John Kendall nodded. "The intention is, of course, to unite the houses of Lancaster and York. Inspired by Bishop Morton, no doubt."

"But how can that be? If the boys are bastards then Elizabeth of York must be one as well."

"A new government under a Tudor king, which God

forbid, could legitimize them. Stillington's oath could be countermanded."

I shook my head. "If that were done and the boys were again legitimate then the elder would succeed to the throne. Henry Tudor would have no claim."

"If they were still alive," John Kendall said grimly.

I sat and stared at him. He drew out his dagger and started to pare his nails.

"Yes!" I said suddenly, making him jump. A piece of fingernail flew across the room and he swore.

"That is what happened!" I said, ignoring the interruption. "That is it! She has been given proof that her sons were murdered!"

"Oh yes?" he inquired with raised eyebrows. "By whom? By Dickon?"

"No, no!" I told him. "By Buckingham. I see it now!"

"By Buckingham? How so?"

"Because Morton was in collusion with him. Morton has started the calumnies again, you said. So he must have a sure knowledge of their fate. Who could have given him that but Buckingham?"

He eyed me carefully. "It is possible," he admitted after some thought. "It is possible, but . . ."

"It is more than possible," I insisted. "They were in Buckingham's care while Richard was away on royal progress, you remember? He had the opportunity then."

"The opportunity, maybe. But what advantage was it to him? They had already been proclaimed bastards."

"The same advantage you said would accrue to him by adhering to Henry Tudor. Their existence would threaten his claim to the throne. And 'Stone Dead Hath no Fellow'," I quoted. "And he could have told Morton that he had done it to save Henry Tudor the trouble."

I got up and brought more wine while John Kendall considered what I had said.

At length he spoke. "Your argument that Buckingham killed the boys has weight," he admitted. "But the same arguments could be used to show that Dickon saw to it."

"Nonsense!" I said scornfully. "Dickon would know very well that he would be the first to be suspected. He would at least wait until his crown was more secure. Besides . . ."—I waved a finger at him—"how is it that Elizabeth Woodville,

61

who first promises her daughter to Henry Tudor, now releases her into the care of Richard of Gloucester? It is a deadly blow to the Tudor ambitions."

"I don't know," he muttered.

"Because," I went on, "she knows that Buckingham has killed her sons and will have no more to do with the Lancastrians. There it is," I concluded. "Dickon has somehow proved to her that the boys were murdered by Buckingham."

"It could be so," he admitted. "For he went to see her privately in sanctuary. And when she came out they said she was weeping bitterly." He scratched his chin with the point of the dagger. "But in that case why does he not produce the bodies and refute the Tudor calumny?"

"Because he does not know where they are. And that . . ." I waved my finger again "is further proof that Dickon, at least, did not do it."

"How?"

"Because if he had killed them he would know where their bodies are, and would produce them as you suggest. The corpses would only show how they came by their death, not who caused it."

He nodded and said, "Um."

"What of the Constable of the Tower?" I asked him.

"Brackenbury? Oh, him? His mind is centred on his stomach. Give him a roasted ox and a sharp knife and he hears and sees nothing until the bones are left gleaming. If Buckingham visited the boys in their apartment, as was his right, being Constable of England, Brackenbury would not be concerned."

"But they were put upon his responsibility."

"Aye, but in Buckingham's carc. He, or anyone else with authority, could come and go as he pleased for all the interest Brackenbury showed. The guard would not impede him."

"The guard? What does he, or the servants say?"

"How can I know? I did not question them. Besides, I hear that since the rebellion the servants have been dismissed. Probably the guard too."

"That seems to show they are dead," I pointed out. "So all that needs to be done is to find their bodies."

He sat up. "Great God! If you meddle in this we shall be looking for yours too." He sighed and put the dagger back into its sheath. "It is evidently better if you do not return to West Minster as yet."

"And remain in hiding here like a mole?"

"Of course you must!" It was Matilda, returning unheard again.

I swung round. "How much have you been listening to?" I demanded.

"Enough to know that your life is in danger."

"You were listening at the door," I accused her.

"I was." She was defiant. "For a long time. And I am glad I did."

"Damnation!" John Kendall said. "I should have been more circumspect."

She whirled on him. "There was no need, sir," she said. "Master Morane is my man. Do you think so ill of me that I would betray him?"

"He thinks ill of every woman," I grinned.

"The fewer people that hear our conversations the better," he muttered. "Then there is less for the executioner's tools to drag out of them."

"You sound as if your conversation has been treasonable," Matilda said.

"Not so!" he replied hotly.

"Even if it was it would be no matter to me," she said. "It is high time there was an end to these murderings, and wars and battles. If Henry Tudor can bring peace to this land by marrying Elizabeth of York, then let us have Henry Tudor, I say."

"Now that is treasonous talk," John Kendall said sternly. "I will not listen."

"I mean no offence to you, Master Kendall," Matilda said quietly. "It is what other people say too. The nobles do nothing but fight and kill each other. They care nothing about the laws of their manor, of the tenant who has been put out unjustly by his landlord, the peaceful traveller robbed in the tavern . . ."

"That is not the case today," John Kendall told her. "Edward the Fourth and the house of York have brought good order these last twelve years."

"But still there is talk of war and rebellion."

"It will be the fact if the Tudors land," I told her. "Have you not thought about that?"

63

"No, Henry," she smiled at me. "I had not thought about it."

"And King Richard needs everyone's loyalty," John Kendall said.

"Loyalty?" she demanded. "And what is that? People who slave for their bread have no time for such high ideals. As for me, I have been loyal but to one man . . ." She looked at me. "But now Henry Morane claims it . . ." I started to say something, but she went on quickly. "And he will deny it, but it is there just the same. What can a man know of a woman's loyalty? It is unseen, unspoken, and given often without hope of return. How then can we give loyalty to a king, a man dressed in fine clothes whom we rarely see, who can cut off our heads or increase our taxes with but a passing thought, when there is another man close to us all the time?" She stopped for breath, then turned to face me. "And that is why, Henry Morane, I will not let you return to West Minster."

I grinned at her. "And if I don't go back and earn a salary again how can I keep you in clothes like that?"

John Kendall chuckled suddenly, but Matilda's face was strained. "It is too much risk," she persisted.

"It is," I agreed solemnly. "I would not dare to parade you in dresses that were out of date."

Her dark eyes studied me for a long time. "You try to steer me aside with flippancies," she said, "but you cannot change what I feel." Then she shrugged helplessly. "But as you are determined to go, Henry, then I shall go with you. Your story will need a witness."

John Kendall gave a long sigh and got to his feet. "Yes," he said, "perhaps, after all, it is better to settle the matter. It is not good to lie in a hole like a frightened rabbit. And now is as good a time as any, while the Stanleys are not at Court . . . Glory be!" he exclaimed suddenly. "I had forgotten the men waiting for me!" He moved quickly to the door. "They will be buzzing like curious bees, especially as they may have seen a woman come in here after me. Oh, Good Lord, let not Agnes hear about this visit of mine . . ."

As he went out I looked at Matilda and laughed. After a moment she came to me and laughed too.

11

WE TOOK a boat from the steps of the Old Swan, although it was farther away, for it was at Dowgate Creek that the watermen knew Matilda, and where John Kendall had tied his boat the day before. I felt it better for her not to be noticed being taken by me to West Minster. It was probably a vain thought, for the brotherhood of the river is all embracing, but it was the least I could do for John Kendall's reputation, in case it got to be known he had called on a woman living in the city near Wall Brook.

The tide was flowing fast from the Great Bridge behind us, so that a vessel with but one oarsman could carry us without difficulty, and be cheaper too. But the fellow, seeing the two of us, promptly demanded three pence, and I was about to remonstrate with my fist when Matilda laughed and kissed him through his beard. At that the hairy face cracked apart in a smile and he settled down to pull at his oars with great venom, the breath whistling like a flute between his ancient teeth.

We passed Dowgate within minutes and then Queenhithe docks, where there was much activity on a sea-going vessel, loading her in time for the next tide to take her through the draw-port of the Great Bridge and down the river, maybe to Flanders, or even across the ocean to Scandinavia. Soon afterwards we were off the Black Friars and the steep walls of Baynard's Castle, with the great spire of Saint Paul's hanging over them like a finger beckoning the sky.

There were boats putting out from the Fleet, probably carrying lawyers to our destination at West Minster, and other craft hauling themselves alongside the wharves of the big houses whose gardens now began to line the riverbank. These were larger boats, pulled by many oarsmen close to the edge to avoid the strength of the tide, bringing pigs and sheep and poultry snorting and cackling for the nobleman's table. Others bore huge casks of ale and mead from the breweries of Brent, and all carried flags and pennants, even standards, bespeaking the owner and his pride in his vessel. The great barges of wool for Queenhithe and the docks beyond the Bridge would not appear yet, for they would wait for the tide to turn and carry them down, judging the hour accurately so that they shot the Bridge before the current grew too strong.

On the other bank all was quiet. The early wildfowler crouched silently with his net, trying for the marshbirds as they skated between the reeds, leaving noiseless trails of ripples behind them in their unceasing search for fish.

Matilda had turned round and was looking back at the line of buildings against the sky. She smiled at me and said, "London is truly the greatest city in the world."

"It is," I agreed, "when the sun shines like this. But when the dark winter mist comes down at night and hides one bank from the other . . ."

"Aye! And strange creatures swim in the water," the boatman said. "Huge serpents with shining eyes and twisted tails, monsters with three heads, each with a pair of forked tongues licking and spitting at everything that passes!"

Matilda swung round with wide eyes, but I laughed and said, "Tell me of the one with the shape of a woman."

The old man coughed and spat over the side. "Well, anyway," he replied, "a whale was caught at Mortlake a hundred years ago. That I know, for my grandfather told me of it. Its teeth can be seen in the church of Saint Mary. I will take you there for another six pence if you do not believe what I say."

"But I do!" Matilda said, "although I have never seen a whale."

Then the Clock Tower at West Minster came in sight and I wondered if the Time Keeper had been told of the brightness of the morning and was about his business checking with the sundial. But at that moment a bell in the tower was given six tremendous blows by the hammer so that I started as if a cannon had gone off and cursed aloud.

"We should be at Mass," Matilda said.

"Maybe," I agreed. "But the clock will not be correct by an hour or more. It seldom is, except when the sun shines."

"It is shining now," she pointed out.

"Aye," I laughed. "But if I know Master Preston he will still be abed. He sleeps late every day, certain that it will rain. When he wakes and sees the weather he will beat his clerk near to death for not rousing him."

"Why doesn't he rouse him, then?"

66

"Because Old Rufus is certain it will rain too."

When she had done laughing she said, "But does he not have striped candles and water devices to set the clock by?"

"Oh, yes, he uses them, such as they are. But the big sundial is the most accurate. And now he will have to wait an hour before the bell is struck again. King Richard once talked of a clock with a pointer, such as are used in Germany, so that all can see the time, but no doubt other matters have erased it from his mind."

"No doubt," Matilda agreed, and said no more until we were afoot.

The sentry put the butt of his halberd on the floor, folded his hands together round the shaft and leaned against it. He lifted one of his thumbs slowly as he eyed me.

"Haven't seen you for a long time, Master Morane. Faring well?"

Grey eyes were narrowed in his wrinkled face. He was a veteran from the days of Towton, and had served in the bodyguard of three kings. A man who would never retire to farm the land the monarch would give him, but would keep his post until the day they found his bones rattling like dice inside his cuirass, and then they would know that he was dead.

I told him that I had come to see the King.

His thumb waved slowly, like a huge snail. "He's in there. But Master Kendall told me to tell you to wait out here."

He had seen me come and go from the royal chambers often enough, and was puzzled. He looked from me to Matilda and back again. "I hope you're not in any trouble," he said, and I knew he meant it. Then, embarrassed, as I evidently was in some kind of trouble, he cast around for something else to say.

"King Dickon's in a fair bad temper these days." As soon as he had said it he realized that it was an even less happy remark to make, and he coughed.

His confusion ended when the door behind him opened quickly. He stiffened and brought the halberd across his body with a swift movement. It was Francis, Lord Lovell.

Lovell eyed Matilda appraisingly and then beckoned to me. When she moved forward to follow he waved her away with an imperious hand. I went inside. He shut the door behind us and looked me up and down.

67

"And now, my absconding scribe, we will hear what you have to say."

I straightened up and glared at him. "Not you, my friend, but the King will hear me. If you choose to eavesdrop that is your affair."

The flesh below his ears and chin went pink. Francis, Viscount Lovell and Lord Chamberlain, was one of the three reputed to be closest to the King. The others, Sir Richard Ratcliffe and Sir William Catesby, were not of noble lineage either, and this fact had on occasion been used as a criticism of the government. The people, it seems, prefer to be ruled by what they think is the wisdom that comes from a long line of proven breeding. Lord Lovell himself had only acquired his title by marriage, and could never seem to forget it. A heavy-set, muscular person, he wore his hair long and curled, and the fur-lined brocades that clothed him gleamed with precious stones. The embroidered hem of his coat reached half-way to his knee, and below it one hose was red, the other in stripes of blue and yellow, while the toes of his soft leather shoes were slashed to show velvet linings before they swept upwards into sharp points. Yet, in spite of his dress and the perfume he used, Lord Lovell was no fool. Neither was he a reluctant warrior when it came to battle, for I had seen him spur his horse at a group of spearmen at Tewkesbury and, single-handed, slay them all.

He met my glare and snarled. "That sounds to me precious close to slander, scribe. To eavesdrop is a . . ."

"The same when absconding is imputed, my Lord."

He stood for a moment while he regained his composure. It did not do to lose one's temper with someone of lesser rank. "You take offence quickly, I see?"

"I do, my Lord," I replied. "But I did not come here to quarrel with you. I came to see the King."

"Then take the dagger out of your belt first, or I might impute something worse."

I had forgotten the dagger. I drew it out and laid it on the table beside the door. By then he had turned his back on me and walked away. I followed him across the room.

Catesby and Ratcliffe were there, as was to be expected, as well as John Kendall. King Richard was sitting in a huge, carved wooden chair with a single cushion. His shoes were beside him and his feet were stretched out towards the fire.

He had looked up, and dark, suspicious eyes were watching my every step. His face had always been pale, but now it was white, and new lines had appeared at the corners of his eyes and between his brows.

I walked up to him slowly and went down on one knee, with Lovell now close behind me.

"Sire," I said, "I beg pardon for my absence."

There was a long silence while the dark eyes inspected me. They had seen me often enough before, but now they were looking at someone different. I met his gaze for a few moments and then looked away, partly through apprehension and partly through not wishing to seem impertinent. This was a man who had the power to have me disembowelled at the wave of a hand. But I had confidence he would not do so lightly, as his brother might have done. He would want proof of guilt first.

"Well?" he inquired at last. "Is that all you have to say?"

I looked up at him again. "I did not come to make excuses, Sire. And any explanation I make would only be a repetition of what your Secretary must already have told you."

From behind me Lovell said, "A concocted story, eh?"

John Kendall swung round, but the King waved him back. "I will hear it from you," he said to me. "And get to your feet."

I stood up gratefully. He listened to me with attention, and when I had finished he grunted. Putting his feet into his shoes he got up and stood inspecting me. Underneath his fur-trimmed black coat he wore a brown silk tunic with narrow stripes of gilt. The gilt was the only brightness he wore, and even his fingers carried but one ruby-set ring. I saw again how immensely wide he was across the shoulders, with a neck like an ox, so that it seemed his thin legs would never support such a body.

"Now let me see the marks," he said.

I struggled out of my shirt and they all crowded round to examine the scars. That on my chest was still wealed and angry, and I guessed that the one on my back was the same.

"A sword thrust, certainly," Richard said. "And from the back to the front." He moved away and put his thumb into

69

his belt. "But it could as easily have been given you while fighting for Buckingham."

"It could have, your Grace," I agreed. "But it was not. The first I heard of the rebellion was from Master Kendall yesterday, and he told me that there was no fighting, or very little, and that in the west country. I have a witness outside who can testify that the wound was made in London, and she . . ."

"A woman witness, eh?" Catesby muttered.

"A woman, Sir William," I admitted. "But a witness. And possibly the priest who came to shrive me when she thought I was dying. Although he may be difficult to find as he went away disgruntled when he found no money on my person."

I saw John Kendall grin.

"You speak boldly," the King said, "for someone who has only one witness, and a woman at that."

"Sire, she can swear . . ."

"Oh yes, I have no doubt she can swear to anything. She has been tending to your wounds and has no doubt formed an attachment for you, eh?"

I shivered, for the room was not warm, except for that part close to the fire. Richard noticed it and waved at me to get dressed again. I did it right quickly, thinking hard all the time.

"And," he went on, "she would swear to a different story under torture, no doubt?" He was watching me closely.

"She would, Sire," I said, and heard John Kendall draw in his breath. "But, as is well known, any person under pain will swear to what is required."

At that Richard's eyes narrowed suddenly, and then he nodded. I saw a trace of something like a smile cross his face. He turned on his heel and walked back to his chair. When he was seated again, he said, "Now tell us who it was that ran you through."

I thought that John Kendall would have told him. But there the question was, direct and dangerous.

"My Lord," I said, "as he was behind me I could not say who he was."

The dark eyes watched me, unblinking. "You could not *say* who it was? But do you *know* who it was?" My evasion had been swept aside, but I knew that it was as much as my life was worth to mention the name of Sir William Stanley even in this privy company.

I said, "Not for certain, Sire. All I can remember is that he laughed."

"He laughed, eh? Then perhaps you would recognize that laugh?"

I shook my head. "One laugh is much as another."

Lovell made a sound of impatience. He bore no particular grudge against me, I knew. It was John Kendall he was trying to make trouble for. They were all jealous of him, of his competence and wisdom, as lesser minds often are. If they could make trouble for his clerk it would be trouble for him too. I saw Catesby's mocking smile, and even Ratcliffe looked contemptuous.

"In fact, your Grace," I said, "the very laugh that Lord Lovell gave when I came in could have been the same."

That wiped the smile off their faces. In the startled silence that followed I saw John Kendall stifle a grin. But the King remained unmoved, staring at me.

"I doubt if it was my Lord Chamberlain," he said quietly. "He does not have the reputation for running people through the back."

I bowed a little. "It was not suggested, Sire, and . . ."

"But whatever he said to you as you came in . . ."— Richard's eyes went past me and I heard Lovell cough— ". . . he no doubt regrets." Dickon had missed nothing. His gaze came back to me. "Are you unwilling to say who it was until I have it dragged out of you?"

"Not unwilling, Sire. Afraid. Any name mentioned by someone like me would be slander. The more so if there were no proof or witnesses."

He nodded slowly. "You would repeat your previous remarks about torture?"

I could only incline my head mutely.

"And the woman you were associating with at that time? Did you know that she was his?"

I looked up at him again, and nodded, but there was relief in me now. The identity of my assailant was not to be pursued further. Now I was sure that Dickon knew who he was, and that John Kendall had told him. He had pressed me hard, but it was to see if I could be trusted to be discreet. And the reason for the questioning in front of the others was

71

now clear too. For the imputation must have come from Lovell or one of the others that I had deserted my post to join Buckingham. To have John Kendall's privy clerk desert to the rebels would have brought his disgrace. But the King was speaking . . .

". . . and so, Master Morane, for someone of your station, you were acting very foolishly, were you not?" He glanced at his Secretary, and then I knew that John Kendall had also told him why I had continued the liaison with Alice.

From behind me Lovell spoke. "Whatever my reputation, Dickon, if I had been in that position I should have run him through for the same foolishness. The only difference being that I should have seen to it that he was dead."

That brought a laugh from the others, even the King's face easing somewhat. Then he grew stern again, and faced me.

"Master Morane," he said, "you have had the courage to come back and answer any imputations that might have been made, and that I will respect in any man. Yet," he added, "your case remains one of suspicion."

It had to be so, of course. He could not let me go free, or the curiosity of the others would be aroused and they would begin asking questions. At least that was what I thought, and the constriction in my chest grew. It was as if Stanley's sword was still in it. So it was to be imprisonment on suspicion, then? I hoped it would not be the Tower.

King Richard looked at Lovell and then at the others. "We will hear no more of this matter, my friends," he told them. His brows came down over his eyes and they were suddenly not friends any more. He was the King, and giving his command. "It would be unfortunate," he went on, "if whoever it was thrust his sword through Henry Morane heard that he was still alive, would it not?"

Catesby nodded vigorously and Ratcliffe said, "Yes." I heard a grunt from Lovell, but there was no need to look at John Kendall. Yet I was apprehensive as to what might happen if Sir William Stanley heard that I was still alive and helpless in the Tower.

"Henry Morane," King Richard said, "your case is one of suspicion. You therefore cannot remain in my Secretary's service." He waved me away and turned to John Kendall. "Find him employment elsewhere than at West Minster."

I turned away, almost blind with relief. At the door I heard him saying, ". . . perhaps in London. I am informed that the Recorder has need of clerks . . ."

Matilda was there, fearful because I had been so long. But when she saw my face she threw her arms round me. I heard the sentry's halberd thud on the floor as he began to cough furiously again.

12

CHRISTOPHER Urswick, Recorder of London, in spite of the King's information, did not seem to be in need of clerks. Most of the work he did himself, and the clerks that he already had seemed to be little engaged. As the King's information was rarely inaccurate I was somewhat puzzled. I knew that I had been sent away from West Minster only because Sir William Stanley might encounter me there again, and my survival from his sword-thrust the King did not want disclosed, but for what reason he wished to keep it secret I could not guess.

Urswick himself welcomed my arrival with no great enthusiasm, and put me to work on tasks that were not only tedious but seemed to have no meaning whatsoever. After a month I suggested to him that I might be employed on work more fitting to my capabilities.

I am of normal stature, but he stood no higher than my shoulder as he looked at me, a slight man with thinning hair the colour of beach sand, and eyes as dull as the pebbles that lie upon it.

"You were at West Minster?" he asked, as if I had just announced the fact.

"Yes, sir. Clerk to the King's Secretary."

"Does the King's Secretary have so little work these days that he can afford to dispense with a clerk?"

"He was ordered to find me other employment."

"Ordered?" Christopher Urswick looked surprised. I found it hard to credit that he had been apprised of this a month before. "Ordered?" he repeated. "There is only one person who can give orders to the King's Secretary."

"Just so, sir. It was King Richard himself."

It took him a few moments to consider that. Then, "Why would the King concern himself with the affairs of a clerk?" he muttered, as if to himself. "Unless . . . unless . . ." He decided not to finish what he was going to say.

I said it for him. "I was attacked by a thief and left for dead. Being absent from my duties for a long time did not serve me well. I am now fully recovered, though," I added, giving him a level stare.

"But the King's Secretary would have retained you?"

I could see that he, too, was thinking of the Buckingham rebellion. I shrugged. "It was not in his disposal, sir."

So it was the Buckingham affair after all? A gleam of understanding swept across his pebble eyes as if they had suddenly been washed by the receding tide. He went back to his desk and sat there for a long time, sucking at the feathers of his pen.

No more was said about the affair. I laboured on for several weeks at matters of little importance, while the other clerks jockeyed with each other for the more interesting duties, such as delivering letters to other parts of the town. Once out of the Recorder's office it would be a long time before they returned; a letter to Baynard's Castle, for instance, no more than half a mile away, took several hours, and when its bearer returned his breath would be foul with wine. Some missives would be for other towns, and then the clerk who took it would be away perhaps a week, limping from hours on horseback and boasting, blear-eyed, of the country wenches he had pleasured on the way. But the boasting was made far from the ears of Christopher Urswick.

In spite of my boredom by day I was entertained enough when work was done. I had given up my lodgings and moved my few possessions to Matilda's house. That had been no great chore as, apart from clothes, there was only my one piece of armour, a sword, and a vicious-looking bill-hook that I had taken from the grip of a dead Lancastrian at Tewkesbury. There had even been a time when I thought I might never need them again, as Edward the Fourth had imposed his peace on the land these last twelve years. But now, with defections to Henry Tudor's standard in Brittany increasing, there was an air of unease and uncertainty about the country, as there is in a village when the first case of plague occurs.

Matilda had found employment with a baker, but her work did not entail her labouring in front of the ovens at night. Instead, it was her task to arrive at dawn, open the shop and set out the wares on the shutters for all to see. The baker was astute enough to realize that it was not only the prettiness of his confections that made people buy, but the attractions of his assistant that first brought them to look. Matilda told me that the cakes and pastries were so compelling

75

that she had to be careful not to eat too many herself, not so much because of the ire of her employer but because of her girth. That was, however, easily kept in check by my fitting both hands together round her waist each night when I returned. On the occasions when my fingers failed to meet she took great fright and abjured all forms of pastry until they did. It was a pity that her employment came to an end after three months when a well-baked frog was found in one of her master's loaves.

The bakery was closed by the sheriff, the baker himself and his two assistants being placed in the pillory. Although the two men were released after a few hours, one of them was an apprentice, and any hopes he might have had of becoming a master-baker were brought to nothing. As to the baker himself, he was confined for a week, in a prison cell by night and in the pillory by day, until his crime was expiated. The sentence seemed to me to be excessively harsh, for once the frog was removed the bread would have been good enough to eat, especially by a hungry man without the price of a loaf. But then the City of London prides itself on its laws concerning food.

The baker certainly paid for his mistake, for not only were his head, hands and feet caged while the hot summer sun beat down upon him, but a man confined in that posture is a prey to all the malicious members of the community. His sentence stated that stale bread should be burned under his nose, but not that dead frogs and other loathsome creatures should be added to the pyre. It was a great occasion for urchins too, who reduced their prices for removing chamber pots from three to five for a penny for the pleasure of emptying their contents over the poor fellow's head. And it was as well he was removed to the prison at night, for there is no telling what the more depraved might have done to his person after dark.

I had been wondering for some time when I should see John Kendall again, for I dared not return to West Minster, when he encountered me at the bear-baiting. It was by the pit at Smithfield, where a monstrous black creature from Russia—or so its owner swore—had been put out to match the best hounds that could be set against it. Although not a spectacle that Matilda enjoyed very much she liked to be with the gay and colourful crowd that always assembled on such occasions. For my part I went to see the cunning of the dogs more than the people.

The huge bear snarled, its chain rattled against the post, dogs yelped, blood ran, and sand flew in all directions. The crowd cheered when three hounds lay dead, and many coins spun into the arena for its Muscovite owner. He was a charlatan, of course, for on occasion his talk lapsed into the English of a Londoner, but the crowd loved it, cheering each time he forgot his Russian accent. It was when the fourth dog, caught before it could turn, limped away with its shoulder nearly clawed off that the chain snapped and the bear lurched forward to fall clumsily on to its face.

A renewed cheer from the spectators changed quickly into the deep moan of panic as the bear got to its feet, scattered the rest of the dogs, and began to climb over the edge of the pit. It was all I could do to hold Matilda tight while the crowd surged away round us, for she seemed to be in more danger from being trampled upon by people than from the animal.

The bear, reaching the surface of the ground, stood up on its hind legs waving a bloodied claw and looked about it. There it hesitated, taken aback by the unaccustomed number of people and, seeing no dogs, was about to turn round towards its familiar pit when three men, more intrepid than the rest, advanced upon it with swords. When it saw them the animal snarled and swung a massive paw, sending two of them reeling away with torn faces, while the other, wisdom finally overcoming valour, dodged aside and ran for his life. The beast, maddened again with blood, sank back on to four feet and began to shamble towards where we stood.

I spun Matilda round and shouted at her to run away quickly. She started to protest, but I gave her a shove that sent her stumbling off, then swung round drawing my dagger and cursing myself for not having brought a sword.

The beast, seeing me, came to a halt and stood up to inspect me better. I held my ground for as long as I dare, to give Matilda time to get away, but my stomach was a-twist and I felt my breath coming faster. If the bear kept still, so would I. But as to whether I should be able to outpace it when it came for me I had not the slightest idea. My attention was entirely fixed on the hate-reddened eyes and the saliva drooling from the sharp white teeth, so that whether it roared at me or not even to this day I cannot remember. Then it shook its head twice and came slowly down on to all-fours. It was time for me to run. But I found I could not move.

I seemed to be rooted to the ground, and barely heard the yell of command and the rasp of bowstrings. For the City Archers, seeing their target clear for the first time, had let fly a volley of arrows that brought the creature down in front of me, blood gushing from its mouth.

As I swung away the world went round with me, so that I had difficulty in keeping my balance. Then I saw Matilda on John Kendall's arm, crying like a babe.

And when I came to them she stamped her foot and said, "I hate you, Henry Morane! I hate you for frightening me like that!" Then her arms were round me and she was sobbing at my chest.

"Never mind," I said soothingly. "Next time I will kill it myself, so that there is only one hole in the fur. Then you shall have it for a coat."

With that she drew away and eyed me. "Dear God! I believe you would! Oh, how I hate you ... !" Then she smiled, and added, "Sometimes."

I saw John Kendall grinning and asked him what brought him there.

"I was coming to see you after the bear-baiting," he replied, "although it appears that my visit might nearly have been wasted." He glanced across at the archers who were congratulating themselves on their shooting. "They left it a little long, I thought," he added pensively.

People were now streaming back past us to look at the body of the dead monster. There were exclamations of amazement and awe at its size, and not a few words of execration for its owner. But that worthy had not waited to hear them. Once his charge had left the pit he had jumped down to pick up as many of the coins as he could before making a hasty departure.

I was about to speak to John Kendall when I felt someone staring at me. It was one of my fellow-clerks, the foxy-faced one who had boasted of his prowess with the country wenches. I waved a hand at him and at first he seemed embarrassed, then he waved back, his glance moving to Matilda before he was lost again in the crowd.

"I was wondering when I should see you again," I said to John Kendall, "And now . . ."

"And now," he interrupted, "the King has work for you."

"Aha!" I exclaimed. "So I have not been forgotten! I am to work in West Minster again?"

"No." John Kendall shook his head. "In Brittany."

13

WE WALKED through Saint Paul's yard, under the great spire that reaches upward of five hundred feet, and past a friar in one of the pulpits who was out-preaching all the others about the tortures of Hell that await all sinners. He had come to the sin of adultery as we went by, and was denouncing it violently, his strident voice describing in detail the abominable indignities that awaited such sinners in the Hereafter that it quite frightened Matilda, who looked at me wide-eyed and clutched at my arm. I grinned down at her reassuringly and put my hand over hers.

The Chepe, as was to be expected, was lined on both sides with market stalls, and progress through the bawling, bickering, haggling mass of people was difficult. The fruit stalls were the most sought after: strawberries, figs, raisins and grapes were all there, laid out below black clouds of circling flies that had probably accompanied them all the way from where they had been picked. Matilda had a fancy for figs, she said, and I spent several minutes shouting above the din at a one-eyed old dame before she would take the price I offered. There were wines too, from all over Europe, and one enterprising fellow was even selling bottles of water from the Tiber itself.

Out of curiosity I asked him the price, and when he said it was four pence I told him it was outrageous. He winked and said that the waters of the Tiber carried the effluent from the privies of the Vatican itself, so that it was very nearly Holy Water. John Kendall gave him a speculative look and told him that he would sell three times as many bottles at half the price. At that he held up his hands in feigned horror. Did we not know that the cost of bringing the bottles all the way across Europe was enormous? There were mountain passes, some filled with snow, and others frequented by brigands, many of whom would steal the water in preference to gold. Why, there were even towns where bottles had been sequestrated by the Mayor for the cure of a recent outbreak of plague. There were deep, mysterious forests where witches abounded, moving silently through the trees to snatch bottles from the very packs of the horses . . ."

"Why would they do that?" Matilda asked innocently.

"To alleviate their pregnancy, my lady."

"But how on earth can a witch be gotten with child?" she said.

"Aha!" He put a grimed finger against the side of his nose. "If the man is a warlock then anything might happen. Witches bring forth all manner of beings. Not merely toads and snakes, but two-headed dogs and creatures with horns like the great rhino-sorcerous of Ethiopia, and on occasion the Devil himself, his spiked tail between his teeth . . ."

Matilda gave a little shriek and crossed herself quickly.

"Spare us the details," I told him, taking her by the arm.

"Sir," he said respectfully, holding out his cap. "At least give me a penny for a good story."

At that I laughed and gave him one. He held out a bottle. "Take it, sir. There is a man coming who looks as if he might buy. Take it, sir, for nothing. It will seem as if I have sold it to you."

I doubted that, because it was Urswick's clerk, and he was no simpleton, but I took the bottle to placate the fellow.

As we turned off the Chepe Matilda said, "Throw it away, Henry. Throw it away unopened. For if you break the tallow and free the contents God himself might not know what stink will emerge."

"Maybe not," John Kendall chuckled. "But the Holy Father surely will!"

A few minutes later we came to a corner where one of the houses had a thatched roof. They were becoming rarer in London since the laws against them had been made, but John Kendall pointed at the bush hanging outside the door and took me by the arm.

"A tavern," he said. "It will save time if we talk there, for my boat is nearer here than at your house." He nodded to Matilda.

She took a fig from her basket and bit into it. "I am agog to hear what business calls Henry Morane to Brittany," she said.

"It is the King's business," he told her sternly. "And it is better you do not know."

"Piff!" she said, throwing away the core of the fruit. "I will go on to the house and warm some ale. If I ply him with

81

enough of it he will tell me." She went up to him, gave him a kiss, blew one at me, and walked away down the street.

It was a small tavern, with but one trestle, and no other person except the landlord. We sat down and called for mead. When it came John Kendall made a face and put down his mug. "Thin and insipid," he announced. "The bees that accounted for this were starved . . ."

"We are not here to talk about the quality of the mead," I told him. "What is this about Brittany?"

He pushed the mug aside and leaned forward. "Duke Francis of Brittany," he told me, "is a firm supporter of the Lancastrians. He is giving asylum to Henry Tudor and his uncle, Jasper . . ."

"Yes, yes," I said. "All this I know."

"But Duke Francis has been stricken with the head sickness again."

"Again? Has he had it before, then?"

"Yes. It is of the brain, and recurs with him as it did with King Henry the Sixth. He has periods of delusion, and when they come he is not fit to govern. At those times the Lord Treasurer, one Pierre Landois, has the power . . ." He reached out for his mug and looked up to call the landlord, but he was not there.

"Finish what you are saying," I told him. "We can drink later."

"Yes. Well, now there is a message from Pierre Landois saying he will, for fifty thousand crowns, deliver up Henry Tudor."

"Jesu! Fifty thousand crowns!" I sat up. "How did you get such a message? By letter?"

He nodded. "If it had been by word of mouth we should not have trusted the man who brought it. Whereas this fellow . . ."

"Who was he?"

"Have patience, and I will tell you. A ruffian named Will Slaughter presented himself at Court and demanded to see the King. Being known as one of Buckingham's men who fled to Brittany after the rebellion he was arrested on the spot. He then announced that he carried a letter for the King which, if it was not read by the King himself in Slaughter's presence, would be to his disadvantage. Lovell, who had been summoned, thereupon relieved him of the letter and opened it. Seeing its contents, he had Slaughter taken to Dickon. It was the message from Pierre Landois I have mentioned."

"And will Dickon accept the offer?"

"He has already. Slaughter was sent back with its acceptance."

"He sent Slaughter back? He should have kept him under arrest and sent someone else."

John Kendall made a grimace. "This Slaughter is a wily bird. He has somehow persuaded Landois of the sanctity of his person. The letter stipulated that the reply must be brought by no one else, or the bargain would not be made."

"He took a risk. Suppose Dickon had not accepted? Slaughter would have lost his head."

"He might," John Kendall agreed. "But there was little risk. Landois knows that the person of Henry Tudor is worth more to Dickon than the head of a fellow like Will Slaughter."

"Aye," I nodded. "A Tudor corpse is worth more . . ."

"Not so!" he said quickly. "The essence of the bargain is that he shall be alive and well. Henry Tudor is to be paraded through London for all to see."

"And be strangled quietly later."

At that he grew angry. "Don't be a fool, Henry Morane. A dead Tudor would only make way for another pretender."

"And a live one would be a focus for further Lancastrian plots."

"Precisely! But as there will always be plots of one kind or another it is better they are channelled in one direction, channels that can be watched and laid bare if necessary. Besides," he added with a smile, "they might implicate others of whom the King may have suspicion, but no proof.'

I saw what he meant. "And has any more been heard from Landois?"

"Oh yes! Slaughter came back with details of how the bargain is to be effected."

"Then he is a fool. Once the details are settled he will be seized."

"The details are not all settled," John Kendall replied patiently. "The time of the exchange is agreed, but the Breton port at which it is to take place is not. It is known only to Will Slaughter."

"A few minutes on the rack will drag it from him."

"It would," he agreed. "But Pierre Landois stipulates that fifty thousand crowns *and* Will Slaughter are to be handed over before he parts with Henry Tudor."

I grunted. "The fellow must have a smooth tongue to persuade the Breton Treasurer of his value."

"Not too difficult. Without him the bargain could not be carried out."

"And this Pierre Landois? Can he be trusted?"

"Who knows? But if he cannot then no great harm is done. If he does not deliver the prisoner then we do not deliver the gold." He chuckled. "And Slaughter gets his throat cut."

"Hah!" I said. "So it is all very simple! The trap is waiting to be sprung at some Breton port of which no one but Slaughter knows the name. Where he and Landois can seize the gold or, failing that, seize its bearer for ransom."

John Kendall chuckled aloud. "And how much ransom do you think you could command, Henry Morane?"

I gave a long sigh. I had seen that coming.

He went on chuckling. "You are a resourceful fellow, Dickon knows. If Landois does not hand over the Tudor then you are to bring the gold back. As you say, it is simple."

"Simple?" I got to my feet and stood glowering over him. "Simple!" My raised voice brought the landlord in. John Kendall told him to consign his mead to the river and bring us beer. When it came I seized my mug and sat down, glaring at him.

"Fifty thousand crowns," I told him, "would buy a company of Swiss mercenaries for a month. An army might be waiting for me."

He waved an airy hand. "You will have an escort, of course."

I put my mug on the table. "Ah!" I said. "How big?"

"Twelve archers."

I looked at him, dumbfounded. Then I said, "Twelve archers? And what in the Name of God can they be expected to achieve?"

"That will be for you to decide," he replied, inspecting the ceiling.

I was about to burst out again when his eyes came down to meet mine. "Calm yourself, Henry," he said, "and consider. There will be no army waiting for you. It would mean

84

the loss of secrecy. If the Tudor is worth fifty thousand crowns to the Dukedom of Brittany how much more would he be worth to the King of France? And even if his person was not worth so much the fact of his betrayal would be. It would give France the excuse she seeks to punish her rebellious vassal of Brittany. This so-called vassal, which is to all intents and purposes an independent state."

"The same would apply when it is found that the Tudor is captive of the English King."

"By then it would be too late. It would be announced that he had been seized in a raid from England. There would be exchanges of hostile utterances between Brittany and England. Hackles would be raised for the benefit of France." He smiled. "And then it would all die away."

He watched me while I considered it. "Even so," I said after a moment, "an escort of twelve archers . . ."

"They are all picked men. And the ship will carry no more."

"The ship? It is arranged too?"

"Of course. It waits to sail from Lyme on Tuesday." He looked out of the window. "And if this weather holds you will be completing the bargain with Landois by Thursday."

"Body of God!" I exclaimed. "I am to be at Lyme by Tuesday! But what of the gold? And the escort?"

"Calm yourself! It is all arranged. The gold is ready, and the escort waits."

I sat down slowly and stared at him with mounting anger. "And if everything has been arranged why didn't you come to tell me before taking a holiday at the bear-pit?"

This time he laughed outright. "Because," he chuckled, "as you are to leave tonight there would have been little point in telling you earlier. It would have given your Matilda that much longer in which to try and persuade you not to go."

14

THE wind was foul, dead against us from the south-west. The sky was the colour of stale milk, with massive, iron-dull clouds surging low over the sea to crash silently into the Dorset cliffs where they broke, gathered themselves, and swept over the top to deluge the countryside beyond. It had been raining for four days.

I looked at the sea and shuddered. Long, rolling lines of grey water, as regular as a Roman legion, advanced one after the other upon the shore, boiling and crashing into angry white foam, to recede again hissing like a thousand serpents. It was not a day for a cruise to Brittany.

He stood there, his curling white hair and beard flattened by the wind, shouting at me that it was a pity we weren't going the other way, to France or Flanders, as on a day like this we could have gotten there in double-quick time. I shouted back, but not loud enough for him to hear, that I thanked God we were not going to France or Flanders or anywhere else on a day like this in that angular contraption of rotted timber and frayed cords that he called a ship. Whatever he replied seemed to be no more than a loud laugh, so perhaps he heard me after all. But then shipmasters are like that, creatures controlled by the moon.

I waved at him and walked back slowly to the flea-ridden inn which was the best hospitality that Lyme could offer. It seemed a long time since that sunny afternoon at Smithfield when the bear had broken loose, yet it was only four days ago. Four days of rain and mud, where the roads had become impassable, forcing us to make detours across open country and keep losing our direction. In spite of that I and my escort of twelve archers had completed the journey in that time, taking turn and turn about with our sixteen horses, and changing them for fresh mounts and drays whenever we could. It was the cart that caused the most difficulty. Eight barrels of gold were no light weight even for the great beasts that drew it, and even more when the wheels went down to their hubs in mud. And while it was not easy for eight tired men to find accommodation in the hostelries of the towns we passed through it was a lot worse for the five whose turn it was to guard the cart. It was not surprising that the archers, Lincolnshire men all, grumbled most of the time, although their murmuring was kept in check by their leader, one Joseph Anderson, a black-browed veteran with a completely bald head. I learned later that he was descended from the Danes of the old East-Anglian Danelaw, and when I asked him how he came about his first name he muttered some tale about his father, whose frequent and prolonged bouts with a mixture of ale and mead invariably ended in a religious fervour, and who had been in one of those humours when his twelfth son had been baptized.

And now we, guarding a cart loaded with fifty thousand crowns, had to wait in a rat-infested place like Lyme before the weather would allow us to start upon our hare-brained expedition.

At least Matilda had said it was hare-brained, and she was probably right. I had told her I could not avoid it, but she would not listen. She had seen me at Death's door once, she stormed, and if I approached it for the second time it would surely open for me. Was it not better to disobey the King's command and go to the Tower than to certain destruction in Brittany?

And what would be the point of that, I replied, for if I was in the Tower I wouldn't be able to see her? There was no reason why I shouldn't return from Brittany safely, and besides, I should be well rewarded. But she had cried and said that there could be only one reason why I was going there, and that was to attempt some harm on the Tudors, and that I had orders to kill him, no doubt, in which case I should certainly be caught and hanged. It would be better if once I arrived there I deserted to the Tudor standard, when at least I should be safe.

At that I became exasperated and told her that even if I were to do such a thing I should be as much a prisoner there as in the Tower.

"You would not!" she had cried. "Because you would be coming back very soon with Henry Tudor's army to depose the monster Richard!"

"He is no monster," I retorted. "And would you have me a traitor, deserting to some chance-taking usurper rather than doing my small part in seeing that the present authority remains secure?"

"And what is Richard but a usurper?" she inquired coldly.

I shrugged. "Whatever anyone calls him he is still the King," I replied, picking up my sword. But she would not kiss me away, and I walked out sombrely. And now, in the midst of my despondency, the only thought that came to me was that I should have brought my cuirass as well, for it would have been some protection against the rain. Such is the way the human brain works.

After leaving Matilda and failing to revive my spirits at a tavern I decided that it would be courtesy to tell Christopher Urswick that I was leaving his service. He would be in his office, I was sure. For he always seemed to be there.

So engrossed was he with what he was writing that he did not hear me come in, and when I coughed he swung round, wide-eyed. When he saw me his expression softened. I told him that I was leaving his service, and he replied that he had been expecting it, because my capabilities were clearly greater than he could use. Then he said that nevertheless he was sorry, and I knew that he was sincere, for I in turn had come to like and respect the quiet, sandy-haired Christopher Urswick. There was one small favour I could do him, he added, and I agreed readily. It was merely to deliver a letter to a ship at Queenhithe and, it being a holiday and all his other clerks elsewhere, it would save him having to deliver it himself as the vessel was about to sail with the tide.

As I walked away it occurred to me that he had not asked what I was going to do, but I put it down to his natural polite reluctance to question other people about their affairs.

The letter was addressed to the Keeper of Hammes Castle, which was in English territory just outside Calais. Hammes was known as being one of the less pleasant places at which to be stationed. Surrounded by marshes, which brought the fever, it was a grim and forbidding work. A soldier from there once told me that he would sooner be stationed in Ireland, and that remark alone is enough to show the dreariness of Hammes. Then I remembered that it was at Hammes where the Lancastrian general, the Earl of Oxford, our old opponent at Barnet, was still imprisoned. To be of the garrison there was bad enough, but to be in one of its dungeons was a hundred times worse. I felt a touch of sympathy for the Earl. He deserved a better fate than Hammes.

My thoughts returned to the present as I splashed out of

the rain into the tavern of Lyme. There was a room I could have for the night, it seemed, if I would wait while the fire was lit. It was a long wait, for the landlord's tale about the attempted Tudor landing to support Buckingham the previous winter was interminable. But not having anything better to do I listened patiently. After all, it was the only event of importance that he was ever likely to be able to talk about during the rest of his humdrum life. In the end the serving-wench came to lead me up a narrow stairway to a room under the eaves where it was not possible to stand upright except near the door. There was a stove glowing with wood sparks near the tiny window and I went over to it to warm my hands while she stood and watched me. She was a prepossessing piece, and her eyes held invitation, but my thoughts were elsewhere, so I gave her a shiny new silver penny and sent her away.

Hardly had her bare feet echoed down the stairs when the door opened again and a tall, cadaverous fellow moved inside quietly. Before he could take another step my sword was out of its sheath and the point against his throat.

He held his arms out away from his body and said in a cracked voice that if I would allow him he would put his hand inside his tunic and show me the King's Writ. I nodded warily and stood back a little while a skeletal set of fingers scrabbled around and finally came out with a paper which he unfolded and thrust towards me. It was an ancient trick to offer something with one hand while a dagger waited in the other, so I took the paper on my sword-point and waved him back against the wall.

It was the King's Writ, true enough, signet sealed, which Richard was in the habit of using at that time. Addressed to all men, and dated a month before, it commanded assistance and service to one Will Slaughter who was about the business of the Realm.

I folded the paper, gave it back to him, and looked him up and down. He was aptly named, six and a half feet without the clogs he was wearing, and as thin as a spear. I asked him what he wanted from me.

"A passage in the ship you use," was the reply.

I nodded. There was a small black insect moving under his matted hair. "Then you will have to ask the shipmaster, not me," I told him.

"I will," he agreed. "But I thought it fit to make known my presence to you first, as you seem to be in charge." He paused to clear his throat. The sound that emerged was like an ass braying suddenly at midnight. "You have heard of me?"

I scowled at him. "Take your warrant to the Master and, if you can satisfy him that you are the person named in it and have not murdered the real Slaughter to obtain it no doubt he will consider it his duty to oblige you."

The skull-like face parted to expose dark and broken teeth, then he went off down the stairs, whistling like a cooking-pot.

15

IT WAS soon after birdsong that the door opened and Joseph Anderson came in with a bowl of soup. He growled the time of day.

"I would prefer to see the wench's face to yours," I growled back.

He gave an evil grin in the half-light. "She has had a busy night, and is indisposed. But the weather has changed. The wind is less and the sun will come up soon. We sail today, so the shipmaster told me."

"You have been down to the ship?"

He nodded. "It seems we have another passenger. A bean-headed vagabond waving the King's Writ. At least, that's what he said it was. Although even if I could not read it I could at least see the seal."

"I have met him," I said. "He calls himself Slaughter, Will Slaughter."

"Aye. And he and the shipmaster have met before."

I frowned at him. "And how do you know that?"

"They were friendly. Until they saw me. Besides," he added, "any decent captain would have thrown a scrawn like that off the ship, King's Writ or no." He paused and studied me. "Any fool can guess that the barrels we carry contain gold, or even hazard that you are a Lancastrian absconding with his treasure, since we are going to Brittany."

"Jesu!" I exclaimed. "I am not a Lancastrian! I have the King's Writ too!"

"Aye," he agreed scornfully. "They seem cheap these days."

I grew angry. "And how do you know we are going to Brittany?"

"Oh," he said airily. "The shipmaster told me."

"He is very free with his information."

"He was last night," Anderson chuckled, "with a dagger against his back."

"Last night? Yet you wait till this morning to accuse me?"

"There was no hurry. You would not get far with eight barrels of gold." He grinned. "I had other business to attend to. More pleasurable business."

I glared at him. "And you think I am a Lancastrian?"

"I do not. You are quick to take offence, Master Morane. What I said was that anyone, seeing all the gold you carry, might think so."

"You mean that Will Slaughter?"

"Not only him. The landlord kept you talking late. It was to ensure that you did not hear his messenger leave on horseback."

"Great God!" I exclaimed. "He sent a messenger about the gold? Who to?" Then I eased. "But wherever he sent it it will be too late. We shall have sailed."

Anderson chuckled. "That is true. And in any case the message will never arrive. The man, one of his ostlers, lies bound against our cart. He has been complaining all night that he has an important message for the King. That you are a traitor and must be held." He laughed again. "At least it shows that the landlord is loyal. Although how he thought the King would receive it in time to stop you I do not know. Now," he added, looking at me hard, "I am asking myself why we carry all this gold to Brittany. It is for Dickon, I know, and therefore can only be to buy something." He grinned. "And what else could be worth all this money but the Tudor himself?"

"For a soldier you think too much and too loud," I told him.

"Aye," he agreed. "But only to you, Master Morane, whom I have orders to escort and protect."

"And I may need it," I said. "For now that I have seen Will Slaughter I am uneasy, the more so since he seems to know the shipmaster."

"God's Hooks! You think they plan to turn pirate and seize the gold?"

"It is possible."

"Then I will go forthwith and wring his scrawny neck."

"That would be murder," I told him.

"Then after we are at sea. His Writ can float away on the waves."

"And treason too," I added sternly.

He gave a fearsome grin. "Then it seems I must wait until we are in Brittany, where the Writ does not run."

"He will have friends there, maybe."

"Friends?" The black eyebrows went upwards. "A

scrawn like that with friends? Hah! So more than one neck will have to be wrung."

I kept my face impassive. "We shall see. But if he misbehaves himself before that I shall be right pleased to help you."

He looked at me, burst into a guffaw, slapped me on the shoulder, and went out.

Although the sky was clear the wind was still strong enough to riffle the sea, so that we were swept along like an empty bucket in a mill-race, with streams of spray and water surging along the deck. My insides lurched in motion with the vessel, but in a different direction, so that I began to feel uneasy. The eleven archers lay about the deck, as damp and miserable as newly-hatched chicks, and the six members of the crew looked at them with condescension as they went about their duties. Of Will Slaughter there was no sign. He had gone into the dog-kennel that passed for the master's cabin, the latter being occupied with the steering. It was as well, for I was beginning to be happier away from the presence of Will Slaughter.

Landfall was made off Normandy in the late afternoon, and we crawled along the coast till dusk, when anchors were thrown out and we prepared for the night. Ships rarely navigate after darkness has fallen, and then only when they belong to someone else, so that risks may be taken. This vessel, I knew, belonged to the shipmaster.

With the anchors down the ship swung round to hang from them, drifting up to them and then away again to be pulled up with a jerk, like a puppy in play with its teeth at one end of a belt and tossing its head violently to loosen it from its master's grip. Great stones were brought from the stern and laid in the middle of the deck. Wood was placed across them and, after much cursing, a fire was started. One of the sailors stood by with a leather bucket of water in case embers set the planking ablaze. Soon a huge cauldron was gurgling and bubbling with puffs of steam, and the aroma of boiled beef overcame the tar and tallow of the ship. In spite of the endless jerking against the anchor ropes I found I was hungry. Even Will Slaughter came out of his kennel and took a mug of soup. I could see his eyes in the firelight watching me as he drank it, but Anderson's dark eyes were on him too. And although he did not wait for the beer kegs to be broached, but went back to his cabin soon after eating, I slept little that night.

As I leaned against the side watching the hills of Normandy stand out grey against the dawn I heard a shuffling and turned round. Will Slaughter was coming to stand beside me.

He yawned twice before he spoke. "You know the full purpose of this voyage, Master Morane?"

"Would I be here if I didn't?" I said tersely.

His skull-like face cracked into an unpleasant smile. "It is a great deal of money," he observed.

The shipmaster was relieving himself at the steering post. When he had finished he came along the deck and stood on the other side of me, watching what he had done. When it came floating by he straightened and said, "The tide is flowing. We sail in half an hour."

"A great deal of money," Slaughter repeated.

"No doubt you have arranged your share," I said to him.

"And you, yours," he replied, grinning. "But it could be greater."

I looked round. The crew were stirring, and some of the soldiers were sitting up to groan. I could not see Anderson.

"It could be greater," I agreed. "In fact I could take it all for myself if I wished. So there is no need to try and bribe me."

He pretended surprise. "Who spoke of bribes? Here," he said, putting his hand inside his tunic, "see this . . ."

His words were intended to divert my attention, for "this" was a butcher's knife some nine inches long. I had, however, been expecting something of the kind, for my hand closed over his before the blade had been withdrawn from his clothes. It was not him I feared, though. It was the shipmaster standing behind me. At any moment there might be the hot thrust of steel into my back. I shoved Slaughter away, twisting the knife out of his grasp, so that it fell tinkling to the planks. Then I swung round, moving sideways, hands outstretched to grab the shipmaster's weapon.

There was no need. He stood there, his face redder than I had seen it before, with Anderson's hairy arm round his neck.

"Gently, gently," the Archer-captain told him. "It is better that sailors do not concern themselves with matters other than the sea."

As Slaughter came back and stooped to retrieve his weapon I brought my knee hard against his chin so that his jaw slammed shut like a vizor and he went over backwards.

"Arrest them both," I said to Anderson.

An instant later Slaughter stood with his arms pinioned behind him, his face dark with fury.

"You cannot arrest me!" he shouted indignantly. "I have the King's Writ. It runs on this ship as good as it does in England!"

Anderson gave a deep chuckle. "Shall I lower him over the side to cool him off?" he suggested. "I am no lawyer . . ." he chuckled again, "but I do not think the King's Writ runs under water."

The sailors stood gazing open-mouthed at the scene. One of them said, "Look! The captain is a prisoner!" Then he fell back spitting blood and teeth as an archer hit him with the butt of his dagger. There was no trouble after that. They stood quiet, eyeing us curiously.

I turned to the shipmaster. "What is your name?" I said. I wanted to be sure it was the same as John Kendall had told me.

"Ned Bennett," he replied. "And owner of this ship which sails in the service of the King of England. If you do not release me forthwith I shall have you arrested for treason and mutiny on the high sea!"

"Well, then Master Bennett," I said, laughing. "Do you know to which port we are bound?"

"I do not. I take my orders from Master Slaughter."

"Not any more," Anderson told him.

Slaughter was standing with a twisted smile on his face. "You will tell Ned Bennett where to sail," I said to him.

"When I am freed," he answered.

"Let us not be so arrogant, my friend," I said quietly. "Either you direct us to our destination or I will have the anchor tied to your legs and drop you over the side."

He paled a little. "You would not dare," he said. "Your duty is the success of this mission."

"My duty is to safeguard the gold unless it can be exchanged," I told him. "If it cannot be exchanged then you, who are already attainted for treason, become worthless to me. In those circumstances my orders are to deal with you as I think fit."

I turned to Anderson. "Have your men bring the anchor and rope." Looking at Bennett, I added, "One anchor will do for both of them."

"God in Heaven!" the shipmaster exclaimed. "It would be murder!" Then he gave a knowing smile. "Ah! But you dare not! Who would sail the ship?"

"We do not need to sail it," I pointed out. "Over there is France. We have six sailors and six oars." I looked up at the sky. "But in this weather it will not be too far to return home."

His insolent smile vanished. I beckoned to Anderson. "Come on," I told him. "We can reach England by nightfall once this is done."

"I know the place," the shipmaster said sullenly. "I will take you."

"You will?" I inquired with mock surprise. "In that case I only need to dispose of Will Slaughter."

"You cannot kill me," Slaughter snarled. "Or the Tudor will not be handed over. It is one of the conditions."

At that I laughed out loud. "Once they see the gold we have brought do you think they will worry about someone like you?"

One of the archers made an exclamation. "Body of God! We are to take the Earl of Richmond back to England as captive!" He rubbed his hands together. "I for one will be in the first rank at Tower Green to see him dealt with. They say this Henry Tudor, like all Welshmen, has a member as big as a horse."

The others roared with laughter.

"Shut your mouth!" Anderson swore at him.

Slaughter drew himself upright. "And do you know this Earl of Richmond, Master Morane? When he has been in London but once, and that years ago as a boy?"

I hesitated, and Slaughter's smile grew wider.

"In fact you do not know him by sight," he went on triumphantly. "And I am the only one that does. Therefore it will be wiser for you to keep me alive so that I can vouch they have given you the right man."

"God's Hooks!" Anderson muttered. "You think we trust you?"

"There is no one else," he replied with a sneer.

I frowned, and turned to the shipmaster. "Ned Bennett,"

I said to him, "where was this ship at the time of the Buckingham rebellion?"

"Why . . . er . . ."

"Was it not one of those that brought the Tudors to land at Poole and turned back when the rebellion failed?"

"Er . . . yes. But I have sworn allegiance to King Richard since."

"Another turncoat," Anderson said. "A rat who sees the Tudor cause for what it is."

"Be quiet!" I said to him. To Bennett I went on, "I know you for what you are, my friend. Your allegiance turns with the price that is offered. But at that time you were part of the Tudor fleet at Poole."

He nodded, and dropped his eyes.

"Then you, too, have seen the Earl of Richmond?"

He nodded again, and Slaughter gave a snarl.

"Nevertheless the Earl of Richmond will not be handed over until I am safe in Brittany," he insisted.

"You have already told us that," I reminded him. "But if the Earl of Richmond is not handed over you will not be safe in Brittany either, will you?" I laughed at him. "In fact you will not be safe anywhere at all, my friend. And it will give me pleasure to slit you from the navel to the gizzard and skewer the King's Writ to your buttocks."

"Why not do it now?" Anderson suggested. "It will be a sight to see, although the smell might overpower us. His insides will be a stinking mess of corruption . . ."

"Double his bonds and lock him in the cabin," I ordered, and Anderson stopped, glaring. He beckoned to one of the archers.

When Slaughter had been taken away I said, "And now have an anchor hoisted to the top of the mast and lashed so that one sweep of a knife will let it fall."

"What is that for?" Anderson wanted to know.

I answered him loud enough for everyone to hear, but my eyes were on the shipmaster. "So that if this man does not behave himself the anchor will drop through the bottom of the ship."

"Then we shall drown," Anderson protested.

"*We* should not," I replied, facing the crew. "For we should be in the rescue boat you have there in the stern." I was not sure if we would, though, for thirteen men and eight barrels of gold would probably sink it too, but I went on confidently, "Your fate, then, will be in the hands of your master. It would be better, therefore to ensure his good conduct."

A sailor with a scar beside his nose stepped forward.

"We know nothing of this, good sir," he said. "Ned Bennett's conduct on this voyage is for his own conscience." He turned to look at his companions, saw them nod, and went on, "I say kill him once we get to Brittany and we will sail this ship back ourselves, Tudor or no. We may not know navigation but we will find a way. But to have the anchor hoisted up there . . ." his eyes went to the top of the mast ". . . might break it, snap the mast . . . and even if it does not it is too dangerous, when it may fall from any accident. Why sir, it would be too frightful for simple seamen to be looking at all the time."

I nodded. "As to breaking the mast I will take that chance. But as to it being frightful to watch, I agree. Once we have finished our business in Brittany it will be brought down." To the shipmaster I said, "As for you, Ned Bennett, whether I kill you then will depend on my digestion. If the Breton wines are all they are said to be, why, then I might be in an amiable mood. But make no mistake . . ." I waved a finger under his nose. "For Slaughter will direct us if you don't. His life depends on it too."

"I have already said I will take you there," he said sullenly. "And back to England too. But do not sink my ship."

Anderson suddenly slapped his thigh. "Oh, ho, ho!" he said. "So much fuss over the puny lick-arse Earl of Richmond!"

"Why not?" I said. "Or do you think you know him too?"

"Know him? God's Hooks! Was I not one of the men waiting to shoot him as he came ashore at Poole?"

16

BY SUNRISE we were running before the wind with Jersey on our right, and noon had not long passed when we were off a small village consisting of no more than a single line of houses on the other side of a dusty track that ran for a few hundred yards along the edge of the sea. Opposite the centre of the village, where a larger house stood, the shore had been banked up with timbers and a narrow jetty ran out into the water. We dropped the sail, oars were put out, and we came alongside ponderously.

All the houses were shuttered tight. Apart from animals lying in the dust, and chickens pecking idly at nothing, there was little to be seen. If anyone had noticed our arrival he was not coming out to welcome us in the heat of the afternoon. The village would not arouse itself till evening when its fishing boats returned.

"Is this the place?" Anderson said, pulling Slaughter forward. "It doesn't seem as if anyone is expecting us."

"That house there." Slaughter, with his hands tied behind his back, jerked his chin towards the largest one. "It is the tavern. A man called Geoffrey de Vannes will be waiting there. That is, if he has not already lost patience at our delay."

"Then that will be your misfortune," I told him. "Take him away," I nodded to Anderson. "And bind his feet as well now."

"I am hungry,.' Slaughter said.

"And if he moves slit his throat," I went on, ignoring the interruption. "I don't like the looks of this place. Have four archers cover me while I go ashore. But let them not be seen unless I call. I want no hostile action on our part to be observed—yet."

"I am hungry," Slaughter said again.

I turned and looked him up and down. "You will either have your next meal after Henry Tudor is on board this ship or you will never need to eat again. And as I see no sign of anyone bringing us a prisoner you can begin your prayers and ask the captain of archers to shrive you. He is the nearest to a priest I can think of."

"Captain Anderson a priest?" one of the archers said.

"Oh, ho!" He gave a great guffaw, which was joined in by the others.

"My father would have had me one," Anderson growled as he dragged Slaughter away. That brought more laughter from his men.

The larger house stood apart from the others so that there was a narrow alley on each side of it. Behind the row of dwellings wooded ground stretched upwards, and from the alley on the right ran a lane which wound up through the trees and over the hill. It was the way in and out of the village, for I could see now that the track along the shore ended in grass where the houses ceased. I climbed on to the wharf and found myself lurching across the planks until my legs had assured themselves that they were on steady ground again. A brown and grey cur got laboriously to its feet and walked across to sniff at my shoes. Satisfied, it waved its tail idly and turned back to its bed in the dust. Once there, it had the problem, common to all dogs, of finding the exact position it had vacated. After several anxious circumambulations it finally gave up the quest and flopped down in disgust, looking at me with a reproachful eye as if I had been the cause of its discomfort. The dust was thick, for whatever the weather had been in England it had not rained here for weeks. But then of course England is reluctant to share its weather with others.

A few shutters moved to allow those behind to inspect me, but I ignored them and went on to rap on the door of the tavern before pushing it open to go inside.

Its room covered the whole area of the house, with a narrow stair at one side leading to an upper storey, and a door next to the window at the back through which a white-haired old man was bringing a tray with a tall, dark-green mug. Seeing me, he smiled a little, and jerked his head towards a much scored trestle. The man sitting there was very young, elegantly dressed, and with a sword at his belt.

He was gnawing at a chicken bone, offering occasional bites to the girl on his knee, while his other arm was round her, its hand exploring her body. Beside him on the bench was his cap, green, with a long pheasant feather. I went over to him and bowed politely.

"Geoffrey de Vannes?" I inquired. "I am Henry Morane of London, come here to offer my respects to His Grace, the

Lord Treasurer, Monsieur de Landois." I spoke slowly, not having used Breton French for a long time.

Brushing aside the wench, he got up to face me. He could only nod as his mouth was filled with chewing, but he threw the bone out of the window. My eyes followed it and saw it kick up a small puff of dust in the yard outside. Beyond it was an open barn, and in its shadows a cart. There was nothing unusual in that, but the cart was covered with waxed and tarred cloths, and from under them protruded the iron snout of a gun. I looked back slowly, concealing my surprise. He had by then swallowed enough to be able to speak.

"Sieur de Vannes," he corrected, and looked me up and down insolently. As he lifted a many-ringed hand to brush away the crumbs from his mouth I saw the shine of steel through the laces of his tunic.

"You have been a long time," he said. Then, waving the landlord and the girl out of the room, added, "You have brought the gold?"

I nodded and jerked a thumb in the direction of the ship.

He strode past me to peer out through the door. When he came back there was a frown between his eyes. "Why is it not being brought ashore?" he demanded.

"It will be," I assured him. "As soon as I see the merchandise you have to sell."

"Merchandise? Oh, I see! You mean the Earl of Richmond?" The frown grew deeper. "He has not yet been brought. In the meantime, as I said, I want the gold carried here."

I gave him a friendly smile. "And in the meantime, as *I* said, the gold remains where it is."

He looked me up and down again and then sneered. "We shall see about that," he murmured quietly.

Still smiling, I went up to him and rapped my knuckle against his chest. It made a metallic sound. "We shall indeed," I said evenly. "Now run away and tell your master that I'm waiting." I saw the girl watching me from the door, aghast.

He took a pace backwards and put a hand on his sword hilt. I reached out and covered it with mine, putting my face close to his. The chicken he had been eating had been well-spiced with garlic.

"Listen to me," I said, and I was not smiling any more. "I

did not come here to fight battles with such as you. I am here on a mission from the King of England. If you do not believe I have the gold you can come aboard and see it for yourself."

He shook himself free, but his hand stayed away from the sword. "I shall do nothing of the sort! The money must be delivered first."

I made an expression of disgust. "You will come to no harm on an English ship," I said as I turned away. Seeing his cap, I picked it up and threw it at him. At the door I said, "If you do not come with me I shall give orders to sail. And when King Richard hears of it he will be in a towering rage. And so will His Grace the Treasurer when the letter reaches him," I added for good measure.

"Letter?" he said. "What letter?"

"The one I shall send before I leave." I saw a glint in his eye. "Make no mistake, my friend. I shall see that my messenger leaves here without you being able to stop him. And on your own horse too." With that I went outside and started walking towards the ship.

By the time I had reached the dock I heard his footsteps coming after me. I waited for him and pointed at the barrels on deck.

"Choose any one you wish," I told him. "And I will have it opened for you to see the contents."

He nodded, but his eyes were for Anderson and his eleven men standing alert and watching him. Whatever plans he might have had this small show of force had made him think again. Then he saw Will Slaughter and stiffened. That worthy gave him a rueful, snaggle-toothed smile of recognition. Geoffrey de Vannes scowled and turned to me. "Have that second barrel opened," he ordered.

It was taken into the cabin and the top prised off. He gasped at the waterfall of shining coins that fell from it. I told him that the others were the same and he nodded thoughtfully. Back on deck he studied Slaughter for several moments before climbing on to the wharf.

"We shall return with the . . . er . . . merchandise," he said, "within four days."

"Four days?" I echoed.

"Four days," he repeated. "Perhaps less. But the . . . goods have to be secured and brought here, you understand?"

"Do you mean that you haven't seized him yet?"

He sneered down at me. "Did you expect we would have him prisoner and waiting for you?" he inquired. "And suppose you had never come? Oh, no, my friend," he laughed, "you English are only to be trusted when we can see the colour of your money."

With that he turned and strode off to the inn. A few minutes later I saw his dust between the trees as he rode away up the hill.

17

"FOUR days!" Anderson said. "God's Hooks! That will give him time to bring an army! Are you going to wait?"

"Not here," I told him. "We'll anchor fifty yards out tonight, and tomorrow I'll go ashore. There are some questions I want to ask the innkeeper. After that I will decide what to do." I glanced at Slaughter. "Put him back in the cabin."

"I am hungry," he said defiantly, "and wish to relieve my bowel."

"Not in my cabin!" the master protested.

I shrugged. "Lower him over the side," I told Anderson. "And let him do what he will. He will at least come up clean."

Before dusk two small fishing boats came in to tie up against the pier. Their crews looked at us curiously as they passed, but greeted us with courtesy. The villagers came down to meet them and take their catch, but more to discuss us, the strangers. Their voices came clearly over the water. I heard one woman saying she had seen the great noble himself go on board our ship and be sent scuttling away like a frightened chicken. One of the fishermen thought that we must be English, for who else would be mad enough to carry their anchor at the top of the mast? "English!" The word was taken up. If so, we must be pirates. Then a calmer voice pointed out that we had been there all afternoon and had taken no hostile action, and anyway the dogs had not barked at us. One of them had even wagged its tail at the man who came ashore. Perhaps we were from the North, another man said, from Danemark perhaps, because if we had been English the village would have been burned by now . . .

The talk went on until dark, when the weak, flickering lights went out one by one.

At dawn, soon after the fishermen had gone out again, we stripped our clothes and hung naked over the side to wash ourselves. Anderson saw the fresh red weals on my back and chest, and pursed his mouth to whistle, but made no comment. His own body was scarred enough. And after we had done I took the vessel back to the pier and went ashore, leaving him in charge.

The village had come to life. Children peered at me round doorways, while older, patient eyes watched me from the windows as I walked towards the tavern. Puppies snarled and wrestled in the sand, chickens scampered out of my way, and I could hear the satisfied grunt of hogs. It was morning, the sun was coming up, the visitors came in peace, and the bullying nobleman was no longer there.

As I went through the door the serving-wench pointed at me and told the landlord that this was the man who had knuckled the great Sieur de Vannes. The old man beamed and set a brown flagon in front of me. I thanked him and asked him how long de Vannes had been there.

"Two weeks, M'sieu. He and his men . . ."

"His men? I didn't see any."

"Nevertheless there were two. They watched you from the barn out there." He waved a hand. "But now they have gone with him."

I nodded. I ought to have realized that someone like de Vannes would have retainers. "And the cannon in the barn? Has it been there as long?"

"It was brought a week ago." He came up and took my arm. "M'sieu, it is no affair of ours in this village, and we are much affrighted."

I gave him a reassuring smile. "There is no need to be afraid. We come in peace with business for your Lord Treasurer."

His reply was a gesture of resignation. "You may come in peace, M'sieu, but guns do not. I know them too well." He saw the interest in my face, and added, "In my younger days I was assistant to Gaspard Bureau."

There was no need for him to add any more. Thirty years before all Europe had watched with astonishment while the artillery train of Jean and Gaspard Bureau had driven the hitherto invincible English armies out of France. A new method of warfare had arrived.

"But rest assured, M'sieu," he added hastily. "I am an old man now, and my past connexion with the Bureau brothers is not known to the Sieur de Vannes."

I grunted and went out of the back door. The innkeeper followed me into the barn. Lifting the tarred cloth away I saw that the barrel of the gun was strapped securely to the floor of the cart with broad iron bands. The muzzle pointed out of the back, the other end from the shafts, under which was a thick pillar of wood which could be lowered to the ground to raise or depress the barrel. The wheels, much thicker than those on an ordinary cart, ran on wide axles. It was a heavy affair, and immensely strong; a weapon which, unlike the cannon I had seen before, could be moved about easily and trained to fire in any direction. But, like all guns, it would take a long time to load.

"The shafts are very strong," the innkeeper explained. "For when the gun is fired it will leap backwards into the air, and when it descends again their points will dig themselves into the ground and prevent the cart from running away."

"I know," I said. "But why is it covered?"

"Because it has already been filled with powder," he replied, pointing at some barrels by the wall. "I heard them say that it would save time, for it could be fired the quicker, and the powder would remain dry. It has not rained here for many weeks," he added.

"Then it has been loaded with a shot as well?" I asked him.

He shook his head. "They were not certain what kind they would want to use. Those . . ." He pointed at three stone cannon-balls "or the smaller shot in the bags over there. Or . . ." he indicated other bags ". . . those. But what they contain I do not know. There seem to be pieces of iron and broken stone in them, but for what purpose I cannot guess. The guns I knew were for breaking down castle walls and towers. And for blowing apart the ranks of the . . ." he glanced at me ". . . the enemy. The slaughter they did was tremendous . . ."

A sudden thought crossed my mind, I half got up, but the landlord was speaking. "You will forgive me, M'sieu? But at that time the English were our enemies."

I nodded absently. I knew what the other bags were for. Small stones and pieces of iron fired at a ship would bring down its mast, smash its oars, and tear its sails and ropes to shreds. I said, "Yet it has been left unguarded. Were they not concerned?"

He spread his hands out. "Where could it be taken,

M'sieu? And who would do so? And even if you were to try and take away such a monster on your ship it would surely sink it."

I went back into the tavern thoughtfully. When he joined me, I said, "We would buy six barrels of wine, forty chickens and three hogs, if you and your neighbours wish to sell. We will pay the prices of England," I added, "which are greater than yours."

His chin went up. "To pay us more than we can obtain in the market, M'sieu, would cause us offence. But I will go and see what can be done. Meanwhile the woman will serve you." He went away shaking his head.

She came in, a smile across her broad face. "Good sir, would you have wine? Or apple juice which has more fire? My master says you must not pay. But had he not said so I would have paid. For it is a rare thing to see a nobleman humbled like that."

I grinned at her. She was tall, and thick across the shoulder, with a deep bosom. She could have overpowered Geoffrey de Vannes easily if she had wished. I told her so, and asked her if she had had cause to.

"I can hold my own with any man I choose," she said defiantly.

"Any man you do not choose, you mean," I laughed.

At first she was puzzled, then she, too gave a deep laugh, gripping my arm like a vice to lead me back into the yard. "See that cannon, sir?" she said. "I can almost heft it round myself."

"I don't doubt it," I agreed. "Maybe you helped lift the powder barrels when they loaded it?"

"They did not ask me. Although I could have." She looked at me with eyes as brown as hazel nuts. "I could have, sir. But I would not have. For they spill powder and I would not wish to be set afire."

"Not with powder," I agreed with a straight face. "But there are other means."

The brown eyes gazed into mine and she laughed again. "I could hold my own if I chose." Her hand gripped my arm once more and she led me to the orchard behind the shed.

The apples were small and not yet fruit, and the trees that bore them twisted painfully out of the long grass. A bearded goat considered us with a reproachful stare and then walked away snickering. She dropped my arm and turned to face me.

". . . if I chose," she repeated, and she was breathing hard. But it was as well she did not choose too much.

18

AS WE came out from the apple trees I heard a sudden shout from the ship. I ran through the tavern to see Will Slaughter galloping towards me, his hands still bound, and a loose rope trailing from one of his legs. He saw me too, and swerved into the lane beside the inn. I leaped after him, to be brought up short by an arrow shearing through the air in front of me followed by a warning yell from Anderson. He stood on the pier, his bow taut, another arrow fitted. I gestured at him to stop, but it was too late.

An arrow is faster than a running man, especially when his hands are tied behind his back, and in that narrow alley Will Slaughter could not dodge. He had a chance, though, for if Anderson missed again he would be through to the safety of the trees beyond. But as soon as Anderson had loosed his next missile I saw him laugh and hand his bow to one of his men. I ran round the corner and Will Slaughter was there on his knees, coughing in the dust, the feathered end of the arrow twitching a foot from his back. As I reached him he fell on his side and I saw the barb right through him, smeared with bright red blood.

He glared at me and muttered, "May God Damn You, Henry Morane!" Then he coughed blood, his eyes rolled upwards, and he was dead.

I got up to see three archers holding back a crowd of curious villagers, and Anderson retrieving his first arrow. He came back to put his foot on Slaughter's shoulders and pull out the other, but the barb held and the shaft broke in his hands. He swore and looked at me.

"Ned Bennett had started to cut him loose while we were intent on you," he explained. "You were a long time and we were concerned," he added.

I scowled at him. "And you left Bennett on board by himself?"

"Aye," he grinned, "but well tied up and with a dagger at his throat." He looked down at Slaughter. "Well," he said, "at least it saves you the trouble of wondering what to do with him."

And that, I thought wryly, was about the best epitaph that

Slaughter merited. Then a jingling of harness in the trees made us look up quickly.

"Get back to the ship," I told Anderson, "and stand ready."

"It is too soon for them to be bringing the prisoner," he muttered. "Better I wait with you to see who it is."

"Get back!" I roared, and he turned away reluctantly.

The villagers had also heard the horsemen and had melted into their houses, shuttering the windows. Mounted visitors could bode no good for them.

The first rider came out of the trees, saw me, and brought his mount to a halt. He jumped down, threw his reins to one of the others, paused to look down at Will Slaughter with raised eyebrows, and then stepped over him to stride along the alley towards me.

"Monsieur de Morane?" he inquired, sweeping off his plumed cap and bowing. He wore his hair long and curled, and the dark skin of his face emphasized the whiteness of his teeth as he smiled. He was tall and handsome, but without any disdain in his eyes as he looked at me. I wondered how many female eyes were peering at him through the shutters.

I smiled back at him and agreed that I was Henry Morane, and he said, "Ah! I am glad. For my master has been concerned at leaving you unattended. He sends his apologies for the departure of the Sieur de Vannes, but trusts that you will understand that the news of your arrival had to be brought to him and ... er ... as it was later than expected ..." His voice trailed away with embarrassment.

I waved a hand. "No offence has been taken," I assured him.

"Good!" He bowed again. "I am Jean Toussaint, Seneschal to His Grace Pierre Landois, Lord Treasurer of Brittany, who rules the country during the sickness of Duke Francis the Second." He smiled. "And I have to tell you that carts are being driven here with meats and wines and pastries for the delectation of you and your men."

"That is right royal of you," I replied. "In the meantime will you drink with me in the tavern here?" I added, "There are some questions I would like to ask you."

He hesitated, then waved at his men to look after his horse, and followed me inside. He made a grimace at the quality of the wine, but I drank mine down heartily. Then, staring into my empty cup, I said, "It is not often one sees a cannon in a place like this. Are you afraid of pirates?"

"Pirates, M'sieu?"

"Yes." I looked up at him. "English pirates."

His eyes met mine, and he put both hands on the table. "It is a direct question, Monsieur de Morane," he said after a moment. "And strange to one who is accustomed to the language of diplomacy." He gave a sigh. "But—yes," he admitted. "I must confess that we had our doubts as to how the bargain might be honoured. Not," he added quickly, "on the part of your King Richard, but then we did not expect he would come here himself." He smiled. "Perhaps in our place you would have taken the same precaution." When I did not reply he went on, "But now that we know you have brought the money and the man called Slaughter lies dead outside I am sure our anxieties are ended."

"But mine are not," I told him. "For it was part of the bargain that he would be delivered up to you alive, as well as the money."

He waved a hand. "I do not think it will be a condition that is difficult to overlook."

"I see," I said. "So you did not trust him either?"

Toussaint shrugged. "Let me put it this way, M'sieu. Slaughter made his bargain with us for your King Richard. Yet we have seen him swear allegiance to Henry Tudor, Earl of Richmond. To make a bargain with such a man is hazardous, and precautions are necessary."

"Yet you yourselves give asylum to the Earl of Richmond and now wish to trade him for gold."

His smile faded quickly. "That could be taken as an insult, M'sieu," he said quietly.

"It is not meant as one. It seems to me a question that any-one might ask." I grinned at him. "Unless he was versed in the language of diplomacy."

At that he smiled again. "You are a direct man, Monsieur de Morane, as I have already observed. I can see that we need have no doubts about your integrity, at least."

"Thank you." I bowed as far as the table would permit.

"And for that reason I will explain." He sighed. "It was our liege lord, Duke Francis, who offered asylum to the Tudors, although it was against the advice of many of us, including Pierre Landois who, as Treasurer, is only too well aware of the state of our finances. He is a careful man, M'sieu, and did not think it wise to wager our slender resources against the possible rewards promised by the Earl of Richmond should he obtain the throne of England." He spread out his hands. "You see the point?"

I nodded. "So the Tudors were being supported by their promises?"

"Yes. Promises. Whereas Pierre Landois and I prefer to deal with such authority in England as already exists. All is not well in our relationship with our overlord, France, and if trouble were to boil we might need England's help."

"Which might be more quickly forthcoming from a Tudor king if you had assisted him to the throne."

"That is true," he admitted. "But he would have to get there first. Meanwhile we could not expect the King of England's help by giving asylum to his enemies. And, as our Lord Duke is suffering from sickness of the brain and does not know what is happening it is an opportunity to remove the cause of any dissention." He spread out his hands again. "I speak quite frankly, M'sieu."

I laughed. "And I will speak even more frankly. Not only do you have the opportunity of removing the cause of any dissention, but you have the opportunity of making a large profit out of it as well."

His face froze for a moment, but in the end he smiled. "It is a point," he admitted. "But possibly you, in our circumstances, might have done the same."

"I might," I grinned, "but I would have used someone other than Will Slaughter. Is that why you did not have the Earl of Richmond tied up and waiting for us?"

"Exactly! We were not to know if Slaughter would return with force and try to seize the prisoner without paying for him."

"And now we have to wait four days before you can carry out your part of the bargain. At least that is what Geoffrey de Vannes said."

"Four days?" He shook his head. "He was being too careful." He got up and went to the window. "It is a fine sunny day, and so his capture will have been effected this morning. In the gardens of the mansion which Duke Francis has given him the Earl of Richmond walks each day after Mass, sometimes alone, sometimes with his uncle Jasper, but never with any others. It seems he takes little thought for his own safety." Toussaint shrugged. "He will be brought to you by tomorrow, possibly this very evening."

19

AWAY in the distance I heard a bell commence its sonorous toll. "Vespers!" Toussaint said, getting up. "You will come?" he asked me.

"I didn't see a church here," I said.

"No. In the village over the hill. The people here attend."

"I don't remember them doing so yesterday, or hearing the bell."

"Possibly," he agreed. "Perhaps the priest was busy with his farm." He smiled. "But now that I am here they toll the bell like good Christians."

"No offence is intended," I told him. "But it is my duty to stay with the ship."

The peals of the bell were interrupted by the noise of another party descending the hill, a much larger cavalcade than the three men who had accompanied Jean Toussaint.

"Ah! The carts for you," he said, going to the door. But it was not carts drawn by plodding oxen. It was a score or more of mounted men headed by Geoffrey de Vannes.

"Seigneur!" he said, bowing from the saddle. Dismounting, he handed Toussaint a roll of parchment. The latter stretched it out. His face tightened as he read it, and he looked up at de Vannes.

"You know its contents?" Toussaint asked him.

De Vannes nodded. "Of course. Everyone is talking about it back there . . ." He jerked a thumb behind him. "There has been treachery. It seems that our guests have rejected our hospitality and left the country. His Grace the Treasurer is in a tremendous rage and has hanged all those who were attendant upon the Tudors."

I looked at them incredulously. Then Toussaint spoke to me.

"The Earl of Richmond and his uncle," he said, "fled to France an hour before our men arrived to seize them. They could only have been warned a few minutes before, because instead of taking Mass they went out of the other door of the church and called for their horses." He stopped and shook his head slowly. "But who warned them the Lord Treasurer does not know. As de Vannes has said, there has been treachery." He put a hand on my shoulder. "And so, my friend," he said, "it seems that we are unable to carry out our part of the bargain after all."

I swore. Henry Tudor could only have been warned by a message from England. The wind that had delayed us would have blown a ship to France more quickly, and with fast horses the word could have been carried to Brittany. But if these Bretons had seized him when the bargain had been made our delay in getting away from Lyme would not have mattered.

"The carts will soon be here," Toussaint said. "Although I regret I cannot stay to entertain you. Our orders are to return forthwith."

"Thank you," I said. "But we will go too. There is daylight left and we must sail."

"Do you not trust us?" de Vannes sneered.

Toussaint glared at him. "Come!" he said. "Have the gun-cart harnessed and escort it back to Rennes. See that it is there by sunset tomorrow." He held out a hand to me and walked over to his horse. I saw him raise it again as he and his men rode into the trees.

I gave de Vannes a curt nod and turned towards the ship.

"There is just one more thing, my friend," he said.

I stopped and eyed him. "Yes?" I asked.

"We will now have the gold brought ashore."

"We?" I repeated. "Are you speaking for the Lord Treasurer? Or just for yourself?"

He waved an impatient hand. "Let us not waste time. Have your men place the barrels on the wharf." Two of his men rode up close to me.

I stood, legs apart, and faced him boldly, but my stomach was like a bowstring. "If you do not let me return to the ship," I told him, "I cannot be responsible for what my men will do."

"Aye!" Anderson called from the vessel. "Four arrows are trained on you, Monsieur Lick-Arse." His Breton was atrocious, but he conveyed his meaning well enough. The horsemen stopped, and de Vannes scowled.

My stomach unwound itself. I turned my back on him and walked, slowly and with stiff legs, towards Anderson. He winked at me as I came near. I saw that the anchor had been let down from the mast and gave a long sigh.

"Shall I kill the shipmaster?" he asked me.

"No. Untie him. I will deal with him in England. But if he does not get us away from here quickly . . ."

Anderson chuckled. "He is already untied, but he will try no more treachery. He is as frightened as you were just now, the difference is that he shows it."

As we cast off the lines I saw the shipmaster trembling. He pointed suddenly. "Look!" he shouted.

The gun was being wheeled out from behind the tavern.

"Push away harder, then," I told him, as the water appeared between us and the shore. I put my hands to my mouth and called to de Vannes.

"If you try to use that cannon on us many of your men will be killed," I warned him.

"And if you do not surrender the gold your ship will be sunk," he shouted back. "And any that survive to reach the shore can look forward to a lifetime in prison."

"God's Hooks!" Anderson said. "Do those ignorant nincompoops think they can sink us with that war-engine?"

"It seems they do," I replied, watching the shipmaster scuttling up and down yelling at his men to row harder.

"It will take them ten minutes to load it," Anderson said complacently. "And when they miss it will take another ten. By that time we shall be beyond range."

"It is already loaded," I told him. "It has been filled with powder for a week. All that it needs is a missile placed in the barrel."

"Aaaah!" he growled. "Even so, the first shot will be a miss."

"They will not use a single cannon-ball," I explained. "See those bags being brought up? Each is filled with stones and broken iron. One of them rammed down the barrel and fired at us will tear the rigging to pieces."

"Then we will row the ship home," he said.

I turned on him. "With all the oars on one side broken too? And the men who work them killed and wounded?"

"Then in God's Name why do you stand there talking?" Ned Bennett screamed. "Where are the archers? Shoot at them!" He swung at Anderson, his face working. "Or cannot you men shoot above fifty yards?"

The bald-headed archer-captain's face grew purple. He seized the shipmaster by the throat and would have strangled him then and there had I not pulled them apart. I hit Bennett across the face.

"Be quiet!" I told him sternly. "Attend to your duties. The archers will see to theirs. They cannot shoot while your men are rowing, you fool! Where could they stand to aim?" I eyed the distance to the shore. "Right!" I said to him. "Stop your men rowing now, but have them ready to start again as soon as I tell you."

"Stop rowing?" Ned Bennett's voice was shrill. "And have my ship torn to pieces? And have those of us who are not killed lie and rot in a Breton dungeon for the rest of their lives?"

I hit him again, harder this time. "Stop rowing!" I roared at the sailors. "And lie down away from the oars."

They didn't wait for confirmation from their captain. As one man they pulled in their sweeps and lay flat on the deck.

The archers stepped over them and drew their bows. The distance was no more than a hundred yards. At that range the blast from such a cannon would be murderous. But Anderson's men stood quietly, braced with one foot against the ship's side and bowstrings drawn back to the ear, waiting his signal. He watched the shore with narrowed eyes, then his lips drew back over his teeth. "Shoot!" he growled.

Twelve arrows swept across the water like angry bees. They converged on their target so closely that I would swear some of them nudged the others aside. And almost before they reached the guns there was another flight on the way.

The men standing by the cannon went down as if they had been swept by a scythe. They fell in heaps, some collapsing like the sacks they carried, others rolling over screaming and clutching at the cruel shafts in their bodies. The man with the ramrod spun round and stumbled across the street, two feet of English wood in his back. But the rod stayed aloft, its end describing a shaky circle as he staggered. Then the circle grew wider until the rod swung right round and fell from his grip. But he reached the tavern door, and might have gained safety had not another arrow pinned him to the wood, where he hung until the weight of his body drew out the point, and he fell inert to the ground.

"Stop shooting!" I said, and the archers cheered. The cannon still lay in its cart, but there was not a man near who remained on his feet.

"Get to the oars!" I shouted at the sailors. "Row for your lives before they can try again!"

"They won't ask for any more of that medicine," Anderson said grimly.

But he was wrong. The gun was already charged and it would take no more than a few moments to ram home the missiles and put fire to the touch-hole. And Geoffrey de Vannes must have seen that we could not row and shoot at the same time. I saw him, mounted now, riding along the street, shouting at his men. They came out hesitantly and moved towards the gun. Some of them dragged away the bodies of their comrades while others manhandled the gun to correct its aim. Another man picked up the ramrod.

We were end-on to them by now, and presented a smaller target, but the spread of that deadly hail could not fail to hit us. I considered the advantage of turning sideways and giving them another volley, although the distance had doubled. But we could not go on doing that indefinitely or we should never get away from the village before dark.

"Put a man in the stern and let him see if he can pick off the rammer," I said to Anderson.

"I will see to it myself," he muttered, moving away.

But not only were we farther out, the motion of the water had also increased. Accurate shooting would be difficult. The first two arrows missed, and each time Anderson swore. And then it was too late. The bags of iron were down the barrel. A man was already standing at the back of the cart, holding a smoking match. A few more moments and we would feel the shock. I braced myself against the deck to hide my fear.

Suddenly the man stumbled and fell to his knees, an arrow through his neck. I heard Anderson give a loud grunt of satisfaction, and the shipmaster cheered. "We are saved! We are saved!" he shouted.

I turned on him savagely. "Be quiet, you fool! We are not safe yet."

We were by no means safe. Although it took a few minutes to encourage another man to pick up the match the range was now two hundred yards, and Anderson's next arrows all missed. He reached the distance easily enough, but our lurching platform spoiled his aim. And now that those on shore had seen that only one man was shooting at them they grew more confident. I heard their yells of triumph.

"Come back here," I called to Anderson. "It is too late to go on shooting. And if you stay where you are you will be the first to be hit when the gun fires."

"They won't come anywhere near us," he muttered as he came up.

"French guns blew us out of France," I told him. "There can never be another Agincourt."

"What?" he roared. "The longbow can still outshoot a cannon!"

"Maybe," I said, watching the distant man put the smouldering match against the end of the gun. "But not for much longer . . ." My last words were drowned by the explosion from the shore.

It was the loudest noise I had ever heard, almost breaking my ears. Even the great thunderstorm after Tewkesbury was nothing to this. I felt the ship jerk under me, then shudder like a frightened ox. Behind the huge billowing cloud of smoke from the shore I saw the gun leap straight into the air, taking the cart with it, and then come lurching down, smashing it to splinters. One wheel flew off, rolling with great loops across the street to disappear right through the entrance of a house. I prayed that there was no one standing too close inside.

Then, as the smoke cleared, I saw the barrel of the gun. It lay on the ground, split apart like a daffodil-flower, and spouting red and yellow flames. The sand round it was a deeper red, for not one man there remained alive. I looked round at the ship, at the crew, and at Joseph Anderson. They stood unscathed, but immobile, like statues, wide-eyed and open-mouthed, with unconsidered sweat pouring down their faces.

The Archer-Captain was the first to collect himself. "Mother of God!" he said reverently. "The gun blew up!"

His words roused the men. When they saw what had happened they began to cheer. The shipmaster, great gouts of tears on his face, tried to throw his arms round me. I shoved him aside and swore at the men.

"Get back to work!" I stormed. "Get back to the oars! When you get back to England you can give Thanks to God for your deliverance, but until then you work for me, and by His Very Buttocks I will kill the first man that slackens." I turned to the side and jerked the foulness of my stomach into the sea. When I came back I added, more quietly, "Meanwhile you can start praying for the poor souls of those around the gun."

"I will hear Mass as soon as we are ashore," Anderson said. "It was the Hand of God that saved us."

"Aye," I muttered, as if to myself, "and God helps those who help themselves."

"He does, for sure," Anderson agreed. "He caused me and my men to shoot well . . ." He stopped suddenly, puzzled. "But even if we had not shot well the gun would still have blown up when it was fired . . ." He put an elbow on the gunwale and studied me curiously. "So why did you say that?"

"Because the serving-wench at the tavern was as randy as a goat."

He looked at me as if I had gone mad. I saw his expression and could not help a smile.

"She had the strength equal to a man," I told him. "She could heft the gun-cart round by herself, she swore. And so, although I had appeased her ardour, as I thought, she still had lust for more. 'Again!' she demanded, and was like to have broken my arm if I failed . . ."

Anderson chuckled.

"And so, God Help me, I told her that more than four times within the half-hour would summon the Devil himself to her . . ."

Anderson stopped chuckling and crossed himself quickly.

"At that she took fright and said she wished she were a man so that she could, as men do, take pleasure all the time without a thought of the Evil One. And so I laughed and told her it was better for me she was not, but if she wished to act like a man she could use the loading stick and ram great clods of earth up the barrel of the gun . . ."

I looked towards the shore where the last rays of the sun picked out the smoky redness of the wreckage.

"But the Lord Himself must have known," I said to Anderson, "that I was ignorant as to what precise effect it would have."

"God's Hooks!" he muttered as he turned away.

20

JOHN Kendall was waiting for me at Lyme. He had a large escort, some eighty men, camped outside the village, its very size bespeaking the importance of the expected prisoner. When I told him my mission had been unsuccessful by only a few hours he shook his head regretfully, but when I told him that it had been betrayed he sat up straight and inspected me with narrowed eyes.

"Betrayed?" he said. "Are you sure?"

"What else?" I told him how the Tudors had been warned of my arrival.

"How could that have been, I wonder?" He examined his fingernails while he considered it. Then he raised his eyes to mine and shrugged. "Ah, well!" he said. "It is the fact, it seems, and nothing can be done now. It was an attempt worth making, though, and it would have been foolish not to have tried. And," he added, feeling for the hilt of his dagger, "it has had some advantage. The very fact that Henry Tudor was forced to flee to France proves his insecurity, and how little confidence and even less authority he commands. Dickon will at least be pleased to know that. The gold is safe?"

"It is. Not one crown is lost."

"Dickon will be pleased to hear that too," he smiled.

"Then perhaps he will reward the archers well, especially their captain. But for them the gold would be at the bottom of the sea."

"It is in my competence to make any payments," John Kendall said. "And I will bear that in mind. And the shipmaster?"

With that I told him the story of the voyage, and he pursed his lips. "Is the man under restraint, then?" he asked, pulling out the dagger and starting to pare his nails.

"No. But his ship is. He will not go far from the sight of it. And I need your advice as to the precise charges to bring . . ."

There was a sudden commotion outside, and the shipmaster came running in to the tavern.

"My Lord Secretary! My Lord Secretary!" he said breathlessly. "I have not yet been paid for the use of my ship!"

"Indeed, Master Bennett?" John Kendall inquired coldly. "And you must have been back in Lyme for nearly an hour!" He clicked his tongue.

But the irony was lost on the shipmaster. "Aye, and the tide sets along the coast," he said. "I wish to leave for London with it."

"Now here we have a man who should be well rewarded," I said, and Ned Bennett swung round, startled. He had not noticed me. I moved forward and added, "He is worth every inch of the six feet of rope I would give him."

The redness went out of his face as suddenly as if it had been wiped off. He stammered something and made to go, but I pulled him back by the scruff. "This is the man," I said, "who plotted with Will Slaughter to murder me and seize the gold."

"Not so!" he protested. "It was Slaughter that forced me to it."

"You admit it, then?" John Kendall said dryly.

"And it was Bennett here who released Slaughter so that he nearly escaped," I said.

The shipmaster turned to me desperately. "He forced me to, Master Morane! He forced me to!"

"How could he have done that when he was tied up?"

"He said that if he was taken back to England for trial and made to give testimony it would go hard for me. Whereas if he got away there would be no one to give testimony against me."

"You believed that?" I said. "Why, I for one could swear . . ."

"But I made no attack on you!"

"Only because the Archer-Captain restrained you."

"But I had no weapon!"

And then I remembered we had not searched him.

John Kendall saw my face and cleared his throat. "Whatever the facts of that incident," he said, "there is this other. That you released a man under arrest for attempted murder."

"I did not know what he had been charged with! Nothing was stated. He was merely arrested. And he had the King's Writ," he concluded. His manner was more confident now.

There was silence for a moment. Then John Kendall addressed me. "Nevertheless there seems to be enough to warrant a hearing. Do you wish to bring charges, Master Morane?"

"I think I will," I said, although I knew that John Kendall thought my case was weak. "We can prove that he had a prior acquaintance with Will Slaughter," I went on. "And, being used for a felonious purpose while on the King's business, his ship will be forfeit."

"You have no case at all!" Ned Bennett said. "And my ship can only be taken from me by process of law, which I know from previous suits the King's justice will be reluctant to do when it is a man's livelihood."

John Kendall knew it too, but he said, "A means of livelihood is not of much importance if its owner is hanging from six feet of rope."

Ned Bennett sneered. "What case is there?" he said to me, but I was at the window looking down over the harbour.

"As to your ship being taken without due process of law," I chuckled, turning round to him, "I am not so sure." I waved at the window. "It seems to me that it is already being taken."

The shipmaster rushed past me to look outside. "God in Heaven!" he exclaimed. "My own crew!" He swung back wildly. "They are sailing away with my ship! Have them stopped, sir, for Pity's Sake," he wailed.

John Kendall held up a hand and trimmed the edge of a fingernail. He examined the result carefully, saying, "Mutiny, forsooth!" Then, turning to the shipmaster, he laid the dagger down and addressed him solemnly. "Now, Master Bennett. It seems it is your turn to bring charges."

"Charges?" he yelled. "I'll have them hanged! Each and every man of them!"

"Yes," I agreed with a serious face. "Charges should certainly be brought. The Court will be interested to hear the circumstances, and the crew's testimony as to his cowardice in Brittany, especially when ships' captains are reputed to be a breed of men without fear." I nodded wisely. "But it will not be amused to hear of his conniving with Will Slaughter to seize the King's gold, which at least two of us can swear to . . ."

But the shipmaster did not wait for me to finish. He scuttled out of the room quickly.

While we were laughing John Kendall said, "And how

much did you bribe the crew to take the vessel, Henry Morane?"

"Nothing," I chuckled. "The assurance of a safe-conduct from the King's Secretary was sufficient."

His laughing stopped abruptly and the veins in his neck began to swell as if they would choke him.

It took three quarts of ale before I had him pacified. In the end he shook his head slowly. "Jesu!" he said, "this stuff is drivel beside the London beer." Looking into the bottom of his mug, he added, "But that in Pontefract was not so bad. The Bretons there found it too strong . . ." He paused, still inspecting the bottom of the mug.

Bretons? In Yorkshire? I was taken aback, but kept my face impassive. I would not let John Kendall score off me as easily as that.

When I remained silent he looked up at me, his eyes glittering. "I said . . ." he began.

"I heard what you said," I told him. "Now I presume you're going to tell me that I have been tricked. That my mission was a waste of time."

"No, no!" he said quickly. "With fifty thousand crowns how could that be? No, no, Henry," he repeated, "your mission was the very one Dickon hoped would succeed. At this very moment Lord Powis waits at Southampton with a thousand archers for the word to sail for Brittany."

This time I could not help showing my astonishment.

A faint smile crossed his face and he put his dagger away with a gesture of satisfaction. He had scored at last.

"Our friend, Pierre Landois," he said, "has sent an embassy to Dickon. Openly, that is. It is in Pontefract now. And we have both signed a treaty, publicly, to abstain from war, or piracy against each other, until next April."

"Then what is Lord Powis waiting with a thousand archers for?"

"Hah!" he chuckled. "But there is another clause to the treaty, a secret one, that in return for a thousand archers to fight against France the Breton will hand over the Tudor to to us. Wait!" He held up a hand to silence me. "Let me finish." He banged his mug on the trestle to summon more beer.

"As regards this secret clause," he went on a few moments

later, "both Landois and Dickon know full well that Brittany is in no condition for war with France. They also realize full well that this clause cannot remain secret for long, with every other man in the Breton delegation a Tudor spy. Therefore they judged that when the Tudors hear of this clause they will make no move until the expedition sails." He took a swallow from his mug. "It will never sail, of course, but the archers had to be assembled to lend verity to the clause. That was why you were sent, earlier, and before the Breton signed the treaty. Landois and Dickon had already been in communication about it."

"Aye, so you told me," I said. "Through a known traitor such as Will Slaughter. Did you think you could trust him?"

"Of course not! I told you that too. It was another reason why you were sent. A pity you did not bring him back for trial, though. His execution would have been a lesson to others."

"His head would have disgraced the others on London Bridge. But it was a pity, nevertheless. Questioning would have produced further information . . ."

"Torture was unnecessary. His guilt was proved."

". . . because Slaughter was not only Buckingham's man. He was also, at one time, a servant in the Tower apartments."

John Kendall sat very still. "How do you know that?" he said.

"I recalled that when Dickon was Lord Protector his nephew complained about the state of his apartment there. Dickon was concerned about the Prince's welfare and called for the wage-roll of the Tower servants. I brought it for him, and one of the names on it was William Slaughter. It is a name easily remembered. And," I added, "Buckingham, as Constable of England, had access to all places such as the Tower."

"I know, I know," John Kendall said irritably. "You have already suggested that it was Buckingham who saw to the end of the boys there. Now you say it was Slaughter who actually did the deed." He pursed his lips. "Then why did you allow him to be killed instead of bringing him back?"

"Because I did not connect him with the matter until the innkeeper in the Breton village mentioned the word, 'Tower', followed by 'Slaughter' shortly afterwards. I intended to question him when I returned to the ship. But his legs were freed, as you heard, and he tried to run away. The Archer-Captain did his duty according to his rights and shot him. He misunderstood my signal to desist." I ended with a shrug.

"Well," John Kendall said, "perhaps it is not of such great importance any more, as the matter of the Tower is closed." He leaned forward. "But what is of importance," he added, "is the fact that the Tudors were warned of your coming. Have you thought about that?"

"I have. I think it was de Vannes, who then tried to steal the gold for himself."

"But how could he have taken it away without being caught? Pierre Landois would soon have found out that he had seized it."

"I think he and Slaughter planned to seize the ship and take the gold to France for the use of the Tudors."

John Kendall shook his head. "I think not. I think he merely seized the opportunity when the attempt failed. Consider the sequence of events. If what you say is correct then de Vannes would have tried to seize the ship immediately you came. He would not have gone away to tell the Treasurer of your arrival."

"No. He went back to warn the Tudors as well. Besides, he only had two men with him the first time."

"Precisely! If he had been planning to seize the gold he would have had the gun-crew waiting. The Tudors would already have been warned, and ready with their horses and baggage, waiting only the word of your arrival, which any of his men could have taken. They would not have had to rush out of the church helter-skelter without their baggage." He shook his head again. "No, Henry, your reasoning will not do."

"But someone warned them."

"Exactly! And we shall have to think closer. Much closer to home. Give it your attention while I am reporting to the King at Nottingham."

"Nottingham?"

"Aye. The Court is there meanwhile. So are the Stanleys." He got up. "I start for there with the gold before dawn, and so I sleep early. Lord Lovell is riding to meet me with his own men. He will be more disappointed even than Dickon to see the gold instead of the Tudor," he added. At the door, he said, "Come and take Mass with me before I start. Unless you are in greater haste."

"I am for London," I said. "But I will see what I can do."

"Ah! Poor London!" he said, without looking at me. "London has lost its Recorder."

My throat suddenly grew small. "Its Recorder?" I repeated.

"Aye. Christopher Urswick. The man you clerked for." His eyes came down to meet mine, and there was no expression in them. "He took ship secretly to France soon after you had left. But it could not have been he who warned the Tudors, could it?" he inquired casually. "For how could he have known of your mission?"

I sat staring into my ale mug for a long time after he had gone.

21

THE sun came up and laid a brilliant yellow square on the
floor beside me. I blinked and cursed the landlord for not
closing the shutter, as all good villagers are supposed to do
after dark. They believe that the night air brings nausea and
the sweating sickness, and my first thought that morning was
that they were right. But as I woke I saw that it was not the
night air, for Joseph Anderson was on the floor too, flat on
his back and snoring like a whale. I watched his beard,
picked out with grey by the sunlight, rise and fall with the
sonorous noises that came through it. Nothing looked less
unhealthy than that roaring monster.

I cursed the landlord again before I saw that the shutter
was hanging from its hinges. The trestle was smashed and
Anderson was still gripping one leg of a broken stool. Then I
remembered the fight. We had been set upon by the village
ruffians; I had brained one with my beer mug, but what
happened after that was difficult to recall. I felt hastily in my
pockets for the money John Kendall had given me and sighed
aloud when I found it was still there. At that moment a
shadow passed over the window and a man looked inside. It
was one of the Lincolnshire archers.

"All well, Master Morane?" he inquired wearily.

"No," I groaned. "I am ill. What are you doing here?"

He was a young fellow with a long serious face. He said,
"We have been taking turn and turn about to guard you
and our captain. It seems that you outstayed him in a
tournament of ale, but when certain bad characters tried to
help themselves to your wages we had to drive them off.
Since then we have feared their return with reinforcement."

"My thanks," I said to him. "You will be rewarded.
Meantime bring some men to help him to the well, and have
others start to haul up water."

He turned and whistled and I heard footsteps. Two men
came in, surveyed the damage, inspected their leader,
grunted twice and lifted him up bodily. Anderson woke with
a start and began to lay about him with the stool leg. The
men dropped him and dodged away swearing, and then he
recovered his senses and gave them apology. Seeing me, he

muttered, "God's Hooks, Henry Morane! Do I look as sick as you do?"

We staggered outside to the well, where Anderson would have fallen in had I not grabbed him by the legs. Buckets of water over the head revived him and he said it was the second time I had saved his life.

"We could have hauled you up again," I pointed out.

"Aaaah!" he growled. "But the snakes and toads down there would have gotten me first." He spat something green out of the water he had been drinking.

Once back in the tavern the hot soup provided by the landlord brought me well again. Then I offered to pay for the damage.

"That is right handsome of you, sir," he said, and gave me a figure quickly.

It was too quick and I was suspicious. Some questions and a few threats brought forth the information that John Kendall had already made it good. Some more answers told me that he had left only an hour before. He had come from his camp outside the village to bid me Godspeed before leaving, and had seen my state, and so had gone again. When Joseph Anderson heard that he was for throwing the landlord down the well then and there, but the terrified man backed out quickly and hid himself away until we had gone.

I parted company with the archers at Salisbury, but that night there were no drinking contests, for we were on our separate ways with the dawn, they for Norwich and I for London, the gold in my pockets jingling like the tiny bells fools and acrobats wear. I rode hard, keeping alert for robbers and other vagrants, but saw no sign of any. The road had been well kept by each manor through which it passed, and the undergrowth, in keeping with King Richard's laws, had been hacked away for a hundred yards on each side. That alone prevented an unwary traveller from being ridden down without warning by brigands. Whatever rumours they might spread about Dickon they could not deny that he kept the countryside in a state of peace.

Here and there I overtook merchants, some wealthy and with long retinues, who wished to dally and pass the time of day. There were friars on foot who stopped me and begged alms, but to all I was in a hurry. For it was dawning on me that everything John Kendall had said had been carefully worded, and even his final message of "Godspeed" had been to the point. It was a warning in friendship I could not afford to ignore. I would have to reach London before the messengers from Nottingham. And once John Kendall had recounted my story to the King and to Francis Lovell those messengers would surely come.

It was evening before I reached the old Saxon capital of Kingstone, and the sight of the Thames almost had me believing that I was in London at last. But there were still twenty miles to go and my horses were as tired as I was. After an impatient night there the grey morning sky saw me riding over the hill through the great forest, and in the afternoon I was in South Wark with the buildings on the Great Bridge looming up in front of me.

London Bridge was as difficult as ever to cross quickly. The houses and shops that lie along each side of it seem to grow wider with each passing week, and their shutters, used as market stalls, seem to protrude farther and farther into the carriageway. Once twelve feet wide, today the road at some places had hardly room for two carts to pass, and at others none at all, so that drovers have to back their vehicles amid much swearing and shouting. Backing a team of oxen or drays is difficult enough, but when there is a solid mass of people behind, it becomes almost impossible.

It seems to grow darker all the time, too, more and more like a tunnel, as increasing numbers of houses on each side have high overpasses constructed across the road to join with those on the other. There had once been a toll, too, to keep out idlers, but the citizen of London, always insistent on his rights, had caused it to be abolished a long time ago, with the result that pedestrians come and go as they please, from the clerk or trader hurrying about his business to the mindless throng of sightseers who get in everyone's path.

The Great Stone Gate, rebuilt not many years before, guarded the southern end, with the Arms of the City emblazoned over the arch and statues in niches on either side. The latter, needless to say, had long been decorated with all kinds of filth. I eased my horses through the gap and then came to a standstill, blocked by a mass of people.

A man on horseback might have the advantage in a crowd, but not on London Bridge, where no one gives way, not even to an elephant from Africa. It is the natural aversion of the Londoner for the mounted man, the symbol of authority. I soon got down and led my animals on foot. My place on the saddle was promptly taken by a swarm of urchins, chanting and shouting, but I accepted them good-naturedly, encouraging them to clear the road for me. Then an intelligent-looking brown scarecrow offered to lead my horses to the other bank before their harnesses were stolen, and I accepted quickly. I knew his kind, he would expect a high reward, but he would ensure that nothing was taken. For even horses have been stolen on London Bridge under the very nose of their owner by cutting their harness and leading them away, while he stands helpless, hemmed in by the crowd.

We made better progress after that. The drawbridge from the New Stone Gate was down and we crossed quickly. No one is allowed to linger on its wooden floor, because it is ageing and will not carry too many people and vehicles at once. Those waiting on the other side for the bridge to be raised for a ship to pass through roared derisive encouragement when I put my foot into one of the holes in the roadway. There were three such holes, acting as gun-ports when the bridge was raised, and which had served their purpose at the time of Fauconbridge's rebellion some ten years before, allowing cannon to fire through at his troops on the other side of the gap.

Two thirds of the way across the road widened into "The Square", next to the Chapel of Saint Thomas, but it seemed just as full of people as the rest of the Bridge. At one time jousts were held there, but that was before the Chapel was built, for even though its back hung far out over the river, the front of it encroached on the Square.

Once across and under the crumbling ruins of the old Roman fort I paid my guide well and asked him if he knew anyone nearby who could stable the horses. At that he smiled, showing me he had a golden tooth, and said that his name was Ali, and that he had an uncle, who kept a shop on the Bridge, but who also kept another place and could look after them. The uncle turned out to be a Saracen merchant, one of those who had long settled in England, and whose integrity must have been beyond reproach or he would have been singled out and murdered years before. He offered to buy the animals for a good price, or better, to exchange them for a roll of silk he said had come all the way from China. But I refused because I was going to need the horses, and besides I did not know where China was, only learning afterwards that it was another name for Cathay.

After that I made my way through streets that grew more familiar, until I came to the house that I knew so well.

22

THE shutters were closed and the door was fast against me, but I banged on it and soon heard the bolt being drawn. It opened no wider than to allow a cat to creep out, and I saw Matilda's anxious face.

"Oh Lord Jesu!" she said, and her eyes grew very wide. She stepped back for me to enter and then our arms were round each other.

"Henry," she murmured against my chest. "Only the Good Lord knows how many times I have prayed to Saint Christopher for your safe return."

She was crying, or would have said more, but in any case I gave her no opportunity, and her tears were soon stilled.

It was a long time later, as we lay gazing through the window to the yard where the tree, now well-covered with leaves, had once gauntly beckoned me to her house, that I said, "Christopher Urswick has absconded."

Some moments elapsed before she grasped what I had said, then I heard her gulp and her hand came away from me quickly.

"He left without warning," I added in the same casual tone. "There can be no other reason than that he has gone to join the Lancastrians."

She sat up abruptly, letting the coverlet fall from her. I rolled over lazily, propping an elbow under my head to inspect her better.

"You think I went to him?" she asked in a small voice.

"I am sure you did. To ask his help in preventing my journey."

She eyed me carefully, then, "Yes, I did!" she said defiantly. "I was sure you were going to your death. Do you understand that?"

"Oh, yes, I understand that, my sweetheart. That is why I know you went to him. But Christopher Urswick is a very clever man. He extracted from you the purpose of my journey, didn't he?"

"Why . . . yes, I think he did." Her dark, anxious eyes were fixed on mine. I sat up and put a comforting arm round her shoulders. "What happened?" she asked. "Did you not bring the Tudor back?"

"No. He was warned before he could be seized. And now I am sure that the warning could only have come from Christopher Urswick. And I was the one who carried it," I groaned.

When she asked me what I meant I told her about the letter Urswick had asked me to take to a ship at Queenhithe.

"Dear God!" she said, and buried her face against my neck. "I might have killed you more surely than I was afraid of."

"You might have," I agreed, "if the Tudors had been strong enough to have had an army waiting for me. As it was they had no time but to escape."

"Then it is as well. You are safe, and Henry Tudor has escaped. For if you had brought him back he would not have had long to live."

"As to that I cannot say," I replied. "But a man does not like to be made a fool of. Nor to fail in what he sets out to do."

"You do not fail with me," she said, raising her mouth to mine.

I kissed her and then held her away. "I must take you away from here before tomorrow is out," I told her.

"Why? I cannot see . . ."

"Because John Kendall has also guessed that you told Urswick where I was going."

She caught her breath. "Are you sure? But how?"

"It is evident someone did. And it could not have been I."

"Oh! Will he tell the King?"

"He will not need to. He said as much when he was talking to me. Dickon and Lovell are astute enough to see it for themselves. As soon as he tells them that the Tudors were warned they will think of Urswick, and ask themselves how he knew. Then Lovell will recall my connexion with him, and yours with me."

"But it need not have been Urswick! It could have been someone else."

"It could have been," I agreed. "But Christopher Urswick is the first they will suspect. And Lovell knows you, my sweet apple. He saw you that day at West Minster."

"He may have seen me, but he does not know where I live."

"John Kendall does. And his first loyalty is to the King."

She was silent at that, and I said, "Have you family or friends where I could take you till suspicion dies away?"

Matilda got off the bed and pulled the coverlet over her shoulders. "Henry," she said, "you worry too much. Even if Lord Lovell has suspicion of me what can he prove?"

"Prove?" I said, suddenly angry. "You are not a fool, Matilda. He will question you. You know what that means."

"I know, I know," she nodded vigorously. "But King Richard will not harm a woman. You have told me that many times. Or is it not true after all?"

"It is true enough," I said patiently. "Dickon would not put a woman to torture. But Lovell would."

"Hah! So your King Dickon will not torture a woman, but will allow someone else to do so. Is that not the same thing?"

I got up and took her by the shoulders. "If I really thought you were so stupid, woman, I would beat you. Do you not understand? Lovell is riding to join John Kendall. He will hear the story of my failure before the King does. Do you think he will ride all the way back to Nottingham to obtain the King's permission to seize you? Why, if he can obtain a confession from you it would be a personal triumph for him, and confound John Kendall utterly." I shook her a little. "Understand this, Matilda," I went on urgently. "Lovell's men will be here by tomorrow. You must be gone before that. Now, where am I to take you?"

"If I go, will you stay with me?"

I nodded. "For a while at least, depending on where . . ."

"I have a married sister at Kingstone."

"Kingstone! Why, I stayed there last night on my way back from Lyme! This sister of yours, how is she?"

"Her husband is a master tanner and they keep a large establishment."

"Big enough for me to stay also?"

"Oh, yes!" Then Matilda shook her head. "But she is a careful body, and very strict. We would not be welcome if she knew we were not married."

I grinned. "You think it better we should be?"

"Of course!" she smiled.

"God's Hooks!" I exclaimed, borrowing Anderson's

expletive. "It is a sorry man that has to receive a proposal of marriage from a woman."

"You did not! It was you that asked me!"

"Did I?" I frowned. "But if we were married I should have to be faithful to you."

"And would that be onerous?" she asked with asperity.

"I cannot say. I have not tried."

"Not tried? You have not tried to be faithful to me?"

"Not since we were married. I have had little chance."

"But we are not married!"

"I know," I said sadly. "That is why."

"Dear God!" she exclaimed, throwing her hands in the air. "Would that I had taken up with a lawyer, then I might have understood him better!"

"In any case," I laughed, "there would not be time to wed before we go."

"Then I do not think I want to go. Henry," she said seriously, "are you sure it is necessary?"

"As sure as you are now going to prepare food. We must leave by first light. I have horses."

She smiled. "It is a long time since I sat a horse."

"Then we will take the river. But that is a long way."

"The river winds!" she sang. "Round and back and round again." She stopped and laughed and her eyes were bright. "And it will take a week! We will spend each night at a different tavern. At Chelsey, at Shene, and at . . . Oh, it doesn't matter where, because each one will be better than the next . . . and at one of them we will find a priest to marry us quickly . . . they say that if one has the money . . ."

"Go and get food," I told her, smacking her across the buttock.

There were meats and pastry and poultry, and as I gnawed the chicken I remembered Geoffrey de Vannes. I did what he had done. I threw the bone out of the window into the street. It was snapped up immediately and a crunching noise followed.

"It is not yet dark," Matilda said. "The dogs roam early."

I nodded and got up to fetch the wine. As I moved past the open shutter the crunching stopped and I heard the animal padding away. I looked out casually and then went suddenly tense.

"You are right," I said, closing the shutter quickly. "The

136

dogs roam early. There are three men along the street who wear the livery of the Hound."

"What does that mean?" she said idly, carving at the bread.

"The Hound," I told her, "is the livery of Lord Francis Lovell."

23

"DEAR God!" Matilda gasped. "They are coming for me!"

"Who else?" I said. I waved towards the yard. "We shall have to go out that way. And immediately."

"I will fetch a bag for my clothes."

"No time for that."

"But I must take some clothes, Henry! I cannot go in only what I am wearing!"

"I will buy you all you need," I began, then stopped. What she had said gave me a thought. "A moment," I said, peering through the shutter. "I can only see three of them." Turning back to her, I said, "Now listen to me. And be very quiet."

"Yes, Henry?" she whispered.

"Do you remember the night you went to fetch my clothes?"

"Could I forget it?" she smiled.

"You said there was a way to Sir William Stanley's house through the back?"

She nodded. "Through the yard. It is very narrow, and has many corners as it winds between the backs of the houses."

"Good. Do you know if anyone lives there now?"

"A woman. Another of his whores, no doubt."

"A woman?"

"Don't be a fool Henry Morane," she whispered fiercely. "Did you expect otherwise?"

"No," I grunted. "I suppose not. But now I have a better thought. Do you know her?"

She shook her head. "I have seen her, that is all."

"Right!" I said. "Then go and bring her here."

Matilda's face was a picture of astonishment. "Bring her here, Henry? But how?"

"I don't know," I admitted. "But I want her here. I could bring her by force, but that would take too long. Another woman could persuade her better . . ."

"I have it!" Matilda said suddenly. "I think I see what is in your mind." She laughed quietly. "Leave it to me," she said, and turned to the yard.

"Wait! Suppose Sir William Stanley is there?"

"You can leave that to me also," she said confidently. "But I do not think he will be there before dark." She went out quickly.

I made to follow, for I was suddenly afraid for her, but then decided it was better to see what was happening outside. The three men were standing by the door, muttering among themselves.

"This is the place?" the tallest one said.

"For sure," another replied. "The sealing wax is on the door sill."

I cursed John Kendall for remembering that.

"Then we will go in," the first one said. He reversed the dagger and banged on the door with the butt.

I waited quietly until he got tired of it. A different voice said, "She is not at home."

"We must make sure. We cannot return without being sure."

"The door is thick. It will be hard to break down."

There was a silence, followed by the movement of feet. Then, "The shutter will break easily, but the window is too narrow for me."

The tallest one said, "Then Alan will have to go through and open the door for us."

At that moment I heard a shout in the distance. Then Matilda came in clutching a great bundle of women's clothes, with other garments draped over her. She looked like a milliner's assistant trying to find her way to market. I could not help smiling, and she smiled back briefly.

Dropping the clothes on the floor, she stood back, breathing hard. "The woman is near behind me," she panted. A rattling at the shutter made her jump.

"Quick!" I said. "Out through the back! Don't let the woman see you! Wait for me at the old Roman fort by the Bridge."

Matilda nodded quickly and disappeared. Almost immediately there was another shout and a woman came rushing across the yard. She was large, as big as the wench in Brittany, and her flaxen hair was askew, streaming all over her face. She charged inside and stopped short, glaring about, her cushion-bosom heaving like a ship.

"Where is the bitch? The thieving bitch!" she roared, her voice echoing round the room.

Then the shutter was stove in with a crash and a small, wizen-faced man came squeezing through. He saw her and halted abruptly. For a few moments the two of them stood staring at each other wide-eyed. The little man was the first to recover. He made for the door like an eel, drawing the bolt with a quick movement.

"Ah!" the tall one said as he came in. "My Lady!" He bowed with mock gallantry. "So you were inside all the time!"

She looked at him with jaw dropped, quite unable to speak.

"Well, well," the man said, waving at the pile of dresses. "You were expecting us, then? Clothes gathered and ready to leave?"

The woman finally recovered her speech. "Who are you?" she demanded. "And where is that thieving bitch?" She gazed about, still bewildered.

Alan chuckled. It was an unpleasant noise from that ferret face. He moved towards her. "Now, Mistress Matilda," he said placatingly, "make no trouble, or it will be the worse for you."

"Mistress Matilda? I am not Mistress Matilda!" The woman stamped her foot. "I am . . ."

"Yes, yes," the tall one agreed, "you can explain that to Lord Lovell, for he is most anxious to see you." He went behind her quickly and seized her arm, so that she screamed.

"What are you doing! I don't know Lord Lovell!"

"Maybe not," Alan chuckled. "But he wants to know you."

She screamed again and the tall one clicked his tongue. "We shall have to bind her mouth," he said to the third fellow, a younger man with bright eyes, who nodded and began to tear up one of the dresses.

The last she could shout before the cloth went round her face was, "Sir William Stanley will hear more of this!"

"Sir William Stanley, indeed!" Alan said, pushing her towards the door. "Maybe he will, but I cannot think why."

When the noise of footsteps had receded I came out from behind the arch and peered cautiously round the room. Not long afterwards I made my way out through the yard.

Matilda was sitting on the stonework where the wall had crumbled away. I put the sack I was carrying on the ground and sat down beside her. A small urchin was trying to sell her an apple. I gave him a half penny for it, at which his eyes opened wide and he scampered away before the fool could realize his mistake. Matilda was laughing.

"Sir William Stanley likes his whores very fat," she said. "Over ripe, like this apple." She threw it over the wall into the river.

"What did you do?" I asked her.

"There was a coil of thin rope in the store-room," she said. "So, before I went up the stairs I tied it across the doorway at the level of my ankles . . ." She saw my puzzled face, smiled, and went on, "Then I went up, unannounced, and when the woman saw me she asked me who I was. I did not answer, but started to help myself to as many of her dresses as I could find. At that she yelled and picked up a cudgel of some kind. So I did not wait to look for more, but ran down the stairs as fast as I could. I could hardly see for the clothes that were draped over me, and I nearly forgot the rope that I had tied." She laughed. "But it served its purpose, for she tripped over it, and I was able to reach you before she did. Otherwise she would have caught me, and as she is a lot bigger than I . . ." She stopped and eyed me with concern. "What happened? Did they take her instead of me as you had planned?"

I nodded.

"Ah!" She spoke thoughtfully. "But I hope she does not suffer harm. I would not like to think . . ."

"She will not suffer," I told her. "The only hurt will be to her dignity. When Lovell sees her he will have to let her go."

Matilda eyed me and smiled a little. "Yes. He will have to. But there will be trouble for his men who made such a mistake."

I began to laugh. "There will be more than that for Lord Lovell when Sir William Stanley finds out he has stolen his whore."

24

THE sun was low along the river and the water was at the top of the tide, and very smooth, so that the brightness was hard to gaze into. Matilda shaded her eyes and peered towards Baynard's Castle.

"That is where I should like to live," she said. "Have you been there in the course of your duties?"

"Aye, on occasions," I replied, my thoughts elsewhere, "when Dickon conducts his business from there instead of the palace at West Minster. In any case it is too big for us, we could not afford the servants." I looked at her and smiled. "Besides, I think King Richard would be loth to give it up. Where else in London would he live in privacy?"

"Can he not do that at West Minster?" she laughed, stretching her arms behind her head. "But perhaps I like the one I have. Is it safe for us to return yet? I need to bring clothes."

I pointed at the sack beside me. "All I could find are in there."

"Stuffed in that bag? Not even folded?"

I frowned at her. "Do you think I had time for such niceties?"

"Then I must go back and smooth them!"

"Your sister will have smoothing stones and irons," I said. "And you will not need the clothes until then. It is wiser not to return. Whether Lovell has discovered his mistake by now or not, he will have set a watch there for my arrival."

"But you are not under suspicion!"

"I ought not to be," I agreed. "But he may consider he needs me for evidence to prove that I told you of my mission before he can charge you with repeating it to Urswick."

Matilda eyed me for a few moments, her brow wrinkled. "Then you are in no harm if he does not find me?"

"And neither will you be," I grinned. I added, more seriously, "But he has had no great affection for me since the words we exchanged in front of Dickon that day, and there is no telling what he might do if he caught me."

"But if I cannot be found?" she persisted.

I swung round to her. "Now what is this?" I said sternly.

"My first care is to see that you reach your sister in King-stone and stay there in safety. You well know that if you are taken I should not hide."

She put a hand on my knee. "I know that, Henry Morane," she said quietly. "And for that reason I will let you take me to Kingstone. But after that, what will you do? Will you wait there also?"

"That depends," I grinned. "on whether your sister's looks are better than yours."

Her eyes blazed. "I believe it might, you . . . you Win-chester Gander!" She reached up and slapped me across the cheek.

A passer-by, an old greybeard, stopped and stared at us. He waved a bony finger at me. "A ducking-stool, young man. The only way with shrews. Teach them early."

He put the finger away inside his cloak and shuffled off, shaking his head. "And the longer they are under the water the better," he muttered. "Such a state the young are com-ing to these days . . ." Avoiding a pile of refuse, he vented his feelings by clearing his throat and spitting at it.

We sat and watched him, laughing, when I saw Ali thread-ing his way through the crowd on the Bridge. His gold tooth was not evident, for his face was stern and set. When he approached I hailed him and his expression changed to one of relief.

"It is well I have found you," he said quickly. "There is a gentleman searching for you. At least, he is asking questions of the sentries at the New Stone Gate and wants to know if they have seen a person such as you, sir. A man, he says, travel-stained, and with two riding horses, who has crossed from South Wark since noon."

"Lord Lovell!" Matilda exclaimed.

Ali nodded. "At least a Duke, to judge by the gear he wears."

"Why should you think he is looking for me?" I asked him, not feeling any need for concern until I was sure.

A thin line of gold appeared as Ali gave a sly grin. "Good sir, my uncle was curious about you. He sent me to follow you. Which I did, and waited. Then there was a commotion at the house into which you went . . ." He spread out his hands. "Then I, too, became so curious that I could not go. The men who caused the turmoil wore the same livery . . ."

143

I silenced him with a wave. "Your curiosity has been worth at least that," I said, giving him a groat.

The silver coin disappeared into his coat faster than the gleam of fish in muddy water. He nodded quickly and waved his hands again.

"Good sir, it is better you do not wait here."

"One moment," I said. "Did you hear what the sentries told him?"

"Oh yes! They said that such a man as he described had passed that way in the afternoon."

Matilda said, "Oh!"

"No need for concern," I told her, putting a hand on hers. "The sentries would say that to anyone of his station, expecting to be paid well. And Lovell would know that too. He is no fool."

Ali nodded vigorously. "But he has also been asking the shopkeepers along the Bridge. They would not expect payment, and therefore would not tell him lies. You have been noticed."

That was different. "Where is Lovell now?" I asked him.

"Over there." Ali pointed. "That is where I saw him last. By the broken house called The Common Siege."

It was not far away. The Common Siege was the house which had fallen over into the river three years before. I got up.

"Come," I said to Matilda. "We will go to his uncle's house and get the horses."

Ali nodded his agreement and set off, with us close behind. There were fewer people about by the time we reached Fish Street Hill, which was a relief after the crowds on and around the Bridge. But as we turned into the Lower Part of Thames Street I saw two men approaching. They wore the badge of the Hound. They might have known me from the days I used to be at Court, so I took Matilda by the arm and guided her into the nearest church, that of Saint Magnus. A few moments later Ali came and knelt beside me.

I turned and looked at him with mild surprise. He saw me and frowned. "Did you think I was not also a Christian, sir?" he said.

I had no reply to that. But there must have been a time, not so long ago, when his ancestors had called us infidels.

"How did you come to be at the New Stone Gate?" I

whispered to him. "Is your shop all that way along the Bridge?"

"No, but the drawbridge was being raised," he replied. "And when that happens everyone goes to watch. They say that one day it is going to fall down, and if that happens it will be a sight not to be missed." He saw that Matilda had risen and stood up, rubbing his hands together. "Especially if it falls on a ship as it passes through. But even without that there is always a great argument to listen to when the shipmaster is asked to pay the new toll. Six pence now!" He chuckled. "And each one swears that he will never again take his ship through to Queenhithe dock and pay such an outrageous price. This one swore so loud that the very skulls above the Gate rattled on their spikes."

Matilda looked at him and shuddered. "It is a dreadful sound when the winds blows through them," she said.

"New heads do not rattle," I said grimly. "When the wind blows their hair streams about them and they nod slowly." I went towards the door. "And if ours are not to nod too it is time we moved on."

Ali went outside to see if the way was clear. When he came back, he said, "The sun has set. It is much darker. The gates will be closing, so that the sentries will require payment to let you through. You, and especially your good lady, will attract attention at any of the Gates, even more so if you use those on the Bridge."

If we went through any of the gates of London after dark Lovell would find out about it the next day, even if he wasn't having a watch set at them already. I had told Matilda that he only wanted to seize me as a witness, but in fact if she were attainted as a traitor it would be I now who would be condemned for harbouring her. She, as a woman, would not be executed by Dickon, I knew, but I would have no excuses. The urgency was, therefore, to see her safely hid away at Kingstone and then, if I were taken later, I could deny any knowledge of her whereabouts. And my denial would be accepted, I was sure, without any need for the use of the rack. At least, I hoped it would be.

It was better, therefore, that Lovell did not learn that we had left London, when he would confine his search to the City until in due time other matters assumed greater importance. Then Ali was speaking again.

"Sir," he said, "it may well be that your Lord has been asking questions of all the nearby horse-copers, knowing that they could not be taken to the house you visited. You said he was no fool."

"You mean that your uncle may already have been questioned? But would he speak?"

Ali shrugged his thin shoulders in a gesture of resignation. "He would have no choice."

"Good!" Matilda said suddenly. "Then we shall have to go the way I wanted to. We shall have to take . . ."

I put a hand over her mouth quickly. She mumbled something against my palm and then tried to bite it.

"Don't say any more," I warned her. "Ali will not wish to know what we intend to do."

He nodded quickly. "That is very wise of you, sir. If I am asked I shall know nothing."

I took my hand away from Matilda's face and she spluttered at me, "If you do that again, Henry Morane, I'll . . . !"

"There!" I told her. "Now Ali knows my name!"

She stopped and glared at me. Ali gave her an impassive look and said, "I will go now." He went to the door and turned back. "Your horses will be safe with my uncle. For as long as ever you wish to leave them." He bowed to Matilda and then he was gone.

She turned to me and said, "Have you known him long? Is he a friend of yours?"

"Long enough," I grinned, "for me to know that he can be trusted."

25

WATERMEN after dark charge double price. That did not matter, as my pockets held money, but I was not sure how far it was to Kingstone. Little more than half a day's ride on horseback, the river might wind for twice that distance. And at further stages it might be too late to find a boat at all. Men of the river, too, have to sleep sometimes. I explained this to Matilda as we walked down the cobbles to the wharf.

"Then we shall find taverns," she said cheerfully. "For by the river it will take half a week."

"How do you know that? Have you been by river before?"

She laughed and shook her head, making the dark hair stream over her shoulders. "Of course not! I have always been in London. But a boatman said so when I told him I had a sister in Kingstone."

I groaned. "So a boatman knows that too?"

She took my arm. "So long ago, Henry, that he will have forgotten. Besides, he was an old man, and may have died."

"Killed by your witchcraft," I said shortly.

She let my arm go quickly and stopped to stare up at me. "Never speak like that, Henry," she said. "Never, never!" She began to tie up her hair. "I had forgotten it was loose," she explained, and I knew that witches were supposed to let their hair run free.

When she had pulled the hood over her head I kissed her and said that we could take a boat as far as Chelsey, where I knew of a horse-coper who, if he was still awake, would lend us horses. Lovell was not likely to pursue his inquiries so far afield.

To that she replied that she had no better scheme and that she would leave it to me and trust in the Holy Virgin.

There was only one boatman at the wharf and he was asleep, curled up inside his cloak with his lantern flickering on the planks beside him. I was about to stir him when I noticed that the tide was on full ebb. He would want triple price to row us against that current, if he was willing to do so at all.

Matilda had seen the tide too. She whispered, "He will not take us until the river weakens."

"That is why he is asleep. He is not expecting custom until then. But I have a better plan. I will buy his boat."

She drew in her breath. "But you cannot row it all the way yourself!"

"When the tide begins to flow again the current will help us as far as Tiding-Turn if need be, many miles past Chelsey."

"But until then what can we do?"

"Row across to the other side and wait under Saint Mary Overy at South Wark. It will be quiet by the trees there. And the boatman will be sure we have gone under the Bridge, and will say so if asked. Then it will be said we have gone to the docks and taken ship to France."

"Could we not do that, in fact?"

I turned and regarded her with astonishment. "To France?" I asked her. "Run away to France?"

She shook her head. "To Burgundy, perhaps. I have heard it is a pleasant place. We could set up house there . . ."

I stopped her talk with a kiss. "I will not run away," I told her. "Neither will I try to shoot the Bridge. A boatman knows how, maybe, but even then only one with experience would try when the tide runs like this."

She peered out across the swirling current. "It is very strong," she said anxiously. "Should we wait till the tide slackens?"

There was a feeble light to be seen from the other bank. "It is not very far," I said, stirring the boatman with my foot.

He groaned and opened one reproachful eye.

"How much for your boat?" I asked him, jingling two coins together.

He opened both eyes, wiped a dirty hand across them, and muttered that it was late.

"I did not ask for you to row," I told him. "I'll buy your boat."

"Buy my boat?" he repeated, as if he was still not with his senses, but the glitter in his eyes in the light from the lantern belied it.

"Three angels for it," I said. "As it lies there in the water."

"And take my livelihood away?" he whined.

"You can buy a new one for two angels."

"And wait a month for it to be built?" He cleared his throat and spat into the water. "And I would live on six shillings and eight pence while I waited? Good sir, I could not."

"You could live for six months on that, as you know well."

"Five angels and it is yours."

I dropped four coins on to the planks in front of him. One of them rolled towards a crack, and as he lurched forward to save it I helped Matilda into the boat. As he straightened up he saw us and yelled, "Hey! I have not said I will accept!" But he was clutching the coins.

As he shambled towards us I threw two silver groats at him. "There," I said, "and that is three times the fare you would have charged for taking us through the Bridge."

He stopped short. "Mother of God!" he exclaimed. "Have you taken leave of your senses to try and shoot the Bridge on this tide! Not even I would dare it, especially in the darkness." He picked up the groats. "You will be drowned, both of you! And your beautiful lady will be hauled up from the bottom with fishes on her bosom and slime in her hair!"

His voice faded away in the darkness as I pushed off into the current.

26

"I KNOW him," Matilda said a few moments later, throwing the cloak away from her face. "Nick Benson. It is as well he did not see me, for he will talk about this for weeks."

"To our advantage, maybe, if he thinks we made for the docks down river."

We were near midstream, where the current was strongest, when it caught us and sent us whirling round like a child's spinning-top. The lights from the houses on the Bridge seemed very near. Matilda saw them too and made an exclamation. I pulled at the oars until the sinews seemed to be leaping out of my back, sending the sweat running down on to my buttocks. The current now ran deadly smooth and implacable towards the torrents round the piers.

London Bridge stands on nineteen stone arches, all of different spans, and most of them changing in shape too, their tunnels growing wider or narrower to a boat as it passes through. A few arches are as much as thirty feet across, others only fifteen. Each end rests upon a pier, where it joins the next, and each pier is surrounded by a row of stakes, the encircled space being filled with rocks and stones, making a huge starling. To a watcher from the sky the Bridge would look as if it floated across the river on giant shoes.

Thus while the greatest arches might stand thirty feet across before they reach the water, the passage between is less than half of that, and each starling encloses a foaming torrent that swirls away from its stakes to join its neighbour in a wall of water like an arrowhead some twenty feet beyond. At slack tide it is pleasant to shoot the Bridge, provided the stool-houses are not being emptied, for it is the biggest wonder of the modern world, a sight to be seen by all from Europe who can afford the journey. It had stood for two hundred and fifty years, and while it will almost certainly last another thousand, it is not one to be caught against in a swiftly moving tide in the darkness of the night.

I hauled in one oar and gave all my strength to the other. We lost several yards while I did so, but then we began to hold our own, for my effort countered the circling motion of the current. In that manner we had travelled nearly half-way across the river when the oar snapped in my hands with a crack like a breaking tree. I fell flat on my back, the stern shot upwards, and Matilda lurched forwards across me. By the time we had recovered ourselves one of the arches was looming towards us like the black entrance to Hell.

There was no chance of avoiding it now. The only hope was to try and steer the boat through without it being crushed against the piles on either side.

I seized the remaining oar and thrust it into a notch in the stern. It would have to serve as a rudder. I saw Matilda watching me, her eyes wide with alarm, but the noise of the water roaring against the starling drowned all speech. I pointed beyond her to the anchor lying in the bows and made signs to her to pick it up and throw it between the piles as we shot past. It was only a small fluke on a thin rope, suitable for holding the boat among river weeds, but it was all we had.

She understood what I meant and bent down to pick it up. At least she would be too busy for the next few moments to be afraid. But now she had her back to me and there was no means of warning her to stand clear of the rope as it coiled out after the anchor. She stood up, legs apart to counter the rolling of the boat, holding the tiny anchor by the shaft. I yelled at her to get down or she would be pulled off her feet, but she heard nothing above the rushing waters.

The current took us at tremendous speed straight towards the middle of the arch. On either side of us it rebounded from the piles in steady waves, smooth and hard as glass, which led downwards as if on a slide out into the river beyond where, its top a-gleam in the starlight, I could see a solid wall of water. I breathed a short prayer to Saint Christopher, for if the anchor failed to hold we should be swept against it and smashed to pieces.

Then in one instant I saw Matilda framed by the dark archway, skirts flying and hair streaming as she stood up holding the barbed weapon like an Amazon of the sea, and in the next her arm was outstretched and she had cast it.

Sebastian, or whichever Saint it is who protects those who fling, must have been watching over us, for the hook caught firmly between the stakes. But then the rope snaked out, grew taut, and the boat swung round violently to be brought up

151

with a tremendous jerk, so that Matilda lost her footing and fell over backwards. She gave a piercing scream, clawed frantically at the gunwale, and went spinning over the side.

I let go of the oar and threw myself headlong towards her. By the Grace of God I got a grasp of one wrist and held her, half in the swirling water and half over the gunwale, for what seemed an age while the boat thudded under us. But in the end I recovered my strength and slowly hoisted her back over the side.

She lay in the water that swirled about the bottom of the boat, panting and gasping for breath, while I rubbed the pain from her arms. I saw her lips move and put my head close.

"What happened?" she asked. "Where are we?"

"We are alive, at least," I shouted. "And, thanks to your aim, hanging by a rope's thread from a starling of London Bridge. If you had missed we should surely have been drowned." I pointed at the steep wall of water behind us.

She murmured something that sounded like, "Dear God!" and then neither of us spoke for some time. I watched the thin rope anxiously, but at least it seemed to be new, and might hold together better than the oar had done.

It could not have been long before our ears grew accustomed to the steady roar of the torrent, for I heard what Matilda said next.

"And even if we had survived that wall of water we should have but one sweep for our progress afterwards." She saw my expression and looked past me towards the stern. "Oh! Has that oar gone too?"

I gave her a grin of reassurance. "Better without it. With only one oar I should row round in circles, getting us nowhere."

She smiled through the spray on her face. "That is not true, Henry Morane. For I have seen watermen moving their boats with an oar swept from side to side at the back." Putting her hands under her she tried to get up, but the boat was bumping and jerking against the rope so that it was impossible to stand. I held out a hand to her, and soon she was sitting beside me on the thwart.

"This seat is quite soft," she announced, feeling beneath her.

"It should be," I chuckled. "It is your sack of clothes."

"Jesu!" she exclaimed, trying to rise. "They will be all spoilt!"

I held her down. "They are wet of course, but otherwise should have no more damage than your sister can have repaired."

She considered me for a moment and then shrugged. "I hope so, for nothing can be done yet. Meanwhile we will use them to kneel on while we make a prayer to Saint Christopher for our safety so far."

"Aye," I agreed, "and add one to the Holy Virgin that the rope holding us does not snap."

She looked towards the deeper darkness of the archway and shuddered.

We knelt quietly for a little while, holding ourselves steady against the gunwale, then Matilda got up. "A swan!" she said suddenly.

I looked at her with astonishment and then cast about us to see where it was.

"No, no!" she laughed, "I meant that if I were a swan I could have sailed through with ease."

I gave an exasperated sigh. "In any case they rarely come this way," I told her. "They have learned by now that they can be killed by stones thrown from London Bridge. Roast swan is a dish for . . ." I saw her face fall and couldn't help laughing. "Besides," I added, "any that do pass the Bridge are for the table of the Tower Constable."

She peered at the gaunt battlements, grey against the night sky, and shivered again. "I can well believe it," she replied. "Just now it looks more of a prison than a palace." She turned back to me. "What can we do now?"

"Wait until the tide changes and sweeps us back to the other side."

"How long will that be?"

"Who knows? As much as six hours, maybe."

"Six hours! Bumping about like this? I am wet to the bone and cold already."

"It may not be so long if the rope breaks," I said grimly. "But at least if you were a swan you would not be cold." I put an arm round her. "Sit close and let me keep you from being bruised more."

"The swan comes to the Constable," she said, snuggling

beside me. An arm went round my shoulders. "I need to be kept warm too," she murmured.

There were better places than a hard, bouncing, spray-ridden rowing boat in which to enjoy each other, but for a while at least neither of us cared whether the rope snapped or not.

27

FAINT gleams on the water showed that lights were beginning to be lit. It would soon be dawn. I looked back and saw that the steep wall of water had vanished. The turbulence round the starlings had subsided, and there was now a smooth channel between them. The tide was slack once more. I stretched to ease the ache in my back and clambered unsteadily forward to haul the boat closer to the piles.

"Saint Thomas's Chapel is not far from here," Matilda said. "Perhaps no more than three or four arches away. It has an undercroft to which steps lead up from the starling. There is a wharf . . ."

"I know," I said. "It is used by sailors visiting the Chapel to ask Blessing for their voyage."

"If we could reach it we could ask for Blessing too. And maybe ask the priest to marry us."

"We could," I agreed. "If I could leap from starling to starling like a mountain goat, pulling the boat after me." I turned and smiled at her. "Even for you, my sweet apple, I cannot walk on water, neither can I swim well enough, not like your swan." I hauled at the rope. "First we must get away from here. Weddings can come later."

She stood up quickly, setting the boat rocking. "You miserable monster! You never really intend to marry me at all, do you?"

"Come up here," I laughed, "and lend your weight to mine so that I do not haul the bows into the air. Otherwise I cannot get close enough to climb up the piles and release the fluke." I held out a hand for her.

She ignored it and came up beside me. "Be careful," I warned her. "Do not upset the boat."

"I have a mind to," she replied icily. "And push you over the side. Climb up the stake, then, and release us."

"I think I had better," I chuckled, "for the sake of my safety." I seized one of the piles. Then I swore out loud and took my hands away quickly. The wood was covered with the shells of sea-creatures that had made their homes there. I washed the blood off my palms in the river while Matilda laughed.

"It serves you right," she said, tearing a piece off her skirt. "Now wrap this round your hands and try again."

I unhooked the fluke and started to pick my way across the rocks, towing the boat round behind me. Once on the other side of the starling I called down to Matilda.

"Tie the boat to a stake while I throw the anchor across to the other side. When it catches I'll climb down to you and haul us across."

"This channel is much wider," she said doubtfully. "See if there is a hole in the arch above you that leads up into one of the houses. Some have them, I know."

"I have already looked," I told her. "But it is too dark to see properly."

At the fourth attempt the hook caught and I went to the edge of the starling. It was a long way down to the boat.

"Throw your shoes up to me," I called. "I can put them over my hands to save them as I slide down."

"My shoes!" she exclaimed. "I will not! Better you be wed with sore hands than I barefoot! I will not!"

"Then I'll jump. And sink us when I hit the boat."

"Jump then! And God have Mercy on you for deceiving a poor wench!"

I jumped, but into the water, and soon Matilda was helping me aboard. "Sometimes I hate you, Henry Morane," she said, putting her arms round me. "But I hope you never hate me."

"I have no need to," I replied, seizing her quickly and putting her across my knee. "There is always this." I smacked her three times across the buttocks.

"Ow!" she yelled, wriggling free and nearly upsetting the boat. I laughed, reaching out for her right hand, knowing it would fumble for the dagger, when she stopped suddenly and grew tense. "Look"! she pointed.

There, in the growing light of daybreak, was a boat.

I pulled her down quickly and, without a word, hauled us into the shadow of the piles. When we bumped against them I could see that we were at one of the wider passages.

She was watching me curiously. "Why do you do that?" she asked. "There are three men in it, rowing this way. If we hail them they will tow us."

"Keep quiet," I warned her. "They may not be as well-disposed as you think. Men who come in boats at night without a lantern are better not interfered with. And that boat carries a sizeable cargo."

"Barrels!" she whispered. "Wine barrels."

I nodded. "I can see them." Two men were rowing hard, while the third stood at the stern, steering with a tiller. "Wine from Burgundy or France," I said, "from a ship arrived at the docks. They are probably trying to evade the Royal Customs."

"How can you know that? They might be going to the Chapel and could tow us there."

"Indeed they might," I agreed, "with all that wine for the priest." I laughed quietly. "I hear they drink like sea-sponges."

She stuck an elbow into my side so hard that I gasped.

"No," she said a moment later. "They are heading for this arch. It is probably the widest."

"Aye," I said, "and maybe too wide for me to throw the anchor across, and reach the other side before they get here. So we'll have to hold the boat close up against the piles and hope they do not see us. And keep very still. If they are the kind of rogues I think they are then they will not like us to see them. Throats are slit very easily in the darkness of London Bridge."

The two oarsmen were stripped to the waist so that the sweat on their bodies shone like morning dew. Fifty yards from the Bridge they stopped their oars and waited for the helmsman to take his bearing. I could see his face screw up with concentration as he straightened the boat and gave the signal to start pulling again. He had not noticed us yet, although I did not think he would as his mind was busy on the steering, and if the others saw us it would be after they had passed when they might be going too quickly to stop. And if they were in the hurry they seemed to be they might not waste the time to turn round and attack us.

I held Matilda still as the heavy boat approached. The wine barrels were stowed amidships, between the men at the oars and the steersman, so that if they did decide to attack us they would at least be separated by the cargo to begin with. I thought about what I should do, and loosened the dagger in my scabbard. Matilda felt my movement and she, too, grew tense. Then, as they reached the archway the two

157

oarsmen pulled in their sweeps and rested on them, letting their way carry them through.

Alongside us in the gloom one of them spoke suddenly. "How much farther is it, Jack?" he asked the helmsman.

"A mile, no more," came the reply. "You will see the carts waiting for us in the marshes soon."

Now I knew that their business was clandestine, for no honest man takes a cargo of wine to load on to carts by the Lambeth Marshes, where only wildfowlers and vagrants dwell.

The other fellow cleared his throat and spat into the water. "Ar," he said idly, watching the spittle float by. "And if no one's there to meet us I'll broach part of this cargo myself . . ." He lifted his eyes and stared straight into mine.

It seemed to take him an age before he realized what he was looking at. Then he shouted an oath and pointed at me. But the helmsman's wits moved faster. Quick as a bee he stooped down and picked up a spear.

Hand weapons I had expected, but a spear I had not bargained for. There was nothing I could do but throw the anchor at him. The fluke, followed by the rope, sailed over his head. It was enough to divert his aim, for the weapon soughed past me to thud into the woodwork of the pier.

I heard Matilda gasp, but I had no time for her. If the man could expend one javelin he must have more to spare. In that I was right, for I saw him stoop down for another. He had it in his hand as I jerked the rope back hard. Even if the anchor did not catch in the boat the rope might disconcert his aim again.

But this time it did more than upset his throw. The fluke caught in his shoulder, spinning him round. I gave the rope another, more violent heave, sinking the hook deeper into him, and would have pulled him overboard had not the tiller held him back. The force I had used dragged our boat right up to theirs, and as we collided he fell forward and began to scream.

In that instant I had leaped on board the other boat, ignoring him, for the other two were clambering over the barrels towards me. The first had a battle-axe in his hand, and the other carried a morning-star. These, like the spear, were weapons of war, and I felt my stomach constrict. But there was no time to ponder on their unexpected appearance in a cargo boat, for the first man had already jumped down and his axe was high.

The weapon must have been unfamiliar to him, though, or he would have sliced me apart then and there instead of raising it to strike downwards. I ducked aside quickly and thrust the point of my dagger hard up under his breastbone. The breath went out of him in a long groan, and then I brought up my knee and shoved him off the blade.

I would have seized his weapon as it fell from his hand but the third fellow was above me with the morning-star. I stood and faced him with my bloodshot weapon, my stomach free again, and the lust of battle over me. Even a morning-star was not going to be proof against my blade.

Yet such a mace, loaded with sharp spikes, is a devastating weapon. It can smash armour like glass, breaking the bones and flesh under it into pulp. Nothing can stand against it, especially when it is wielded from overhead, as from the seat of a horse. And this man was overhead, crouched on the barrels. I would have to keep away from him so that he had to jump down. Then, if I was quick, I might have him before he recovered his balance.

Or so I thought. But there were two others behind me, wounded, it is true, but I did not know how sorely. The screaming had stopped, and the one with the battle-axe was silent too. Perhaps they were creeping up towards me. I would have to use guile.

The fellow on the barrel-top was the slow-witted one. I halted abruptly and gazed up, open-mouthed, at the arch above him. Although he must have known that the tide was low enough for him to be able to stand upright without endangering his head he was taken in by my age-old trick. He turned to look up too.

With that he was mine. A dagger-thrust through the knee sent him stumbling over the side, and by the time he could open his mouth to scream the water rushed in, choking him. He did not even have the wit to let go his heavy weapon, so that the weight of it carried him down. One huge bubble came up, and that was all the trace he left. I swung round, breathing hard, ready to deal with the men behind me, and then I saw Matilda.

She was standing over them, a gout of blood as big as a ripe plum hanging from the end of her Italian dagger. Her breath was coming in gasps and her eyes were as wide as silver dishes. She gazed at me blankly for a few moments and then was in my arms, crying like a babe.

"I had to do it, Henry!" she said, amid great sobs. "I had to kill them! Both of them! The one with . . ."

"There now," I said soothingly, holding her tight.

"The one with the anchor in him was crawling towards you with another spear. He was so intent on you that he never saw me . . . but it was the other one . . . Dear God!" she cried, tears welling down her face. "He was already dead, I am sure, but . . . but I had to kill him again to make certain!"

"The better for that," I murmured, smoothing back her hair. "A woman's bravery costs so much more than a man's. But it is finished now, little one." I took the dagger from her unresisting hand and held it over the side, afterwards wiping it on my sleeve. "There," I said to her. "Take it and see if you can broach a barrel with it. Your prayers have brought us a boatload of wine. We must make the best use of it."

She looked up at me with reddened eyes and smiled a little. Then she took the weapon and started to prise at a cask. At first she pecked at it like a bird, but soon her strokes grew stronger.

I watched her for a few moments before turning back to heave the bodies over the side.

28

MATILDA'S strokes at the wine-cask were having little effect. I told her to stand aside while I swung the battle-axe at it. It was a weapon about three feet long, balanced so finely that it felt no more than a part of my arm, and with a double blade, one side curved outwards and as sharp as an infant's tooth, the other shaped like a butcher's cleaver. But it was for thrusting as well, for the end carried a long spike of the kind used for prodding through the eyeholes of a vizor. The whole head was of steel, and shrunk on to a haft of ash, so that it was a formidable weapon indeed. I was glad that I had not been struck with it.

The fact that they carried battle weapons was curious, and I could only think that they had brought them from a ship which, carrying a cargo such as wine, would need to be well armed against the pirates in the Channel.

I gave the barrel a hefty stroke and split it right down. Wine poured out all over us and soon the deck was awash.

"Hurry!" Matilda said, leaning down to cup her hands against the broken stakes. "Or there will be none left."

"It cannot all gush out so quickly," I said. "That barrel must be a tun."

It was heady stuff, and sweet, and I told Matilda not to drink too much of it or she would stagger over the side. That brought the fire back to her eyes and I knew she was herself again. She looked me up and down.

"I may not be able to drink as much as you, Henry Morane," she said coldly. "But so far I have not put it to the test. Ah!" she said, cupping her hands against the barrel again. "My feet are chilled."

"They may well be. The wine is over our ankles."

She stood up quickly, full of concern. "Henry," she asked me, "will the boat fill with wine and sink?"

I grinned at her. "If it does it will be the first I ever heard of sinking that way."

"But will it?"

"No, of course not! The boat has already been carrying the weight of the wine without sinking. We are merely letting it out of the cask into the hull."

She eyed me doubtfully, then sat on the gunwale and splashed her foot in the swirling liquid. Her toes came out dripping red and I wondered how much blood was mixed with it.

"It it fills the boat then it must sink," she insisted.

"If it does then we have our own boat." I pulled it closer and got to my feet. "Come," I said, "It is time we moved from here."

"Henry, I know what we will do! We will take the other barrels to the priest. It will be his fee for marrying us!"

I shook my head slowly. "Better not. He would want to know where they came from. And even if he was unlike other priests and was not curious his clerks would talk about it. No, my sweet," I went on, "we cannot go near the priest now. Look outside." I pointed. "It is daylight, and there will be other boats on the river. We must leave this one to fend for itself. We have oars now, and can go . . ."

"Could we not sink it?"

"Not easily. We should have to break it into small pieces, and that would take a long time. Even then the pieces would float. But before that the bodies will be discovered, because they will float too. Then," I went on emphatically, "the Hue and Cry would be raised, and every vessel would be stopped and questioned."

"So we cannot be wed at the Chapel, then?"

"There are other Chapels. We . . ." I stopped. There was a shadow at the entrance of the arch.

"Quick!" I told her. "Lie down! Another boat is coming. The waterman must not see you as well as me."

"Lie down? In this wine?" she asked indignantly.

There was no time for argument. I pushed her down and put my foot on her head to keep her there.

The waterman rowed inside the passage, put up his oars to clear the starlings, and floated towards me.

"Hey!" he called. "The best of the morning to you! What have you there? Whole casks of wine?"

"I wish it were," I said dolefully. "Or you would not see me resting like this. Barrels of fish in brine is all." I could feel Matilda squirming under my foot.

The waterman sniffed and spat over the side. "It smells like Gascon," he announced. "Or even the treacle they send from Burgundy."

162

"I think they must be Gascon fish," I replied. "For I can hear them churning about in a barrel as drunk as an abbot on Palm Sunday."

At that he burst into a roar of laughter that kept him until the end of the passage. Then he put out his oars again and rowed away, still chuckling.

Matilda came up spluttering. "By the Holy Virgin!" she exclaimed. "I will make you pay for that, Henry Morane!" Then she started to cough and I beat her on the back, so that she leaned over the side and spouted wine.

"Come," I told her, picking up one of the oars. "Bring the other with you and we'll go from here. The tide is beginning to turn and will take us fast up-river."

She muttered something and lifted the heavy oar with both hands, then held it over to me. As I reached for it she dropped it on my toes. I swore and danced with pain, while she stood back triumphantly.

"There!" she cried. "Now maybe you will learn not to humble me with your foot!"

I rubbed my toe until the pain had gone, considering what we should do. In spite of what I had said earlier the wine boat would have to be destroyed now, especially the barrels, as one waterman had seen me with them, and there might be others coming through. I thought about how to do it and decided that the quickest way would be to broach the casks and let them flood out, then smash the bottom of the boat so that it sank as low as possible in the water and we could roll the empty casks overboard. That way the water would wash out the evidence of the wine, at least, and the barrels might sink with the weight of their iron hoops. I explained this to Matilda, and she thought it best too, so I picked up the battle-axe and split the next cask. But when no wine flowed I stood back, puzzled. I smashed out the stave and peered inside. Steel, not wine glittered back at me.

"What is it?" Matilda said. "Is there no wine in it?"

"No," I said. "No wine. A barrel-full of weapons. Battle-axes and maces and such-like."

"Dear God! What does that mean?"

"It means," I told her, "that I understand now why those men had weapons of war so easily to hand. They were carrying a cargo of them. If the other barrels contain the same there is enough to equip a hundred men."

163

"But why? Why should they be . . . ?"

I swung on her. "Because," I said grimly, "no one would be carrying a cargo like this in such a clandestine manner unless to arm men for a rebellion."

She looked at me with wide eyes. "What can we do?"

"Nothing. Except sink this boat as quickly as possible. The weight of the weapons will carry it down like a stone."

"Should we not report it to someone?"

"And who would believe us? That we, one man and a woman, captured it from three armed men?" I shook my head. "No," I went on, "whatever devilry someone is up to will be stopped by the lack of these arms. Besides we don't know from which ship it came." I took an axe from the barrel. "Here," I said, "take this and help me beat out the bottom of this boat."

By the time the water was gushing in through the hull the tide was setting back strongly, and it was with some impatience that I waited for it to sink.

"Heigh ho!" Matilda said as I rowed out into the morning sunshine. "The current runs like a fish and we shall be in Kingstone by sunset."

"The tide only runs with us for half a day," I told her. "And when it changes my hands are in no condition to row against it." I held one up. "The sea-shells tore them and the oars will tear them more."

"Oh!" she said with concern. "They should have attention! They must be bathed and bound in wine . . ." She stopped suddenly when she saw my face, and presently began to laugh too.

29

WITH the tide running strongly there was little work for me to do, so that we were soon past West Minster and the chance of being noticed by any of Lovell's men who might have been posted to watch the river. And at that time of the morning there was considerable traffic, both crossing and going with the tide. A small boat would not be conspicuous, especially as Matilda kept the hood over her head and could, from the bank, have been taken for a man.

On the Lambeth side there was nothing to be seen. If anyone lay on the narrow wall of earth that crossed the marshes watching for a cargo of wine and weapons he showed no interest in us.

After we had passed the great Abbey and Palace Matilda undid her cloak and shook out her hair. Two men in a boat close to us looked at her with astonishment. Their craft had a small sail and was keeping station against the current while they trailed long nets in the stream. They shouted us a greeting for the new day, and the younger one whistled and blew kisses at Matilda, to which she responded with a smile, and I with a glower. But when his head turned round on its neck to follow us the older man cuffed him and told him to attend to his business, which was for salmon, not geese, and soon the whistling died away mournfully behind us.

At Chelsey I put in at the steps and went to look for the horse-coper, but as I walked I decided that as we were making so well in the boat we could well continue that way. To travel from Chelsey on horseback would mean a long road round on the northern side of the river and crossing into Kingstone by its bridge, the first to span the river upstream from London. We should not reach it before dark, when the place would be full of thieves and cut-throats. For Kingstone contained only less evil at night than London itself because it was less in size. And even if we were to reach it by sunset it would be near impossible to cross the narrow wooden structure against the stream of market carts returning to places such as Hampton and Sunbury Cross at the end of the day.

With these thoughts in mind I turned back to the stage, to find Matilda the eye-ful of the watermen there. I had to admonish them sternly not to talk of our visit, as I was a privy servant of the Archbishop of Canterbury taking one of his geese back to Brent, and if news was spread of such a high priest of the Holy Church having a goose as beautiful as this one it would go ill with anyone who spread it. At this they were suitably awed, and I gave them each a penny to impress their silence, which would probably thus be prolonged for nearly half a week.

Matilda's eyes sparkled with amusement as I recited the tale, for old Thomas Bourchier was close on eighty, and could hardly mumble through Mass.

Before we came to Brent the tide grew slack and then changed against us, making it impossible to reach Kingstone that day. We put ashore at a stage where there was a tavern, and near where it is reputed that Julius Caesar first crossed the river to reach London. The innkeeper had some pieces of time-blackened bronze which had been found not far away, and which he swore were parts of a Roman helmet. Whether it was true or not we were too weary to care, but the legions of fleas that inhabited his place were real enough, and were only exceeded in size by those in the church where we went to offer Thanks for our safety. Its priest, however, was nowhere to be seen, but the clerk told us he was away in the woods with his dogs and his hawk, hunting rats, and would be back for Vespers.

But even if there had been no vermin in the tavern we found it impossible to sleep for the din. There was music, dancing, and shouting, so that in the end we gave up and joined the crowd to make as much noise as the rest of them. The innkeeper, extracting lugubrious sounds from his crumhorn, put his instrument aside to serve us, but when he saw my hands he clicked his tongue and went to fetch cloths to bind them. The cloths were soaked in mead, which he said was an infallible cure told him by an apothecary of Mortlake, who was famed for his remedies.

Whatever the reputation of the apothecary the bandages took away the soreness of my palms. I borrowed a rebeck from a fellow who was so drunk that he was trying to blow it like a horn, and plucked a few notes, to which Matilda gave me loud encouragement with a discordant song. At this the others roared their appreciation by clapping their hands in unison and banging their mugs against the wall. When I gave the rebeck back to its owner and patted his face for thanks he grinned at me and tried to blow it again. The effort sent him sprawling on to his back, where he smiled amiably at me and forthwith went to sleep. It had been a good day for salmon, it seemed, and the fishermen were spending their catch. Although to judge by the tallies carved on the landlord's stick the catch had been spent long before.

With the dawn I was wrestling with two lusty fellows by the river bank, and Matilda was asleep on the grass nearby with a goat chewing appreciatively at her skirt. It was not long before the animal, delighted with the taste of the drapery, which still gave off the fumes from its soaking in wine, gave a greater tug and Matilda woke with a start. Seeing us standing there laughing, she got up, kicked the goat on the nose, and stalked away into the inn with her skirt trailing behind her like a battle-torn banner.

After that it was an hour before she would speak to me, not saying anything at Mass, even though the priest was in attendance. And even when the landlord brought us a huge kettle of soup for us to break our fast she still kept silent. At last, when the morning tide died away against the current of the river at Tiding-Turn and I rested on the oars to observe that we could have been married by the priest at Brent she turned on me and swore that she wouldn't marry me even if I was Emperor of Africa himself.

At that I laughed quietly and said that we were not far from the bridge at Kingstone.

"What has that to do with it?" she demanded.

"It is where they duck scolds," I replied, keeping my face away from her.

"Oh? So I am a scold?"

I shook my head. "I didn't say so. But anyone seeing you now might think so."

"Dear God!" she exclaimed, looking at herself. "What am I to do? I cannot go to my sister in torn and wine-soaked clothes like these!"

"There is the sack there." I jerked a thumb at it. "What is in it may be rumpled, but . . ."

"Then take me ashore where there are trees, and I will change them."

I leaned on the oars and I looked at her. "The Emperor of Africa, eh?"

167

"Henry! I did not mean that!" She put her arms round me and the boat slewed round. "Please take me ashore."

"So now I am to be beguiled, is that it?"

She took herself away quickly. "I will not be laughed at!"

"We were laughing at the goat, not at you."

"And that," she said stonily, "is about as true as your story of me and the Archbishop of Canterbury."

I grinned at her and pointed at a team of oxen on the bank drawing two heavily-laden barges of wool bales. "The trees are on that side," I said, "as you can see. And the other bank is meadow grass."

"There are bushes farther on," she said. "They will have to do."

They grew down to the water and I pulled in between them. The clothes were mostly damp and some smelled of wine, but Matilda found a sober dress that was no more than rumpled in a few places and, to my surprise, made me turn my back while she pressed it on.

"Keep the boat still," I heard her say, "so that the ripples die away and I can see myself in the water to make up my hair."

"At the bottom of the sack is a silver mirror," I told her. "I had a mind that you might need it."

Two arms came round me from behind. "Henry Morane," she said, "you are a great solace! You think of everything!"

"Everything," I agreed, chuckling and turning round. "Even to a quiet place in the meadows of Tiding-Turn."

30

THE bridge at Kingstone was an intricate mesh of wood, due to the constant strengthening and repairs that had to be carried out, and there seemed to be nowhere to pass through except the central porch. But that was filled with an endless procession of barges and boats larger than ours which took the right of way amid vociferous arguments with each other. Above, on the roadway, there were arguments too, more prolonged, for the crossing was longer, and carts starting the journey over would almost certainly meet another coming the other way so that both became stopped, impeding all traffic until the matter was settled.

In order that the flow of traffic should not be held up, therefore, the Wardens of the Bridge had imposed a fine of six pence on carts that met head-on in this way, and both carters had to pay it. Such a ruinous penalty quickly had its effect, for no carter would start his crossing until the way was clear, sending a runner across first to ensure it. Thus runners from both sides would often meet in the middle, when negotiations would commence, usually with clubs, and the afternoon sport of the denizens of Kingstone became less of watching the cock-fights than cheering and laying wagers on the contestants on the bridge.

It seemed that we should have to tie up the boat by the Hospital and complete our journey on foot when such a contest on the bridge ended with a fellow who, climbing on to the parapet to get a better swipe with his club, had his legs adroitly taken from under him by his opponent, and toppled into the water. All traffic stopped immediately and the bridge and banks became lined with spectators to watch him drown.

"We must save him!" Matilda exclaimed.

Marvelling at the irrationality of women, who one day will stab two men with a dagger and the next will be a monument of concern for a drowning man she has never seen before, I pulled towards the fellow. Shouts of disappointment followed me as I pulled him into the boat, but at least, when his coughing and spluttering was ended, he was able to express his thanks by showing me a passage through the bridge and guiding me to a mooring place beyond the Bishop's Hall.

The way to the tannery of her brother-in-law, Matilda said, was now through the market place and over an ancient stone bridge that crossed the Hogsmill stream. I asked her how she knew it so well, and she told me that she, and her sister, had been born there. That gave me some surprise, although I had never asked her before, accepting without thought that she was a child of London.

Market places are the same the world over, and Kingstone was no different, being filled with a thrum of people milling aimlessly between counters and covered stalls, their vendors trying to shout their wares and abilities loud enough to drown the next. Fortune-tellers with their tarot cards laid out in front of them gave strident accompaniment to astrologers waving mystic symbols that no one could understand. But these were quiet compared with the noise that came from the pig-butchery on the other side where fat, smiling, smooth-faced men, their leather aprons running blood, held still-squirming pieces of pork aloft for all to buy.

Then we were transfixed suddenly by a piercing scream that came from a tooth-drawer's chair when he stepped back and held his red and white morsel triumphantly in the air. I was tugged by bawds, no more wholesome than a horse-gelder's cat, and cuffed them away whining and complaining that but for a farthing I could have them in the Egyptian style, and even if I did not want that they had a younger brother.

We came to a haberdasher's stall and Matilda stopped, exclaiming that the ribbons and laces were better value than in London. While I stood beside her impatiently a ruffian snatched at her bag of clothes which hung from my arm, but the battle-axe was inside it and shore through, so that he scuttled away like a coney holding his thumb in his mouth. The next stall was a mercer's and she must stand there entranced too, so I walked away to listen to an apothecary calling on all who were sick or let blood, or who were cast down with ague, or fever, or stone, or pleurisy, or strangulation, to take his cure of powders made from crushed worms and lilies and mixed with a secret elixir from the sweat of Saint Jude himself. I was rapt at the man's success, for although his cure cost as much as three pence, there were scores that bought it. When he paused for breath I grinned at him, and he chuckled and winked knowingly, showing me the calloused gums under his beard.

At that moment it thundered, and soon the rain came. The place emptied as if by astrologer's magic, most of the crowd running to the Moot Hall or the Church. Stalls were quickly covered with canvas, the owners taking shelter beneath them, and once the place was clear I found Matilda easily enough. I took her hand and led her to the Cranes, where we sat and drank mead, waiting for the shower to end.

"You seem to know of this place," she said.

"The Cranes? Yes. I slept here on my way from Lyme. Three days ago."

"Three days? Is that all? It seems like three years since you came back. Do you think Lord Lovell will have given up the chase by now?"

I nodded. "He will want his men for other purposes. But he will leave one near your house while he reports to Dickon that you have gone. He will also say that I have not been seen either. And only one conclusion will be drawn from that. I shall have some explaining to do if I am found."

"Then we must see to it that you are not found. At least with me."

I did not know what she meant by that remark until later, and did not have time to ask her then, for she went on, "Maybe the priest here would marry us before I meet my sister. She is very devout and proper, and . . ." she shrugged "I would prefer it in the Chapel of Saint Mary." She pointed across the market place. "Over there, under the spire of the Church. The Chapel of All the Kings."

"All the Kings?"

"All the Saxon kings were crowned there, it is said. And the coronation stone lies there too, to prove it."

"So does the pickled body of Saint Luke in the Vatican, but who is to say that it is really his?"

"Unbeliever!" she taunted. "For God's Sake do not let my sister know that I have married a heretic!"

"She won't," I assured her. "For it will not be in King-stone. If you were born here the marriage would soon become talked about, and would reach her ears quickly." I finished my mug. "And if she is as devout as you say she will in any case be appalled that we have been living in sin. What

171

did she have to say of your last man, Sir William Bourchier?"

Matilda's eyes glinted. "Don't say it like that! He wasn't my last man. He was my first!"

"Oh, so?" I said airily. "Then there are to be others?"

She banged her fist on the trestle. "Henry Morane!" she cried. "Why do you twist everything I say? You know very well what I mean."

I laughed and covered her hand with mine. "I merely asked what your sister thought of Sir William Bourchier. Or did she never know of him?"

She shook her head. "No. I was sent away to be brought up in a noble household. To be My Lady's dresser."

"Which one?"

"Bourchier's, of course," she smiled.

"And where was your sister sent?"

"She was not sent anywhere. As the eldest daughter she remained at home with the dowry." She smiled again. "I am surprised you know so little of ordinary customs, Henry Morane."

I nodded slowly, as if to myself. It seemed that the practice of sending children away from home to be educated with other people's families was spreading to the merchant classes. It was a long-standing custom with the nobility, but in their case it brought a wider field of experience. For lesser folk it seemed pointless. Why have the brats merely to exchange them for someone else's?

"And your sister?" I asked her. "Has her dowry brought her a marriage of contentment?"

"As to that," she replied, getting up, "let us go and see."

31

MATILDA'S sister was married to a worthy citizen named Edward Coombe, and ran a large, well-furnished household, even to having glass in the windows of the main hall and the solar. Master Coombe, narrow in frame and stooping with great height, because of his sparse white hair appeared to be much older than his wife, until one saw the shrewd eyes of a man who had encountered many a horse-coper in his time, and was still ready to encounter more. Yet he was a kindly man, and offered us a room of his house for as long as we cared to stay and asked no questions. But I knew that he would satisfy himself about us soon enough.

Eleanor, his wife, was as different from Matilda as a barrel is from a bunch of grapes. Very fat, with a great fold of chin presaging the surplus flesh that lay farther down her body, she was not a cheerful person such as many stout people can be. She commanded her servants and children in a high-pitched whine, and was clearly not too pleased to see her young sister again, nor at the alluring contours that were all too evident under Matilda's gown. Nevertheless she took us in without hesitation and herded Matilda away to be bathed and dressed as became a member of the household.

Of the children I was surprised, after what Matilda had said about her own upbringing, that they were the Coombe's own. It transpired that Master Edward had fixed ideas on the subject of education, and those, like all his other ideas, held sway in the end in spite of his wife's different opinions. There were two small girls, ruthlessly imprisoned in miniature versions of adult clothes, and a boy of some ten years whom his mother referred to as Matthew, but on addressing him called him "You".

It was a well-managed household. There were prayers before and after each sitting down to food, and more in the morning and evening. The servants kept closely to their appointed places, and there was no familiarity such as takes place between master and man in the establishments of the nobility. But then the family, especially on the distaff side, which has sprung upwards from its equals has to exercise more care to remain above them.

Nevertheless it was an establishment like many others, part of the backbone of England, and its members the salt of the kingdom. Although it seems to me that an overdose of salt can spoil a fine meal and lead to a thirst for something different.

Eleanor, as Matilda had warned, was avid to learn our circumstances, and we had agreed that I would say I was a baker whose premises had been burned away with fire, so that we had no place to live meanwhile. Even though it was a lie it was better than to tell her that I was an out-of-work scrivener living in sin with her sister. She heard my story with an expression of sympathy on her face that concealed the satisfaction of hearing another's troubles, which is common to many people, but she was somewhat put out to hear of the gold I carried in spite of my explanation that it was what I had saved from the fire. She did not approve of a mere baker possessing more money than a tanner of hides, even though the latter was a person of more consequence, especially in a small place like Kingstone.

Master Coombe eyed me sceptically and cleared his throat, then observed that gold should be kept in a safe place.

"To me, sir," I replied, "there is no safer place than under a sword blade."

He nodded without saying any more. But it was an unusual kind of baker who guarded his gold with a sword.

"As for us," Eleanor said, "the wealth we amass is kept in a great iron-bound coffer in the cellar of which only Edward has the key."

"That would not do for me!" Matilda said lightheartedly. "I can keep count of it better when it is in Henry's pockets."

Eleanor shot a quick glance at her husband, and I saw him repress a smile.

It was at supper a few nights later, when the clatter from the kitchen at the other end of the hall had died away, that Edward Coombe asked me if I had considered setting up a bakery in Kingstone. The master-baker was an old man, and while he had apprentices and a journeyman none of them would buy his business from him. They were all going to London as soon as the old man died. Kingstone was small, and they were ambitious to enter the great city.

"Then why does the journeyman not go now?" Matilda asked. "While the apprentices are bound to their master, he can work for whom he chooses."

Edward Coombe looked at her with some surprise. For a woman to be aware of matters of business was new to him.

"The journeyman will benefit from the baker's Will," he said. "It is common knowledge."

There was no hint that our welcome was ending, or that their hospitality would not continue, for they were kindly people. I said, "No, I will return to London, take lodgings there, and see what can be done about restoring the bakery." Matilda gave me a sharp look. "I brought my wife here after the shock, and if you will I should like to leave her with you a week or two further. Tomorrow I will buy horses and travel back soon."

"Now what is this?" Matilda said when we were alone together.

"I must return to London and see what is happening. To stay in Kingstone, cut off from the world, I am in no mood for."

"But would you leave me here?"

"Not for long," I said, putting an arm round her. "But here you are safe for a while."

"Dear God!" she cried. "To be safe is one thing, but to live a life as tedious as this is another! I would return with you and take my risk, except that if I am found with you it would be you who would suffer." She broke away and looked up at me archly. "Aye, Henry," she said, "you had better not be away too long. Master Coombe has an air of competence about him that might appeal to me if I were left alone to my own devices."

"Ho, ho!" I laughed. "Your sister's husband too!"

"Poor Eleanor is but a country cabbage."

"Even a cabbage can be sweet when the outer leaves are stripped."

"You dare!" Her eyes flashed. "You just dare! I have not yet thrown away that dagger."

"I know it," I grinned. "That is what kept me from the bawds in the market place."

32

THE bedroom was large, although the smaller of the two which stood at the opposite end of the hall from the kitchen. Between them, on a slightly higher level, was the Solar where Edward Coombe, as master of the house, would retire for privacy and none, not even his wife, might enter except by invitation. Below the Solar, and only approachable through it, was the cellar where the iron-bound chest lay quietly in the dust.

Above these rooms was a loft, reached by a ladder outside, where the children slept on straw, and their noise subdued by Mistress Coombe banging on the ceiling boards with a long stick kept for that purpose. The hall itself was walled with carpets, and the floor rushes changed daily from the plentiful supply growing by the river.

It will be seen that it was a modern house, even to having the stool-room outside and away from it. Clothes were no longer hung in there for protection against moths and fleas, but kept in great chests in the hall and bedrooms, and consequently smelled the sweeter.

The bed we had was of feathers, wide enough for four people, and surrounded by drapes to keep out any cold airs that might escape past the fire. Towards dawn the sea-coals in the grate would have dwindled to a spark, but not long afterwards a boy would come in through the arras from the hall and tend to it, and then maidservants would bring sheets and towels and a huge ewer and basin to bathe Matilda.

They would draw the drapes aside and lead her out naked to stand on the warmed sheet while they washed her with a perfumed cake of soap that must have cost at least a penny. When that was finished they would stand her on another sheet and dress her. It was a most decorous business, and the first morning, when I peered through the drapes they were drawn across me quickly by the older maidservant. I essayed a wink at her before my face was covered, but was only met with a frosty frown.

When Matilda had been led away into the hall two menservants came to put me through a similar process. But I told them to leave the steel and I would wash and dress and scrape my stubble myself, and they departed, stiff-faced, as if they had been chided for being delinquent in their duty. Later, when I met them and gave them a half-penny each they unbent a little and wished me a good morning.

When prayers were done we ate our breakfast, after which Master Coombe must depart for his tannery next-by. What occupied him there all day was a mystery to me, for he had three clerks and a treasurer as well as an army of skinners and salters, but as he brought home more funds for his coffer in the cellar each evening there was little point in probing further.

It was one morning before he went that he asked me if I knew of any well-educated tutors in London, because the boy Matthew would soon reach maturity and something had to be done for him. The very question showed that he knew I was no baker, for such a person would, if he educated them at all, send his children to a school of the parish.

"Yes," his wife put in, "I have taught him his horn-book and figures, but he needs a wider study." I saw the boy watching me with an apprehensive smile on his face.

"I do not know of any," I told him, "but I will find out. Meanwhile as I need to exercise myself, if you will permit him to walk with me I will question him and see what he knows." The boy's smile grew wider.

"Perhaps we could hunt in the great forest!" he exclaimed. "I can bring my crossbow!"

"No!" Eleanor said. "I will not permit that. The forest is a dangerous place . . ."

"But I will be with Uncle Henry!"

"Hold your tongue, Matthew, when your Mother is speaking," his father said.

"I will look after him," I said with a smile at Eleanor. "But if I, too, am to go hunting, I shall need a bow. Matthew," I said to him, "you can show me where to buy one."

"The boy does not know . . ." Eleanor began.

"Oh yes, Uncle Henry! I know where! A fletcher named Hayward has a shop in the market."

His mother gasped, and her husband turned away quickly. I knew that he did it to hide a smile.

33

K INGSTONE bridge, seen from the level of the street, is a narrow, swaying structure that looks as if it will fall sideways into the river at any moment. A line of drays, loaded with beer, lurched unsteadily across, brushing pedestrians against the wall, while runners shouted vociferously at each other on the far side, where other carts, bringing wheat and beans from Middlesex, waited for them to cross. It was too narrow for us to walk over without being crushed by a cart-wheel.

"We will use the ferry," I said to the boy.

"Over there, uncle." He pointed at a house with a bush hanging before the door, denoting that it was a tavern. "The ferryman is there. The house is the most unseemly and bawdy place between London and Southampton."

"What do you know of it?" I asked him.

"The servants talk. Why, they say that inside . . ."

"Where is the fletcher's?" I asked him quickly.

I bought a stout bow and a quiver of clothyard arrows. I could do nothing less with the boy at my side, but I was apprehensive as to whether I could draw such a monstrous weapon, it having been a long time since I had done so. To be an archer requires a special skill and great strength, and not every man has the strength or skill to become one, let alone aim and fire six arrows in a minute of time. The boy had his crossbow, a slender affair built for a woman, with the horns drawn back by a lever which is called a cranequin, though why a French word need be used instead of the English "crank" I have never discovered. Perhaps it is to show one's superior education in these matters. The crossbows I had met before were of the heavy kind used in battle, where massive steel springs have to be drawn back by a windlass while a foot is thrust through a stirrup at the end of the stock. Yet even the war crossbow, while as powerful as the English yew, could not fire so fast or be so accurately aimed, but then of course it does not need a strong man to shoot with it.

The ferryman refused to take us across, and I would have struck him had he not been so bemused with ale, so in the end we crossed the bridge on the back of a brewer's dray and set off away from the road into the forest that lies on the Middlesex side.

"See that crow up there?" Matthew said. "Watch me kill it with one bolt." He lifted his little bow.

"Wait until there is something bigger," I told him. "And why kill the crow? You cannot eat it. And besides, it has its uses."

"It is a bird of ill-omen," Matthew said. "And what uses can it have?"

"If you were to kill all the crows in the world," I told him sternly, "there would be nothing left to eat up all the refuse. Great piles of filth would grow so that no man could pass along a village street without being tainted."

"But there are dogs," he argued. "They will eat the offal. I would not shoot dogs."

I had to think quickly. "Ah!" I said, "there are dogs, it is true. But they only eat the larger pieces. The crows remove the tiny bits that dogs will not consider."

"And we cannot eat crows," he agreed after some thought. "Do you only shoot things that you need to eat, Uncle Henry?"

I nodded solemnly as we pushed our way through some tall bracken, now sere and brittle and crackling as we passed.

"And yet my father says you have a battle-axe."

I halted suddenly and eyed him. "What of it?" I said.

"So you must have fought in many battles, and killed many men." His pale face looked up at me. "But you do not eat them, do you?"

"No, Matthew," I laughed. "Men do not eat men."

"But you kill them."

"That is different. In battle if I did not kill a man he would kill me. It is self-protection."

He nodded sagely. "Then I could shoot the crow if it tried to kill me? If it swooped down with beak and claws ready to tear me into little pieces?"

"Indeed you could," I assured him.

And for the next hour he examined each bird we saw hopefully, in case it showed a warlike tendency towards us. His face fell as each one flew away.

It was the same with the deer. Those that we saw did not allow us to approach, and we were no hunting party with dogs and horses to ride them down. In one deeper glade young Matthew saw a wolf, or swore it was, and I did not dissuade him even though I grew tense and had my hand ready for my dagger. I would sooner have trusted that than the longbow, although an archer like Joseph Anderson would have laughed at me.

In the end Matthew shot his crossbow at a distant coney while it was twitching its nose in the sunlight, and by the Grace of God the bolt only missed its white scut by inches as it scampered away. That was good enough for him and he went home proud of his near success, boasting that with a little more practice the next coney would not live so long.

At supper that evening, after prayers had been said, Edward Coombe told me that new Acts of Parliament had been proclaimed by the sheriff that afternoon which prohibited certain importations, especially of leather. He rubbed his hands together and said that, with the new process of Caxton's, he would be able to buy a printed copy of the new law and study it at his leisure. I observed that, if the importation of leather was prohibited, it would be to his advantage.

"Not so much for me," he replied. "It is levied against goods that are already made, purses, bags, jerkins and so forth, whereas I, a tanner, sell my leather for that purpose, especially for shoes. Nevertheless," he steepled his hands together "they will be to the advantage of English shoe-makers and other handicrafters, not only of leather, but of other manufactures such as silk lace and ribbons . . ."

"And so prices will rise," Eleanor put in sourly, "for the thieves here can charge what they will."

". . . Even small things like handbells and scissors," Coombe went on, ignoring her. "And . . ." he smiled "the sheriff also read a proclamation against the merchants of Italy."

"Italy?" Matilda said. "Why of Italy?" I grinned at her. I knew she was thinking of her dagger.

"Because," Edward Coombe told her, "they sell too much here in England."

"So now they cannot?" she said.

"Oh no!" he almost chuckled. "King Richard's new law does not forbid them to sell. Not at all! They may sell what they like, apart from the importations I have mentioned, but they cannot take the money for what they sell away from

England. They must spend it here," he concluded triumphantly.

"Hah!" I said, "so we shall have to buy good English daggers, then." I could feel Matilda glaring at me.

Edward Coombe eyed us curiously. "Aye," he said, "and no longer may a merchant from Italy or any other country give house to a man from his own land. The King has proclaimed that the households of foreign merchants are full with their own people conniving and plotting for secret profits, to the detriment of the people of this realm."

I laughed. "You do not approve of foreign merchants, then?" I said.

"Oh yes!" He laughed this time. "So long as they do not carry out their trading here. And it seems that King Richard does not either."

"Richard of Gloucester is a villain," Eleanor said suddenly, and we all turned to stare at her. She eyed us defiantly in turn. "They say that the two sons of King Edward are dead, and that Richard had a hand in it."

"Now where have you been hearing such a tale?" her husband asked her.

"The priest said so. Not only that, but he killed the poor old crazed king, Henry the Sixth, in the Tower with his own weapon, and likewise his son after the great battle of Tewkesbury, when the boy lay defenceless from a wound."

"The priest said that too?" Edward Coombe inquired.

She nodded vehemently.

"Then it is just as well Dickon does not hang priests," I put in, "for such talk is treasonous."

"It is as well he does not hang women either," Edward Coombe said, his sharp eyes on his wife.

"But these are the rumours that everyone hears," Matilda said. "You cannot hang a rumour." She faced me. "And I, for one, think that they may well be true."

I gave a long sigh. "It is strange, is it not," I remarked to the table, "how women, one and all, are not partial to King Dickon. Is it because, I wonder, he is no huge, handsome figure of a man, swiving every woman he encounters, like his brother Edward was? And because he has a wife to whom he remains faithful?"

"He is not!" Matilda said. "He has two bastards, as is well known."

"Born before he was wed," I pointed out. "Is that a sin?"

"All fornication is a sin!" Eleanor exclaimed. "The Holy Writ states it to be so!" The points of her eyes turned on me. "Can the murders be denied? Of the boys in the Tower? And the lad at Tewkesbury? All of them little more than children? If so, why does he not do it?"

"That is for him to decide," I answered, restraining my irritation. "But as to Tewkesbury it is simply not true."

"How so?" Edward Coombe demanded curiously. "Is that for certain?"

I nodded. "And in any case he was no lad, being eighteen years of age and in full manhood. Although," I added, "whether he was the son of Henry the Sixth or the Earl of Somerset is not certain." I waved a hand. "Yet there is no doubt that he was the son of the former Queen, Margaret of Anjou."

"Lad or not," Eleanor insisted, "he was known as Prince Edward and was killed by Richard of Gloucester after the battle."

"As your priest says, Mistress Coombe?" I growled. "But I have said that it is not true and can be proved. Before the battle," I went on patiently, "King Edward himself proclaimed and had it published to all commanders, that the person of the so-called son of Henry the Sixth was to be preserved alive."

"That may be," Matilda said. "But he was killed."

"In the fury of battle," I agreed. "His chest was stove in by a morning-star wielded by Lord Scrope, and even today I swear that His Lordship does not know he did it." I had their attention now, and went on, "The prince was in full plate, but the shield he carried bore the arms of Lancaster, no more. It seems to me that when he was dismounted he lost his own shield and picked up another from a fallen man . . ." I grinned sardonically "unless he had it from the commencement of the battle and was trying to conceal his identity . . ."

I glanced round and saw the servants' heads filling the space between the arras and the archway into the kitchen.

". . . And so, even though he was on foot he made with his sword at the legs of any horse that came close enough. He brought one down, and was about to thrust his blade through the helmet of the rider as he lay gasping on his back, when Lord Scrope saw it . . ."

One of the servants coughed, and the arras was drawn across quickly.

". . . John Scrope swung his mount as if it had been no bigger than a fox and roared his challenge. But the prince was too intent upon fitting the point of his sword into the eyehole of his victim's vizor to see his doom. The crash of the mace on his breastplate could be heard above the din of battle round them." I paused and eyed my audience in turn.

"And," I went on, "it was only after the issue was decided and the burial pits were being dug that King Edward remembered the lad and sent to find him." I nodded reminiscently. "As he was not with his mother, Margaret of Anjou, who had watched the battle from a distance, it was first thought that he had escaped, but she swore it was not so and that King Edward had killed her son. Then the cadavers were examined and he was found, although hard to recognize . . ." I looked at Matilda and added, "And it was Sir William Stanley who took it upon himself to carry the news to his mother."

"Sir William Stanley?" she said wonderingly.

"Aye," I nodded. "Who else but a carrion crow like him?"

34

THIS time I stabled the horses at South Wark and crossed the Bridge on foot. It was evening and darkness was not far away, but the people were as thick across the road as ever. On the other side, I walked along the bank a little way to look back. The tide was again swirling out between the starlings and I watched the waves with awe, thanking Saint Christopher once again for our safe passage through that night.

"There is no one there," a voice said beside me, and I swung round quickly. It was Ali, smiling his golden smile.

"I saw you pushing through the crowds, sir," he said.

"You miss little," I told.

He shrugged and held his hands out sideways. "To see all is to know all, Master Morane."

"You remember my name too?"

"To forget nothing is to remember everything."

"Yes, yes," I said impatiently. "Then if you've seen everything tell me if the house is still under guard."

"Two men wearing the livery of the Hound stood nearby for three days, and one at night, or most of it. But for a week now they have been gone." He put a hand on his cap and shaded his eyes with the other. "I am like the hawk," he said. "I see everything and miss nothing."

"What of the woman they arrested and took away?"

"The woman they arrested? Oh yes! She no longer lives in that house. There is another. More fat, and the belly on her . . ."

I didn't hear the rest of it. I was thinking that Sir William Stanley must have settled his problem with Lord Lovell. It might even have crossed his tortuous mind that there was something about Matilda's house that needed investigation. He might have learned of my connexion with her somehow.

". . . And she was brought there by a fellow wearing the badge of the Hart," he concluded.

That told me no more than that Stanley still kept the place.

Then Ali caught my sleeve. "Tomorrow," he said earnestly, "I regret to tell you that I shall be able to help you no more." I looked at him curiously, and he went on, "Tomorrow I take ship for Venice." He spread his hands out again. "With the new laws concerning Italy and foreign merchants I have to go there to make certain arrangements for my uncle."

I looked down at his face, blank with innocence, and grinned.

Having wished him well, and paid him accordingly, I went round to the gate behind the house. It was still barred but, seeing no one, I climbed the wall quickly and hid in the kitchen. Of the other two cottages that backed on to the yard one was still unrepaired and empty, and the deaf old harridan who occupied the other would not notice me if I kept out of her sight. I peeped in through the window and saw her on a stool by her iron stove, absorbed in her needle-work. Ali had been right, no one was watching Matilda's house any more.

The place was dim behind its closed shutters, and cold with loneliness. But there was wine, and I took it, sitting on the bed until it was dark outside, thinking of all that had happened since the night Alice had been killed by Sir William Stanley. By then the wine had taken hold, and I fell asleep, cursing him. And in the morning light it seemed safe for Matilda to return, so I would go all the way back to Kingstone and fetch her.

On the Bridge I stopped at one of the stalls and bought gifts for the Coombe family: a goblet of Venetian glass for Edward, and a comb of horn, inlaid with pearls, for his wife. For the two girls I bought similar, smaller combs, and for Matthew a new-fangled gun which could be held in one hand. It was from Pistoia, also in Italy, and I wondered sardonically how the merchants would smuggle the money I had paid for my gifts out of the kingdom. Perhaps they would wait until Ali had completed his "arrangements".

The pistoia, as the merchant called it, was tiny enough for a lady to carry in her girdle. It seemed to me to be a very complicated weapon for a woman to use to defend her honour when a dagger would have done as well, but perhaps there are special circumstances in Italy where honour has to be defended at longer range. At any rate it would be right for Matthew, as it had a small barrel and fired a leaden shot no bigger than a pea. With it I bought a horn of powder, lead and a mould for the shot, and my only concern was in case he

185

might blow himself up with it, if his father allowed him to fire it, that is. I grinned to myself as I thought of the probable decimation of the poultry at the Coombe establishment.

But my humour faded quickly when I reached Kingstone that evening. Edward Coombe was the first to greet me, and his face was sad. Without preamble he told me that Matilda had gone away that very noon, with the explanation that it was better I were left to myself. It was a remark he did not understand, he said, and he showed some indignation when he repeated it, for a wife who deserted her husband deserved no more than the whip and the pillory.

He put a sympathetic hand on my shoulder and told me that Matilda had asked for ink and paper and wax and had written a letter which, if I would come into the Solar, he would give me. He added that he kept a flagon of wine in the cellar which had grown old and which he kept for occasions such as this, when its potency would assuage all gloom.

I followed him, he nodding all the while, not so much for what Matilda had done but because she was his wife's sister. For my part I said nothing, waiting to see what the letter said before I knew what to think.

"Henry, my fierce and only darling," the letter ran, and Matilda's writing was as full of curves as her body. "You must know why I cannot stay with you. If you are taken with me, the woman who betrayed the King's secrets, it will go hardly with you. You will deny this, but I know that it is so. And without me you can say that you have never seen me since you returned from Brittany. I know we have talked about this before, but it is right to say it again. But I am only gone until the day when the Tudor comes and kills the . . ." she had written 'Monster' and then crossed it out ". . . and then we shall be together again . . ."

I groaned out loud. If I had to wait for that then I should never see Matilda again.

". . . and can be wed as you desire . . ." the 'you' was heavily underscored ". . . and use the bed no longer in Sin, the bed on which you came back to life for me and which is the only life I know or want. And when you are with other women do not forget me for I shall be alone, and when these troubled days are over . . ."

She had written no more, nor even signed her name.

I swore and screwed up the letter and threw it into the fireplace. The red wax melted and ran down the paper, falling from its edge in droplets that blazed like tears of blood.

Edward Coombe nodded sombrely and said nothing.

"She is afraid for me," I told him, for I owed him that. "There is suspicion of her betraying a secret, and the King wishes to question her. The suspicion is wrongly founded, but she thinks I will suffer if she is found with me."

He looked at me for a long time, then nodded again. "Aye," he said, "I did not think you were a baker. It is unusual for a man of bread and cake to know so much about the battle of Tewkesbury."

I grinned at him. "That's why I spoke of it at such length," I told him. "So that you would realize that I was not. It is unfair to deceive one's host."

"Aye," he replied. "I thought that was what you were trying to tell me." Then he smiled. "Well, at least my wife still considers you a baker." He held out his hand and I took it.

"I do not think you will wish to stay here longer now," he added. "But you are welcome this night."

I shook my head. "Thank you, but no. Matilda's leaving would cause Mistress Eleanor some embarrassment, the more so if I stay alone."

"She does not know yet," he said, to my surprise. "She has taken the children out since the forenoon visiting the priest . . ." he chuckled suddenly ". . . no doubt to tell him that Dickon did not murder Prince Edward." And then his face became melancholy again. "I will tell her some story, probably that you both went off together. And if there is any assistance you need, although I do not wish to meddle . . ."

I knew what he meant, and said my farewell to him. Edward Coombe was a man I had come to like.

35

MATILDA would return to London, I was sure, and it
did not take long to find out from the watermen that a
woman of her description had taken a boat downstream that
same noon. The boat was very fast, they assured me, with
two men at the oars and, as the tide would be with them
once they passed Tiding-Turn she would be in London that
very night. Although once in London, I thought morosely,
she could easily hide from me. Yet it seemed certain that she
would return to her house sooner or later, whether Dickon
stayed on the throne or not, so I decided to go and wait
there. It would be a matter of patience, and mine would
outlast hers.

As it was almost dark when I left Kingstone I went no
farther than the great forest that lies across the road to London and slept there in the bracken until the morning cold
woke me. There were no other travellers until the sun rose,
but I questioned the early countrymen I saw and soon found
the track to the village of Putney, where I knew there was a
ferry.

I already had horses with Ali's uncle in London, and so I
sold mine to a one-eyed coper by the river. He told me that
he had hated those animals since one had kicked out his first
eye, but as he had knowledge of them and no other means of
livelihood he prayed every morning to the Holy Virgin that
another would not kick out the second. He had been a
peeping-tom, of course, and would have had his eye removed
for it, for there were no other marks on his face which a hoof
would surely have made. But I accepted his price because I
was in a hurry, and because it was a tale used to make a bargain which I had not heard before. After that I took a boat
to West Minster.

The Palace was empty, as I had expected, but the sentry
was the same grey veteran who had been on duty when I last
saw the King. I learned from him that the Court was not
returning yet, for he had not been alerted for it. He told me
that Dickon would stay in Nottingham all winter, for it had
been winter when Buckingham had raised his rebellion, and

the threat from the Tudors was not to be taken lightly at any season of the year.

It was with something of shock that I realized that it was not yet a year since Buckingham had tried his throw and I lay next to death in Matilda's bed. I asked the sentry how he knew all he spoke about.

That the Tudor was plotting another attempt at Dickon had been common talk at Court before it left, he replied. And he hoped it was true because he found keeping sentry at an empty palace was tedious and he longed for more stirring matters.

I left him and went to John Kendall's house. I found it was still open and his wife, Agnes, there also. She was pleased to see me. I was someone to complain to.

"No, Master Morane," she told me, "I have not seen my husband since he went away with the Court. And it has been at Nottingham all summer, which you would think was long enough for John to have set up our household there. But no, he has probably taken house with another woman, and here I am, neglected and starved . . ."

She did not look it, but I did not say so.

". . . except for the messenger he sends at rare times with pittances for me to keep the household, and nothing for the clothes that should befit the wife of the King's Secretary. I am still wearing the dresses of last year, and with winter, which will soon be upon us, I don't know what I shall do . . . One would think that for Christmas . . ."

"Your dress becomes you well, Mistress Kendall," I said gravely. "To me, a man of humble discernment, did I not know you, and had I been asked, I would have said that you were the wife of an earl at least . . ." Before she could say anything I went on quickly, "And I know that Master Kendall has no thought but for your welfare and if he has not yet taken you to Nottingham it is because he has not yet had the opportunity of setting up a household suitable for your station." I paused for breath, but my flow of loquacity had silenced her.

After studying my face for a few moments, she said, "Do you think so, Master Morane?"

"I know it, Madam," I said. "He talked of little else." It was a lie well spent. She smiled. It made her face more comely, even more than a smile does to other people. For her eyes were so wide apart, almost at the sides of her face, that when her features were in repose she had the expression of a sheep.

"Mistress Agnes," I asked her, "I beg pen and ink so that I may leave a letter for his next messenger to take back to him."

With that she clapped her hands and ordered them, together with a silver jug of a pale wine that soon lay inside my belly as gently as morning dew on a forest cobweb.

I wrote a very short letter: "John, my friend," I said, "I am in London and much bewildered for there is no one here I know." I signed my name and sealed it, and then joined Agnes in another bowl of wine. The message would tell him that I was not with Matilda, and the next move was his. I hoped it would be with the knight, the messenger-piece, or even a pawn, but not with the King.

Saying my farewell to Agnes I walked back along the Strand to London. I had half a mind of seeing Matilda gazing into one of the shops, perhaps a dressmaker's, or one where gold and silver smiths were at work, but it was raining and the way was muddy from the streams that trickled down from the gardens on the other side.

I walked along quickly, avoiding the muck thrown up by the horses and ox-carts, to the Strand's narrow footbridge with its slippery planks, which in dry weather the more fastidious riders would walk their mounts over to avoid muddying the animal's feet in the ford, to the imprecations of pedestrians who were thereby forced to wait. But now, it being muddy everywhere, horsemen used the ford as it was quicker, and I crossed the bridge without difficulty. I stood there for a moment to look back at the the old Savoy, once John of Gaunt's great palace, but now a fire-blackened ruin inhabited by rogues and other bad characters. It was here that the street extended into a wide avenue of trees until it joined the Aldewych Way at Strand Cross, but the gold-smiths and milliners along it were all shuttered up against the weather.

Temple Bar frowned down at me as I walked under it. One day, I promised myself, I would burn its ugly structure to the ground. And then I had forgotten it as I was slithering down the lane to the Fleet Bridge and trying to keep my feet. It was on the other side, climbing up the hill to the Lud Gate that I lost them and fell into the mire, to the guffaws of the guards there. When I got up I cursed them so fluently that they stood aghast, and it was my turn to laugh. In the end we were clapping each other on the back and I was taken into the guardhouse to drink warm beer by the fire and dry my feet.

After that I went to Matilda's cottage and prepared to set up house on my own. It was such a dismal business that, two days later, I found employment in a counting-house to keep myself occupied.

36

IN SPITE of the sentry's confidence that the Court would
stay at Nottingham all winter King Richard and his
Government returned to West Minster early in November.
There was to be no Tudor invasion that winter, it was considered, not so much due to the season but because they were
having difficulty in raising the necessary forces in France.
The Court of Charles VIII, it seemed, was having doubts
about the success of the venture. They lacked a general, too,
for the Earl of Oxford, the only soldier of any competence
whom Henry Tudor could rely upon, was still a prisoner in
Hammes Castle.

A week or so afterwards there was a treason trial which
drew much attention, and I went to the subsequent execution partly on the chance of seeing Matilda. Although it was
a spectacle that would not attract her, she might go to
mingle with the crowds, as she liked to do. Such events were
festive occasions, for only those close to the scaffold could see
what went on, the majority enjoying themselves more at the
temporary market of shops and stalls that was set up around
the perimeter.

Two men had been charged with treason; John Turberville, a shipowner, and William Collingbourne. The former
had escaped with life imprisonment, and it was Collingbourne
who had to be dealt with that day. Formerly a gentleman-
usher in the household of Dickon's mother, he had bribed a
man eight pounds to carry a message to Henry Tudor urging
him to land in England at once as Richard was about to make
war on France. It would be clear that if such a war commenced the Court of Charles VIII would be fully occupied,
to the detriment of the Tudor cause. It was a stupid message
to have sent, for even if Dickon had been planning to land an
army in France the preparations for it would have been
noticed by better spies than Collingbourne. But, stupid or
not, it was a dire act of treason, and he would have to suffer
the full penalty.

He had been found guilty by a commission specially
appointed by the King and composed of the highest in the
land, it being the first arraignment on this charge since

Buckingham's rebellion. There were the Dukes of Suffolk and Norfolk; the latter's son, the Earl of Surrey, and the Earl of Nottingham. There were also viscounts and barons, including Thomas, Lord Stanley, who seemed to pop up like a cork whenever the waters were murked by the taint of treason. It could not be denied that Collingbourne had had a fair trial.

Yet the affair might not have drawn so much attention but for the rhyme Will Collingbourne had nailed to the door of Saint Paul's itself:

> "The Cat, the Rat, and Lovell our Dog,
> Rule all England under a Hog."

Without the other, more serious charge, the seditious couplet would have merited no more than imprisonment and people would have laughed, as indeed Dickon himself was said to have done when he read it. But Catesby, Ratcliffe and Lovell—the "Dog", with his device of the Hound—were personally insulted and demanded of the King that Collingbourne be hanged forthwith. But Dickon the "Hog"—from his badge of the Silver Boar—had refused, saying that the foolish couplet did not merit the ignominious death by the rope and that he was to be tried on the treason charge alone.

I had not expected that there would be such a crowd, but all London seemed to have turned out and Tower Hill was packed so tight that even the cutpurses and pickpockets would find it hard to ply their trade and escape through the press. I went early to be next the scaffold where I could look back over the crowd from time to time, yet even if I could have been able to pick out Matilda among that mass of people I should have no chance of reaching her. But none of that eager sea of faces was hers and at length I turned round again towards the line of billmen that guarded the scaffold. The apprentice executioner had already climbed up and was fanning the flames in the brazier with his leather apron. It was when his master mounted the steps that the crowd broke into a cheer.

They were of a size, those two, but the master was bald behind his mask and his chest a carpet of greying hair. He eyes the crowd disdainfully, no doubt wondering which of them would one day be stepping up for his attentions, but I saw his assistant's eyes glittering in their caverns as he moved his head round to survey the cheering throng.

The noise died away slowly as Will Collingbourne was led up to the platform by two of his jailers and then the Tower drummers began their melancholy beat.

He was an esquire of about fifty, as bald as the executioner, but with a small beard in the old-fashioned manner, and he stood facing his tormentors bared to the waist and with his hands bound behind him. His expression was calm, but I saw his legs a-quiver. He looked at them for a long time, then turned his back and stood towards the new, unseasoned wood of the gallows. The grey-chested one stepped past him and seized the rope that hung from them, knotting it round Collingbourne's neck while his assistant tore off his breeches and tied his ankles together. A few moments later the unhappy man was in the air, his two legs thrashing as one, while his face purpled and hoarse sounds came from his tortured throat. The drummers ceased their beat abruptly and the crowd stood very quiet.

Then, as his struggles grew less and he became erect, the executioner drew his long knife and sliced off his privies with one sweep of the blade, holding them aloft on the point for all to see and then throwing them into the brazier. A great sigh came from the onlookers.

A moment afterwards the apprentice cut the rope and Collingbourne fell to the boards, writhing and moaning. I was sorry for him that he did not die on the gallows, but these executioners were an expert team. I moved my head away a little as a puff of wind brought the smell from the brazier into my face.

"And now, Master Collingbourne," I heard the master say from behind his blood-spattered mask, "how will this suit you?" He held up the knife and, while his assistant lifted the helpless man up by his armpits, thrust it into the bloody mess where his genitals had been.

As the drummers lifted their sticks to beat again I heard Will Collingbourne groan out loud. "Jesu!" he moaned, "yet more trouble!" And, as the knife was twisted and his bowels pulled from him, he died.

It was a lesson to all traitors, and it was not lost on those who saw it. The crowd, so full of cheer at the commencement, watched silently while his body was cut into quarters, each dripping piece being held aloft and displayed before being carried away by the bailiffs to be impaled on the New Stone

Gate of London Bridge. Yet there was one more moment of cheering when the executioner, having removed the head, seized it to raise it aloft and dropped it, for it was bald, and had to pick it up again by the ear and hold it out sideways. But this time the jeers were for the hangman, not the victim. He stood for a moment, glaring at the crowd, then tossed the head contemptuously over the platform and stalked away down the steps. I saw him pause to curse one of the drummers who had vomited over his instrument but that was not surprising as the poor fellow stood directly under the nauseating stink of the burning entrails.

And on the next day I heard that the Earl of Oxford had escaped from Hammes.

37

LIVING by myself in that empty house soon brought me into a state of melancholy. If Matilda really intended to abide by her decision not to return until the Tudors invaded it would mean waiting until the spring, at least, and a long dreary winter by myself I had no stomach for. Once the Tudors did come and could be roundly defeated the miasma of suspicion and treachery could be cleared away and the country could settle down again to a life of order and security. For Henry Tudor was the last hope of the Lancastrians, and when he was disposed of there would be no one with even half as tenuous a claim to the throne as he had. The case against Matilda, if there was any, could be settled for a fine at most, for Dickon was not one to bear a grudge over a matter that would not hold importance any more.

What delayed me from moving out and finding lodgings was the thought that John Kendall could find me more easily where I was. Now that the Court had returned I could have approached him, but felt it prudent not to do so. It was for him to judge the moment.

In the end he came, although when the banging on the door commenced I half hoped that it would be from a softer hand than his. But he stood there, a hesitant smile on his face, and when he came in he looked round cautiously.

"She is not here," I told him. "And I don't know where she is."

He nodded a little. "It is as well. For Lovell sent his men here once to take her for questioning. And he may send again." He studied my face. "You'll know why."

I brought him wine and a pastry, and when he sat down to eat it I said, "So it is as you hinted at Lyme? That she is alleged to have held conversation with Christopher Urswick?"

He nodded again, his mouth full, then said, "But not with intent of treachery. At least I was able to assure that. Her fault is with looseness of tongue."

"For which it could be cut out," I snarled.

"Depending on the gravity of her guilt," he agreed. "But I doubt if Dickon would go that far. Anyway," he added confidently, "it is Urswick who is the traitor. He has been proclaimed so at Saint Paul's."

I gave a sardonic laugh. "I have not been there of a Sunday of late, but the list of traitors must take an unconscionable time to read through these days."

"Aye," he agreed sadly, "and it gets longer. Sir James Blount is now on it too. You will have heard that, at the instigation of Urswick, he freed the Earl of Oxford from Hammes, and together they joined the Tudors?"

I grunted and turned away to get more wine. Christopher Urswick had me to answer to as well. I had not forgotten that evening when he had given me a letter to take to a ship. The letter had been addressed to the Keeper of Hammes, and it was easy to guess now that it had contained more than a warning to the Tudors of my coming. I cursed myself for my stupidity, and I cursed Urswick more. But I knew my rage was mostly directly against myself for I still could not resist my liking for him.

When I put the wine down in front of John Kendall I said, "It is a long time since I sent my letter to you. Is Agnes well?"

"She is well, but . . ." he gave a sour grin ". . . complains that with the season of the year she needs new clothes."

I laughed. "Any woman would for Christmas." Except Matilda this year, I added to myself.

"But with the return of the Court I have been over-busy and have little time for flippancies." He looked up at me. "And I do not have so many reliable clerks just now."

"Well," I said, sitting down, "at least I am glad to see you again."

"You may not be. I did not come here to exchange pleasantries. The King wishes to see you."

I straightened, although it had been what I was expecting. "And Matilda?"

He waved a hand. "I will tell him she cannot be found. He will not doubt me. And so you will have to answer for her, if you can."

"When?"

"Tomorrow. After Matins. Be at the water-gate of Baynard's Castle."

"Baynard's Castle? But that is his personal household!"

"Where else, as he wishes to interview you privately?

Would he have you appear at the Palace with preparations for Christmas driving everyone scatterbrained? With lords and ladies running hither and thither like ants on a honeypot, colliding with servants and tradesmen? Besides, Lord Stanley is Steward of the Household, as you know, and his brother . . ."

"Yes," I said, "I know. Has Sir William remarked on my absence?"

"He has. But dare not appear to be too curious. Only once has he mentioned it, to my knowledge. He said he had not seen my privy scrivener for some time and wondered if you were sick." John Kendall chuckled quietly. "But Dickon overheard and replied for me. He told him that Henry Morane's whereabouts were not precisely known, but it was believed that he was in Brittany." He got up laboriously. "Which was true at the time," he added. "Lord Lovell will be attending on you tomorrow at the water-gate. See to it that you do not bring a dagger. And," he concluded, his eyes taking in the room, "it would be better if this house did not show traces of your stay."

"I will find lodgings tonight," I assured him. "What of Will Slaughter?"

"Will Slaughter?" He frowned. "Oh, him? I have found that there was one of that name as servant in the Tower apartments. But nothing can be proved now. Aye, and Duke Francis of Brittany has regained his reason and Pierre Landois is disgraced. He was lucky not to lose his head, they say. But the Duke has given orders that henceforth all English ships are to be seized and their crews imprisoned. There have been sea fights. In fact a state of war exists, in all but name." He shook his head. "Which proves to me that Duke Francis must still be mad. What can he hope to gain by fighting us if he wishes our help against France?"

"Will Dickon ask me about Slaughter?"

"He might, although I think the matter is closed." John Kendall gave a satisfied grunt. "But it has taught him not to have me signet-seal writs for him to write in the names afterwards. It is important that I know the names of his spies when the writs are recorded."

"Then if the records are read the names of the spies are known."

He was affronted. "The records are secret," he said stiffly.

"Only known to me and Dickon. **Suppose** the writ had been stolen from Will Slaughter?"

"Aye," I said with a straight **face**, "suppose it had! By someone other than I, who could **not** be trusted to tear it up and throw it into the sea!"

38

BAYNARD'S Castle might be King Richard's London home, but it was Middleham in the far-off Yorkshire moors where his heart lay. For it was at Middleham where he had met his wife, Ann Neville, and where the happiest part of his life had been spent. Where he had governed the turbulent North for his brother Edward and gained the respect of its people for his impartial rule and for the justice he dispensed. But now, as King, with greater responsibilities, he saw them less often, but they still loved him. The city of York was his to a man. From the north sprang the roots of his strength.

The short voyage along the river brought to my mind Matilda's remarks about Baynard's Castle, and I looked at it with more interest as we approached. There was little to see, though, for its back was to the river, and the grey curtain went sheer down to the water when the tide was high. But now, with the narrow slits in the walls squinting down at me, there was a line of slimy rocks at its base and the arrow-pointed tracks of pigeons in the mud between them. Alongside the slippery stone stairway that led up from the water there was a boat tied, a boat with twelve oarsmen lolling on their benches and the banner of the Hound at its prow. The waterman hesitated, eyeing me cautiously. I did not appear to be important enough for him to land me there without a reprimand from the guard, but when the latter beckoned us forward he let his breath out in a sigh and pulled the last strokes to land me on the other side.

At the top of the steps Lovell himself was waiting. When he saw me he ceased the impatient tapping of his foot and his eyes fell to my belt. But I had my dagger ready, handle towards him, and he took it with a wry smile. He had to have the insult, though, for he told his men to run their hands over me in case there was another weapon concealed in my clothing. After that he signalled me to follow him through the water-port and along the passage to the stairs that led up to the square, eastern tower.

The air was clear and cold, and the day bright with the steel of December sunshine. As we passed the narrow windows the seabirds outside spread their white wings and flew away with much squalling, circling wide out over the river to resume their perches on the roof tiles when we had gone. There were none on the battlements, though, for three people stood there, all girls.

They turned when they saw us, and the tallest waved at Lovell. "Why, Uncle Francis," she called, "we were watching for you to take your boat away again."

It was a courtesy title she used, for I knew her immediately as Dickon's niece, not Lovell's. She was Elizabeth of York, sister of the missing princes, whom Henry Tudor had publicly sworn to marry. I bowed and looked at her, not yet nineteen years and tall for a woman, as tall as I, but slender like a willow, and with brown eyes that shone with the freshness of youth. The cool sunshine gleamed on the pale, shoulder-length hair that fell straitly from her fur-trimmed cap. She had the large, rounded face of Edward, her father, and something of his build. Comely enough, and pretty in spite of her height, but only beautiful because she was a princess. But, even so, too beautiful to be married to a bumpkin like Henry Tudor.

"From up here your boat looked like a summer beetle as it was rowed across the water," she said to Lovell. "But Cicely and Bridget did not see you come, so I called them . . ." She saw me and stopped. "But who is this you've brought?"

"Never you mind," Francis Lovell told her, but his tone was softer than his words. No one could be harsh to Elizabeth of York. "You should not be up here to catch your cold. Take your sisters down to warm themselves by the fireplace."

I stood aside as Cicely took the hand of the younger one and, as they made their way towards the stairs, they put out their tongues at him. Lovell made his face into a fierce glower and they giggled as they went down. He smiled, waved Elizabeth towards the door, made a sign to me to wait, and went down the stairway at the other side.

Elizabeth stopped and eyed me. "Who are you, sir?" she asked.

"Henry Morane, Your Grace. Once privy clerk to the King's Secretary."

"John Kendall's clerk?" she repeated. "Oh, yes, I have seen you before, I remember, but some time ago. But then it is not often I am at Court, much less in London. I am here for Christmas," she added, going across the battlement again. "It is a wonderful city, is it not? The greatest in the world! And look at that Bridge over there! Do you know," she said, turning back to me, "that I have never been upon it? I should love nothing better than just to walk across it and see the shops and the people, and perhaps hear Mass in Saint Thomas's Chapel there."

I went and stood beside her. London Bridge stood out bold and clear in the bright sunshine; even the great causeway joining it with Bermondsey went on like a wall beyond the roofs of South Wark.

"When the weather is warm enough," Elizabeth of York went on, "I have a stool brought up here and sit and watch it. See!" She pointed. "There are nineteen arches. I have counted them. And a drawbridge that is raised to let tall ships pass through. But I expect you know all this, Master Morane?" The brown eyes, level with mine, were alight with an innocent envy.

"Too well, Your Grace," I replied, trying to summon a smile.

"Oh, and you needn't call me 'Your Grace'," she laughed. "I and my sisters are commoners now, you know, since the law was passed about our bastardy. Cicely was very vexed about it, but I am not. It is much trouble being a princess and, besides, I may be permitted to marry an Englishman now instead of some foreign prince I have never seen, or even that Henry Tudor."

I made no reply, but I didn't think that, as the daughter of Edward the Fourth, her bastardy would last long if Henry Tudor ever did achieve the throne.

At my silence she turned and inspected me. "Do you not think so, Master Morane? That is it better to be a commoner?"

"I have never been anything else," I replied. "But to me you will always be Elizabeth of York, a princess, no matter what any law says."

"Now that," she laughed, "would be treason if Uncle Dickon were to hear of it. Are you not afraid of him? Everyone else seems to be."

"Sometimes," I admitted, "but I respect him more."

She stood back and eyed me. "That is a very straightforward remark," she said quietly. "And it is strange to hear, for I have not heard anyone else speak like that. Some of them even say, when they think I cannot hear..." her voice lowered "... that he made away with my brothers in the Tower. What do you think of that?"

"People with malice in their hearts will say anything," I replied. "They should be stopped."

"But I cannot do so if I am not supposed to hear. Oh!" She clapped her hands suddenly as a seagull flew near. "If only cousin Henry could have been brought to London to confess to it then all this talk could have been prevented!"

So, I thought, she too believes that her brothers are dead, and that Henry, Duke of Buckingham, was responsible. And she must have had a better reason than I for thinking so, for she could only have been persuaded of it by her mother. And her mother would never have taken her and her four sisters out of sanctuary into Richard's care unless she had been sure that Richard had no part in it. Would she have accepted his hospitality for herself and her daughters for all this time, and more, would she have written a letter to her other son living in exile with the Tudors telling him to come home and live safely with Richard?

I looked up and saw Elizabeth of York eyeing me with concern. I cleared my throat and said, "He could have been, Mistress Elizabeth, for he was taken alive, and did ask for a last audience with the King. Perhaps if he had been allowed it he would have confessed..."

"Now who is it that is supposed to have confessed, and to what?" a voice said from the doorway. We both swung round to see Elizabeth Woodville standing there.

Her dark hair under the wired veil was greyer now, but her eyes were as deep and as beautiful as ever as they studied me. "Why," she said, "it is Henry Morane! It is a long time since I saw you."

I bowed low. "A year and more, Madam. Since the day I nearly glued you to Mistress Shore with sealing wax."

"Was it that day?" She laughed. "You have a memory, Master Morane."

"I could not forget." I told her.

The dark eyes left mine and clouded a little. "Poor Jane," she said, "she has done her penance, but I fear that living with her husband again is even more. And how do you fare, Master Morane?"

"No better than I could expect, Madam," I grinned. "I wait audience with the King."

"Up here in the cold? It is not like Dickon to freeze a man before seeing him." She held out a hand to her daughter. "Come, Elizabeth, at least I can see that you are not allowed to freeze. Cicely told me you were still up here gazing out over London." She glanced at me and smiled. "Although at least Henry Morane is a knowledgeable man to have as guide. I once heard tell that he knows more of London than the Sheriff himself."

"That, Madam," I replied with a straight face, "is because I have spent so much time keeping out of his way."

They laughed and waved at me as they went below.

39

LORD Francis Lovell would have been very annoyed if he had known that Elizabeth of York had stayed to talk with me, for I knew that he meant to leave me up there alone and cold before I saw the King. I waited a long time before I heard someone climbing the stairs. Then a corpulent usher appeared, wheezing and panting puffs of white steam into the wintry air like an ancient steed trying to recover from its last charge. He led me below, to a room that looked out on to the courtyard where at least twenty carts were being unloaded, the barrels being rolled away into a low arch which would be the entrance to a cellar.

I swung round as Lovell came in pulling his white-furred cloak round him. He waved at me imperiously and I followed him into a room where a huge fire blazed in the hearth. With his back to the fire, talking to John Kendall, stood King Richard.

He nodded to Lovell, then looked me up and down, hands on hips. His face was pale, paler than I had seen it before, and it was not with the cold. I bowed and made to go down on one knee, but he waved me up.

"Welcome to you, Henry Morane," he said. "We have not seen you since your return from Brittany, where you did well . . . or as well as a man could have done in the circumstances that attended your mission." He paused. "But those circumstances were tainted, and we wish to learn how it came about."

I inclined my head, but kept my eyes on him. "It seems, Your Grace," I said, "that Master Urswick . . ."

"Yes, yes. We know about Master Urswick. He stands condemned by his own action. What we require to know is how he came about his information."

I started to speak, but he held up his hand. "Now, Master Morane," he said, "we will come to the point. What is alleged is that the woman you consort with, Mistress Matilda Nicholas, spoke of your venture to Christopher Urswick . . ."

There it was, the direct charge, and my heart beat faster.

". . . She has not been found to answer to the allegation, and it is our wish that you tell us where she is."

I hesitated, then looked him in the eye, "My Lord," I said, "I do not know where she is."

Lovell, behind me, said, "Hah!" But Richard's black eyes remained on mine, unblinking.

I stared at him for as long as I thought prudent, then dropped my own.

After what seemed an age, he said, "Am I to believe that?"

I looked up again. "It is true, Sire."

He nodded a little. "I know you for an honest man, Henry Morane," he said slowly. "But where women are concerned no man is entirely honest. There seems to be some equivocation about what you say. I can smell it."

"My Lord," I replied, "you may not entirely believe me. And that I cannot mend. But as to the allegation against Matilda Nicholas it may be that I can be of assistance . . ."

Lovell snorted again.

". . . in that I may be able to refute it."

John Kendall made a noise like a soup-kettle as he let out his breath.

"You think you can?" Richard's eyebrows were raised. "Then proceed."

I summoned my wits as they all looked at me. "First, Your Grace," I said, "there was no reason why she should betray my mission . . ."

"That is not the charge," Richard said tersely.

"She would not betray it," I went on doggedly, "either deliberately or inadvertently, for she knew Christopher Urswick only by sight. And a man of importance such as the Recorder of London does not grant audience to all and sundry . . ."

"She could have written him a letter," Lovell said.

"Aye, Francis," Richard said, looking at him, "if she had learnt to write."

"That she can do, My Lord," I said, and saw him nod at the admission. "But to write a letter is a deliberate act, and bears a more serious charge than that of a loose tongue."

A faint smile crossed the King's face. "It seems, Henry Morane, that you should have studied law." He scratched his chin. "But perhaps you have?"

"No, Your Grace, but . . ."

"Is that all you have to say?" Lovell asked. "Because, so

far, I cannot see any refutation of the charge. All you can assert is that it was unlikely she saw the Recorder because he may not have been disposed to grant her an audience." He gave an unpleasant laugh. "It is like baiting a bear with toothless hounds. All bark and no bite."

I turned round and stared at him, a sudden realization blinding me like a flash of lightning.

"By your leave, My Lord Lovell," I told him, "it is not all I have to say."

"Then proceed," Richard said, "But do not dwell too long on uncertain possibilities."

"There is but one more point, Sire," I said, and saw John Kendall looking at me dubiously.

"My understanding is that the Recorder absconded promptly," I went on. "And so in any case there was little time for her to have gained an interview with him. Therefore, with deference, I submit that Urswick had his own spies, and that one of them apprised him of my plans."

"Ohoho!" Lovell chortled. "So now he invents spies! Perhaps he can tell us their names!"

Richard gave him an irritated look. "Hold your peace, Francis," he warned. To me, he said, "Well, Master Morane, can you tell us their names?"

"Of one, my Lord. One of his clerks, John Tanner."

"John Tanner? And how would this John Tanner have come by his information?"

I said, "May I have your leave to speak with your Secretary, Sire?"

Dickon studied me carefully and then nodded. "But so that we all may hear."

John Kendall came forward, his face a wide map of puzzlement.

"Do you remember when we met at Smithfield?" I asked him, and he nodded. "And as the bear was killed a man waved at me from across the crowd?"

"Aye, I remember," he agreed, frowning. "A sharp-faced fellow. Was that Urswick's clerk, John Tanner?"

"It was. He, like the other clerks, had come to know that I had worked for you, and was curious as to your business with me."

John Kendall nodded again. "He may have been, but . . ."

"And do you remember the charlatan who tried to sell me a bottle of Holy Water, as he called it?"

"Yes. In Chepe Side. He told a trumpery story."

"And pressed a bottle on me to make it look as if I had bought it? So that a fellow who was approaching might be induced to buy another?"

John Kendall hesitated. "I remember that," he said carefully. "But I do not recall if it was the same fellow who was following."

"A pity," I said, and turned back to the King. "Yet I would allege, Sire, that this John Tanner, curious as to my business with your Secretary, followed closely and overheard us speaking of my mission."

Dickon stared at me for a long time. Then he said, "And where is this John Tanner now?"

"I do not know, My Lord."

"Have you tried to find out?"

"No, My Lord. Because the memory of the incident has just come back to me."

"Just come back to you? After all this time?" The black eyes narrowed.

"Of a truth, Sire. It was when my Lord Lovell referred to toothless hounds and bear-baiting that it came to me as lightning comes from a cloud. I suddenly remembered seeing John Tanner at the bear-baiting. And now . . ."

Lord Lovell let out his breath in a snort of derision.

"And now I will find him," I finished.

"If he is to be found," Richard said sternly, "it will not be by you. Francis," he said to Lovell, "see to it." I heard Lovell turn away and whistle for one of his men.

"And," Dickon continued, "see to it that he arrives here." There was a glint in his eye. "I should not be pleased to hear that he has disappeared while in your care."

I turned to Lovell. His face was set. They were good friends those two, but there was no doubt who was the master.

An esquire came running in. "Take everyone in the Recorder's office," Lovell ordered. "And bring them here." He turned back to the King, shrugged, and stuck his thumbs into his belt. I watched them both, the inside of my stomach hardening into a block of ice.

John Kendall spoke up. "My Lord King," he said, "that will be considered a high-handed action by the Mayor of

London. He will resent such interference of his citizens without a Writ. There should have been one."

Richard considered him for a few moments and then sighed. "Aye," he agreed. "You are right, as usual, Master Kendall. I am too impulsive. Then fetch your instruments and I shall dictate a letter to My Lord the Mayor with due explanation and apology." He looked at me and a thin smile came over his face. "And who better to write it down than Henry Morane?"

"Who is Recorder now?" I asked John Kendall when we were back in his room.

"Recorder?" he said, "Oh, one Thomas Fitzwilliam." He was busy turning over a heap of clothes. "Pounce Box!" he muttered. "Where in the Name of Saint Agatha can it be?"

"Why do you need it?" I asked him.

He straightened up and looked at me angrily. "Great God, man! Where you never my clerk? Don't you know that a Writ has to be on parchment? And that parchment has first to be cleaned with pounce?" He cast round the room, flinging clothes in every direction. "All this living out of little boxes! The sooner we move back to West Minster Palace the better! Then I can have my office again and everything will be in its proper place!"

"But we are writing a letter, not a Writ."

He threw a pair of boots on to the floor so hard that a tile cracked in two. "Body of God!" he shouted. "Why didn't you tell me?"

"I thought you knew," I said midly.

He stood, glaring at me, and I said, "Why all this excitement, John? What is eating at you?"

"Because of the trouble you make! All this concocted story of a mythical John Tanner! Wouldn't it have been better for you to have admitted that your woman told Urswick about your mission? Then the affair could have been settled quickly . . ."

"As to that we shall see," I replied evenly. "But I do not understand why the King concerns himself with such a matter. Matilda must be of small importance to him, and the incident could well be forgotten."

"Then I will tell you," he said, speaking slowly and patiently, as if to an unlettered peasant. "He may have other missions for you in mind. And if it is proved that your Matilda has a loose tongue, why, then he will see to it that . . ."

"The offending member is cut out," I said bitterly.

"Not necessarily. She could be kept in a prison."

"A prison?" I repeated. "You mean a dungeon deep under the ground such as are in the Tower and other castles. It would be better for her to lose her tongue than that."

"I meant imprisoned under care, such as Bishop Morton was in the Duke of Buckingham's. For instance, she could be kept in my care."

At that my humour came back and I began to laugh. "Do you think I would trust you with her care? Oh, ho! I should have to find one of those old-time chastity-belts!"

He gave an angry puff and walked out of the room, leaving me to bring the ink and paper.

The letter was written and being sealed when Lovell's men brought in three trembling clerks. Two of them I knew, and they looked at me with awe. It was clear that they thought I had denounced them. They went down on their knees in front of the King.

John Tanner was not among them, and I said so straight away.

Dickon's face was strained as he stood over them. "We extend our apology for bringing you here so summarily," he said, and they gazed up at him with astonishment. "We wish to ascertain the whereabouts of your fellow clerk, one John Tanner. You may rise," he added.

The got up slowly, unbelievingly. It was a long time before any of them could speak. Then one of them stuttered, "I . . . we . . . Sire . . . we do not know. He left . . . went away . . . at the same time as our master . . . Ur . . . Urswick." The other two plucked up their courage and started nodding vigorously. "With our master!" they exclaimed simultaneously.

Dickon eyed them in turn and they quailed. Then he gave a wry smile and turned to John Kendall. "Give them a noble each for their trouble and send them back."

They went out as if waking from a dream. I, too, was almost in a similar state, for my only hope at the beginning of the interview had been to try and persuade the King of the improbability of Matilda communicating with Urswick, and it was an argument that I had doubts of protesting with sincerity as I knew it to be false.

And it had been Lovell who had inadvertently shown me a way out.

40

I DID not see John Kendall until after the new year had
come. Christmas had been wet and dismal, although the
shops had tried to bring cheer with great displays of gold and
silver work, and beads and glass from all over Europe. Mud-
spattered waits sang their carols and damp bellmen rang
their tunes, but they brought no joy for me.

Although Matilda was now free of taint I had no way of
telling her, not knowing where she was. I hired a fellow with
a long, inquisitive nose to search for her. From the description I gave him he produced a score of wenches, most of
whom were willing to share my bed, and some would have
taken possession of it had I not sent them scampering for
their clothes with a hearty smack across the buttocks when
daylight came. Even that did not stop the arguments about
money which followed as inevitably as the sunrise. In the end
I paid off the fellow with the long, inquisitive nose. He
would never find Matilda, and wenches that followed each
other could all have been sisters, so alike were they in their
performance, and so tedious when not on the bed.

March began with a thin fall of snow, and I moved my
belongings back to the house, hoping that with the spring
Matilda might decide to return. My first visitor was John
Kendall.

He shook the white film off his cloak and warmed his hands
at the brazier. "I have called somewhat belatedly," he said,
"to thank you for the Yuletide gifts you sent to Agnes and
me." He smiled. "I trust the one I sent you did not come
amiss."

I laughed. "I have not yet decided where it should be
placed," I said, waving a hand at a corner of the room. It
stood there, a plaque of beaten silver in a carved wooden
frame. The silver had been worked into a design depicting a
woman in full-armour tied to a post above a pile of logs.
Around her were angels, their hands untying the bonds
that held her, and underneath were the words: "The Maid
Freed from the Faggots."

There had been many such pieces since Joan of Arc had been
executed, all with the suggestion that she had been a Holy

Person and had somehow escaped before she had felt the flames. It was a subject about which I knew little, happening some fifty years before, and rarely a topic for discussion. It seemed that the Duke of Bedford had exercised his authority towards a French spy with a harshness which might have been merited towards a man, but not towards a woman, or at least so it was inferred. But John Kendall had not chosen it for its political implication. The allusion was clear.

"The escape of Matilda from the tongue-screw," I said. "Very appropriate."

"I trust she has appreciated the sentiment," he said.

"I hope she will. For I have not seen her since."

"Not seen her? But there is no need now to hide herself!"

"Find her and tell her that," I said savagely.

He scratched his chin. "You could have her proclaimed at Saint Paul's as free from taint," he suggested.

"Hah!" I said scornfully. "There are so many names proclaimed for treason that no one waits to hear if any are absolved."

"I could have her name read first. It would cause interest."

"It would cause a sensation," I said. "And she would think it was a trick. You know how she feels about . . ."

"Yes, yes," he said quickly. "We shall have to think of something else. But in time she will be found." He glanced across at the plaque and said, "Yet your trouble is nothing compared with Dickon's. His wife is dying as she walks. Even at Christmas her illness was apparent, at least to me, for all the brave show she put up, not missing any of the festivities or balls where the radiance of her countenance and the splendour of her gowns almost outshone those of Elizabeth Woodville and her daughters."

"But isn't her sickness for the loss of their son?"

"At first it was thought so. But that was a year ago. And now the physicians have told Dickon that her illness is mortal. Worse, that it is contagious, so that he must no longer even share her bed-chamber. Ah, God!" he exclaimed. "Even to think about it tears at my heart. The Tudors can come and be killed, but the mortality of Queen Ann is inevitable before that. Dickon sits there, staring into the fireplace, and hears nothing. Ah, God!" he repeated, "Whatever sins he may have done he is paying for now!"

"You think the Tudors really will come?"

"Yes. We have certain news. It will be in the summer. It will have to be by then at the latest, for Henry Tudor cannot remain a pensioner of the French Court any longer without so much damage to his reputation that his cause could never recover. We know that King Charles's Regent has promised him men and ships, and he is to move to Rouen in the spring and set up camp." He looked out of the window. "If spring ever comes, that is." He gave a wan smile. "Now that the Earl of Oxford has escaped from Hammes," he added, "at least they have a general to lead whatever he can collect for an army."

"But why will the French give him aid?"

"Because that foul-mouthed Bishop Morton has told it that Dickon intends to invade France." He sighed. "As if Dickon did not have enough on his mind just now without considering a foreign adventure! Aye," he went on with a growl, "and Morton has also spread it that Dickon is poisoning his wife so that he can marry Elizabeth of York himself and so thwart the Tudor promise. So that he can marry his own niece! Even Satan himself never stooped so low with his calumnies!" He crossed himself.

"That goes beyond foolishness," I said. "For how could anyone believe such a story?"

"They might," he muttered, "if it was repeated often enough."

"But he can easily thwart the Tudors by marrying Elizabeth to another prince. There must be many in Europe who would take her hand."

"No doubt," he agreed. "But she does not want it, and Dickon humours her in everything. Neither does he see her married to anyone but an Englishman. And in any case . . ." he shrugged "he does not take the threat of these Lancastrian rebels seriously."

"Do you?" I asked him.

"I?" He looked surprised. "Well, perhaps not. Proper precautions have to be taken, of course, but Henry Tudor is little known here, and he can only rally to his cause the followers of those nobles who desert to him. The common people would not care."

"And of the nobles there is only the Earl of Oxford."

"There may be others here in England who would defect once he lands."

"Then cut off their heads, or at least lock them up."

"Aye," he said sombrely, "if we knew who they were." He held up his mug for me to fill again. "And you, Henry Morane, think you have troubles." He drank, wiping the dregs off his mouth with the back of his hand. "When did you last see your Matilda?"

"At Kingstone," I replied, and told him how we got to be there.

"Now that is interesting," he said when I had finished. "About the pirates in the wine-boat . . ." for I had told him all that had happened, even bringing the battle-axe to show him. "The ship they came from would have belonged to John Turberville, who was arraigned for treason with Will Collingbourne."

"I saw the execution. But Turberville escaped that penalty."

"Because not enough could be proved."

"But treason is an act against the King's person. Is not smuggling wine against the laws of his Customs the same thing? Against his person?"

"It is." He nodded. "But does not merit castration and the removal of his bowels, at least in Dickon's view, as it is not an act directly giving aid and comfort to his enemies. But . . ." He got up and took the battle-axe, swinging it gently at his side and holding it up for me to see. "This is from France, as you must have noticed."

I nodded, and he went on, "And there was suspicion that Turberville was smuggling in a shipload of arms such as this for disaffected persons who might rise against the King." He put the axe on the table and sat down. "If we had been able to catch him on that voyage," he said grimly, "there would never have been any taint against Matilda. She would have been well rewarded instead."

I put my head in my hands and groaned.

"But as to her whereabouts," he went on, "you say you last saw her at Kingstone?"

"Yes. But she left there, I thought for London, but I cannot find her here."

"Well, then," he said slowly, "if she cannot be found in London is it not possible that she has returned to Kingstone?"

I looked up and stared at him.

41

JOHN Kendall was right. I found Matilda at Kingstone, and she was in a pretty state of impatience too. The winter had been a long dreary tale of mud and early darkness, and the Coombe family had not enlivened her spirits by their, or at least her sister's unremitting devotion to the calls of their parish.

She had set off for London that morning to stay with friends, she told me, taking a boat manned by two stout fellows who agreed to row her as far as Tiding-Turn, where she would be able to get another boat for the rest of her journey. They had been stout enough, and lusty too, trying to rape and then rob her at a small rush-lined creek which they had evidently used before for the same purpose. But with Matilda they had encountered no defenceless woman, which they ought to have realized for defenceless women do not travel alone, and she had buried her dagger into one and forced the other with the point at his back to return her to Kingstone. The one she had killed was probably the better off, for it was the other one's body I had seen hanging from a gibbet as I rode into the town. In spite of its mildness the winter had preserved the corpse well enough, at least as to the parts the rats had not consumed, and I had ridden by waving my cap at it, thinking that the Sheriff of Kingstone was offering a fine notice to all travellers that the town took short shrift with thieves, whether on the King's highway or the river.

Yet Matilda was not pleased that I had discovered her, and even when I told her that the King had heard her case and that all suspicion was removed she did not believe it. But I had expected that, and showed her the paper attesting it, signed by John Kendall and stuck with his seal, which I had taken the precaution of obtaining from him. Even then she feigned a reluctance to return to London, which I saw through as quickly as a coney-catcher's card trick, until I said that I needed her help to remove the three women who had taken house with me and who were costing six times as much as she would. At that she went straight off to pack her bags, for she had two now, and rode beside me right through the great forest before she said a word. Even then it was only to tell me that she was returning to London for no other reason than that she was sick of the tedium of Kingstone, and if she really did find traces of other women there I could move out forthwith, or have her dagger in my gizzard. She had now convinced herself that I was entirely at fault in not finding her sooner to tell her that it was safe to return. The brain of a female is truly a marvellous and intricate affair, surely compounded by God in a moment of aberration.

When we reached the house she was somewhat mollified to find that I had laid in a stock of meats and wine, and after half a dozen cups of the latter she let fall, almost with shyness, that the irritation of spirit had left her and she was feeling better. I took her to the bed forthwith, and afterwards she admitted that her sickness might have been due to the lack of my physical presence. When I grinned at her and remarked that Edward Coombe could not have been as satisfactory as she had hoped she threw her wine cup at me, and from that point onwards our former relations were resumed.

It happened a few days later—it was the sixteenth of March, 1485—that the sun's orb was obscured by the moon, and darkness fell upon London. It was a natural phenomenon, of course, but it frightened Matilda. She clung to me and said that it was a warning to adulterers and others who lived in sin, and that we should be married forthwith. When the eclipse was over we went out into the streets and mingled with the crowds who had been watching the spectacle. Many of them were blinded by the too sudden return of the sun, and were careering about with their hands over their eyes bewailing their misfortune and calling on the Holy Virgin to restore their sight. In their miserable state they were a fine target for pickpockets and other thieves, who had not had such a good day for a long time.

A little while later we found ourselves beside the Church of Saint Lawrence Jewry, so I took Matilda inside with the others who were giving Thanks and sent one of the clerks to fetch the priest. While we were waiting I inspected the gewgaws that adorned the church. Three enormous eggs hanging by strings I recognized for those of an ostrich, but near them lay the bones of a creature strange to me. The neck itself was as long as I was tall, and at the end there was the skull of a calf, but with two little studs instead of horns. When the priest told me that it was the head and neck of a came-leopard, a monster that inhabited Africa, I was little the wiser, but what aroused my interest the most was a needle floating on parchment in a bowl of water. It was from Cathay, he said, and in whatever position the bowl was put the needle swung round so that it pointed to the north. While it should have pointed to the east, to Jerusalem, he went on, it was of great value to navigators, but it seemed to me that it would be of little use in rough weather when the water in the bowl would not remain steady.

There were other curiosities that the priest wanted to show me, but Matilda was tapping her foot with impatience, so I told him our business. At that he demurred, saying that news had come only an hour before that Richard's Queen, Ann, had died that very dawn. There would soon follow a pro-clamation of a State of Mourning, he knew, and it was as much as his living was worth to celebrate a marriage. I left the Church in a melancholy state, no less than Matilda, although my sorrow was partly for Dickon.

"Three weeks!" she said. "That's how long Mourning will last. And no priest will marry us till then!"

"Three weeks goes fast enough," I told her. "And, besides, we have lived together for a year and more. Who is to know that we are not married!"

"I do, for one!" she cried, and ran away from me through the crowd. I followed her home and found her weeping on the bed.

Three days later John Kendall called, to tell me that I was for Nottingham.

42

"**I** WILL not have it!" Matilda stormed. "We are about to be wed!"

John Kendall smiled at her. "My felicitations, Mistress Nicholas." To me, he said, "And high time too, Henry Morane. But is there any reason why the contract cannot be made in Nottingham?"

"You mean I can go too?" Matilda cried, and when he nodded she threw her arms round him and kissed him.

When she had done his face was very red and I laughed. "It seems she is not sure which one of us she wishes to marry," I remarked to the ceiling. To John Kendall, I said, "So the Court goes back to Nottingham again?"

He nodded. "Aye. To the Castle. But you will have to find lodgings in the town, for Lord Stanley, as Steward of the Household, is still at Court."

"Why to Nottingham? And is there work for me?"

"To Nottingham because it is the centre of the realm, and we are not yet certain where the Tudors intend to land. As to you, why, Dickon had a mind to send you to France."

"To France?" Matilda gasped, putting a hand to her mouth.

He shook his head. "But I dissuaded him of it, pointing out that you are known to the enemy now. By sight at least to Bishop Morton and the Earl of Oxford, and more closely to Christopher Urswick. If you were seen spying there it is likely you would never return."

"True enough," I agreed. "He wanted me to spy there?"

"To find out where the Tudors intend to land. They have moved to Harfleur, and the French have promised them men and ships, and money. If we can discover their intentions it will save time, and be less expensive, to frustrate them."

"Henry Tudor will keep it very secret," I pointed out. "Discussing it only with his Uncle Jasper and the Earl of Oxford. There will be no need for plans on paper."

"The shipmasters who sail his fleet will have to be told where they are going."

"Not until after they have sailed."

He nodded. "That is what Dickon has already considered."

"And even if he should seem to discuss his intentions with others," I added, "it is likely they will be false plans, to mislead any spies that might hear."

"That is a further argument," he admitted. "But, while in any case spies must be sent to see what they can learn, he has agreed that it would be too dangerous for you to go."

"Too dangerous?" Matilda inquired ironically. "Does King Richard then have concern for lesser people such as Henry Morane?"

"He has concern for everyone." John Kendall smiled. "And as for Henry Morane, why, there will be other work for him to do."

"Hah!" she said, and turned away to fetch wine.

"It looks as if we shall have to speculate as to their intentions," John Kendall said.

"That will not be difficult," I replied. "They are certain to attack Calais first, and have a secure English base to work from."

"Dickon has thought of that. Sir James Tyrrel has already gone there with reinforcements. He is putting Guisnes in a state of defence, and without Guisnes Calais cannot be taken."

I nodded. The Castle was some five miles south of Calais, commanding the approaches from Ardres and Boulogne. Guisnes and the smaller fortress of Hammes behind it were the outlying defences of the English pale in Europe. No, I thought, the Tudors could not take Calais.

"But Sir James Tyrrel has been holding Glamorgan and South Wales," I pointed out. "Who will replace him there?"

"There is no need," he said, taking a pastry that Matilda had brought, "The eastern border of Wales is all Yorkist land, and Shropshire, next to it, is held by Sir Gilbert Talbot."

"And the rest of South Wales?"

"Rhys ap Thomas is the greatest chieftain there. He has sworn fealty to Dickon, pronouncing that the Tudors will have to pass over his belly before they cross his lands."

"Then that is secure," I agreed. "Which leaves England to consider. The north country is solidly for York, the east coast is tight under the Duke of Norfolk, the south . . ."

"Lovell has the fleet ready at Southampton. And without Calais they can do little harm there. And in the west, even if

Devon and Cornwall are no hotbeds of enthusiasm for Dickon they are even less for the Tudors." He chuckled. "And they already know what kind of reception they would get if they tried Poole again."

"So all that is left," I said slowly, "is North Wales and Lancashire, where the Stanleys lie."

John Kendall gave a grim smile. "I was wondering when you would come to them, Henry Morane," he said. "Yes," he added, "there are the Stanleys."

Apart from the King himself, the wide lands of the Percies in Northumberland and those of the Howards of Norfolk, the Stanleys commanded more force than anyone else. Their intervention on the side of the rebels would cause us much trouble, especially if Henry Percy chose to sit upon his estates in Northumberland and await the outcome.

"The Stanleys should be put in prison until the Tudors are defeated," I said.

"On the contrary," John Kendall replied. "Dickon has already sent messages to Lancaster and to Chester proclaiming that all men there should follow their lords, Sir William and Thomas Stanley."

"Great God!" I exclaimed. "Why has he done that?"

"Think on it, Henry. To arrest two of the most prominent men in the country would show fear, or at least a lack of confidence which would encourage his enemies. Not only that, but what would the men of Lancashire and Cheshire do if their leaders were imprisoned? Would they not be more likely to join the rebels?" He put his mug down and shook his head slowly. "No. Dickon is right. We shall have to hope that when the time comes the Stanleys can be trusted."

"I have had little time for King Dickon," Matilda said suddenly. "But if he were to be betrayed by a man such as Sir William Stanley then I would be on his side."

We both looked at her with surprise. Then John Kendall said, "Good for you, Matilda Nicholas!"

She got up and went to kiss him. This time he smiled and said, "I seem to be better off with your favours than your future husband."

"I haven't married her yet," I told him. "It will depend on how comely and willing the wenches of Nottingham are."

For that I got a slap across the face.

"At any rate," John Kendall went on, "if the Tudors land

in Cheshire, and even if the Stanleys join them, they still have to march on London."

"Aye," I grinned, "with King Richard's army in front of them, and Norfolk and Rhys ap Thomas on either side."

"And possibly the Earl of Northumberland behind him."

"Why 'possibly'?" Matilda asked him. "Is his loyalty in doubt too?"

"Not so much his loyalty as his apathy," John Kendall said, eyeing her sombrely. "At times Henry Percy shows little concern for affairs outside Northumberland."

"Yet he is Commissioner for Yorkshire," I pointed out. "They will come, at least."

"They will indeed! The men of Yorkshire, by their spirit alone, could account for Henry Tudor."

"Then let's hope he puts it to the test soon," I sighed. "Although I would not care to be in Henry Tudor's boots."

"I too!" Matilda put in. "I would sooner have Dickon than a man who has to depend on Sir William Stanley."

"Now I am doubly glad I am not in his boots!" I chuckled.

43

EVEN in summer Nottingham Castle was cold. Fierce winds surged along the stone corridors, scattering the floor rushes and keeping the drapes in constant motion. The town at the castle-foot was cold too, but more from the manner of the inhabitants than the weather, for they had no love for the soldiery that had been thrust upon them. While the inns and taverns did a violent trade, and the vintners and other suppliers to the Court increased their profits by more than they had ever dreamed, they, too, would not be sorry when the army had gone. Profits were pleasant when they came easily, but not if their city were to suffer the brunt of war.

King Richard had moved back to Nottingham Castle at the end of June. "The Castle of his Care", he called it, for it was to Nottingham that news had been brought to him of the death of his son. Now that his wife had died as well I wondered if it would unman him, for everyone knew how close they had been. Yet the threat of the rebel invasion would keep him occupied, and for that reason alone it was no bad thing. Once Henry Tudor had been dealt with, either in battle or at Tower Hill afterwards, Dickon would settle down again, all sorrow past, or at least I hoped so. And even if he did not marry again the Yorkist succession was assured, for John, Earl of Lincoln, had been named, and he, the son of Dickon's sister and the Duke of Suffolk, though young was already showing his forthrightness.

While it did not seem to me to be important any more whether Lord Stanley knew I was still alive or not, John Kendall had emphasized the point, and it was for that reason I moved along the corridor cautiously and, following his instructions, found his office exactly, drawing aside the arras to see him sitting at a table hard at work, paring a fingernail with his dagger.

He looked up at me and frowned. "You are late, Henry Morane," he accused.

"A long, hard climb up here," I told him. "And I had to be sure I came to the right office first time. How is Dickon?" I asked him.

"Dickon is well," he replied. "And so am I, even though you did not ask."

I grinned. "It was not necessary. Seeing you sitting there as robust as ever."

"Robust?" He got up and stretched himself, looking down at his fat paunch as he tried to hold it in. "Robust enough," he remarked, satisfied. "There is work for you."

I waited, looking through the window at the sunny fields that stretched away northwards. It was a fine day for a battle, or a wrestle in the grass with a country wench.

"This morning," John Kendall said, "Lord Stanley asked leave of the King to go to Lancashire and attend his estates. He pleaded that he has been away a long time and their administration is suffering."

"His brother is there," I pointed out. "As well as his son, Lord Strange, to attend to them. Besides, as Steward, his close attendance upon the King is necessary."

"We know all that," John Kendall said impatiently.

"Then of course Dickon won't let him go. It is too thin an excuse."

"Exactly what we all said, Ratcliffe, Catesby and I. But Dickon has given him permission." He sighed. "And it can only mean one thing. That the Tudors are preparing to move from Harfleur."

"Haven't your spies confirmed that too?"

"Spies?" he snarled. "They've found out nothing. Useless!"

"Then why has Dickon . . . ?" I began.

"Because he says his loyalty must be proved. However," he smiled a little, "there is one condition. Stanley must send his son, Lord Strange, to the Court in his place."

I laughed. "A hostage, eh?"

"Obviously! And Lord Stanley knows it too. He was in some dilemma, but he accepted with as good a grace as he could muster."

"And where is the work for me?"

"To attend upon Lord Strange, who does not know you."

"To watch him in fact. To see that he does not try to escape?"

John Kendall sheathed his dagger, got up and put a hand on my shoulder. "Henry Morane," he said, "your perspicacity is unlimited."

224

With that sarcastic remark I left him and went back to the town to prepare to move from our lodgings. Matilda was delighted.

"Can I move too?"

"I doubt it," I told her. "There are too many lords and and nobles up there for me to be easy about you."

"What does that mean? That you do not trust me?"

"Oh, I might," I conceded, "But the Earl of Lincoln is there. He is the handsomest of the Suffolks and, as Richard's heir, I wouldn't put it past him to have you for the next Queen."

"Monster!" she protested, and I smacked her across the buttocks and told her to be quick about packing while I went for a cart.

"Then there will be no hurry," she replied. "For you'll be an hour haggling over the price. I will have time to deck myself."

"You stay in those clothes," I told her. "I don't want our arrival to cause a sensation. In fact some dirt on your face would not be amiss."

"You want me to enter as a servant?" she said hotly.

"My servant, no one else's," I said, and went out quickly before she could find a missile.

George Stanley, Lord Strange, was pale and thin and very young. Or he appeared so, for he was twenty-five years of age and had been married for six of them. He took his title from his wife, Joan, only child of the former Lord Strange, and by her right attended the House of Lords, although I had never seen him there.

He was no more than half-brother to Henry Tudor, though, being the eldest child of Lord Stanley's first marriage. It was Stanley's present wife, the horse-faced and intriguing Lady Margaret Beaufort, who was the mother of Henry Tudor. Such are the intricacies of England's noble houses.

King Richard made the new arrival welcome, feasting and entertaining him with all the courtesy that befitted the heir of Lord Stanley. All day long there were attendants upon him, so that never once was he out of anyone's sight, and even after dark I made the rounds to see that the nightmen were at their posts.

While waiting for news from France King Richard occupied his time in hunting, which was his favourite sport,

225

and as the weather that summer was warm there were few days we did not spend in Sherwood Forest. Most of the Court, and its ladies, went too, so that great pavilions were set up and trestles laid for the huge feasts that followed in the evenings. Lord Strange, also an enthusiast for the chase, shot an accurate crossbow, his bolt bringing down more than one stag when halted with the dogs baying round it. I had perforce to accompany him, and always be on my guard, although care had been taken to give him a nag that was not overfond of galloping too far.

Matilda attached herself during the day to the entourage of Elizabeth of York and her mother, so that she was not always at our tent when I returned in the evening. The first time I chided her for this she replied that Elizabeth of York was a sweet girl.

"Unspoilt," she said. "And I hope she does not have to stay in Nottingham Castle too long." She threw her head back. "But here," she went on, looking up at the forest, "is a place I could stay at for ever. All the grass, and those oak trees. See, Henry, they have fruit on them now!"

"Acorns," I told her. "Food for pigs in winter. Take care you do not become too close to Elizabeth of York. Whatever the law says, she is still of royal birth, and her person is of special importance."

"She needs help," Matilda said. "More than her mother can give her."

"Help?" I said. "What kind of help? She has all the attendants anyone could need. Besides, she has four sisters."

"They are but children!" Matilda exclaimed. "She needs a friend."

A week later the pavilions were folded up and the Court went back to Nottingham. But Richard stayed a few more days, keeping Lord Strange with him, so that I had to remain too. It was one evening, after my charge was asleep, that I received a summons to his presence. With him was only John Kendall.

"How now, Henry Morane?" the King said. "Is the guard alert?"

"As always, Sire. But Lord Strange sleeps."

"He has made no attempt to escape as yet?"

"None, Sire."

"H'm! He probably waits for the Tudor landing. When it

comes you must be additionally vigilant. Tomorrow we return to Nottingham."

I bowed and waited. What he had said was not worth summoning me for. I wondered what was to come.

The black eyes were narrowed and inspecting me carefully. "It has been brought to my attention," he said slowly, "that you are living in sin with this Mistress Nicholas. Is that true?"

I dropped my eyes. "It is, my Lord. But only because we have not yet had the opportunity of making the contract. We were to be wed in London but . . ." I waved an apologetic hand ". . . I was summoned here."

"So? And yet you brought her with you? Knowing that I do not look with favour at fornication in my Court?"

"Your Grace!" I looked up at him again. "I did not bring her to Court. We had lodgings in Nottingham. We hoped to marry there . . ."

John Kendall cleared his throat. "It was my fault, Your Grace. I overlooked the fact that they were not wed when I had them move to the Castle."

Richard's eyes swung on him. "Your fault, eh? Then had you better not rectify it forthwith, Master Kendall? There is the Chapel at the Castle." He waved a hand. "Alert the priest. Tell him to marry them. And if there are niceties of law or custom that have to be dealt with then tell him that it is my command. Or better . . ." he gave a thin smile "have a Writ made."

John Kendall bowed slightly. "That will not be necessary, Sire. The priest has already been told. He merely awaits your approval."

"My approval?" Dickon's eyebrows went upwards. "Oh! Because it is a Royal Chapel, eh?" He turned back to me.

But I was looking at John Kendall. So the priest had already been alerted, had he? Then he was part of the plot too. I could see it now. It wasn't Elizabeth of York that needed help so much as Matilda. Because how else would Dickon have known we were not wed unless his niece had told him? But the royal eyes were on me and I turned back to meet them.

I bowed and said, "Thank you, Your Grace. It is what we have been planning for a long time."

"A long time? Since she took care of you when Sir . . . someone thrust a sword through your back?"

"Even so, Sire."

He grunted. "Have you a sponsor?"

I was about to reply when John Kendall spoke. "I will stand for him, Your Grace," he said. "And . . ." He hesitated. "I . . . er . . . have been asked to convey a request from the Lady Elizabeth . . ."

Richard swung on him. "The Lady Elizabeth? Which Lady Elizabeth? My niece, or her mother?"

"The Lady Elizabeth of York," John Kendall said. "She asks your permission to attend upon Mistress Nicholas."

I stood, stunned. They had been as thick as a pair of thieves!

"Body of God!" Richard exclaimed. "She wishes to attend as maid to the bride?"

John Kendall nodded uncomfortably.

The King eyed him for a long time, then turned back to inspect me. At length he spoke. "If that is her desire," he said quietly, "then I have no objection." He saw my expression and his face twisted into a smile. "If my niece is to attend the bride, why then perhaps the King of England may be present too, as a witness."

I began to stammer something when there was a commotion outside. The sentry held back the flaps to let in Sir Richard Ratcliffe.

"Dickon!" he said. "The Tudors have landed in Wales! Four days ago!"

44

RICHARD'S pale face showed no emotion. "Where?" he asked him evenly.

"At Milford Haven. In fifteen ships. Catesby is outside questioning the messenger."

"Fifty ships?" Richard's brow wrinkled.

"No, no!" Ratcliffe said. "Fifteen, not fifty."

"Fifteen! Body of God!" He went to the flaps and addressed the sentry. "See that the messenger has food and wine, and rest. I will talk with him in Nottingham tomorrow." I saw him beckon to Catesby, who followed him in.

"Did I hear you correctly?" Dickon said to Ratcliffe. "Only fifteen ships?"

"Aye," the Yorkshireman muttered. "No more than two and a half thousand men."

"Added to those who join him here," Sir William Catesby said darkly.

Richard turned and stared at him. "You think so? Well . . ." He shrugged. "We shall see. We shall see now who the traitors are. Now, Master Kendall," he said, "as soon as we are back at Nottingham in the morning have summonses sent to Francis Lovell at Southampton, and to Sir Charles Brackenbury at the Tower to bring the men of London, all to join me at Leicester. And," he added, his brow thickening, "send immediately to Northumberland to exercise his Commission of Array, especially at York, and to march south forthwith."

"There is plague in York, Sire," John Kendall said. "I doubt if they can send many men."

"They will come, bringing their coffins with them if need be," Ratcliffe chuckled. "I know them."

Richard laughed. It was the first laugh I had heard him give for a long time. His spirits had risen. There was prospect of action now. "And, Master Kendall," he said, "do not forget John Howard of Norfolk. He will never forgive me if he misses a battle."

"He can smell one a hundred miles away," Catesby murmured. I was surprised to see that he looked nervous.

"One thing more," Dickon said to John Kendall. "While

Sir William Stanley is responsible for North Wales and will be marching to cut off the rebels, his brother's place is now at my side." He turned to stare at me. "Write to Lord Stanley therefore, and tell him to bring all his forces to Leicester and join me there immediately."

Matilda was waiting for me at Nottingham Castle. "You have heard the news?" she said anxiously.

"Aye," I told her. "The priest is waiting, it seems."

"No, no!" she said with impatience. "About the Tudors?"

"Oh? The Tudors?" I replied airily, taking her hand, "Come, the priest is waiting. Let us get the business over before the King loses his good humour."

"The business?" she cried. "You call us being wed 'the business'?"

"The best I have ever carried out," I said, kissing her.

"I've a mind not to go through with it after that," she told me, returning my kiss.

"Then Dickon will hang me," I answered. "It is for you to decide."

"The King? Dickon? What is this about the King?"

"He attends as witness."

"Oh! Dear God!" she exclaimed, smoothing back her hair. "I must have time for my toilet . . . clothes!" She turned on me. "You didn't tell me that!" she accused.

"Neither did you tell me of your plotting with Elizabeth of York and John Kendall. As a conniving woman you deserve the ducking-stool as soon as we are wed."

She smiled up at me. "If that is your first wish as soon as we are wed, my Lord . . . ?"

"Hah! We have done the other times enough. It will be a new . . ." I moved forward quickly and drew the dagger from her sheath before she could get her hand to it. "One of these summer days," I told her, throwing it to the floor, "you will hurt me with that."

"When that day comes," she said, her eyes flashing fire, "it will be the best thing for you!" With that she stamped out of the room.

Yet she came to the Chapel soon enough, for I knew that the threat of keeping Dickon waiting would bustle her. First came Elizabeth Woodville, dark and stately, the wisps of grey in her hair lending dignity to her appearance. She bowed to Dickon, then drew her veil aside and smiled at him. Then, close behind, Elizabeth of York trod quietly in her slippers, a full hand taller than her mother, her golden hair falling beyond and underneath her veil. As for Matilda, the first thing I saw was that she had changed her gown. Where she had acquired it I could not think, for it was of silk, and pale blue, with a wide sash of cambric tied in a bow. And when I saw that the veil on her head was one that had been worn by Elizabeth Woodville, I looked more closely. She and the former Queen were of a size. She was almost a part of the entire Woodville family now, I thought, smiling. And then the priest was going through his incantations.

"My felicitations to you, Mistress Morane . . . Madame," Dickon said afterwards, and, bowing to her, then kissed her quickly on the cheek. Matilda gasped and stammered something, her face as red as the ruby I had put on her finger. I saw him smiling as he went out, followed by John Kendall, for there was work to do.

"Now," I said, turning to the two Elizabeths, "my thanks to you, Ladies, although, but for your station I should chastise you both for conniving."

Elizabeth Woodville laughed. "At least that would be something I have not undergone since I was a child, Master Morane. Come," she said to us, taking her daughter by the arm. "We must take wine, at least, in my chambers, for there will not be time for more now that our enemies are in the realm."

"Aye," Matilda whispered to me as I kissed her. "What is to happen to them now?"

But Dickon had already been considering where to send Elizabeth Woodville and her daughters. He sent for me soon after, and John Kendall was with him, pen in hand, which he passed to me.

"Master Morane," he said, and his face had a different complexion. There was even a trace of colour in it. "Write an order for the following to be housed in the comfort befitting their station: John de la Pole, Earl of Lincoln . . ."

"Where to, My Lord?" I asked him.

"Oh! Yes!" He gave a short smile. "I was discussing it with Master Kendall and forgot you were not present . . . To the Household of the Council of the North, the Constable of the Castle at Sherif Hutton . . ."

"The Earl of Lincoln," I repeated as I wrote it down. He would not like that.

"He will not be pleased at that," Dickon said to John Kendall. "But as my heir, his duty is to the realm and not to fight by my side."

John Kendall grunted. He, too, knew that Lincoln would put up a hearty protest.

"And young Richard, Earl of Warwick . . ."

Clarence's son was but ten years old. Had it not been for his father's attainder for treachery he might have been king today.

". . . and John of Gloucester . . ."

Dickon's bastard son before his marriage. John of Gloucester was a likeable fellow, but quite hare-brained and with rarely a serious thought in his head. Dickon loved him, the only son he had.

"And you," the King concluded, addressing me, "send for Mistress Woodville and her eldest daughter. Master Kendall can write the other names."

I bowed and went outside to call a messenger.

"What now, cousin?" Elizabeth Woodville said as she came in.

"Away from here, My Lady," Richard replied, returning her smile.

"Well, thank God for that!" she replied. "I detest all castles, and especially this one. They smell of sweat and war." She waved a hand at Elizabeth of York. "My daughters too, I presume? Where are we to be sent? I hope not a place like this."

"It is better," Richard promised. "The castle of Sherif Hutton in Yorkshire. It will be as comfortable as befits you . . ."

"Oh, yes!" Elizabeth of York clapped her hands. "I know it well! It is . . ."

"Shush, daughter!" Elizabeth Woodville warned her. "Do not interrupt the King!"

But young Elizabeth was not abashed. She smiled widely at the King. "Uncle Dickon!" she exclaimed. "I have but one favour to ask! I . . ." She saw me suddenly and stopped.

"What is it, girl?" Richard asked her.

She dropped her eyes.

"Speak up!" I told her. I could sense what was coming.

"I was . . . I was going to ask, My Lord, if Matilda . . . Mistress Morane, could accompany me . . ." another anguished glance at me ". . . as serving woman . . ." Then he looked me straight in the eye. "But I had forgotten she was wed!"

Richard nodded, then swung round to stare at me. "That is not for me to decide," he said. "She has a husband now. Even though that husband is going to be busy on affairs of the realm."

45

WHEN the time came Matilda parted from me in a flood of tears, cursing me and my decision, and threatening to abscond her post and stay with me and the rest of the Court. But, with the Tudors now rampant in the country, and as yet no one knowing their intentions, it was clearly better for her to stay with Elizabeth of York until the business was settled. In the end she accepted my decision and, penitent for her bad temper, set off with the cavalcade as it wound its way down the steep track from Nottingham Castle. Before it disappeared round a spur at the cragfoot I saw her face, pale in the distance, upturn for a last look at me and I waved. Then her head turned away quickly and I knew she was crying.

Monday, August the Fifteenth, was the day of the Assumption of Our Lady, and King Richard took care that the Festival was devoutly observed. No proclamations were sent, and little business was done, although John Kendall told me that we were to move south to Leicester soon to meet the Duke of Norfolk's forces, now assembled under his banner of the Silver Lion, and marching north from Bury Saint Edmunds.

In the afternoon the wind shifted and storm clouds gathered in the west. It seemed as if the sunny days were ending. I was with John Kendall when he was summoned to the King. A messenger had arrived and the news he brought could have been sent by those same clouds. Henry Tudor had reached Shrewsbury two days before. He was now in England.

King Richard was taken unawares when he heard it. He took a step backwards, with blanched face, and cried, "Treason! Treason, by God!" Then he recovered himself and spoke to Ratcliffe.

"Dick," he said quietly, "we are betrayed. For the Tudor rabble to have reached Shrewsbury can only mean that Gilbert Talbot and Rhys ap Thomas have let them pass. Or even joined them," he added after a moment.

It was bad news indeed. Talbot alone, as sheriff of Shropshire, had two thousand men under his command. I wondered about him. It seemed that he might still be festering from Bishop Stillington's tale of the Lady Eleanor Butler, his kinswoman.

"Rhys ap Thomas!" Ratcliffe muttered. "A loyal Welshman! And the Tudors would have to walk over his belly before they submitted!"

"Sir William Stanley must be with them too," John Kendall pointed out. "Or they could not have reached Shrewsbury."

Richard eyed him, nodded and turned towards the window. "It will not save him," he muttered. They were prophetic words, although he himself would never see them fulfilled.

Lord Francis Lovell arrived in sweat and dust an hour later. His contingent, he said, was marching with all speed from Southampton, and many of the sailors from the fleet had joined them. Dickon was pleased to see him, at any rate, for Lovell was not downcast.

"Newport?" he said. For by now the mounted scouts had told us that the Tudors had arrived there the day before.

"Shrewsbury to Newport?" Lovell repeated. "He marches straight towards us here in Nottingham, then?" He laughed deeply. "Is he so certain of the battle, then?"

Dickon smiled. "We shall see. It may be no more than a brave show towards us before he veers in the direction of London. And if he does that, why, we shall be a spear in his back. So we wait and see if he gets nearer before we move to Leicester."

"Two thousand men brought from France," Lovell said. "A present from the French with their fifteen ships, I hear." Then he laughed. "Two thousand men. Not soldiers. Not mercenaries. But jailbirds!"

"Jailbirds?" Ratcliffe asked with astonishment.

"Aye!" Lovell chuckled. "The Court of Charles the Eighth has dredged the jails of Normandy, promising any their freedom that joined the Tudor fleet. A more studied insult to Henry Tudor I could not have thought of myself."

"And so we fight thieves and cut-throats, is that all?" Ratcliffe smiled.

"As well as Talbot's men and probably Sir William Stanley's men," John Kendall said. His face grew taut, "And the Welsh of Rhys ap Thomas."

"How many are they?" Lovell said lightly. "Two thousand more, that's all?" He paused and looked at the King. "But what of Lord Stanley? Where is he?"

Lord Stanley's answer came that very hour. He sent his apology to the King, and would join him if he could at Leicester as he had been ordered, but he was stricken with the sweating sickness, and was unble to move from his bed.

If true, Lord Stanley would deserve sympathy. Although a new disease, it took a violent form. It came in an instant, without warning, taking a man unawares whatever he was doing, wherever he happened to be. A great fever sweeps over him, followed by a fit of sweating so that all the water seems to run from his body. Then there are dreadful pains in the back and shoulder, which move soon after to the stomach and liver. The head splits with agony and the heartbeats like the skin of a drunken drummer. Madness ensues for a while, so that the sufferer is not responsible for his speech. Neither would he be responsible for his actions if he had the strength to move. It was a disease not heard of until some five years before, and there was no cure that was known. Yet, unpleasant as it was, I had not yet learned of it killing anyone. Lord Stanley would recover not too long hence, if he did indeed have the sweating sickness.

It seemed, in fact, that he had been exaggerating. For that night I caught his son, Lord Strange, as he tried to escape out of the window of his castle room.

46

"**B**Y GOD!" King Richard exclaimed when I took the
shivering youth to him. "His father will have cause to
sweat now!"

It was a stupid thing to do, to try and escape through that
window, for it looked out over the sheer cliff, and Lord
Strange, in spite of tearing the arras into strips, had no great
length to hang from. He would have assuredly fallen, had I
not seized him by the shirt—for he was fully clothed—and
dragged him back inside.

"And now, My Lord," Richard said to him, "we will hear
why you wish to leave us so soon."

"He goes to spy for his father," Sir Richard Ratcliffe said,
"to tell him what strength we have."

"He goes too quickly, then," Lord Lovell said. "He should
wait to see the army that Norfolk brings, as well as the men
from the north under the Earl of Northumberland."

The young man shivered again, but said nothing.

"Rack him," Lovell suggested, grinning under his curling
hair.

"Do you hear that?" Dickon said to him. "Speak now,
Lord Strange, or the rack will do it for you."

Lord Strange looked at him blankly. Then his head rose,
and he shrugged. It was a brave gesture, but it was no use.

I went with them as they marched him below. It was a
duty commanded on me by John Kendall, who had no taste
for such scenes. The King's Secretary, or his clerk, must witness the proceedings and record what the prisoner says. I
had little taste for the business either, for, although I had
not seen it before, I had heard horrid tales of the instruments used by the executioner. If Lord Strange held out he
could suffer worse than I had seen Will Collingbourne.

While they stripped his clothes I busied myself looking for
pen and ink. They were found for me, and I took a stool
under the low arch of the vault. A candle stuck on a spike in
the wall beside me gave enough light, but the rest of the
dungeon was dim, the horns of the lanterns being long
befogged with age. The executioner wore no mask or apron,
and the gleam from his muscles ended where a thick black

mat grew over his chest and stomach. In places the hairs were moving. It may have been a trick of the light. Or it may have been the vermin that they housed.

It was not a true rack such as there is in the Tower, but it would be effective enough. Lord Strange's legs were strapped to a rail at one end, and his arms encased in tight leather gaiters at the other. He lay on the wooden slats between them, through which nails protruded, so that he arched his back at the sudden pain. Then, spreadeagled, with his arms beyond his head, the gaiters enclosing them were attached to pulleys. The pulleys could be turned together by a wheel with a stave through it, as a capstan on a ship. It was a simple apparatus, and would pull his arms out from his shoulders, or his legs away from his thighs. But it would not kill, unless a man died of the pain too soon. If the executioner knew his business he would be released before he died, a crippled, unwieldy thing, like a child's doll with its arms and legs loose, incapable of any movement to help himself. If he did not speak before he reached that point he might just as well be dead.

Cold water was suddenly thrown over him so that he gasped. As he tensed to receive more water the executioner put his weight on the wheel and his limbs grew taut. Another turn and his body was free of the slatted bed, suspended by the straps. Lord Strange gave a deep groan.

"If you wish to remain a man," Lord Lovell said to him, "it is better to speak now. With your legs unhinged you will never do more than crawl, a pitiful thing, creeping along the streets, and mocked by everyone."

Lord Strange muttered something and then lost his senses. The executioner turned back the wheel, letting the body fall again. More water was thrown over him and he revived.

"If I am to be killed," he groaned, "then I will die silent."

"The King will not have you killed if you speak," Lovell said. "You have my assurance of that."

"Your assurance?" the prisoner inquired with as much spirit as he could muster.

Lovell made a sign to the executioner.

"Wait," I said, getting up and pushing past Sir Richard Ratcliffe. He grunted with surprise, but I took no notice. I stood looking down at the naked man.

"As clerk to the King's Secretary," I told him, "I am here

as a witness. Lord Francis Lovell has given you his assurance
and I have writ it down." I waved the paper in front of him.
"If he should break his promise he will answer for it to the
King."

I heard Lovell mutter something and turned on him. "Is
that not so, My Lord?"

"It is so," he agreed reluctantly, but after some little time.

Lord Strange's eyes went from him back to me. "And
before that they will kill you too," he said.

"If they do," I retorted, "the King's Secretary will want to
know the reason."

Lord Strange regarded me for a long time. Then he
sighed. "You might be a braver man than I, then," he said.
"What is it you wish to know?"

I let my breath out slowly, then motioned to the executioner to untie him. He did it reluctantly, glowering all the
time.

But Lord Strange added little to what we already knew.
He told us that his uncle, Sir William Stanley, and his
cousin, Sir John Savage, had been for some time in correspondence with Henry Tudor, Earl of Richmond, as he
called him, and had promised him aid.

"And your father?" Lovell asked him.

"My father must know of it, of course," the young man
replied. "But to my knowledge he has not joined in the
correspondence."

"Give him more rack," Ratcliffe suggested.

"It is all I know," Lord Strange protested. "Would my
father have sent me here if I knew all his secrets? I came
reluctantly in any case. I would have gone to London had I
been permitted, for this fight is not for me." He groaned.
"May I be clothed again?" he asked. "It is cold, and I have
told you all I have. I do not know, even, how many men
have joined the Earl of Richmond, except my uncle and Sir
John Savage." He looked at me. "See that my father never
hears of this," he asked me.

"I will see to it," I promised him.

"I would have racked him more," Lovell told the King
later, with a sidelong glance at me. "For he still has not told
us which way his father's sympathies lie."

Dickon smiled thinly. "It is probably true that he doesn't
know," he said. "As his father himself probably has not yet

239

made up his mind. The Stanleys will fight on the side that suits them best." He put a hand on Lovell's shoulder. "Francis," he said, "if Northumberland brings the men of the North we need not be concerned too much. As to the Stanleys, I will have Sir William proclaimed a traitor forthwith." He smiled again. "Now consider the plight of the rebels. For even if the Stanleys join him, Henry Tudor cannot know if they will really fight for him or not."

Lovell eyed him for a moment and then grinned.

The next day we all went hunting. Sherwood Forest was the best in England, Dickon averred, and how could time be better spent than in the chase while we waited to see what the Tudors would do? Besides, the Duke of Norfolk was not yet at Leicester, and the Earl of Northumberland had farther to come. The Tudors were still marching in our direction, but were yet as far away as Stafford. It was in the evening that we received another shock.

Two men from York came from Nottingham where they had been looking for the King. They were John Sponer, Sergeant of the Mace in that city, and John Nicholson, its Messenger. The citizens of York had heard that the rebels had landed, and wanted to know why they had not been summoned to fight.

Richard's face grew grim. It meant that Northumberland, Commissioner of Array for East Riding, had not made his summons there. Was he intending to stay neutral or, knowing the loyalty of the men of Yorkshire, had he assumed that they would not wait to be called?

Henry Percy, fourth Earl of Northumberland, was a hairy-faced little man with all the character of a squirrel. His grey appearance was akin to one, too. His father, the third Earl, had been slaughtered at Towton, the bloodiest encounter of the civil wars, and, as he had been fighting against King Edward, he had lost his earldom as well. But all that was twenty years before, and since then Henry Percy had been restored as the fourth Earl by King Edward, who never bore grudges against the children of his enemies. Yet Henry Percy had watched the nobles change sides and kill each other throughout the wars, minding his own affairs and staying apart from the quarrels of others. It was a policy that saw him sitting on his estates in the north when King Edward and Richard of Gloucester had returned from exile in 1471 to fight it out with the Lancastrians at Barnet and at Tewkesbury. To Henry Percy it was all the same whether Edward the Fourth or Henry the Sixth was king.

He had supported King Richard during Buckingham's rebellion, it is true, but he had hated Buckingham, and in the event there had been little to do, for the revolt had been in Wales, and it had been unlikely that the meagre forces that Buckingham disposed of would reach far-off Northumberland. But I knew that he resented Richards' popularity in Yorkshire, and the establishment by King Edward of the Council of the North under Richard had been an affront to a man whose ancestors had ruled that part of the realm for generations. The Earl of Northumberland's loyalties appeared to be lukewarm, to say the least. But whatever course he took, we were between him and the rebels.

That afternoon I lost my falcon. She perched on a branch and refused to return to my hand. It was a strange thing to happen, and I wondered if it was a bad omen. I blew the whistle at it, and rode round and round the tree, but she sat there and eyed me bleakly. It must surely be a bad omen, I thought as I rode away in the end, and meant that Matilda would not return. My spirits were low as I returned to the tent to find Sergeant John Sponer asleep on my paliasse and John Nicholson gone back to summon the men of York.

47

KING Richard returned to Nottingham on the evening of Wednesday, the seventeenth of August, where Lovell told us that both Stanleys now had armies in the field.

"So much for the sweating sickness," Richard grunted.

"Then we can hang Lord Strange straight away," Ratcliffe said.

"Not yet," Richard told him. "We have yet to see what his father does."

"The two Stanley forces are apart from each other," Lovell explained. "Neither has joined with the Tudors so far. And they, it appears, seem to have second thoughts about advancing straight across the country towards us. They have left Stafford and there is a report that they have changed their direction towards Lichfield."

"Lichfield?" Ratcliffe said. "That means towards London!"

"Aye," the King agreed. "But we shall have to wait for confirmation." He drained his wine at a gulp. "Meantime I am for bed. Tomorrow's news will tell me what to do."

The first messages in the morning told us that Henry Tudor was at Lichfield.

Lovell gave a loud laugh and rubbed his hands together. "Now we shall have them!" he said. "If they continue on the road to London we shall take them like a hot spit up the backside, no matter what the Stanleys do."

But Dickon did not smile. "Where are the Stanleys now?" he asked John Kendall.

"Lord Stanley moved out of Lichfield ahead of the rebels, Sire," he replied. "And Sir William, still apart from him, remains some ten miles to the north."

"That's good enough for me," Ratcliffe said. "I'll hang his son today."

Dickon turned and looked at him thoughtfully. Then John Kendall spoke.

"It is not wise, Sire, to act too soon in this matter," he said. "Lord Stanley can claim that he recovered from the sickness more quickly than expected, and summoned his men immediately thereafter. He can say that, by keeping close to the Tudors and falling back as they advance, he is acting as a screen for you . . ."

"A likely tale!" Lovell exploded. "And in that case why hasn't he sent us messages to that effect?"

John Kendall could not answer that, of course, and merely shrugged. Lovell sneered and turned his back on him.

King Richard held up a hand. "Yet there may be something in what my Secretary says," he observed. "We will leave the matter of Lord Strange a little longer. Now . . ." he beckoned to John Kendall ". . . have summonses sent to all Captains that we march for Leicester at first light tomorrow. Aye, and send word to Northumberland to overtake us there. We shall see what steel Henry Percy is made of."

I turned to follow John Kendall, but the King called me back.

"A moment, Master Morane," he said, and there was a slight smile on his face. "The time has come for me to give you more serious work."

I faced him, stiff in the legs, wondering what was to come.

"Take horse straight away," he told me, "and ride for the great road to London, Watling Street, that is. That will be the way the Tudors will come. It will be while they are on that road when they will hear that I am at Leicester. And that will be where they will have to decide whether to continue towards London, or swerve back to meet me."

"You think they will swerve back?" Catesby said.

"They dare not do anything else," Richard said to him. "Otherwise, as Francis Lovell has just observed, we shall be up their backs like a hot spit. Remember . . ." he pointed at Lovell ". . . that the Earl of Oxford is a soldier too. He cannot let Henry Tudor march on London with us behind him."

I bowed, and was about to go, but the royal hand told me to wait.

"I wish my order to be very clear, Master Morane," the King said. "I need no reports from you as to where the rebels are. My scouts will tell me that. Your mission is to watch them, and the Stanleys. For, as you have just heard, all three armies are still apart from each other. Before the Tudors decide what to do they will almost certainly have to consult with one of the Stanleys, or both of them if they are both plotting treason. And, apart from any such decision as to strategy, they will have to discuss the detail of their battle tactics." He paused, the black eyes watching me carefully. "It is of that meeting that I shall require to be informed. And," he added slowly, "I shall want to know what is said there."

Catesby gasped, and Ratcliffe let out his breath in a long whistle.

"A tall order, Dickon," he said.

"Not too tall for a fellow such as Morane," Lovell sneered. "He has a rare ability to obscure himself . . . and confuse others," he added after a pause. I smiled a little at that. I knew he was remembering Sir William's woman whom his men had arrested.

The King saw my smile and misunderstood it. He nodded. "I seem to recall that you, Master Morane, may have little cause to love Sir William Stanley," he said. "It may give you added zest to confirm that he is a traitor."

I stared back at him, and the scars on my chest and shoulder began to itch.

Ratcliffe turned to me. "I wish you well, Henry Morane," he said. "You will need all the good fortune you can get."

"He can pray for that in the Chapel before he goes," Lovell said with an unpleasant chuckle.

Dickon dismissed me with a wave. "As to that, Master Morane," he said, "God be with you. And . . ." a wan smile crossed his face "if by any chance Sir William Stanley happens to get killed, why . . ." he glanced at Lovell ". . . I do not think there will be any mourning here."

No, I thought as I went out, and there will be little for Henry Morane either, when he is found dangling at the end of a Tudor rope.

48

IF ONE were able to draw a map of England on the back of a playing card (assuming that the backs of Tarots were blank instead of being filled with Zodiacal designs) it would be simple to draw two diagonal lines from corner to corner, like the cross of Saint Andrew, for the lines would denote the two great highways that cross the country; Watling Street from London to Chester, and Fosse Way from Bath to Lincoln. And not far from where the lines cross, a little way back up Watling Street, lies Atherstone, a village in the county of Warwick.

It was down Watling Street towards Atherstone that Henry Tudor was marching. And it was at Atherstone that he would probably make his decision whether to continue to London, or turn across country towards Leicester, where stood the army of the King.

On Wednesday, the seventeenth of August, Lord Stanley had been at Atherstone, but had left the place ahead of the Tudor advance and had marched five miles in the direction of Leicester, thus still keeping himself between the rebels and the King. Three miles north of him, at the village of Shenton, sat Sir William Stanley, also between Atherstone and the King. There were thus four armies now assembled, lying in the shape of a diamond on its side, with the King and Henry Tudor at each end, and the Stanleys at the top and bottom points. There, over that rolling countryside, three of the armies watched and waited, for the next move was up to Henry Tudor.

I took the road to Leicester straight away, sleeping in a haystack, and arriving there at dawn. The day was clear, and the rising sun sparkled on a long line of steel approaching the city from the south. It was Norfolk's vanguard, mounted men with polished armour and newly burnished shields. Pennons fluttered in the sunlight and the noise of drums and trumpets greeted me. The town's people were there in a great crowd, eager, yet apprehensive. They knew that the rebels were no more than twenty miles away, and that a battle would likely take place not far from their walls. Whether the King triumphed or not they did not care so much, so long as the victor treated them with consideration. But Dickon would, they knew, and of Henry Tudor they had little information, and so their sympathies were with the King and the established order. Those of their men, summoned by

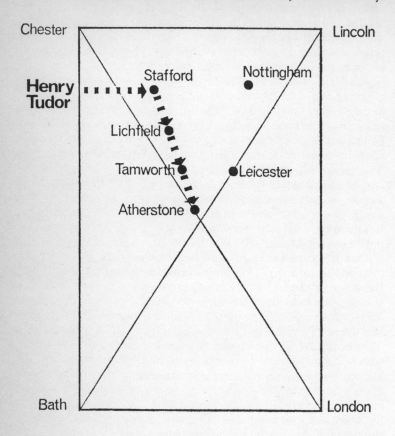

the Array with their bows and bills, were drawn up in three lines at the edge of the market place, smiling shamefacedly through the garlands hung over them by the village wenches. A great cheer went up as Norfolk's first armoured men walked their horses into the square, and more flowers were thrown.

While I breakfasted at the White Boar on soup and beans and three quarts of Leicester ale the rest of the vanguard came in, with John Howard and his son, the Earl of Surrey, following them close.

Surrey, a man no longer young, being forty-two years of age, had grown into the image of his father. The leathery face, and the glance about him as if scanning distant horizons, were the same as the older man beside him. An older man certainly, born some sixty years before, yet appearing no more in age than his son. A hardened pair, those two, and as loyal to Dickon as an oyster is to its shell.

John Howard, first Duke of Norfolk, had fought in near every battle that had taken place since his boyhood. If he had not been busy at Castillon in 1453 he would almost certainly have been fighting the Turks when they overwhelmed Constantinople in the same year. A sailor, too, for he had been in command of the Yorkist fleet during the civil wars that followed. Against Brittany he had captured and held two of their islands off the coast, and the French wanted his person to hang as a pirate. He had fought at Barnet and at Tewkesbury and had slaughtered more Lancastrians than King Edward himself, or so it was reported. He had a nose for battle, as Sir William Catesby had observed.

I went out of the White Boar and crossed the dusty square towards him. Bowing, I told him who I was, and that the King's army would be in Leicester that same evening.

Pale blue eyes looked me up and down. "Hah!" he said at length. "I did not think young Dickon would be far away. Did he send you to tell me that?"

I shook my head. "I came on other business, my Lord, which the King would prefer I did not disclose. In public," I added quickly, looking at the men about us. I told him where the Tudors were, and that the Stanleys were retreating in front of them.

"Why don't they join him straight away and show us the colour of their shirt tails?" the Earl of Surrey said, leaning forward on his saddle.

His father guffawed. "Colour?" he said. "They have no colour. Even their shit is lily-white." He swung to me. "And you, Master Morane? Can I be of service?"

"Aye, my Lord," I replied, and pointed across the square at a group of archers exchanging pleasantries with the village wenches. "Your Lincolnshire men, sir. I have a use for one of them."

He looked where I was pointing, and his rusty eyebrows drew together. "You want one of my archers?" he inquired, turning back to me. "For how long?"

"Until the day before battle is joined, however long that may be. The bald-headed one on the right."

"God's Buttocks!" Surrey exclaimed. "He wants no less than your captain, Joseph Anderson!"

Norfolk chuckled. "It will serve to keep the women from sapping his strength before the fight. Hey!" he called. "Captain Anderson!"

Joseph Anderson took his arm from the shift of the woman it circled and turned to hasten across the square. He saw me, stopped suddenly, grinned, and bowed to his commander.

"You know this man?" the Duke asked him.

"Not too well, my Lord," Anderson replied airily. "Except that when he flourishes the King's Writ all kinds of devilry ensue." He looked me up and down and then back at Norfolk. "A bad character, my Lord. Not to be trusted by women or the King's enemies."

Surrey laughed and spat into the dust. "Two of a kind, it seems," he observed, eyeing me. "I will not ask your business, sir, as it appears to belong to the King. Take Anderson, but bring him back for the fight, or most of him," he added with a loud laugh. He beckoned to an esquire to help him dismount. "Come, father," he said, "the White Boar over there waits eagerly for us. It must be Dickon's own with that device."

We stood and watched the Howards striding across to the inn. "Where to this time?" Anderson muttered. "The pit of Hell?"

"Probably," I grinned at him. "But not so far as Brittany, at least."

49

W E LEARNED from one of the King's mounted
scouts that the Tudors were still at Tamworth, some ten
miles up the road from Atherstone which, now that Lord
Stanley had marched away to Stoke Golding, was a place
devoid of the enemy. It was at Atherstone, therefore, that I
decided to find lodgings for the night.

The inn in the town was called The Three Tuns and the
landlord, after having had such eminent guests as Lord
Stanley and his officers, was disposed to be overbearing
towards less important travellers. A huge, red-faced fellow
with shoulders as round as a cartwheel, he eyed us suspiciously, although we wore no badges or livery. He told us
he could give us a bed and asked us where we were bound.

"If it is any of your business," Anderson told him, "we go
to North Wales for falcons, although a sorry innkeeper like
you wouldn't know that the best falcons come from there."

He nodded, eyeing the great bow that Anderson carried.
"There is war hereabouts," he warned. "Take care that you
are not summoned for it."

"The only thing that will keep me here," Anderson said,
"is a bright-eyed serving-wench, and that not for long." He
waved a hand at him. "Go away and see what you can find."

The landlord set the mugs down in front of us and with-
drew, muttering.

It was an old inn, built in Saxon times, of wood as was
their custom, with a great hall and gallery high up round
three sides of it somewhat below the roof beams. We sat at a
trestle in one corner, with the central fireplace between us
and the entrance. Close beside us was a narrow door that led
to an outhouse alongside the hall and to the courtyard before
the living quarters. On the other side of the door stood the
three tuns for which the inn was named.

"The women all seem to have gone off to follow the army,"
Anderson said with disgust.

"As I have a wife now," I said to him, "I can wait
awhile."

He put his chin on his fist and regarded me with astonishment. "God's Hooks, Henry Morane! I, too, have a wife, but

that does not stop me from swiving any mort who is willing. Aaaah!" He lifted his head and stretched his arms high. "But then of course yours must be new, as I heard no talk of it in Brittany."

I drank my ale and grinned at him.

"As to mine," he said, "why, she has no spirit for the joust when I go home. She spends much time at the Confession soon after I have gone again, I hear. Though what she has to confess about I cannot think. I am a most decorous fellow as far as she is concerned." He cleared his throat and spat on the rushes. The vermin under them scuttled away quickly from the sudden, unexpected deluge. He got up and put his heel on a cockroach, screwing it to the floor. "Tell me about yours," he said. "Or is she so new that it would cause you embarrassment? Yet . . ." he looked at me thoughtfully "you are not so young that you would blush when recounting your tournaments . . ." He stopped as hoof-beats outside ceased at the door and four men came in.

Banging the hilt of his dagger against the wall, the first shouted for ale, and the landlord came running. But when he saw him he smiled and they began to exchange pleasantries. Although I could not see his badges I guessed that he was one of Lord Stanley's men who had recently been staying at the inn. It transpired that they were bound for Tamworth with messages for the Earl of Richmond, as they called him. I was wondering what the messages were likely to be when I saw the second man.

I ducked my head straightaway, even though it was gloomy in our corner of the hall, and a few moments later moved out quietly and, I hoped, unnoticed, through the door beside me. Anderson followed soon after, but not soon enough to make it appear other than casual.

"Now what is this?" he whispered fiercely.

"The leader is Lord Stanley's man," I told him.

"I could have heard that a mile away."

"But the second man . . ."

"The fellow with the notched ear and the scar that makes him appear to smile all the time?"

"The same. And if you were to remove his shirt there would be another, under the ribs. Made by my dagger two years back. His name is Lambskin, and he is Sir William Stanley's man."

Joseph Anderson whistled quietly. "So!" he said. "The Stanleys' men ride together with messages for the Tudor, eh?" His hand went to the knife at his belt. "Then we will waylay them and find out what the message says."

I put a restraining hand on his arm. "No," I told him. "On their way back, when they have the reply as well."

We waited until they had gone before we went back into the hall, rearranging our clothes as if we had gone outside to relieve ourselves.

"Your advice is wise," I told the landlord. "With so many men from the armies about we will not stay in case we are impressed to fight. We will leave now and find lodgings in some side lane."

"But you will pay me for tonight which you have contracted for," he warned.

I shook my head. "Not with the place empty and no one seeking a bed."

"Oh, you will!" the landlord said, picking up a cudgel. "You will pay."

"We shall indeed," Anderson said quietly, drawing his knife.

The landlord hesitated, his face suddenly drained of colour. "You would murder me?" he cried.

"Why not?" Anderson said, grinning ferociously. "If you insist on payment it is the only way we can get it back."

It took a few moments for him to digest that observation, then he threw down his club, shrugged, and walked out through the door.

"I cannot see why I should have to spend the night with my back against a knotted tree-trunk," Anderson complained, "when those messengers are not likely to return from Tamworth before dawn."

"It is a fine night and warm," I told him. "And, even if they do not return before daylight, it was better we left the inn when we did, and not just as they arrived. As it is, the landlord will think we are far away on the road to Chester . . ."

He grumbled something and soon began to snore.

The sun came up early, filtering through the trees of the copse in which we lay. Anderson yawned and stretched himself, presently going over to the horses which were tethered some distance away by a small, clear stream. When he came back, he said, "How long do you think they will be? I need soup and ale for breakfast."

"There is a crow up there watching you." I pointed to a tree. "Shoot it and we can roast it at a fire."

"God's Hooks!" he said with disgust. "When the day comes that I have to eat carrion . . ." Then he saw my face and grinned. "But maybe there are chickens hereabouts, or wildfowl by the stream."

"Do not wander far," I warned him. "And if you hear them coming you know what to do?"

"Aye. You have told me three times already. Are you sure they will come this way?"

"It is the way to Shenton," I said. "At least Sir William Stanley's man will come, and likely the others too, for the lane to Stoke Golding branches from this one farther on."

I was becoming impatient too, for the sun was high in the sky, before I saw their dust. I shadowed my eyes and saw four men, then made a signal to Anderson on his hillock forty yards away. He waved back, then disappeared behind it, and I settled down to wait.

The lane grew narrow as it passed through the copse, so that they had to ride in single file. Lambskin was the second man, and they were all bleary of eye and cursing.

"We could have been back at Atherstone last night," the leader grumbled, "if the Earl of Richmond had been at Tamworth as we had been told."

"He would have been there if he had not gotten himself lost," Lambskin said. "The army was there, at least, and its officers were anxious for him."

"Aye, they would be," the last one said. "A rabble of flea-ridden Welshmen without a leader. Maybe he went to look for an English woman to swive . . ."

I waved twice at Anderson to tell him that his target was the second man. He waited until they came out from the copse, then rose above the grass suddenly and discharge two arrows almost as one. While the others were standing in their stirrups with astonishment he turned, ran down the hillock, jumped on to his horse and was galloping away before they could recover.

The first arrow took Lambskin straight through the shoulder, the second killed his horse. He rolled into the dust yelling and clutching at the shaft. The others were looking down at him when their leader shouted, "Over there!" and they put spurs to their mounts after Anderson.

Lambskin sat in the dust groaning and cursing as he tried to pull out the arrow with his left hand. I dropped from my branch on to him and clubbed him senseless with a blow. Then I brought my horse and threw him over the saddle to take him behind a fold in the ground and await the return of Joseph Anderson.

He came back half an hour later, panting and swearing and wiping at the thorn scratches on his face with the back of a dusty hand.

"Your marksmanship was excellent," I told him. "Better even than in Brittany."

"Huh!" he growled. "I had no moving ship under me this time. I could have killed them all as they stood."

"Oh, no," I said. "The messages must reach the Stanleys."

"Well, at least I shot one of them. He died quickly." He grinned. "After that the others rode away like frightened sparrows." He jerked a thumb at Lambskin, glaring at us through the ropes round his face. "But they'll send back for him. I heard one of them say he wasn't dead."

"He will be when they come back," I said. "Unless he talks to us." A muffled sound came from the prisoner.

He told us what we needed to know before I had occasion to light the fire I had built on his belly. Sir William Stanley had sent a message to the Earl of Richmond to say that he and his brother would return secretly to The Three Tuns that evening so that they could all confer about their plans. Henry Tudor had replied that he would be there.

"God's Hooks!" Anderson said. "Then they'll all be together! We can . . ."

"Hold your tongue!" I told him. "This fellow is all ears."

"Aaaah!" Lambskin said suddenly. "I remember you now! That night . . ."

I clubbed him across the mouth to keep him quiet.

"He knows you, does he?" Anderson said. "Then that settles it." Before I could stop him he had drawn his long knife and slit Lambskin's throat.

I looked down at the blood-drenched body and shook my head reprovingly. "That was too soon," I said to Anderson. "You should have made him walk back to the road first. Now

253

you'll have to carry him. For that is where they'll expect to find him when they come searching. And rob his body, too, to make it seem the work of thieves." I grinned at him. "At least with that dust over you you look like one. And those that got away will report you so, or else a deserter from one of the armies. Whichever it is doesn't matter, so long as the Stanleys still think their conference a secret."

"Aye! The conference! Are we to kill them all?"

"My first duty is to report what they say to the King. And they will have an escort. If we mix in a fight, even if we kill one of them, and are taken, then Dickon will not know what was said." I shook my head. "It will be difficult enough to get close enough to hear what they say."

Anderson scratched at his chin. "Aye," he muttered. "I was wondering how you intend to do that."

50

W E LEFT our horses, and Anderson his bow, at a farm-house outside the town and found our way in there on foot. The farmer took my money gratefully, for he was a poor man and swore by King Richard. Then, when I saw a line of clothes drying on a hedge, I had a further idea, and made him an offer for those that would fit us. If he were not an honest man and betrayed us then, while he might hide our horses for himself, the clothes we wore would show that they came from him and his sons, and they would be implicated. After we had taken them I pointed this out to him, and he was indignant almost to assaulting me, and took much sooth-ing. But I explained to him that in these troubled days it was hard to be sure which men were honest, especially when a Welsh invader was so close and needed men. In his case his honesty was proved and, I assured him, when we came back we would pay him better, and the King would be told of his loyalty.

There was much coming and going in Atherstone, for the Tudor army was approaching, but we made our way to the outhouse of the inn without being questioned, and hid under the straw against the wall. We were not too soon, for a little while later a sentry was posted at the door, and we were hard put to it to prise holes in the wall without him hearing us. The holes had to be prised carefully too, at the seams between the planks, to avoid pieces of wood falling inside. But the sentry was much occupied with coughing, and had trouble with his bowel, to judge by the noises that came from his backside.

When I had finished I could see into the great hall quite clearly, but could not hear unless I removed my eye and put my ear in its place. I saw that the gallery bore a sentry at the farther end, so it was as well we had not considered hiding there. The three tuns themselves, each big enough for four men, stood with their tops removed, so it was clear that they had been examined too. Another sentry trod the creaking wooden floor not far from us, which was fortunate, as his footsteps must have drowned any noise we made.

Inside was Lord Stanley, fatter than before, and his hawk-faced brother, each holding great tankards of ale, and looking expectantly towards the door. Soon afterwards it opened and several men came in, wiping the dust off their faces with embroidered cloths.

Easy to recognize was Jasper Tudor, with his hunched body and triangular nose hanging over a thin mouth that seemed to extend right across his face. Sir John Cheney, the biggest man in England, taller even than the late King Edward and as wide as one of the tuns, towered above them all. Another, Sir William Brandon, I knew too, but the man who led them I had never seen before.

He stood up straight, and was of good proportions, but his face was long and bony and his eyes stood unhappy in their sockets, as if much calculation had wearied them. They were the eyes of a man who had been told many falsehoods, and expected to be told many more. This was, of course, the much-vaunted Henry Tudor, the man I had tried to capture in Brittany. And by his side, in a small polished breastplate, stood the little, sandy-haired Christopher Urswick.

I saw the Stanleys dismiss the sentry near me and then go down on one knee. With that I replaced my eye with my ear to hear what was said.

"Once again, my Lord!" Sir William Stanley said. "My Lord and Royal Nephew!"

He may have had some claim to be Henry Tudor's uncle, but it was a thin one, as his brother was only Henry Tudor's father by marriage. But his presumption was soon put down.

"Nephew?" a voice inquired, and there was a curl to it. "Is Lord Stanley then my father?" It was of a higher pitch than an English voice, but that served to add to its asperity.

Thomas, Lord Stanley, cleared his throat. "A mug of wine, Sire? This inn, unfortunately, does not boast of glasses."

"Thank you, My Lord, but no. I come here not to dally with wine, but to ascertain your plans, as you have suggested. My army is close to Atherstone, and we camp here for tonight, where I will join it."

"I, too, will join my men," Sir William said. "They are at Shenton, and await your command."

"Then have them march to Atherstone and meet me here."

Lord Stanley coughed again. "Would that be wise, Sire? Would it not show my brother's hand too soon?"

"Too soon? Has not Richard of Gloucester already proclaimed you a traitor?" he said to Sir William.

The latter gave a mirthless laugh. But it was Lord Stanley who spoke.

"He has indeed!" he said. "And in my case he has taken my son as hostage for my good behaviour. For my part I dare not endanger his life by moving to your side too soon."

"What then?"

"When battle is joined, my Lord. He will then be too busy to think about my son."

There was a long pause. I was about to look through the hole again when Henry Tudor spoke.

"And you, Sir William?" he asked him.

"In my case, too, I think it better not to show my hand until battle is joined. Even though I have been proclaimed a traitor I think it is a trick. What evidence can there have been? No. I think he is not certain, that is all, and wishes to try and force me . . ."

"And yet to proclaim a man a traitor is not something that is done lightly, and without proper evidence."

"It is with the Usurper of Gloucester."

Another pause followed, then Henry Tudor spoke again. "He may be a usurper," he said quietly, "but do not forget that many still regard him as King. Otherwise he would have no army to fight for him."

"A dwindling rabble," Sir William said scornfully.

Some shuffling went on inside the room and a new voice came to me. I peeped through quickly. It was Jasper Tudor.

"My Lords," he was saying, "we have yet to hear your plans."

"Ah, yes!" Lord Stanley replied pompously. "I was coming to that. Richard Plantagenet is at Leicester, to be joined there, if not already, by John Howard of Norfolk, and later by Henry Percy of Northumberland. But Northumberland will not arrive in time if the first two are brought to battle quickly. Therefore we consider that you should not march on London as it will allow Northumberland to reinforce them, and they will attack you from the rear."

"You suggest, then, that we march from here towards Leicester?"

"Aye, My Lord. That will bring Richard and Norfolk out of the city without waiting for Northumberland. They are

257

both impetuous by nature, and this time it will be to their cost, so that . . ."

"And will you both be marching with me?"

It was Henry Tudor with the question again, direct now, and Sir William Stanley murmured something I could not hear.

Neither did Henry Tudor, for he asked him what he had said.

"On your northern flank, Sire." Sir William raised his voice. "On your left flank, keeping to the higher ground, the lay of which my brother and I have studied. Then, when combat is joined, I will attack beyond your left wing and outflank the enemy."

"And I, Sire," Lord Stanley added quickly, "will be ahead of you on the other side, to the south, in case Northumberland arrives in time to take the rear station. Thus I shall be able to screen him from you. And if he is not there I shall repeat my brother's tactic from the other side." He laughed. "In either case the Yorkists will have no chance."

"You think not, My Lord Stanley?" Henry Tudor inquired coldly. "I trust that you are right, for if not, none of us will have much concern for the future." He added something, which must have been to the others, for the sound of footsteps came from the rushes. I looked through the hole. Sir John Cheney and the rest were going out, leaving the Tudors and Christopher Urswick with the Stanleys.

"Then we are agreed?" Henry Tudor said. "From here I tell my Lord of Oxford to take the road to Leicester?"

There was a murmur of assent.

"Which is what he has already advised me," he said, and there was impatience in his voice. I saw the two Stanleys kneel in front of him and take his hands to kiss. Then they went out, Sir William's arm on his brother's.

When they had gone Henry Tudor gave a long sigh.

"Just so!" his uncle said, "They will fight for us if we are winning!"

Henry Tudor said nothing, and I saw Christopher Urswick reach up to put a hand on his shoulder.

"God's Hooks!" Anderson whispered horsely. "I wouldn't be in his boots for all the whores in Flanders!"

51

NO NOISES were coming from the sentry. I whispered to Anderson to plug up the holes we had made in case any light showed through afterwards, and crawled to the doorway. It was empty. He must have been one of the Stanleys' men and had gone off with them.

It was quite dark outside now and, as the courtyard seemed to be clear, we stole across it and between the houses to an open space on the other side. But there, in the meadow at the foot of the slope beyond the town, was a myriad of lights and the sound of many men. It was the Tudor army, making camp for the night. We turned and went back past the inn, keeping to the alleys between the houses.

"We could have shot them all as they came out of the tavern," Anderson grumbled.

The alley ended at the street, and I stopped at the corner to peer out.

"You might have shot one of them, no more, because the street would have been thick with their bodyguards. And who would you have picked before we were arrested?" I asked him irritably. I stepped out into the street, off my guard because of my impatience, and collided with a man walking fast close to the wall.

He was as taken aback as I was. He stepped away, muttered something, and turned to run. But I was quicker than he was, and grabbed him, hauling him back into the alley.

"Jesu!" he exclaimed. "It is Henry Morane!"

I swore out loud. My prisoner was Christopher Urswick!

"So you have come here to try again to kill the Earl of Richmond!" he said reproachfully.

"I did not try to kill him in Brittany," I told him. "And in any case you gave away the plan."

"Now what is this?" Anderson said, appearing beside me. He peered at Christopher Urswick in the darkness. "Ah!" he said in recognition. "At least we can kill one of them!" He reached for his knife.

I had been promising myself what I would do to Christopher Urswick when I had him in my power. But now, with his disposal at my command, I suddenly lost the stomach to see him despatched so summarily, like a thief in some dark, noisome alley in a place like Atherstone. In my weakness, or perhaps because I had once had a regard for him, I held Anderson back.

"No!" I said. "This man is nothing. A menial, no more. Look at him!" I held Christopher Urswick away from me like a puppet, dangling in the air. His eyes, wide and staring, gleamed at me in the starlight.

"Let him go?" Anderson growled. "Then he will say he has seen us."

"Would you do that?" I said to Urswick, shaking him a little, like a rag doll.

"If you are here to murder the Earl of Richmond then I will," came the brave reply, but his teeth chattered with it.

I set him down. "There," I said to Anderson, "he does not even know why I am here!" I winked at the archer and he understood, grinning sourly.

"And I," I said to Urswick, "did not know until you said so that your Earl of Richmond was in Atherstone." I heard him click with impatience for speaking so forthrightly and could not repress a smile. That, at least, was a score to me.

"All right," he promised. "I will not say I have seen you here. I will accept your word that you mean no harm to the Earl."

"I am weary of this," Anderson muttered. "It is quicker to kill him than to argue. Then we can be on our way." He balanced the knife between his fingers.

"This is for your own good," I said to Urswick, and struck him such a blow with my fist that he went reeling along the alley to fetch up senseless against the wall. We left him there, breathing like a man about to drown, and crossed the street quickly to the open country at the other side.

"I wouldn't have trusted him," Anderson grumbled. "He is sure to say that he has seen you."

"Seen me?" I halted and glared at him. "Seen *me*, Henry Morane? And of what importance is that to anyone? What he does not know is that I saw him first, and in better company." I sighed then. "But if he had known that then I suppose I should have had to have cut his throat."

Anderson swore and spat into the muddy water of a ditch. Then I heard him chuckle, and a hand came on to my shoulder. "But perhaps you are right, Henry Morane," he said. "He really was too small to kill."

52

WE RODE through the night and when we were near Leicester I recalled that it was Sunday and the city's gates would not open for at least an hour after sunrise. Accordingly we slept gratefully in a haystack until wakened by a patrol of armoured men. They told us that they were the screen of Norfolk's vanguard, which was assembling in the Swine's Market and would soon be ready to march. In spite of it being a Sunday, they added, the whole army would be on the move that morning.

Somewhat shamefacedly we rode through the gates, were cursed by the yawning sentry, and then again by squadrons of horsemen leading their mounts along the narrow street.

At the edge of the market Anderson dismounted and gave me his reins.

"We shall meet again without a doubt, Henry Morane," he said. "And probably in Hell. For you will get there first and drag me in after you." He grinned, spat against a wall, and walked stiffly across to a line of archers who greeted him with cheers and jibes, asking him how many country wenches would bear babes in the coming spring. I rode on past them with a wave and came to the White Boar where King Richard and his chief officers were waiting. I was surprised to see Henry Percy of Northumberland with them, his bearded face one great sulk. He had arrived the night before, John Kendall told me later, and had not ceased complaining that his men were tired after their long march and needed rest. He now had a night's sleep past him, but he looked no better. And even though all his men were mounted there was not a single one from York among them.

There must have been a hundred knights and officers outside the White Boar, but King Richard spied me and beckoned me through them.

"Greetings, Master Morane," he called. "What news have you?"

I told him all that happened, but left out the affair with Christopher Urswick. When I had finished he nodded and turned to John Kendall.

"He comes this way for sure, then. Have orders made for

the army to march to Kirkby Mallory." Then he laughed and eyed those round him. "It seems that Sir William Stanley thinks he has been proclaimed traitor as a trick. Hah! No doubt when the time comes he will go to the scaffold proclaiming his astonishment." He turned back to me. "What you have done deserves a reward, Master Morane. I will see to it after the battle."

"It does not tell us more than we already know," Lovell objected. "Their strategy is obvious and their battle tactics like a child. Even with the Stanleys on either flank . . ."

"It tells me this," Richard said sharply, "that the Tudors are fools if they trust the Stanleys."

"They did not seem fools to me, Sire," I said, and Richard frowned. He glanced at Northumberland, who was watching me speculatively.

Norfolk said, "And what of my captain of archers, Master Morane?"

"He is back at his station, My Lord," I said with a smile. "Sore from riding on horseback instead of women, but otherwise intact."

Dickon's brows drew together at that, but Surrey gave a loud guffaw. "Sore because you took them all for yourself, hey?" He clapped me on the back, driving the breath out of my body.

"Go now, Morane," the King said, "and break your fast. Overtake us at Kirkby Mallory and attend me there. You have armour?"

"Yes, My Lord. In one of the carts."

"See to it there, then," he told me, and pressed his horse away.

There was enough time to rest, for I had not long come through that village and knew it to be only ten miles off. I sipped my hot ale and listened to the City's guns making their salute to the King as he rode out. I wondered how long it would be before he rode back again.

It may not have taken much time to catch up with the army, but it took nearly an hour to ride past it, strung out as it was along the country lane. I first came up with the line of supply carts, two abreast, so that I had to take to the fields to pass. There were great barrels of corn and wine, mutton, beans and so on, for the whole countryside had to be scoured to feed an army of ten thousand men. There were cartloads of

262

armour and bow-staves, others heaped high with bundles of arrows, and some bearing small guns suitable for the field. The main artillery train still rested in the Tower. Such big pieces were for siegework, and Dickon did not anticipate any city hereabouts allowing the rebel army to shut itself up inside.

The drivers swore and cracked their whips in the dust at the weary looking oxen, and the women riding beside them shrieked for more speed. They were a motley lot, and I was glad Matilda was not among them.

Ahead of them rode Northumberland's rear guard. All were mounted, on anything with four feet from drays to donkeys, for they had had to come a long way. They were well equipped, with helmets, and padded tunics reaching to the loins. Each man carried a spear and shield as well as a sword, for when the battle came he would dismount to fight.

Next were some two thousand spearmen of the King's troop. They carried no shields, their spears being sixteen feet long in the continental style, a new method of fighting which the Swiss had brought to some success.

The dust they kicked up was a yellow cloud in the sunlight, and the coughing and swearing and spitting sounded as if an army of frogs was on the march. Many were the oaths shouted at me as I rode past, as, being mounted, I was taken for an officer. Yet their spirits were high. Before them was the prospect of an easy battle. It had been fourteen years since there had been an opportunity like this, and most of them thought only of plunder and loot, not the hard fighting that would be necessary before it. The veterans of Barnet and Tewkesbury were easy to pick out. They marched through the dust, grimly silent.

Little other traffic came along that country lane. Anyone seeing that host of soldiers would draw aside and wait until they had passed, but a friar, more arrogant than the others, demanded right of way. At that a bellow of laughter went up and spears prodded at the rump of his donkey, setting it off to career away across a field, wheezing and spluttering, with the Holy Man bouncing astride it. A cheer broke out when he finally lost his balance and fell into the grass. He got up, wiping the dirt off his gown, and shouted at the men. What he said I could not hear, which was probably as well.

Beyond the spearmen I could hear the sound of drums and

263

trumpets. It was the band of Royal Musicians making a brave noise as it marched, while streams of sweat ran down on to their pieces. A little ahead were flags and banners waving in the sunshine, and under them the glittering, plated host that formed the main division. Even though they only wore half-armour their bodies looked to be roasting in the heat. Helmets were tilted back, and not a few breastplates had been removed to dangle from the saddle. Yet King Richard and the hundred or so men round him were in full plate, and rode erect as if it was a cool day in spring. Farther along the road I could just discern Norfolk's vanguard, on foot and four abreast, with the outlying squadrons of heavy cavalry on either side.

Near Kirkby Mallory a halt was called for the army to feed and be refreshed with wine. The carts came up and women filled the iron mugs that the soldiers handed to them. A few fights ensued, but it was for the wine, the women being for later when the battle was done. At least that was how the order stood, although not always kept to.

While this was going on the King summoned his officers to attend him. Word had come from the scouts that the two Stanleys were still keeping their positions at Stoke Golding and at Shenton. The Tudor army had left Atherstone and was marching down Watling Street, but their outriders had been seen scouting towards Leicester.

"They will turn off and march along Fenn Lane," Norfolk said. "It runs straight as a pigeon's flight across the plain towards Sutton Cheney." He looked at Richard. "We came close here in Buckingham's time."

Dickon nodded. "Sutton Cheney is not more than five miles ahead. Pass the order to take that road."

Three hours later we came to Sutton Cheney and whistles blew for a halt. Dickon called his officers together again, for now we knew that the Tudor army was strung out along Fenn Lane, as Norfolk had predicted, and was marching in our direction, although still some hours away. As the others arrived they found Dickon standing near an ancient tumulus that lay beside the road. We climbed to the top and surveyed the treeless, rolling countryside around us.

Sutton Cheney lies at the eastern end of a long ridge which runs alongside Fenn Lane. At the other end of the ridge the ground is higher, where it is called Ambion Hill. A wide, but shallow stream, known as the Tweed River, comes round under Ambion Hill, follows the bottom of the ridge for half a mile or so, where it makes a marsh, and then crosses Fenn Lane under a stone bridge built by the Romans a thousand years ago.

A mile beyond Ambion, where Sir William Stanley still waited, was the village of Shenton, and two miles south of it on another hill Lord Stanley watched from Stoke Golding. It was now apparent that Henry Tudor was seeking battle, King Richard said, and thus he had three alternatives.

The first, he went on, was to continue along Fenn Lane, cross the bridge, and fight their way up to Sutton Cheney. His scouts would have told him that the Tweed was easily fordable south of the bridge, as the weather had been dry for weeks, and the bridge itself would stand the weight of the field-cannon he had brought with him from Shrewsbury. He had but six of these, of the smaller kind known as Serpentines, Dickon said, but once they reached the slope of Sutton Cheney they would be of little use, as they were difficult to train upwards. But, he added with a scowl, there would be some merit to this plan because, as he passed the Stanleys on either side, they could come down and reinforce him. In those circumstances an open battle in the plain would not be to our advantage as the numbers would be nearly even. He glanced at Northumberland as he said this last.

"It seems his most straightforward plan," Norfolk said, and Lovell nodded his agreement.

"Therefore," King Richard said, "tonight I will take possession of that height over there," he pointed "known as Harper's Hill. And opposite Lord Stanley at Stoke Golding. You, John," addressing Norfolk, "will camp midway in the plain, covering the approach from the stone bridge."

"And I?" Northumberland asked.

"You, My Lord, will remain here in Sutton Cheney." He looked round at us all. "My intention should be clear to you. If the enemy adopts that plan he will encounter Norfolk first, and My Lord Northumberland and I will sweep down at him from either flank. Lord Stanley can then do what he will," he added grimly.

"And Sir William Stanley?" Lovell asked.

"Why, Francis, he will have the choice of joining the

265

rebels from Shenton or of marching round the north of Ambion Hill and attacking Sutton Cheney from that side. It will be a long march," he smiled. "And on arriving here he will encounter Northumberland. I do not think he would dare do that on his own."

"It would be even more dangerous for him if we held Ambion, at the other end of this ridge," Surrey put in, and his father growled concurrence.

"I intend to," Richard answered, "and forthwith." He looked round at us again. "But where the enemy camp tonight will show their intentions for tomorrow. Because their second alternative is to march up the lane to Shenton and, with Sir William Stanley's help, attack Ambion Hill from the north-west."

"In that case," Lovell objected, "he will leave Lord Stanley a long way behind him."

"Precisely! Lord Stanley will have to march down from his hill at Stoke Golding and join the Tudors before the battle commences, thus giving away his intentions earlier than he expects." Richard smiled. "It will place him in something of a quandary. Especially as I have his son."

Norfolk laughed. "Aye, that will teach him!"

"Therefore," Richard went on, "three hundred of my men will occupy Ambion as soon as it is dark, without fires or noise, or other signs of their presence . . ."

"Maybe Sir William Stanley will attempt the same," Sir William Catesby put in.

Richard shook his head. "He will not dare, with the Tudors still a distance away. And if he tries it, whether tonight or in the morning, why then my men will hold him until reinforced by Henry Percy along the ridge." He looked at Northumberland inquiringly.

The latter shrugged. "We can be prepared tonight, Your Grace, although my men are tired."

"Tired?" King Richard raised his eyebrows. "Have they not yet recovered from their ride from York?"

It was a bitter jibe. It told Northumberland that Richard still suspected him for not calling up the men of that city.

John Kendall cleared his throat and we all turned to look at him. "You mentioned three alternatives, Sire, and . . ."

"Why, yes I did!" Richard grinned, and waved a hand at him. "Sirs," he said, "you will see that I have a good

266

Secretary to keep my memory sharp. One other alternative, I am reminded." He eyed us all in turn.

Surrey gave a loud chuckle. "It seems to me, Sire, that all that is left for him is to turn tail and make quickly back to Wales."

Dickon smiled and made a mock bow towards him. "Why, sir," he said, "with that you could be right!"

53

WHISTLES were blown, trumpets sounded, and the soldiers, with much profanity, began their march to their appointed stations. The King's men went first, down to the plain and across to Harper's Hill. Then Norfolk's division moved off and pitched camp on the plain itself. The men of Northumbria settled down gratefully where they were.

Three hundred men-at-arms, with swords and shields and spears, set off along the ridge, cursing their misfortune at having to spend a supperless night. But in the end they were not dismayed, for the King had ordered three hundred more to be fed and wined at Sutton Cheney, and afterwards relieve them, so that in due course they were able to rejoin their comrades at the camp fires and take their ale. To Ambion Hill also went four hundred archers from Norfolk's division, as Dickon was not sure of Northumberland's energy in coming to its support.

It seemed to me that, if he was not certain of Henry Percy's loyalty it would have been better to send him to Harper's Hill. But, on reflection, that would have been too close to Lord Stanley for Dickon's comfort. And to have Northumberland in the middle of the plain instead of Norfolk might be risky too, if the Tudors did attack that way. Dickon was no fool. Sutton Cheney was the best place for Henry Percy that night.

As for me, before joining John Kendall at Harper's Hill, when I saw the black-browed archer-captain leading his men to Ambion I decided first to see how the land lay there.

"God's Hooks!" Joseph Anderson said when he saw me. "I thought this hill in front of us would have an ill-omen about it. Now I am sure."

I grinned at him. "It has, indeed. There are the ruins of a village here, once called Ambion. It has disappeared a hundred years since. The Great Plague wiped out every man, woman and child. And no one has been back to rebuild it again."

"Oh, Holy Mother!" he croaked, and crossed himself.

I stood on the highest ground I could find and looked

about me. A mile ahead was Shenton, where the camp fires of Sir William Stanley glittered in the evening. Away over to the left, on a distant height, I could see those of Lord Stanley at Stoke Golding. The seemed like stars come down to earth. Behind me, at Sutton Cheney, a few lights showed. Perhaps Northumberland's men were as weary as he said. Or per-

The Night Before

haps, an awful thought, they had already decamped and were on their way back to Leicester. Yet the sight of Norfolk's and the King's camps were reassuring. Even without Northumberland we might have the measure of the enemy. But where was the Tudor? I peered into the distance down Fenn Lane.

Suddenly I stiffened. There were lights springing up between the Lane and Shenton. It was a part known as the White Moors, and it could only be the Tudors making camp there. I looked back at Harper's Hill and wondered if Dickon could see them from there. I decided it was time for me to ride back and see that he was informed. When he heard it Joseph Anderson grunted approvingly.

"The omens will improve now," he muttered as he watched me go.

I walked my horse slowly between the camp fires of the King's division to find John Kendall waiting for me impatiently outside his tent.

"Where have you been?" he demanded.

I told him, adding that the Tudor army had made camp too.

"Glory be!" he exclaimed. "Do you not think that the King's scouts have already told him that? And orders have already been sent to march back at first light and hold Ambion Hill in strength? I have been waiting for you to write them down."

"Write them down?" I echoed. "Does a war have to wait while orders are transcribed on paper?"

"No, no," he said testily. "But you know that I have to keep a record of such matters."

I went into his tent and sat down at the trestle while he dictated. When he had finished I started to get up.

"Wait," he told me. "There is one more." A smile came over his face. "This one, by chance, is an order for a man called Henry Morane."

I sat down again slowly, my eyes fixed on him.

"Henry Morane," he said portentously, "the King's order is that tomorrow, at sunrise, you ride to Lord Stanley's camp at Stoke Golding . . ."

I groaned.

". . . and demand his allegiance immediately in the Name of the King. If he demurs, or refuses outright, you are to tell him that it will be at the cost of his son."

54

SLOWLY I clawed myself out of a terrifying nightmare. Matilda was stretched to a rack, fully clothed, and I was trying to loose her. All the while the hideous machine was pulling her legs away from her skirts and her arms out of her sleeves, and all the while I was cutting the straps that held her with my battle-axe, but as fast as they were severed another grew quickly in its place, so that I grew frantic for speed, and for fear that the blade would become blunt. She lay there without a sound from her lips, her eyes wide with supplication, while a sea of ghostly soldiery looked on, murmuring and swearing at me to work faster.

At last I woke in a sweat of fear, still half-dreaming and searching blankly round me for Matilda. But all I saw was grass and a line of tents standing out in the darkness against a thin grey band of light behind the hill. But the murmuring and cursing went on, and as my senses came back to me I knew that it was real. The men were being kicked awake by their officers. I grunted with relief, glad that it had been no more than a dream, and then my spirits were immediately dashed again by the recollection of what John Kendall had told me I had to do. I got up, stretched and broke wind, then stumbled across to the nearest soup-kettle.

I rode down the hill in the morning twilight, splashed across the Tweed, and between the few houses of Dadlington. The dunghills there were already beginning to steam and the first flies were making their investigations, but of dogs there were none. The hamlet was quite deserted, for all the inhabitants, like those of Sutton Cheney, had fled, not wishing to be embroiled in other people's wars. On the other side I saw an outrider wearing Lord Stanley's badge. I hailed him and told him my business. He moved up close to me quickly, with sword at the ready, then, seeing I had none, sheathed it again.

"You have temerity, sir," he said.

"I do a duty," I told him shortly, and rode on in silence.

The sentries stopped us and, while a message was sent to Lord Stanley, they searched me with rough hands. Finding no weapon, they stood back, eyeing me curiously. Lord Stanley came soon after, gnawing at a chicken bone.

"Ah, yes!" he said, and I saw that he wore no armour. "Henry Morane, the scrivener?" He threw the bone away and pulled slivers of the flesh from his teeth, while his forehead knitted. "Morane?" he repeated. "I had a vague understanding that you had died." He eyed me up and down and shrugged. "Ah, well, it seems that you did not. I hear that you bring a message from Richard of Gloucester?"

He would not call him King, it seemed, and I waited.

"Well, man? Speak up. What is it?" But I could see that he already knew.

"My Lord," I said, "the King sends you his greetings, and bids you join him with your forces with all speed."

Lord Stanley put his hands on his wide hips and looked round at the officers who had come with him. "Do you hear that, sirs?" He swung back immediately to me. "And if I do not, Master Morane?"

"I am bidden to tell you that if you do not then the King fears for the safety of your son, the Lord Strange."

There was a long silence while I looked him in the eye and held my ground. At length he frowned.

"I am of a mind to have you hanged for that impertinence."

"I do not bring impertinence, My Lord," I told him steadily, although my stomach was tight. "I carry a message, no more, and am bidden to take back your answer." I turned round and inspected those assembled round the dying fire, and then looked back at him. "I have never heard it said against you, My Lord Stanley, that you hang messengers."

One of the officers took a step towards me, but Lord Stanley waved him back. "As you say, Master Morane," he agreed, his eyes narrow in the flesh of his face, "I have never yet hanged a messenger. And I will not let someone like you have the honour of being the first. Take this message back to your Duke of Gloucester then. Tell him that, whatever fears he may have for Lord Strange, I still have other sons . . ."

He turned on his heel and stalked away.

As I rode down the hill from Stoke Golding I could see the Tudor army marching up the lane towards Shenton. Beyond it, Sir William Stanley was already moving out behind Ambion Hill. Norfolk's men could be seen on the ridge, with the King's division close behind it. I put a spur to my horse and galloped to Fenn Lane. Two Tudor scouts saw me and pursued, but I reached the stone bridge before them and soon was among the shelter of Richard's soldiers.

His officers were about him, as well as Sir Robert Bracken-bury, lately Constable of the Tower, with his contingent from London, his hair as white as the ashes of the fires they had left behind them. All had been armoured, except for their helms, and Dickon looked as if he had slept as badly as I. When I gave him Lord Stanley's reply his brow darkened. He beckoned to Sir William Catesby.

"Will," he told him. "Go. See to Lord Strange."

Sir William Catesby paled. Dickon noticed it and said, "Why, man, have you no stomach for it?"

"It is not that, Sire. But should we not wait until Lord Stanley moves . . ."

"Moves?" Richard's voice rose. "Is his reply not move enough? Go! Do as I say!"

Catesby turned and walked away slowly, followed by Richard's angry glare.

He waited until Catesby had gone down the track before turning back to us. "Make no mistake, My Lords," he said. "Today will be notable in this country's history. Over there are the last of the pretenders. Once they are defeated there is no one left to take their place." He smoothed back his hair with the palm of his hand. "Much of the night I have spent in thought," he went on, "and some in dreams . . ." A wan smile flickered quickly across his face. "But of this I can assure you, that after today England will not be the same again, whether the Tudors prevail or not. I am sick to weariness of the constant plotting and treachery that has surrounded me these last two years. From Hastings and Buckingham to certain other gentlemen whom you all know. And I mean to stamp them out as you would a cockroach." He turned on his heel and beckoned to an esquire to bring his helmet.

When it was brought I saw that there was a thin golden circlet round the headpiece. It was the battle-crown of England.

The man holding it faltered a little. "Sire," he said after a pause, "there are no Chaplains in the camp to give us Mass."

Richard swung on him. "Chaplains?" he inquired. "For Mass? Hah!" He laughed bitterly. "No, sir, I did not bring any. For it is clear that if God is with us in this battle he will not look kindly upon us spending time in supplications. And

273

if he is not . . ." his voice grew harsh "then, sir, your prayers will be but idle blasphemy."

Northumberland cleared his throat loudly. "Sire," he said, "my men are all mounted, and can move quickly to wherever they are required. I submit that we do not follow you along this ridge, but wait in Sutton Cheney is case Lord Stanley moves across the plain to attack us in the rear."

"He will march across the plain all right," Norfolk said. "He can do nothing else. But as to whether he attacks towards Sutton Cheney or joins the others at Shenton remains to be seen."

"In the latter case," Richard said to Northumberland, "you will reinforce us quickly."

The Earl nodded.

"You understand that?" Richard persisted.

"Aye, My Lord, it is understood."

Richard turned his back on him and addressed Norfolk. "The men are rested?" he asked. "Then have them take position."

Lovell said, "I have a submission, Sire." He spoke respectfully, for King Richard was no longer in the mood for familiarities. "The golden crown you wear, Sire," he went on, "is it not too conspicuous?"

"By God!" Richard exploded. "Am I not King?" He glared round him, and was met with shamefaced nods. "Then as I live as such I will take my chance of dying that way too." He frowned. "Where is my Secretary?"

"Here, Sire," John Kendall said breathlessly, pushing his way through the others.

We stood and looked at him, open-mouthed.

John Kendall was in full armour, even to a battle-helm. A sword was strapped to his side and he carried a spear.

"Why, John," the King said, appalled, "what is this?"

The fat face looked at him defiantly through the raised vizor. "Did you expect me to stand and watch the fight, My Lord?"

"Body of God!" Richard shouted. "I will not have you in the battle! You have no practice . . . !"

"Sire!" John Kendall interrupted him. "I will ride with you as close as I am permitted. If you forbid it, why I will . . ."

"Yes?" Richard gave a short laugh. "And what will you do? Resign your office?"

274

"Even that," John Kendall said relentlessly, staring at him.

They stood glaring at each other for a long time. Then the King put his hand on his Secretary's shoulder. "Then God be with you, Master Kendall," he said, and turned away quickly so that none of us could see his face.

55

FROM the top of Ambion Hill Sir William Stanley's men were easily distinguishable in their red coats, and nearly all seemed to be mounted. They were standing to arms on the lane that led north out of Shenton. On our left the Tudors were unfurling banners and blowing many trumpets and flutes as they moved along the track towards that village.

"How many of them do you count?" Richard asked Lovell.

"About six thousand," he replied. "No more."

"Aye, about that," Richard agreed thoughtfully. "Two thousand French, five hundred of his friends from Brittany, a thousand more with Talbot and Savage, and the rest Welsh levies raised by Rhys ap Thomas. There are few Englishmen among them, at least."

"And we, My Lord," John Kendall said, "have nine thousand, seven hundred and forty two, if none have deserted or gone sick."

The others looked at him with astonishment mixed with awe, then someone laughed. But Richard said, "That includes the three thousand brought by Northumberland?"

John Kendall nodded without saying anything. The implication was clear.

"Sir William Stanley has fifteen hundred more," Ratcliffe pointed out.

"Aye, and so has his brother," Richard said. "But they will not fight until they see how the battle goes." He pointed across the plain towards Stoke Golding. "See! Lord Stanley has called his men to arms." To me, he said, "What was their disposition?"

"About fifteen hundred men, the same as his brother, Sire," I told him. "But all on foot and armed no better than the Tudors."

Richard grunted. He beckoned to a knight standing by. "Sir Marmaduke," he said, "you are Lord of this Manor, I think. Tell me, is this called the Manor of Sutton Cheney, or of Ambion." He smiled. "My Secretary will wish to record the day as being of somewhere, I think."

Sir Marmaduke Constable shook his head and pointed to

the north. "Up there, My Lord, on that ridge, is the town of Bosworth. This field comes within its Manor."

"Bosworth Field," John Kendall muttered. "I must remember that."

I grinned at him before turning back to look at the rebels. Lord Stanley's men were now descending from their camp and along the track that led to Fenn Lane. It seemed to me that if they were making for Sutton Cheney they would have marched more directly across the plain. But if they were aiming for Shenton then the Tudors would wait for them, but they were not. The Tudor army was already beginning to ford the Tweed below that village. I watched them, their spears glittering in the early morning sun, as they splashed across column by column. The Earl of Oxford's banner was clear enough, for the Star With Streams stood out straight behind its bearer as he rode quickly up and down the column. Then he stopped and others rode to him. A conference was about to begin. I watched them closely and from their gestures it was almost as easy to follow what was said as if I had been present. They could not attack straight up the hill from where they were as the rays of the sun were level with the ground and its brightness would blind the soldiers. It was better to march a few hundred yards round the end of the hill and attack from there. The could not march too far, I thought, as beyond it the northern edge of Ambion was very steep.

The meeting dispersed, officers rejoining their commands, and soon the columns turned to their left and along the bottom of the hill as I had noted. Oxford's division led the way as they marched, six abreast, across the meadow. Behind them came the Tudors, with the great standard of Wales drooping in the sun, and five of the guns they had taken from Shrewsbury.

The ground they crossed was now less open. Grassy hollows and golden ridges of gorse with a sprinkling of trees here and there marked the slope that led down from Norfolk's position. The latter had his men spread round the curve of the hill with the bowmen on the left, being not yet certain from which direction the attack would come. And as the enemy appeared strung out in a thick column before them, the archers began to shoot. Oxford, half-way along the division, stung by the volley, ordered a halt, and whistles

277

summoned his men to face towards us, while bowmen ran in front of them to take position. Much shouting went on, and I could hear commands in English, Welsh and French. They were forming into column for the assault.

After them came the Tudor division led by the white-hooded men of Sir John Savage. Then appeared more than

The First Moves

two thousand following the banner of the Black Raven. They were Rhys ap Thomas's Welshmen, long-haired and wild, armed with a forest of spears. Behind them were the Tudors under their great banner, Henry himself and his Uncle Jasper, with the huge figure of Sir John Cheney seeming to ride above the others.

The Tudor column continued until it was behind that of Oxford's, and then halted too. More archers came from it, and three guns were manhandled into position. Orders were given, but not in French this time, and the bowmen joined their comrades in front and began to shoot. Norfolk's men replied again, and soon the air was thick with flying arrows. I saw men fall in the enemy ranks, but they were quickly pulled aside to be replaced by others. Norfolk's men I could not see too well, for they were below me on the brush-filled slope. Then a serpentine cracked and a stone ball, as big as my fist, appeared in the air, bounded off the grass, tore up a gorse bush by the roots and flung it on one side amid a shower of earth and yellow petals. The bombardment, preliminary to the assault, had begun.

The shooting match went on for about a quarter of an hour, and the guns banged at intervals, although I could see no sign that they did much harm. Norfolk's line was strung out thin, and cannon are only of use against tightly packed men. Oxford had been waiting, it seemed, until the sun was higher, although his polyglot army was taking much goading until it was in the shape he wanted. Then, all at once, there was the sound of many trumpets, the archers retired quickly, and the enemy began to march up the slope. A great cheer came from Norfolk's men as they charged down to meet them.

We sat our horses and watched, King Richard motionless on his great white charger. Before the dust of the fight rose to obscure our view I saw the main ward of the Tudors moving up behind Oxford. It was not their plan, then, to attack alongside him, but to advance in division behind each other, like the French at Crecy, those in the rear making good the losses and reinforcing those ahead. But if it had been arranged that Sir William Stanley would form a line at their left flank he still stood aloof, half a mile away. His brother, having crossed Fenn Lane, was marching across White Moors, a cloud of dust of that shade showing his position. Yet he, too, seemed to move slowly, not as a man hurrying to the aid of his friend. If I were Henry Tudor, I thought, I should be a very worried man.

Clashing of metal, shouts and yells, and the screams of those wounded grew louder as the fight intensified. First Norfolk's line would bend back, his Silver Lion waving closer to us, then Richard would motion to an officer to advance his men to help, and the line would straighten out again as the enemy gave ground in turn. I could see the King glance back occasionally for Northumberland's men, but there was no movement from the direction of Sutton Cheney.

Then, all at once, a tremendous blare of trumpets came from the Tudor lines. "Rally! Rally! Rally!" were the shouts, and Oxford's men fell back quickly to the standards that were raised behind them. A sudden pause came over the battlefield as Norfolk's line stood resting on its weapons, breathing hard in the dust and steam around them and wondering at the new manœuvre. But the enemy would not be allowed to reform. I saw Norfolk raise his sword. Blood dripped from the steel gauntlet that held it.

"At them!" he roared, waving the point in the air, and setting off to stride down the hill. Beside him Surrey waved too, and Lords Dacre and Zouche yelled at their men. Another great cheer went up as the division charged down on the enemy.

This time Oxford's men were in better fettle. Close with them now were their reserves, even though most of them were Welsh, and they were better knit together. Norfolk was attacking the entire Tudor army.

King Richard beckoned to an esquire, telling him to send to Northumberland to make haste. Then he turned and looked across at Sir William Stanley's force, but the red-coats were still motionless on the plain. His brother had, however, now crossed the Tweed, and would soon be with the Tudor ranks. Norfolk needed help. Sir William Stanley would have to wait.

As the King raised his arm to signal the advance I saw the banner of the Silver Lion wave drunkenly over the sea of weapons and then fall. A roar of triumph came from the enemy. A few minutes later a frantic messenger, his face streaked red and yellow with dust and blood, came running to us screaming that the Lord of Norfolk was killed and Surrey taken prisoner.

"Go on, then!" Richard yelled at his captains, "and avenge the Lion of Norfolk!" His last words were drowned by the trumpets as they sounded the advance. The men-at-arms streamed by, their faces set and purposeful, relieved at having to wait no longer while their comrades fought. King Richard drew his sword and held it high.

"Where is the Tudor?" he asked Sir Richard Ratcliffe.

The latter peered through the dust and shook his head.

"I see him!" Sir Ralph Assheton shouted excitedly. "Over there! Behind his division. On that hummock. Over to the right!"

I looked hard and discerned a group of men, some twenty or thirty riders, standing on a low ridge. Above them hung a great flag, listless in the morning sunshine. I could see its white and green ground and then, as a puff of wind stirred it, the Red Dragon of Cadwallader stood out clearly. I gave a shout, but others had seen it too.

Richard bared his teeth and stood in his stirrups, raising his voice so that all the knights and officers of his guard could hear.

"Gentlemen!" he called. "John Howard of Norfolk is down, and Surrey, his son, is taken prisoner. Northumberland has failed us. And Lord Stanley will soon swell the enemy ranks. See!" He pointed with his sword. "His brother, too, has heard the news and assembles his men to close in like the carrion birds they are. The time has come to seize our opportunity." His eyes swept round us and they were bright with fury.

"The hub of all this treachery and double dealing," he went on vehemently, "is Henry Tudor who stands over there. Once he is disposed of England is saved. We ride, therefore, all of us as one, to kill that man, slaughtering all who come in the way."

"My Lord," Ratcliffe demurred, "it will mean riding round the edge of the battle and across the head of Sir William Stanley's column as it advances."

"It will," Richard agreed grimly. "But we shall be there before Sir William Stanley."

"If Northumberland has failed us," Lord Ferrers said, "then the day is lost. Is it not better then, to run and live to fight again on another? After all," he added reasonably, "the men of York are not yet here, nor those of Suffolk. Neither are . . ."

"My Lord Ferrers!" the King roared. "Would you have me leave the crown of England on a gorse bush for Henry Tudor to pick up while I run away to rally the men of the North?" He rubbed his hands together and snapped his fingers for his battle-axe to be handed to him. "Do you gentlemen ride with me or not?" he called.

"Of course!" Ferrers shouted, drawing his sword. "Let us settle this affair today! Now!" A cheer went up from the eighty men or so who formed the guard.

King Richard waved his gauntlet in acknowledgement, pulled his vizor shut and turned his great horse to guide it down the hill.

The Final Stages

56

JOHN Kendall, the skin of his face drawn tight with unaccustomed tension, closed his headpiece. I turned and grinned at him. His eyes glittered back at me through the armoured slits. There was fear in them, but there was exhilaration too.

As for me, I was the least well armoured of them all. A sallet helm, such as archers wear, covered my head down to my ears, no more, and for the rest I had breast and back plates, with other steel on my thighs and forearms. This was by design, though, for I had found that at Barnet and Tewkesbury I was more nimble at avoiding enemy strokes without the weight of heavy armour to impede me. But now, riding to attack the core of our opponents, I was not so sure. And while there were only twenty or thirty of them grouped about Henry Tudor himself there were five hundred more of them at his front. The familiar signs in my stomach began to make themselves felt and my mouth grew dry. I took a tight grip on my battle-axe and could feel the reassuring slap of the sword scabbard against my horse. And after that, with King Richard putting spurs to his horse at the bottom of the hill, I was too busy trying to keep up with him over the uneven ground to be concerned about my fear.

We had about half a mile to go, and at first were unnoticed because of the plentiful sprinkling of bushes and numerous hollows we had to ride through. Then I heard a shout and a piercing whistle blew. A line of archers assembled hurriedly and loosed their shafts, but they were shot raggedly and did us no harm. From over to the left a serpentine exploded, and I laughed out loud. Guns would not stop us either. Neither would the horsemen galloping back from Oxford's ranks to help their leader.

The line of foot soldiers before the hillock gave under the shock of our charge. Richard himself killed two, and a moment later was through them. A serpentine cracked again, but it could not have been the same one to have fired so soon. As I reached the disorganized knots of men who had formed the line a bearded fellow stabbed at my horse with his spear. I swung down and brained him on the spot, hardly pausing, for King Richard and those about him were ten yards ahead.

My horse had hardly taken me that distance when I received such a blow on the head that I went reeling in the saddle. Dimly, I realized that it must have been a cannon shot, for no man could have stood up that tall to do it. As I fell I had enough wit left to move my feet out of the stirrups, so that I rolled across the grass free of my mount to tumble into a thicket of gorse, where my senses left me.

I must have recovered almost instantly, for the two men advancing on me with spears were still several feet away. They were heavily-built and moved ponderously. I clambered through the thicket and dodged away behind some bushes. My business was not with men on foot.

But the sudden effort made my head spin round again, and I had to rest for a moment. I wondered what had caused such a blow and took my helmet off to inspect the dent. But there was nothing to be seen. It must have been the passing wind of a cannon-ball that had unseated me. I sighed with relief and got up, shaking my head to clear away the film from behind my eyes. I must reach King Richard quickly.

And then I saw him, his huge white horse reared up, and Sir John Cheney alongside cutting at him with his sword. But the encounter lasted no more than a moment, with the giant knight sprawling on the ground, his helmet and the head inside it split as cleanly as an apple, and as white too.

Ratcliffe was there, and Lovell, fighting against a knot of men who wore red coats. Sir William Stanley's men had moved quickly. As I ran forward I looked round for John Kendall, but could not see him. The fleeting thought crossed my mind that he had taken refuge in flight, but I shed it immediately. He was not one to do that once his decision had been made. And then, at last, I found him.

He lay on his back, arms spreadeagled, a mountain of flesh covered with plate. A spear still ran through him from under his cuirass and out of his armpit at the other side. I stumbled across to him quickly, tears welling in my eyes, and raised his vizor. But John Kendall's eyes held no tears, nor ever again would hold anything.

I closed his helmet gently and rose unsteadily to my feet. King Richard was forcing his charger through a press of shouting men, his golden crown sparkling in the sunshine. He struck at Sir William Brandon, bringing him to the ground, and the standard of Cadwallader with him. He struck again at another knight, but by then his horse was on its knees and he missed the blow. Leaping off the saddle he swung his axe at those nearest him, and they gave way, but then a man rushed at him from behind and clubbed him so that he fell forward on to the grass, roaring "Treason!" as he saw the red coats of his enemies.

At the cry Lord Lovell turned his horse. I saw him spur it towards Dickon but three men-at-arms with spears headed him off. He swung away from them to be met by three more. He rode on, trying to find a way past them, but there was nothing he could do. King Richard was surrounded. I saw him halt and raise his vizor, peering at the mob. Then he closed it slowly, raised his hand in salutation, and spurred his horse away over the ridge.

Ratcliffe was ahead of me as we rushed to aid the King, but a blow from a mace despatched him immediately. I stumbled after him and saw Dickon try to get to his feet. He was still roaring, "Treason!" as the press closed in on him, axes raised and swords at the ready. There was nothing I could do either, but I went on blindly. And as I reached the outskirts of the throng they drew back with a great sigh and stood to look at what they had done. What ten minutes before had been the King of England was now a bloody mess of steel and flesh and trampled grass. I turned away and let my vomit rise.

Then I heard a shout and knew that I had been seen. I turned back to see weapons raised menacingly as the soldiers advanced on me. I threw down my battle-axe and raised my hands in the air.

But the lust for blood was in them and I knew my end had come, yet I was too full of shame and sick at heart to try to turn and run. I stood helplessly, waiting for the inevitable spear. And then, through the gorse, a horseman came and ordered them back. They hesitated first, and moved away sullenly as they saw who it was. He rode over to inspect me better.

"Jesu!" he exclaimed, and his face paled as if he had seen a ghost. "Henry Morane, as I live!"

It was Sir William Stanley.

57

HE SAT, looking down at me. "Unless you are a twin?"
"No, sir," I said, a fit of rage coming over me and
giving me strength to speak. "The same Henry Morane that
you stabbed through the back."

"And survived too, eh?" A slow smile spread across Sir
William Stanley's hawkish features. "Well, well! But that
can be remedied now." He beckoned to his men. "Take him
over to that tree and hang him," he ordered.

As they rushed forward he suddenly held up a hand.
"Wait," he said, "I have a better scheme." He looked round
at the white-hooded archers among them. "You men," he
sneered, "shot badly today. You should have more practice.
Tie him to the tree instead and let me see if you can do
better at a closer target."

They grinned at that and, knocking me to the ground,
stripped me of my armour and dragged me across the grass.
In a moment I was bound tightly to the trunk. They stepped
back and twanged their bowstrings. But I did not care.
Everyone I knew was dead. There was nothing left for me. I
closed my eyes tightly to keep the tears in check.

It seemed to be an interminable time before the first arrow
tore through my chest. I wondered, dimly, if there would be
much pain, and started to pray that it would be short. But I
found I did not know who to pray to, for there did not seem
to be a God any more. Yet the arrows did not come, and I
opened my eyes to see why they had not.

There, in front of the archers, their bows already taut, was
the slight figure of Christopher Urswick, hands on hips,
frowning up at Sir William Stanley.

"I tell you, sir," he was saying, "that this man is the King's
prisoner."

The King? I thought. But the King is dead. Cut up like an
ox on a butcher's slab.

"You are in error, sir," Sir William Stanley replied
haughtily. "The man is mine. Taken in battle."

"I repeat, Sir William, that he is wanted alive. If harm
comes to him before the King questions him you will answer
for it."

There it was again, "The King!" I shook my head violently.

"And after that?" Sir William sneered.

Urswick shrugged. "No doubt he will be returned to you if you press the point."

Sir William Stanley turned his horse slowly and looked me up and down. I glared back at him at which he shrugged and returned to Urswick.

"As you wish, sir," he said at last. "But I will not forget your impertinence." He dug a spur into his horse and galloped away through the bushes.

They untied me while Christopher Urswick held his sword point at my throat. When I was free he ordered them to bind my hands behind me, and waved the weapon at a distant hillock.

"Over there, Henry Morane," he said brusquely, but his voice was not unkind. "It seems to me that the new King may have a use for you."

CHILD ABUSE AND THE SCHOOL

By Jeanette Willan Fairorth

PALO ALTO, CALIFORNIA

Published
by

R & E RESEARCH ASSOCIATES
936 Industrial Avenue
Palo Alto, California 94303

Library of Congress Card Catalog Number
81-83623

I. S. B. N.
0-88247-615-7

TABLE OF CONTENTS

Chapter   Page

iii

CHAPTER 1

THE SOCIAL, PSYCHOLOGICAL, AND EDUCATIONAL PROBLEMS OF CHILD ABUSE

Historical Perspective of Child Abuse and Child-Rearing Practices

Child abuse is not a phenomenon of the twentieth century only, rather it is a matter of history. Tales of children being maltreated and even murdered by their parents abound in myth, legend, and literature. Of course, it is not merely a matter of tales, they have been murdered and maltreated in fact. However, the systematic conceptualization and identification of child abuse is a recent concern (1960's). Child-abuse reporting laws require physicians, school nurses, and

1

school teachers to report immediately to
the Public County Child Welfare Agency
any child less than eighteen years of
age who on examination "discloses evidence of gross physical neglect or
injury not explained by the available
medical history as being accidental in
nature."[1]

In order to understand the reasons
for abuse of children it is beneficial
to have a historical perspective on the
development of the issue. It should be
noted that this dissertation is concerned chiefly with the abuse of children by
those who have some responsibility for
children (family care, custodial care)
or by those who are closely related to
the family situation (siblings,
relatives, etc.).

Research by the National Center on
Child Abuse has revealed that two
thousand children were killed by their
own parents on 1976 and 200,000 more
were beaten badly enough by their
parents to require medical treatment.
Sexual abuse ranges from exposure and
fondling to intercourse, incest, and
rape. There were 137,000 cases of
gonorrhea reported children under thirteen years of age. (The number of cases
due to youthful promiscuity is not
known.) In 1976, the Pennsylvania
Department of Welfare received 6,400
reports of child abuse, a 300 percent
increase over the previous year.

As was mentioned, violence and
abuse directed at children is not a new
phenomenon, nor is it unique to our
society and culture. Radbill suggests
that children are exposed to less viol-

2

ence from their parents today than in the past and, in fact, many of the past instances of maltreatment of children, then accepted, perhaps, as appropriate discipline, would be defined today as abuse and would be the object of intervention by social or legal authorities.[2] The state's right to intervene coersively or noncoercively in families' lives will be discussed in a later chapter.

Through the years some kinds of child abuse have been justified and rationalized in many ways. In primitive times the explanation involved the believed need to please certain gods or to expel evil spirits. Ritualistic killing, maiming, and severe punishing of children in attempts to educate them, exploit them, or to sometimes rid them of evil spirits have been part of history since biblical times. Forms of mutilation of children have been recorded over the centuries as part of religious and ethnic traditions.[3] This has been referred to as ritual surgery and has included castration to produce eunuchs, footbinding of female children in China, wrapping the neck with wiring, tattooing, and cranial binding as seen in North American Indians.

Throughout the Bible there runs a theme of child murder and abuse. The Bible narrates the story of Moses. The Pharaoh ordered the slaying of children, first by ordering the mid-wives to kill the small ones; then, upon learning that they failed to carry out his orders, he commanded that all male children be cast into the river. Deuteronomy 21:18-21 clearly instructs a father to put a

3

wicked son to death. Proverb 23:14 states: "Thou shalt beat him with the rod, and shalt deliver his soul from hell."

Infanticide has been documented in almost every culture, both civilized and uncivilized, so much so that it can almost be considered a universal phenomenon.[4] Solomon states that infanticide has "been responsible for more child deaths than any other single cause in history, other than possibly bubonic plague."[5]

Infanticide has been practiced throughout history to limit family size, to relieve the financial burden of the unwed mother, and to assure crop growth by human sacrifice to the appropriate god or gods. Children have been slain, abandoned,, and sold into slavery by parents unable to support them, by mid-wives and wet nurses greedy for money, and by rulers fearing loss of their power. Other children, perhaps more fortunate than those murdered or exposed, were mutilated to increase their appeal as beggars or freak performers.[6]

But stronger even than the theme of sacrifice is the theme of the child as a nuisance to be abandoned or as a chattel to be used. Aristotle wrote: "The justice of a master or a father is different from that of a citizen, for a son or slave is property, and there can be no injustice to one's own property." Over the years Western education has made sporadic attempts to influence attitudes toward a more humane view of children, but a historical tradition of

4

viewing children as property of their parents persists.

Whipping children and youths has been the prerogative of teachers from the days of the early Greeks. Five thousand years ago there was a "man in charge of the whip" to punish boys upon the slightest pretext. In England and America teachers are pictured armed with the birch. The severity of punishment by schoolmasters led to Roger Ascham's writing of The Schoolmaster in the sixteenth century, in which he advocated love instead of fear as a motivating element in teaching children.[7] One nineteenth century schoolmaster who kept score of his disciplinary practices reported administering 911,527 strokes with a stick; 124,000 lashes with a whip; 136,715 slaps with his hand, and 1,115,800 boxes on the ear.[8]

Rousseau said that babies in their earliest days were often beaten to keep them quiet. In his introduction to "Emile", Rousseau stated that the usual treatment of babies seems to have been a calamitous mixture of mollycoddling and neglect.

The recurring theme of "Spare the rod and spoil the child" persists in child-rearing practices and is only currently being challenged by the emerging idea that children are persons with rights of their own for which society must take responsibility.

Lloyd DeMause described the following modes of child-rearing in Western culture:

Infanticide mode (Antiquity).

5

Parents resolved their anxieties about taking care of children by killing the child or by perpetrating severe abuse if the child were allowed to live.

A̲b̲a̲n̲d̲o̲n̲m̲e̲n̲t̲ m̲o̲d̲e̲ (Medieval). Parents who were unable to tolerate the care of children abandoned the child to others such as wetnurses, servants, or nannies, or perpetrated extreme emotional neglect if the child remained in their care.

A̲m̲b̲i̲v̲a̲l̲e̲n̲t̲ m̲o̲d̲e̲ (Renaissance). Parents with ambivalent feelings about child rearing continued to care for the child but expressed the ambivalence through projecting onto the child an evil nature and expressing overly ambivalent feelings of love and hate without rationale in the daily care of the child.

I̲n̲t̲r̲u̲s̲i̲v̲e̲ m̲o̲d̲e̲ (18th Century). Parents continued to relate more with the child (as in the ambivalent mode) but expressed the relationship through controls such as praying with the child or through discipline that used guilt rather than physical punishment.

S̲o̲c̲i̲a̲l̲i̲z̲i̲n̲g̲ m̲o̲d̲e̲ (19th Century to the present). Parents viewed the child as an individual who needs continuous training and guidance in order to become civilized. Parents at this stage have given up overt forms of abuse and use covert methods of manipulation,, guilt, and a detached quality of parenting to sustain long periods of contact with children whose increasing needs are too much for the parent to tolerate.

Helping mode (Current). This mode is based on the proposition that the child knows better than the parent what the child needs at each stage of life. This mode involves both parents fully in the child's daily life as they help the child with its expanding needs. The helping mode requires enormous time, energy, and emotional maturity on the part of both parents, especially in the first six years of the child's life, to help the child develop his or her full capacity for emotional and intellectual growth.[8]

After examining over two hundred statements of advice on child rearing prior to the eighteenth century, DeMause concluded that most approved of beating of children severely:

> Century after century of battered children grew up and in turn battered their own children. Public protest was rare. Even humanists and teachers who had a reputation for great gentleness, like Petrarch and Pestalozi, approved of beating children. Bethoven whipped his pupils with a knitting needle and sometimes bit them.[9]

In early agrarian society the idea that a child was a chattel of his parents was a functional, practical arrangement since the family's livelihood depended on the number of hands that tilled the soil and did chores. Later, with the advent of the Industrial Revolution, child labor became a valuable resource because it could be easily controlled and cheaply bought. More economic value was placed upon the child by society; the phenomenon became defined as one of "maltreatment of children." Charles Dickens wrote about the problems of children growing up in an industrialized society.10 Growing concern for the welfare of children led to legislation regulating the use of child labor and shortly afterwards came laws providing for compulsory education and school attendance.

Abandonment of unwanted children was prevalent during the nineteenth century in the United States. In 1873, 1,392 foundlings were left at the New York Foundling Asylum, and 122 infants were found dead in the streets, alleys, rivers, and elsewhere.

In the meantime, another problem had surfaced, one apparently distinct, psychologically and sociologically, from infanticide and abandonment. This was the phenomenon of deliberate physical abuse and neglect. America's first recorded case of child abuse that became a matter of intense public concern was in 1874. The classic case is "Mary Ellen", a child, beaten and starved, found by some concerned people chained to her bed. They quickly discovered there was no law on the books by which she could be rescued. The parents exercised their absolute right to bring up their child as they chose. A visiting nurse and a concerned church group appealed to the Society for the Protection of Cruelty to Animals on the grounds that Mary Ellen was a member of the animal kingdom, was being accorded worse treatment than to the lowest animal, and therefore qualified for the Society's protection. The Society agreed that her case fell under the laws governing the treatment of animals and had the child removed from her home. One year later, in 1875, a Society for the Prevention of Cruelty to Children was organized in New York.

As stated before, child abuse has been part of our culture through the years, but only recently (1960's) has the syndrome or pattern of abuse been identified and described in terms of an emerging understanding of the phenomenon through psychological and sociological principles. The battered-child syndrome was first described in 1860 by Ambroise Tordieu, a professor of legal medicine in Paris. He wrote a paper clinically describing injuries to children that appeared grossly inconsistent with the histories as given by the children's caretakers. He described thirty-two children battered to death by whipping and burning. The same year, Athol Johnson at the Hospital for Sick Children of London called attention to the frequency of repeated fractures in children. He attributed these to the rickety condition of bones, since rickets at that time was almost

9

universal among London children. In 1870, official London records reveal that among 3,926 children younger than five years of age who died by accident or violence that year, 202 were listed as manslaughter, 95 neglect, 18 exposure to cold--all obviously dead of child abuse.

During the close of the nineteenth century and well into the twentieth, children were being brought into hospitals by parents who told tales of bizarre accidents to explain their children's injuries. The advent of the x-ray machine brought an end to many unexplained injuries to children. In 1956, John Caffey, a specialist in pediatric radiology, was among the first to draw attention to certain heretofore unexplained injuries observed in children. He reported six infants having multiple fractures in the long bones and suffering from chronic subdural hematomas (bleeding between the brain and the skull). Caffey concluded that the "fractures appear to be of traumatic episodes and the causal mechanisms remain obscure."[12] Silverman in 1953 reached conclusions similar to those of Caffey and noted the "excellent prognosis of traumatic lesions compared with that of other diseases considered in the differential diagnosis."[13] In 1955, Woolley and Evans wrote an article suggesting the possibility that parents were responsible for the fractures and subdural hematomas and concluded that "it is difficult to avoid the overall conclusion that skeletal lesions having the appearance of fractures,, regardless

10

of history or injury or the presence or absence of intracranial bleeding, are due to the undesirable vectors of force."[14]

In 1962, there was a startling breakthrough contributed by Kempe of the University of Colorado School of Medicine. he coined a new term, "battered-child syndrome." In his article, "Child Abuse: The Pediatrician's Role in Child Advocacy and Preventive Pediatrics," Kempe describes the term "battered-child syndrome":

> When I saw child abuse between 1956 and 1958 in Denver, our house staff was unwilling to make this diagnosis. Initially I felt intellectual dismay at diagnosis such as "obscure bruising," "osteogenesis imperfecta tarda," "spontaneous subdural hematoma". When I served as a member of the program committee of the American Academy of Pediatrics in the late 1950's and became a chairman of that committee in 1960, I discovered that one prorogative of that position was to plan one plenary session. The rest of the committee agreed to a multidisciplinary group presentation of child abuse, provided that I came up with a title that would catch our membership's attention. That is how the emotive term, "the battered-child syndrome," was born.[15]

Kempe and his colleagues undertook a nationwide survey--the first of its

11

kind--of hospitals and law enforcement agencies in an attempt to determine how many cases of physical abuse were reported in the course of a year. The results were a total of 302 cases of the battered-child syndrome reported by seventy-one major hospitals. Thirty-three of these children had died, and eighty-five had sustained permanent brain damage.[16]

In the 1960's, the problem of the physically battered or severely maltreated child began to force its way into the public consciousness. Campaigns to enact child abuse laws in the states started to bring results, and today all states and the District of Columbia have child abuse reporting laws. A major objective of this legislation was to improve mechanisms for locating cases of child abuse and to assure protective services for the victims, their siblings, and their parents. A secondary purpose was to obtain a better understanding of the scope and nature of the phenomenon than was possible when only a few selected cases came to the notice of health, education, welfare, and law-enforcement authorities.

Congress held lengthy hearings on child abuse and neglect in 1973. It found that, despite the progress made, insufficient resource had been directed toward preventing, identifying, and treating the problem. In too many states, the reporting laws were merely "window dressing," providing for the collection of the collection of information but not for adequate services for the child and the family. Even the collection of information was hampered by the wide disparity in definitions of child abuse and neglect from state to state. And when provision was made for treatment, it was often woefully inadequate. Often a complex, multidisciplinary problem is treated through a single agency--understaffed and undertrained --to deal with the ramifications of child abuse and neglect. Furthermore, while the measures for treatment were found to be inadequate, the measures for prevention appeared virtually nonexistent.

By nearly a unanimous vote, Congress passed the Child Abuse Prevention and Treatment Act and the President signed it into law on January 31, 1974. The Act created the National Center of Child Abuse and Neglect as a focal point for federal efforts. Responsibility for the activities of the Center was assigned to the U.S. Department of Health, Education, and Welfare which, in turn, placed the Center within the Children's Bureau of the Office of Child Development.

The Center provides national leadership by conducting studies on abuse and neglect, awarding demonstration and research grants to seek new ways of identifying, diagnosing,, and preventing this nationwide problem, and by giving grants to states to enable them to increase and improve their child protective services.

As a result of this recent surge of interest, the problems of abused children are taking on a new phase in

13

our history. Why child abuse and neglect is such a monumental challenge for the schools has something to do with what the modern school has become. This will be discussed in the following chapter.

Definitions of Child Abuse
Abuse Legislation

Because of the inherent difficulty in the concept, the term "child abuse" continues to post many problems. It seems to this writer that we do not now have a satisfactory definition of child abuse and neglect. According to **Webster's Dictionary**, a definition is "a clear and exact statement of what something is."17 For example, most people would agree that a "table" is a piece of furniture consisting of a flat top set horizontally on some sort of support, usually legs. However, people do not agree on a definition of abuse or neglect.

Although it seems fair to say that traditional definitions as well as those now emerging a redesigned to help protect children from harm, this laudable purpose has not prevented these definitions from being controversial.

The definition an individual favors is historically linked to professional objectives. Researcher, physicians, social workers, protective workers, police, courts, and social planner all have somewhat different objectives. These differing objectives naturally color the definitions adopted.

Gil, professor of social policy at Brandeis University in Massachusetts, suggests that the definition of child abuse depends upon the purpose for which it is to be used.18 Medical practitioners engaged in the diagnosis and treatment of physically abusedchildren tend to use definitions based on physical or anatomical symptoms identifiable in their child patients. Mental health workers who are concerned with emotional abuse in addition to physical abuse prefer to broaden their definitions of child abuse to include psychological damage. Social workers, law enforcement authorities, and others whose interest extends beyond ;the victims of abuse to perpretators of abusive acts focus their definitions not only around observable, physical, and psychological consequences of abuse but also around behavioral and motivational characteristics of perpetrators. Finally, legislators and social-police specialists whose concern is the protection of all children against potentially injurious acts and conditions require comprehensive definitions which take account, not only of clinical, physical, and psychological aspects of child abuse, but also of cultural, social, economic, and political factors which presumably constitute the dynamic sources of this phenomenon.

The definition of child abuse and neglect in the Federal Child Abuse Prevention and Treatment Act (P.L. 93-247) is a good example of the difficulty with applying one definition to a variety of objectives. The Act defines child abuse and neglect as:

15

the physical or mental injury,
sexual abuse, negligent treatment,
or maltreatment of a child under
the ge of eighteen by a person who
is responsible for the child's
welfare under circumstances which
~~indicate that the child's welfare~~
~~under circumstances which~~ indicate
that the child's health or welfare
is harmed or threatened thereby.

This general and broad definition suits
research and demonstration activities
well enough, perhaps. Its lack of
specifications, however, has proven to
be disadvantageous to seeking to comply
with the Act's eligibility requirements
in order to receive grants in aid.
    Donald Kline feels that the above
definition has considerable appeal to
educators since it flows from a sense of
what children are, what they need, and
what they may become. Moreover, this
definition suggests change for improving
the lives of many vulnerable children
who are at risk, not only from abuse and
neglect but also from a wide variety of
socially sanctioned practices which
hinder or prohibit the full development
of each individual.
    The literature reflects a variety
of definitions which range between a
very narrow definition emphasizing
severe physical abuse; for example:

Children with significant physical
trauma unexplained by history or
admitted to by parents; repeated
unexplained trauma, and neglected
children who are seriously suspect-

16

ed of being physically abused and
who have siblings with documented
abuse.[19]

to a very broad definition emphasizing
maltreatment or circumstances in which a
child's health or welfare is threatened;
for example:

> Any act of commission or ommission
> by individuals, institutions, or
> society as a whole, and any condi-
> tion resulting from such acts or
> inaction, which deprive children or
> equal rights and liberties and/or
> interfere with their optimal
> development.[20]

The dilemma over general and therefore somewhat vague definitions versus
specific and therefore potentially over-
narrow definitions will be with us for
some time. Will we opt for specifications, listing precisely all those
actions that constitute child abuse and
neglect, and thus chance inadvertently
excluding actions that need to be
included? Or will we move toward
generality and thus risk misinterpreta-
tion that includes behaviors that should
not be included?

Those who believe that most children and families benefit from the child
protective intervention process
generally want to restrict the
definition.

Barton Schmitt, a pediatric consul-
tant to the National Center for the
Prevention and Treatment of Child Abuse
and Neglect, has identified specific

17

categories of abuse and neglect which help to clarify the intent of P.L. 93-247. These include physical abuse, nutritional deprivation, drug abuse, medical care neglect, sexual abuse, emotional abuse, severe hygiene neglect, and educational neglect.[21]

Based on an extensive review of the then available literature in the fields of law, medicine, social work, education, psychology, and the allied health fields, it appeared to Schmitt that only three attributes must be identified in every case in order for it to be considered abuse: The child (a) is under the age of eighteen, (b) is under the charge of a caretaker, and (c) has suffered nonaccidental physical or psychological injury.[22]

Every state now requires that suspected child abuse be reported but each state defines child abuse differently. Although the definitions do vary, all are a combination of one or more of the following four elements: (a) a nonaccidental physical injury,[23] (b) neglect,[24] (c) sexual abuse (rape, statutory rape, involuntary or voluntary deviate sexual intercourse, indecent assault, incest),[25] and (d) emotional abuse.[26]

The terminology used to describe abuse in most of the statutes follows the suggestions of Kempe and Helfer but is defined in legal terms as a situation:

> where a child . . . is suffering from serious physical injury or abuse inflicted upon him by other than accidental means or suffering ·

18

harm by reason of neglect, malnutrition, or sexual abuse, goes without necessary and basic physical care, including medical and dental care, or is growing up under conditions which threaten the physical and emotional survival of the child.[27]

Every state requires the reporting of nonaccidental physical injuries. Indiana, for example, defines the abused child as one who "has had physical injury inflicted upon him other than by accidental means."

A few states have defined child abuse to include all four elements. Connecticut defines child abuse as a child who:

has had physical injury or injuries inflicted upon him by other than accidental means or has injuries which are at variance with the history given of them, or is in a condition which is the result of maltreatment such as, but not limited to, malnutrition, sexual molestation, deprivation of necessities, emotinal maltreatment or cruel punishment.

The definition of most states fall between these two. A typical example is the Alabama law which defines abuse as "harm or threatened harm to a child's health or welfare. Harm or threatened harm to a child's health or welfare can occur through: Nonaccidental physical or mental injury; sexual abuse, or

19

attempted sexual abuse."

At the present time all fifty states have child abuse reporting laws, as do Washington, D.C., Puerto Rico, and the Virgin Islands. There are individual variations among the states but essentially abuse is legally defined and those who report such abuse in good faith are immune.

The Pennsylvania child abuse law requires physicians, school nurses, and school teachers to report immediately to the Public County Child Welfare Agency any child less than eighteen years of age who on examination "discloses evidence of gross physical neglect or injury not explained by the available medical history as being accidental in nature."[28] It also states that any other adult individual who has reason to believe that a child is suffering from neglect or injury may make a report. The law grants the reporter immunity from liability and requires the County Public Child Welfare Agency to investigate the report within forty-eight hours and to provide services for the protection of the child and preservation of the family unit.

In summary, questions still remain as to whether a definition of abuse should focus on harm to the child (acts of commission which are currently used in the narrow definition of child abuse) or on acts of ommission (which are currently used in the definition of neglect) of the parent or caretaker. What if a parent, intending to harm a child, fails to do so because his blow is ineffective or diverted? On the

20

other hand, is it abuse or neglect if a child is harmed--even grievously--but if, as far as can be determined, the parent did not intend to do harm? These are very real questions, especially in relation to cases where what appears to be "reasonable" corporal punishment leads to serious injury to a child.

These two divergent approaches reflect deeply held views on the nature and causes of child abuse and neglect. This writer believes that a satisfactory definition should incorporate these two concerns, but achieving a practicable mix between intent and actual harm will take much time and effort. Of course, as our understanding improves, we may come to see the entire matter quite differently from any present view. A generalized ethical view may make a specialized concern with children redundant.

In the end, it should be decided that the terms "child abuse" and "child neglect" encompass a wide range of behaviors with multiple causes, and these phenomena will be defined, not in simplistic, one-dimensional terms, but as sets of symptoms that occur in conjunction with each other and tend to characterize a situation.

Incidence of Abuse

Society has advanced from an era when children were simply property, to be handled, used, abused, killed or disposed of at the will of their parents, without anyone else having the right to question why such things were done. But many children today are still

21

victims, and because they are silent victims the magnitude of the problem cannot be known with certainty.

Experts admit that we really do not know how many children are victims of child abuse. Reliable information on the real incidence of child abuse is not available because of differences of opinion as to what incidents and situations are to be classified as child abuse, and also because of the nonpublic nation of many cases. There is some information on the number of legally reported cases. Yet, this information is of limited value since criteria and procedures for reporting vary widely across states and localities. Kempe and Helfer, two pioneers in this field, report that between 250 and 300 cases per million population are recorded in our larger cities each year.[29] Some authorities predict that for each reported case there is a minimum of twenty-five actual cases.[30] Gil reported that fewer than seven thousand cases occur annually,[31] while Light reported a figure of 1,175,000.[32] Based on 1975 data, Gelles estimated that between 1.4 million and 1.9 million children three to seventeen years of age and living with both parents were "vulnerable to physical injuries and violence." Owing to certain characteristics of the family:

The indicated number of children exposed to dangerous modes of violence in 1975 is a "low estimate" Gelles said because only intact families were surveyed (the risk of

22

abuse is believed to run higher in single parent families) and no children under three years were included. Thus he considers that 1.4 to 1.9 million estimate to be a base-line figure; if all children were included it would be much higher.[33]

Assumptions regarding the magnitude of the problem based on these or any other data two or more years old should be made with caution. It should be remembered that P.L. 93-247 was just becoming operational and the nation's social consciousness was just beginning to awaken to the seriousness of the problem.

Gelles further states:

If we can confine our definition to one that calls abuse only those cases where observable physical injury has been deliberately caused by a caretaker, then our incidence of abuse will be comparatively small. If on the other hand we apply the definition provided by the Child Abuse Prevention Act, the incidence of abuse may be as high as tens of millions of children (depending on what we call mental injury).[34]

What becomes clear at this point is that no one knows with certainty the extent of child abuse because the definition of abuse remains obscure.

Because of the apparent severe

23

underreporting, Gil employed a quite different strategy to estimate the national incidence of child abuse and neglect. The Gil data are currently the most comprehensive and in-depth set of reports available on individual cases, collected in a systematic manner across different states. (Reporting levels are known only for 1967 and 1968, the years of the nationwide surveys. Nearly 6,000 cases were reported in 1967 and over 6,600 in 1968.) With a grant from the Children's Bureau of the U.S. Department of Health, Education, and Welfare, Gil collected basic data on every case of physical child abuse reported through legal channels in the entire United States in 1967 and 1968. He then took a well-designed sample of these reports from the 1967 cases, and collected more detailed information. In October 1965, he commissioned the National Opinion Research Center (NORC) to question its standard survey of 1,520 respondents about whether "they personally knew families involved in incidents of child abuse resulting in physical injury during the 12 months preceding the interview." Since forty-five respondents, or 3 percent of the people, reported such familiarity, Gil suggested an upper bound of between 2.5 and just over four million cases of child abuse. He suggested that reported incidents involve nearly exclusively abuse of children in their own homes. He further states:

There are very few reports on child abuse in schools and children's institutions although this kind of

24

abuse is known to occur frequently all over the country. There are also no systematic records of the massive abuse and neglect of children due to inadequate medical care, inadequate education and substandard living conditions as can be found in migrant labor camps, in urban and rural slums, on Indian reservations, and in many other settings.35

It should be noted that these legally reported cases may constitute only a part of the total of child abuse incidents. Since abuse incidents tend to occur in the privacy of the home, all may not come to the attention of individuals or institutions who are required to report, and these individuals and institutions may not actually report all the cases known to them. The reporting may also be subject to some bias. Physicians in private practice may be less ready to report incidents than are those in public hospitals. Consequently, incidents from middle- and upper-class families may be underreported to a greater extent than cases from economically deprived families. Other factors, such as differences in administrative procedures, may also influence reporting.

In conclusion, Gil's survey dealt specifically with cases of physical abuse, and not with severe neglect, psychological, and sexual abuse. No comparable large-scale survey exists on child neglect or molestation.

Some statistics are available, but

due to the lack of uniformity in definitions and reluctance in reporting, no doubt there are inaccuracies in existing data. Since legislation was passed, the number of reported cases appears to have risen astronomically. However, a word of caution about interpretation is in order, since it seems unlikely that child abuse has increased so extensively. First of all, it should be noted that there is no basis to the frequently made claim that the incidence of child abuse has increased in recent years. One simply cannot talk about an increase or decrease of a phenomenon unless one has accurate counts of different periods in time. Such counts are not available, and, hence, there is no basis for comparison over time. What has increased in recent decades is the awareness of, the interest in, and the concern for this phenomenon. It seems that people are responding to educational efforts to observe more carefully, and with the elimination of the threat of law suits, feel more comfortable about reporting and bringing the problem to someone's attention. While then, we have evidence of increases in reporting levels, this increase seems largely due to improvements in the administration of reporting legislation and to growing awareness among physicians and others responsible for reporting.

Causes and Dynamics of Abuse

There is at present an extensive body of literature presenting various theories on the causes of child abuse.

26

In 1974, the National Institute of Mental Health published a bibliography listing 138 different references, and the research in this area continues to increase.

Some authors stress the psychological components;[36] others emphasize factors of social and economic stress, social isolation, high mobility, and unemployment.[37] Others give special attention to the interplay of mental, physical, and emotional stresses. Of the research done to date, Gil's comprehensive national survey is the most widely quoted. He suggests that it is a multidimensional phenomenon rather than a uniform one with one set of causal factors. Gil describes various dimensions of this phenomenon. The basic dimension on which all other factors are superimposed is the general culturally determined permissiveness toward the use of a measure of physical force in caretaker-child interaction, and the related absence of clear-cut legal prohibitions and sanction against this particular form of interpersonal violence. A permissive attitude toward acts of physical violence against children and a tendency to regard the perpetrators of such acts with tolerance were brought out in the opinions expressed by a majority of the respondents in the public opinion survey.

The next dimension of the phenomenon results from specific child-rearing traditions and practices of different social classes and ethnic and nationality groups, and the different

27

attitudes these groups hold toward physical force as an acceptable measure in rearing their children.

A third dimension of child abuse is determined by the environmental chance circumstances that may transform an "acceptable" disciplinary measure into an "unacceptable" outcome, resulting in relatively severe injury to the child. Fourth, there are many environmental stress factors which may weaken or even temporarily paralyze a person's ability to control his impulses and aggressive and destructive feeling toward physically powerless children. A vast array of environmental strains were precipitating elements in a large proportion of the incidents reported.

Underlying these pressures is the traditional acceptability of some amount of physical discipline. While discipline practices vary widely, there is generally understood to be a line somewhere over which parents do not step. In times of intense frustration or terrible personal pressures, parents sometimes do slide over that line.

Theorists have attempted to understand the reason for our society's attitude toward children and violence in order to account for the specifics that cause parents to act punitively enough to render serious physical and emotional damage to children. Kempe believes that the actions of parent-child batterers are based on modeling. That is, parents who were beaten excessively themselves come to be parents who beat their own children. He believes that parents of children who

28

are victims of the "battered-child syndrome" are mentally ill.

Gil suggests that the use of force on children stems from an inherent cultural belief that violence is an acceptable method of solving problems. He suggests that our society is "mentally ill" in terms of its approach to the use of violence.

This writer feels that there is a fairly clear-cut difference between what is discipline and what is abuse. The individual who disciplines has in mind the welfare and best interest and safety of the child. The one who abuses is suffering from a compulsion he cannot restrain. There is also a cut-off point, if not a precisely defined one, between the exasperation of the normal parent who occasionally feels himself letting go and then puts on the brakes, and the unguarded and generalized rage of the abusing parent. That point is the imposition of control, the act of stopping before the hostile emotion gets out of hand.

Fontana suggests that while there is in our culture a relationship between our child-rearing beliefs and the acts of violence against children, it is extremely difficult to accept the possible implication that the deliberate and sometimes ingenious torture inflicted by so many abusing child-care individuals is a natural extension, say, of the bottom-slapping disciplinary practices of nonabusing parents. He says that parents who question themselves in their attitudes, aware of their flashes of anger, who do not blame their children for their own abuse, who are concerned about their disciplinary modes and motivations, who wonder if their instinct to retaliate is normal, who pull themselves short and "count to ten" before "walloping" and then restrain themselves instead, are not the abusers.

In looking at the contemporary social context in which parents must rear their children, it is not that difficult to see why they may experience problems. The rapid pace of social change in this country, at least since World War II, has eroded many of our social support systems for parenting. For some, parenting has become a lonely, frustrating, and sometimes arduous task. Now that those informal processes for sharing responsibilities and know-how across generations and among family, friends, and neighbors have begun to dissolve in many places, it is realized that good parenting requires more than what is left of our instincts; it requires help and support and some practice.

> It is not really surprising, for example, though it is disturbing, that many parents in their twenties have little idea about what to do with a child. They probably have not been around small children since they gave up babysitting in high school--if indeed they ever did that. As our society is increasingly segregated by age and as our average family size shrinks, the chances for each succeeding

30

generation to pick up the care and understanding of children's development in any sort of informal setting diminish greatly.

Not being casually available to learn about child care, they are also not casually available to provide some relief to the parent. Without neighbors or grandparents or friends who will take the children for a few hours at a time, there is little relief from the frustrations or even the boredom that parents surely must feel at times.

Especially with the increasing population density of urban areas, to say nothing of the stress and strains of modern living, people are making increasing demands on their homes as total living environments—havens from the pressures. Children, of course, disrupt the quiet and neatness of that environment and hence have become a source of friction that in other times probably went unnoticed. As families become more fragmented, marriages less stable, the economy less predictable, it is easy to see how all these forces may combine to produce volatile situations in more and more homes.[38]

Lasch's description of society adds another dimension to why parents may experience problems:

In an age of diminishing

expectations, the Protestant virtues no longer excite enthusiasm. Inflation erodes investments and savings. Advertising undermines the horror of indebtedness, exhorting the consumer to buy now and pay later. As the future becomes menacing and uncertain, only fools put off until tomorrow the fun they can have today. A profound shift in our sense of time has transformed work habits, values, and the definition of success. Self-preservation has replaced self-improvement as the goal of earthly existence. In a lawless, violent, and unpredictable society, in which the normal conditions of everyday life come to resemble those formerly confined to the underworld, men live by their wits. They hope not so much to prosper as simply to survive, although survival itself increasingly demands a large income.[39]

The various forms of physical, social, intellectual, and emotional deviance and pathology that may afflict caretakers and/or children in their care constitut the final dimension of child abuse.

Steele, in a booklet "Working with Abusive Parents from a Psychiatric Point of View," states that the phenomenon of emotional neglect is far more prevalent in the life of parents who abuse children than in that of those who do not:

There is a lack of warm, sensitive interaction that is necessary for the child's optimal growth and development. A triad of insufficient empathic love and care, pre-mature and extreme demands for performance, and excessive criticism and physical punishment for failure constitutes the essence of the abuse syndrome.40

According to Steele, there are certain personality factors and traits prominent in abusive and neglectful parents. These include immaturity and association dependency; extremely low self-esteem and a sense of incompetence; difficulty in seeking pleasure and finding satisfaction in the adult world; social isolation and reluctance to seek help; significant misperceptions of the child; fear of spoiling children; a strong belief in the value of punishment; and serious lack of ability to be emphatically aware of the child's condition and needs. According to Steele, "the cumulative effect of this constellation of psychological charact-eristics makes it extremely difficult for the parent to succeed in meeting the demanding tasks of child care."

Child abuse is often referred to as "learned" or "conditioned" behavior. What a child learns, he repeats when he becomes an adult. If a child is reared in an abusive environment, he is likely, when he becomes a parent, to recreate that abusive environment. His child, in turn, learns the same kind of behavior, has children, and repeats the process. Thus, child abuse is often referred to as a "cycle."

To explain the interaction of the factors leading to abuse of children, one authority, Helfer, has created a diagram of the "World of Abnormal Rearing" (WAR), a cycle that manifests itself in an estimated 85 percent of all families who abuse their children.[41]

The WAR diagram shows a cycle of actions, each stemming from the previous one. The cycle begins with a conception that results in a wanted pregnancy. Unfortunately, however, the child is wanted for selfish or unusual reasons.

The child is born, therefore, into an atmosphere of unrealistic expectations. To cope with these expectations, the child learns role reversal, taking care of the parents in a sense instead of being cared for. The child becomes compliant, always doing something for others, which is abnormal behavior for children. When children are reared this way, they do not have a normal childhood and never learn to trust other people.

Distrust on the part of WAR children leads to isolation. Children find that they had better handle their own problems because they are unable to rely on other people when a problem arises. Isolation gives rise to an inability to cope, with the feeling that "I'm no good."

As WAR children reach adolescence, they find that their home and school experience with friends and parents are for the most part disastrous. Their ability to select friends who are helpful and supportive is poor because they have never attained the necessary skills to do so. This also places in jeopardy their ability to select a mate who can meet their needs. The mate who is selected is usually found to be unhelpful. The cycle is repeated as a new child is conceived in the hope that it will meet their needs.

What kind of parents might have the potential to abuse their children? In 1962, Merrill attempted a typology of personality types and identified three main clusters of characteristics: (a) parents who seem to have continual, pervasive feelings of hostility and aggressiveness; (b) parents whose personalities seem characterized by rigidity, compulsiveness, lack of warmth, and lack of reasonableness and pliability in thinking and believing; and (c) parents with strong feelings of passivity and dependence.[42]

What is common to most parents who have been studied retroactively to the problem of abuse is that there is a high incidence of divorce, separation, or unstable marriage marked by considerable marital conflict, and high mobility with many changes of addresses, unemployment, and alcoholism.[43]

Parents who fit "The World of Abnormal Rearing" share the common pattern of considering that their children exist to meet parental needs and expectations, and therefore they ingore or are unaware of their children's needs. These are parents who never experienced early childhood fulfillment or nurturing themselves and have no real preparation to pass on the "imprinting" or learned behavior to their children.

The potential to abuse a child is acquired over many years and has several causes. From the studies published, there seem to be at least four categories relating to the parents' potential for physical abuse. The first category concerns how the parents themselves were reared. Thirty to 60 percent of abusing parents say they were abused as children.[44] The second category is the inability of families and of the abusing parent in particular to use people to help them when they are "uptight" with their children. The third category describes unstable marital relationships. There is a high proportion of premarital conception, youthful marriage, forced marriages, and emotional or financial difficulties in the lives of abusing individuals.[45] How parents see the child is the last category. The parents who have the potential for abuse often expect the child to do things for them at a very early period of life. They often have an inappropriate expectation of the child's level of functioning and the child's capacity to respond at any given developmental age.

Kempe and his co-workers found some patterns of parent-child relationships characteristic of abusive parents, such as a high demand for performance and aggressive behavior toward the child when the demand is not met.[46]

Reference has been made to the

abusing parent or caretaker. Robert W.
Bensel, professor and director, Maternal
and Child Health, School of Public
Health, Department of Pediatrics,
University of Minnesota, suggests,
however, abuse and neglect of children,
particularly those of school age, occur
in other environments and institutions.

It is not only the individuals in
the community such as police and
teachers, who may perpetrate
neglect and abuse, but also the
very nature of the institutions,
through their philosophy and
organization, which creates an
environment in which neglect and
abuse may occur.

Brenton, quoting Kaplan's work on
teacher maladjustment, states that 25
percent of teachers "consider themselves
unhappy, worried, or dissatisfied."
Seventeen percent were "unusually
nervous" and 9 percent are "seriously
maladjusted" as indicated by
psychological testing.[47]
In summary, it can be said that no
single cause of child abuse can be
identified, although the notion long
held by most societies that a child is
the property of the parent and that
"there can be no injustice to one's own
property" has been one of the major
contributors to the problem throughout
history.
It can be argued that the problem
is only symptomatic of greater social
and economic problems. Poverty,
breakdown of the nuclear family, drug

and alcohol abuse, increasing mobility of individual family members and job-related work away from the home for extended periods of time, and cultural and ethnic differences are all associated with the physical abuse, neglect, sexual molestation, and psychological and emotional abuse of children.

Bronfenbrenner relates child abuse to the degree to which the human ecology enhances or undermines parenting.[48]

Garbarino, in a study designed to explore selected features of this ecological model, suggests that efforts be made to deal with support systems provided for mothers.[49] These efforts could include income supports to relieve stress, child-care services to provide relief from the pressures of the parenting role, and educational development opportunities for the parent. He believes that where the human ecology provides adequate support, child abuse is minimized; where support is inadequate and stress great, the "personality" and "cultural" factors cited by Gil are manifested in child abuse.

We come now to what appears to be the most salient conceptual issue in the child-abuse area: namely, whether child abuse is best conceptualized as a pathological phenomenon most appropriately understood in terms of the character traits or psychodynamics of individual parents, or whether it is most appropriately viewed as socio-cultural, ecological phenomenon, with the causes seen as residing in the

38

extremely stressful nature of the parent's ecological niche. In this latter view, special attention is given to the effects of poverty, alienation, and the lack of an effective social support system for the parenting function.

To determine whether child abuse is the result of individual pathology or societal pathology requires an understanding of the causes of abuse. The following may be described as those causes resulting from societal pathology:

1. Notion long held by society that a child is the property[50] of the parent and "there can be no injustice to one;s own property."
2. Culturally determined permissiveness toward use of physical[51] force, i.e., specific child-rearing traditions and practices.
3. Absence of clear-cut legal prohibitions and sanctions[52] against this particular form of interpersonal violence.
4. Environmental stress factors, i.e., unemployment, unstable marital relationships, poverty, etc.

The following may be described as those causes resulting from individual pathology:

1. Personality factors: (a) continual, pervasive feelings of hostility and aggressiveness which leads to excessive criticism and physical punishment for failure. (b) Immaturity with strong feelings of passivity and dependence; low self-esteem and a sense of incompe-

39

tence. (c) Rigidity, compulsiveness, lack of warmth or ability to
be emphatically aware of the
child's condition and needs. (d)
Lack of reasonableness and
pliability in thinking and belief
which leads to unrealistic
expectations.
2. "Learned" or "conditioned"
(modeling) behavior, i.e., parents
who were beaten excessively
themselves end up beating their own
children.
How this individual versus social
conceptual issue is resolved has real
implications for the social efforts that
are chosen to reduce the incidence of
abuse. If one commits oneself to the
individual psychological approach and
selects psychiatric intervention as the
treatment of choice, there are neither
enough mental health workers nor money
to treat all the adults guilty of child
abuse.

This writer feels that it is too
late to view child abuse totally from
the individual perspective. Concern
should be given to the social factors
that contribute to the incidence of
abuse. In the ultimate model for
explaining child abuse, the abuser will
be conceptualized as part of a family
that is embedded in the social,
economic, and political realities of its
ecology.

The complexity of the dynamics of
child abuse argued strongly for multidimensional solution strategies. A
continuum of intervention models ranging
from minimal to maximum levels of

involvement should be examined. Strategies must be matched to profiles of individual needs. Where economic stress is present along with marital instability and isolation, intensive resources will be necessary. When the basic problem is isolation, other strategies and fewer resources might be appropriate. While multiple solutions are often implemented on an ad hoc basis, rarely is evidence collected to support the effectiveness of one solution as compared to another for specific target groups. Yet this information is needed to guide future efforts. Global reports do not contribute to the systematic improvement of intervention strategies.

Finally, and perhaps most important, if one is to be effective in stopping the abuse of children, one needs to examine our society's value system and to reduce the acceptability of man's violence to man, of which child abuse is but one manifestation.

Sequelae of Abuse

An extensive review of the literature from the fields of medicine, law, social work, education, and psychology reveals only a few reports of the sequelae, or after effects, of child abuse beyond the immediate physical effects of the injuries. Only seven published reports were found regarding the sequelae of abuse and neglect among 415 articles reviewed as a prelude to research efforts[53] at Utah State University in Logan.

The earliest report of the sequelae

41

of physical abuse was made by Kempe and
Silverman in 1962.[54] Kempe and
Silverman drew subjects from the records
of 71 hospitals for a relatively large
sample of 302 cases. Of the 302 cases
examined, 85 had neurological damage and
33 of the subjects had died. In 1963,
Elmer reported on 50 cases in which 4
were retarded, 2 had neurological
damage, and 7 had physical defects.
Again, in 1976, Elmer and Gregg followed
up 20 cases to find 10 were retarded and
8 had emotional disturbance.

In 1970, Morse et al. reported on
21 cases drawn from hospital case
records and found 9 with retardation and
6 with emotional disturbance.[55] In the
same year, Gil did a nationwide survey
of 12,610 cases and found 1,639 who were
retarded and 378 who never attended
school.[56] In 1972, Martin followed up
42 cases to find 14 retarded, 18 with
neurological damage, and 16 with delayed
speech.[57] McRae, Ferguson, and Lederman
followed in 1973 with 34 cases to find
12 with retardation, 3 with emotional
disturbance and 3 with neurological
damage.[58] And in 1974, Martin reported
on a longitudinal follow-up of 58
children who were physically abused to
find a high incidence of growth and
neurological problems and impaired
emotional functioning.[59]

According to Martin, there is no
specific profile; however, three
factors are prominent consequences of
abuse:

1. Thirty-one percent of children 4.5
   years of age had significant

neurological damage, and in all cases, learning and emotional behavior was affected;

2. Children both neglected and abused suffered greater deficits in ego functioning, which makes viable the learning process; and

3. Abused children who had been removed from the home had greater difficulty in establishing object constancy and a sense of security. These are also necessary ingredients for children to be receptive and effectively active in the learning process.60

Kempe and Helfer assert that children denied normal developmental experience have greater difficulty in their abilities to make decisions, use others, trust, and become dependent on someone else.61 These are among the behaviors educators identify for determining school readiness.

After reviewing several studies, the lists of behaviors and characteristics begin to sound redundant. But, the information about the school-age child is so critical to the teacher's understanding and empathy of the abused child in the classroom that it cannot be over emphasized. Therefore, to serve as a summary, or develop a picture of the abused student, the following information is most significant. In school, abused children behave fearfully, are clinging, and aloof with peers. With the teacher, they oppose control, are manipulative, unresponsive to praise, and apathetic towards things most

43

children their age enjoy.[62]
They do relate quickly to adults, appearing very bright at first. However, this is deceptive, as it actually reflects the child's ability to anticipate others' expectations. These behaviors which were once strengths, and may have actually saved their life, are now weaknesses in the academic setting.

Hurly also concludes that children subjected to continual severely unpleasant, affective experiences are discouraged in investigating their environments, a condition which has an inhibiting effect on intelligence.[63] In another study, additional characteristics of an abused child have an adverse effect on learning were identified.[64] Primarily, these children had poor orientation and perceptual awareness of the environment. They were isolated, inhibited, immature, and had delayed speech development.

These characteristics resulting from abusive treatment are especially pertinent for classroom teachers to know if they are to be helpful agents. It should be noted that children frequently exhibit some aggression, shyness, disruptive, or other behaviors indicative of temporary problems. This does not necessarily mean they are being abused.

In addition, consideration must be given to which "needs" ought to be met by the schools. Besides physiological needs,, mental health needs, and social- ization needs there are many other needs which, if they were all to be satisfied by schools, would mean teachers would

44

have to take complete charge of a child. Schools are usually thought to have a primarily educational function. It may be difficult to see how this function can remain a primary one if schools take responsibility for looking after a child as parents, doctors, group leaders, and so on are accustomed to do.

The satisfaction of basic physiological needs is a necessary precondition of educability. Teachers ought to be aware that some children may suffer severe deprivation in these respects in order that the teacher may refer the children to those qualified to provide the necessary treatment.

---

[1]Commonwealth of Pennsylvania, Act 91, August 14, 1967.

[2]Radbill, "A History of Child Abuse and Infanticide," in The Battered Child, eds. R. Helfer and C. H. Kempe (Illinois: University of Chicago Press, 1974).

[3]Radbill, "A History of Child Abuse and Infanticide," in Helfer and Kempe.

[4]D. Baken, Slaughter of the Innocents: A Study of the Battered Child Phenomenon (Boston: Beacon Press, 1972).

[5]T. Solomon, "History and Demography of Child Abuse," Pediatrics 51, no. 2 (1973): 773-76.

[6]Education Commission of the States, Child Abuse and Neglect: The Problem and Its Management, Vol. 1, Publ. No. (OHD) 75-20073 (Washington, D.C.: U.S. Department of Health,

Education, and Welfare, 1976).

[7]S. Radbill, "A History of Child Abuse and Infanticide," in Violence in the Family, eds. S. Steinmertz and M. Strauss (New York:L Dodd, Mead & Co., 1973)

[8]V. Fontana, The Maltreated Child: The Maltreatment Syndrome in Children, 2nd ed. (Springfield Ill.: Charles C. Thomas Publisher, 1971).

[9]L. DeMause, "Our Forebearers Made Childhood a Nightmare," Psychology Today, 119755, pp. 85-88.

[10]B. Gross and R. Gross, The Children's Rights Movement (New York: Anchor/Doubleday, 1977), p. 29.

[11]Solomon, "History and Demography of Child Abuse," pp. 773-76.

[12]J. Caffey, "Multiple Fractures in the Long Bones of Infants Suffering from Chronic Subdural Hematoma," American Journal of Roetgenology 56 (1946): 163-67.

[13]F. Silverman, "The Roetgen Manifestations of Unrecognized Skeletal Trauma in Infants," American Journal of Roentgenology 69 (1953): 413-27.

[14]P. Woolley and W. Evans, "Significance of Skeletal Lesions in Infants Resembling Those of Traumatic Origin,: Journal of American Medical Association 158 (1955): 539-43.

[15]C. H. Kempe, "Child Abuse: The Pediatrician's Role in Child Advocacy and Preventive Pediatrics," American Journal of Diseases of Children 132 (1978): 255-60.

[16]Ibid., pp. 105-12.

[17]Webester's Seventh New Collegiate Dictionary (Springfield, Mass.: G. & C.

46

Merriam Co., 1963).

[18]D. Gil, Testimony of Gil, Hearings of the U.S. Senate Subcommittee on Children and Youth, "Child Abuse Prevention Act," 8. 1191, 93rd Cong., 1st sess., March 1973.

[19]H. Martin, "The Child and His Development," in Helping the Battered Child and His Family, eds. C. H. Kempe and R. Helfer (Philadelphia: J. B. Lippincott, 1972).

[20]Gil, Testimony.

[21]B. Schmitt, "What Teachers Need to Know About Child Abuse and Neglect," Childhood Education 52, no. 2 (1975): 58-62

[22]Schmitt, "What Teachers Need to Know About Child Abuse and Neglect," pp. 58-62

[23]B. Schmitt and C. H. Kempe, "The Pediatrician's Role in Child Abuse and Neglect,: Current Problems in Pediatrics 52, no. 2 (1975): 58-62.

[24]M. Wald, "State Intervention on Behalf of Neglected Children,: Stanford Law Review 28 (1976): 625-706.

[25]S. Sgroi, "Sexual Molestation of Children: The Last Frontier in Child Abuse," Children Today 4 (1975): 18-24.

[26]"Emotional Neglect in Connecticut," Connecticut Law Review 5 (1969): 100ff

[27]C. H. Kempe and R. Helfer, eds. Helping the Battered Child and His Family (Philadelphia: J. B. Lippincott, 1972)

[28]Commonwealth of Pennsylvania, Act 91, August 14, 1967.

[29]Kempe and Helfer, Helping the Battered Child and His Family, p. xiii.

47

[30] Ibid., p. 106.
[31] D. Gil, "What Can Schools Do About Child Abuse?" American Education 5 no. 4 (1969): 2-5.
[32] R. Light, "Abused and Neglected Children in America," Harvard Educational Review 43 (1973): 556-98.
[33] R. Gelles, "The Social Construction of Child Abuse," American Journal of Orthopsychiatry 45, no. 3 (1975): 365.
[34] Ibid.
[35] D. Gil, Violence Against Children (Cambridge, Mass.: Harvard University Press, 1970).
[36] C. H. Kempe and F. Silverman, "The Battered Child Syndrome," Journal of the American Medical Association 181 (1962): 17-24; B. Steele and C. Pollock, "Discussion," in The Battered Child, eds. R. Helfer and C. H. Kempe (Illinois: University of Chicago Press, 1964); V. Fontana, Somewhere a Child Is Crying: Maltreatment, Causes and Prevention (New York: Macmillan Publishing Co., 1973); B. Melnick and J. Jurley, "Distinctive Personality Attributes of Child-Abusing Mothers," Journal of Consulting and Clinical Psychology 33 (1969): 746-49.
[37] E. Elmer, "Abused Young Children Seen in Hospitals," Social Case Work 4 (1960): 98-102; L. Young, Wednesday's Children: A Study of Child Neglect and Abuse (New York: McGraw-Hill Book Co., 1964)
[38] Proceedings of the First National Conference on Child Abuse and Neglect, Publ. No. (OHD) 77030094 (Washington, D.C.: Department of Health, Education,

and Welfare, 1976).

[39] C. Lasch, The Culture of Narcissism (New York: W. W. Norton & Co., 1978).

[40] Education Commission of the States, Child Abuse and Neglect.

[41] R. Helfer, The Diagnostic Process and Treatment Programs, Publ. No. (OHD) 75-79 (Washington, D.C.: U.S. Department of Health, Education, and Welfare, 1974), p. 26.

[42] J. Spinetta and D. Rigler, "The Child Abusing Parent: A Psychological Review,; Psychological Bulletin 77, no. 4 (1972): 296-304.

[43] Kempe and Silverman, "The Battered Child Syndrome," pp. 17-24.

[44] R. Helfer, "The Etiology of Child Abuse," Pediatric Symposium on Child Abuse 51, no. 2 (1973): 777-79.

[45] Ibid.

[46] C. Pollock and B. Steele, "A Therapeutic Approach to Parents," in Helping the Battered Child and His Family, eds. C. H. Kempe and R. Helfer (Illinois: University of Chicago Press, 1968)

[47] M. Brenton, "Trouble Teachers Whose Behavior Disturbs Our Kids," Today's Health 17 (1971).

[48] U. Bronfenbrenner, Is Early Intervention Effective? (Washington, D.C.: Office of Child Development, 1966)

[49] G. Garbarino, Helping the Battered Child and His Family (Illinois: University of Chicago Press, 1968)

[50] See Chapter I, "Historical Perspective of Child Abuse and Child-

Rearing Practices."
[51]See Chapter I, "Historical Perspective of Child Abuse and Child-Rearing Practices."
[52]See Chapter III, "Corporal Punishment and the School."
[53]D. Kline and J. Christianson, "Educational and Psychological Problems of Abused Children," final report, Contract No.G00-75-00352, Utah State University, Logan, 1975.
[54]Kempe and Silverman, "The Battered Child Syndrome," pp. 17-24.
[55]C. Morse et al., "A Three Year Follow-Up Study of Abused and neglected Children," American Journal of Diseases of Children 120 (1970): 439-46.
[56]D. Gil, "Violence Against Children," Journal of Marriage and the Family 33 (1971): 637-48.
[57]Martin, "The Child and His Development," in Kempe and Helfer.
[58]K. McRae et al., "The Battered Child Syndrome," Canadian Medical Association Journal 108 (1973): 859-66.
[59]H. Martin et al., "The Development of Abused Children," in Advances in Pediatrics, ed. S. Irving (Illinois: Chicago Year Book Medical Publishers, 1974).
[60]Martin et al., "The Development of Abused Children," in Irving.
[61]C. H. Kempe and R. Helfer, eds., Helping the Battered Child and His Family (Philadelphia: J. B. Lippincott, 1972)
[62]Martin, "The Child and His Development," in Kempe and Helfer.
[63]J. Hurly, "Parental Acceptance-Rejection and Children's Intelligence,"

50

in Readings in the Psychology of Parent-Child Relations, ed. G. Medinnus (New York: Wiley, 1967).

64 E. Rubin, C. Simpson, and M. Betroen, Emotionally Handicapped Children in the Elementary School, (Detroit: Wayne State University Press, 1966).

CHAPTER 2

THE ROLL OF THE SCHOOL AND THE

EDUCATOR IN CHILD ABUSE AND NEGLECT

Reasons for Involvement of the School and the Educator in the Problem of Child Abuse and Neglect

Until recently, child abuse and neglect was not thought to be a concern of the schools. Much of the literature prior to Gil's report strongly suggested that abused and neglected children were of preschool age.[1] In 1969, however, Gil reported that 47.6 percent of the reported abuse cases concerned children of school age. And more recently, Lebsack, reporting on the highlights of data collected by the Children's Division of American Humane Association's National Clearinghouse on Child

Abuse and Neglect, shows 43.13 percent of all cases were from "public and private social agencies, schools and school personnel, law enforcement, courts, and hotlines."[2] The data are supportive of Gil's 1969 findings and tend to confirm the call of many for significantly greater involvement of the schools in the area of identification of child abuse.[3]

The school is in an advantageous position to detect abuse, note repeated abuse, and learn of the child's family background. Once in school, a child's appearance and behavior are observed regularly by a number of people.

There is sufficient evidence to indicate that when teacher have been trained, they become effective participants in the referral process. After teachers were informed of their legal responsibilities in Syracuse, New York, the school system became "the greatest single source of uncovering these problems (abuse) in Syracuse."[4] Project PROTECTION, a federally funded project in Montgomery County, Maryland, has brought a steady increase in child abuse referrals.[5] In the bedford-stuyvesant area of Brooklyn, the SCAN (School, Children--Abused and Neglected) project produced over 1700 referrals in its first months of operation. In the first twenty-five days of operation, a team in the Jefferson County public schools in Colorado reported twenty-two cases.[6] In all instances, teachers were involved in reporting suspected cases of abuse.

The **Guidelines for Schools**

53

published by the American Humane Association in Denver expressed the following philosophy:

> Because schools are concerned with the whole child, seeking help for the child in trouble is quite compatible with educational objectives. The emotional impact of serious neglect and abuse often sets up blocks which inhibit and create learning disabilities for the child victim.

American educational systems and educational personnel can no longer avoid involvement in the growing problem of child abuse and neglect. History records that when society becomes sufficiently aware of a major social concern, it turns to the schools for solutions, e.g., desegregation and drug abuse. The schools are the one institution that touches the lives of many adults and has more contact over longer periods of time than any other social structure except for the home. Child abuse and neglect have been a concern of social work and of medicine for many years, but only recently has education been involved. Why this tragedy is such a monumental challenge for the schools has something to do with what the modern school has become.

The school has become more than a vehicle for cognitive improvement and development. School health personnel deal with many of the health problems of the individual child.[7]

The hot lunch program seeks to

54

ensure that some minimal level of nutritional adequacy is assured to each child. School counselors and psychologists assess not only the cognitive skills and abilities of the child but also vocational preferences and personal problems. Special education teachers make certain that exceptional children have specially tailored curricula and experience to overcome or make the best of handicapping situations. So many things that used to be ignored or thought impossible to deal with are today seen as the routine responsibility of the school. So many things that used to be the responsibility of the natural family are today also the responsibility of the school, among many other institutions.

To see how this has developed and what its implications are requires a look at the not too distant past.

The protection and development of the child have for all past ages been primary concerns of the nuclear or natural family and the extended family. The models of how to rear and care for children were passed by visible example for generation to generation, and usually two generations (parents and grandparents) as well as other family members were engaged in these tasks.

Pioneer and rural Americans depended on family and extended family care for the protection and care of the child. Not only were the mother and father engaged in caring for the child, but brothers and sisters, grandparents, and aunts had special roles that provided natural support mechanisms to promote the physical, psychological, and social development of the child until adulthood.

Child care and protection have always been the responsibility of the natural family in this society. When abuse and neglect occurred, often little was done; nor was it even felt that anyone other than the natural parents had any responsibility to the child.

In family farm settings, young children were important participants in contributing to the economic activity of the family; unit. Families included children and grandparents, and the routine of living involved everyone in a daily tempo of shared activity. The family was a large organic group that required cooperation and participation of all family members.

Industrialization and postindustrialized era greatly changed the role of the natural family and sharply reduced the prevalence of extended family units. Through this process, issues associated with the care and protection of the child also changed. Young children in early industrialization became valuable economic commodities that could perform certain assembly tasks, and the use of child labor spread with industrialization. The exploitation of children by their parents led to legislation protecting the rights of children, formerly the domain of the family.

The first accommodation of the family to industrialization is for the man to enter the wage economy labor force and for the woman to stay at home to manage household activities, including the care of children remaining at home. Thus, in the United States by the 1950's, the rural farm family had been replaced as the typical social unit by the wage economy family, with the male as the external income provider and usually the; most influential family member in setting goals for the family and in disciplining children. The female, on the other hand, had the responsibility of running the household and nurturing the young child. This was the model of family living to which all aspired, and good child care was something assumed to occur naturally with loving parents.

Postindustrialization developments have, however, altered this model, largely through the increased participation of women in the work force, the declining ability of the man solely to provide sufficient income, and the emphasis upon new and often conflicting roles for women as stressed through various women's movements. Today, then, the typical natural family consists of parents and children. Grandparents or other family members do not live in the household and are, at best, occasional visitors. The development and protection of the children are the responsibility of the parents, and other family members or neighbors are seen as having highly questionable authority or responsibility for the children.

As the natural family has been reduced in its size and scope and its responsibility in child rearing, formal institutions have been created to handle roles and responsibilities previously belonging to the natural family.

In one way, the postindustrialized United States is a world of institutions and individuals. The world of the preindustrialized United States was a world of families and individuals. Today, however, we are born in an institution, the hospital; socialized in an institution, the school; earn our economic livelihood in an institution, the factory or office; and die in an institution, the nursing home or hospital.

When institutions fail or when the natural family fails in the care of the child, another institution is there to intervene. This institution, Protective Services, a unit of the Department of Public Welfare, has the responsibility to protect the child when the family does not provide care and protection. Protective Services may act to treat the family to improve its functioning, remove the child for placement with another family or institution, or remove the child for a period of time while awaiting improvement of the family situation and at some subsequent time return the child.

In this world of institutions, then, many major functions that were largely or solely the responsibility of the natural family now lie with professionals and institutions. The process on the last thirty years has extended the professional model in many areas of the health, education, and emotional well-being of the child and consequently reduced the degree to which the natural family is responsible for the development and protection of the child.

Lasch feels that the school has assumed many of the training functions formerly carried out by family, including manual training, household arts, instruction in manners and morals, and sex education.[8]

The modern secondary school in fact, has been called upon to play an increasingly larger role in the education of American youth. THe years since the end of World War II have witnessed an intensification of an old conflict: postwar debates over "life adjustment education" as contrasted with the academic curriculum. John Dewey hoped that a new synthesis of educational theory would resolve certain dualisms in educational thought between vocation and culture, interest and discipline, activity and subject matter, and the child and society could be harmonized within a new educational framework. Then, he believed, would a democracy reap the benefits promised by a new age of science.[9]

Schools have a history of involvement not only with most dimensions of the student's life but also with the family through groups such as the PTA. It is clear, however, that American education has been slow to become involved in child abuse and neglect. The Education Commission of the States' Child Abuse and Neglect Project suggests several reasons for this: A primary reason is the particular nature of the problem itself. The complex and emotional nature of child abuse ;makes ;it difficult to understand. Educators are apprehensive about taking on another major social problem, especially when education is under criticism for failing to prepare people in basic skills. A major difficulty in the perception that child abuse is a welfare problem. Through legislative mandate, departments of social welfare throughout the United States have been charged and challenged with carrying out the public's concern for the welfare of children, while schools have been charged with the education of children. Finally, many people, including educators, are reluctant to become involved in what they feel are legal problems.

Recent legislative trends have left educators with only two basic alternatives: to develop policies and programs dealing with the problem of child abuse and neglect or to wait until policies are imposed through legislative or funding requirements.[10] In short, education must act or react.

An example of the legislative and funding requirements already imposed is the Child Abuse Prevention and Treatment Act (P.L. 93-247). This Act illustrates the imminence of education's choice to act or react.

To qualify for funding under the Act, a state or its political subdivisions must meet several specific requirements. At least three of the requirements in the existing legislation directly involve education:

1. The state must have administrative procedures, trained personnel, training procedures, institutional and other facilities, and multidisciplinary programs and services sufficient to assure that child abuse and neglect are reported.
2. The state must provide for cooperation among law enforcement officials, courts of competent jurisdiction, and all appropriate state agencies providing human services for the prevention, treatment, and identification of child abuse and neglect.
3. The state must provide for public dissemination of information on child abuse and neglect, as well as list facilities ;and prevention and treatment methods available to combat this problem.

Another indicator of the increasing demand of society that schools become involved is seen in the rules and regulations of state and federal agencies. Personnel engaged in the operation of Head Start programs, for example, are required by federal regulation to report child abuse and neglect. Failure to comply with a federal regulation carries the threat of loss of funds for the program.

School Policies and Reporting Procedures

There are thirty-seven states that currently name schools and/or school personnel among those specifically obligated to report suspected cases of

child abuse and neglect11 The balance
of the statutes identify personnel
serving in specified institutions or
indicate that "any person" suspecting
child abuse and neglect shall report.
Only Oklahoma makes no provision in the
statutes to provide immunity from civil
and criminal liability for those who
report in good faith.

In spite of the fact that all
states have child abuse and neglect
reporting laws, few schools have
established policies and procedures
under which the employees of the school
shall report.

According to the Education
Commission of the States' Report No. 85,
84 percent of the state departments of
education, 56 percent of the largest
school districts in each state, and 90
percent of the largest private schools
in each state have no policies regarding
the reporting of child abuse and
neglect.

The guidelines that follow are
practical suggestions to help education
policymakers develop and implement
effective policies suitable to their
particular circumstances and state laws.
They were developed by a task force of
the Education Commission of the States'
Child Abuse and Neglect Project:

1. Since all states require or
   encourage school personnel to
   report suspected cases, every
   school system should adopt and
   issue to all school personnel and
   the constituents of the district a
   child abuse and neglect policy,

particularly a policy on reporting.
2. The adopted policy should inform school personnel of their legal and professional obligations regarding child abuse and neglect.
3. The policy should inform all school personnel of immunities from civil and criminal liability provided in state laws when the report is made in good faith.[12]

One of the problems among school personnel is their lack of knowledge of the characteristics of child abuse. A review by Kline and Hopper, of 475 articles and 20 books discussing child abuse, revealed 53 articles referring to the need for teacher and school involvement. Few of those appeared in journals that school personnel might be expected to read; and even then, the references were general and brief.[13] A few articles in educational journals advised caution and delay in reporting until such time as the school is certain that the child is being abused.[14] This would seem to discourage early reporting which is recognized as the major route through which this phenomenon is recognized and treated.[15]

There are both legal and professional reasons for school personnel to be concerned about the phenomenon of child abuse. Teachers are professionals who have been trained as observers of child growth and development and are aware of behaviors that interfere with academic achievement. They have a professional responsibility to observe behaviors that interfere with a child's academic success and seek the assistance of other professionals whenever they suspect a case of child abuse and neglect. Abuse and neglect are seldom isolated occurrences, and usually abusive and neglectful behaviors recur both in frequency and severity.[16]

The teacher must search for factors that might place a child at risk. In the case of exceptional children, the risk index in high. Whether or not parents admit it, the exceptional child usually fails to match parental expectations of what that child should or could be. No matter how well the parent may cope, the problem of accepting that this child is less than perfect -- less than what was wished for, anticipated, or expected -- is a constant burden for a family to carry.

In one study, it was found that 27 percent of the children adjudged abused or neglected were subsequently enrolled in special education classes.[17] It was also determined that these children exhibited behaviors indicative of psychological problems; they were fearful, shy, immature, withdrawn, depressed, aggressive, destructive, or excessively absent from school, or they engaged in stealing behaviors.

While no one would suggest that all children in special education or all children who exhibit behaviors indicative of psychological problems are abused and neglected, school personnel cannot discard the possible diagnosis of abuse and/or neglect for some of these cases if they are to represent themselves as professionals.

The child win congenital defects is also at risk, and many exceptional children have associated congenital abnormalities or defects. Smith and Hanson studied 124 abused children admitted to an emergency room and found that u7.5 percent had obvious severe congenital defects compared to a 1.75 percent incidence of anomalies in children admitted for emergency care not related to battering.18 Thus, children who have congenital defects are about six times as likely to be abused as those who do not.

Studies done by Oates and Kent found that abused and neglected children tended to be substantially below grade level in reading, math, and spelling.[19]

In view of current knowledge about the coexistence of educational and psychological problems with child abuse and neglect, the professional responsibilities become increasingly apparent.

Educators can develop an awareness of abused children in the school by becoming knowledgeable about the characteristics of child abuse and neglect.

The educator's legal role in cases of child abuse is generally limited to identification. In most states, teachers are mandated to report suspected child abuse and failure to report can theoretically result in criminal or civil liability. (Every state provided immunity from civil and criminal liability if the report of suspected child abuse is made in good faith -- an honest belief by the reporter that the child was abused.

There are two types of liability:

criminal and civil. Justification for civil liability arises when one citizen's rights are violated by another. Unlike criminal liability, the wrong is viewed as being committed against one citizen, not all of society. The citizen who has been wronged may file suit for compensation for personal injury in the form of a monetary award. It may be argued, for example, that when a teacher identifies suspected child abuse but decided not to report, the teacher may have a civil suit brought against her. In other words, a teacher who is negligent in performing her duties may be held civilly liable. Legal considerations aside, educators committed to the well-being of their students have a professional and moral duty to report. The process of protecting a child's safety in cases of child abuse involves three steps: identification, investigation, and intervention. Until there is some form of identification, there can be no investigation and no intervention. The teacher's legal responsibility is to report suspected child abuse. Responsibility for the investigation, for developing a definitive diagnosis and prognosis, and for providing treatment has been specifically assigned to other professionals.

Primary Prevention

The concept of primary prevention of child abuse, neglect, and sexual molestation involves attempts to reach the general population in a sustained effort to attack the causes of the problem. Secondary and tertiary prevention (identification and treatment after the fact) involve efforts to prevent the recurrence of problems in any given case.

McAffee and Nedier have provided the following rationale for the introduction of parent education on a massive basis in the schools.[20] Their rationale is based on the fact that society has been changing rapidly and as a result so have families. According to McAffee and Nedier, some of the indicators of social change are:

1. 60% of American families are metropolitan residents.
2. Many families are having fewer children. The average household size in 1974 was 2.97 persons. In 1973 the live birth rate in the United States was the lowest in history.
3. Many families move frequently, both short and long distances.
4. The number of single-parent families is increasing, both because of divorce and because of parents never married.
5. Over 50% of all women are in the labor force; over 30% of all women with children under 6 work out of the home.
6. Stable, multi-age communities and the extended family have been replaced by communities linked by interests, age and income level.
7. Child bearing among young adolescents seems to be increasing. In our society these young people

have had little or no exposure to youngchildren and even less in how to rear children.[21]

The theory that abused children learn abusive parenting attitudes and child-rearing practices and, in turn, upon becoming parents rear their children based on these learned attitudes and practices is important when related to primary prevention.

The school system's adult education program could offer courses in parenting, child rearing, and family life, including such topics as parent-child relationships and constructive methods of discipline. One may question whether it is appropriate for government to intervene in the family through education and social institutions by offering programs of parent education. The right of parents to raise their children in a manner consistent with their attitudes, values, and beliefs has rarely been questioned in this country. With the majority of this nation's population will agree that all children should be protected against abusive treatment, strategies for prevention can become an emotional arena of debate. To avoid entanglement and arguments, goals and objectives must clearly address techniques for strengthening the family. Educational content must be determined by professionals and by voluntary representatives or the parents themselves. Control must be shared by representatives of both groups if these programs are to have credibility and acceptance as viable

68

strategies.

The PTA could regularly devote meetings to discussions of child abuse and neglect, inviting members of the child protective service, a local pediatrician, or other professionals to speak on various aspects of the problem. Other meetings could focus on problems of child rearing.

Another focus for preventive action involves the curriculum in family life education, child development, sex education, interpersonal relations and other such courses. Units of study could be inserted at appropriate levels from kindergarten through twelfth grade on parental responsibilities, methods of disciplining children, coping with family crisis, the practical and emotional aspects of child care, and ways of dealing with anger and frustration. The goal of the curriculum would be to prepare children to become responsible adults and, more specifically, to become responsible parents.

In summary, while the schools should not be expected to provide solutions to all of the social, economic, and cultural variables that clearly impinge upon the environments where child abuse and neglect appear to be most prevalent, they can provide some measure of primary prevention through instruction on appropriate parenting behaviors and knowledge of child growth and development. They can also provide a substantial measure of secondary prevention by identifying abused and neglected children at an early stage and

soliciting the assistance of other
institutions and agencies in preventing
the recurrence of abusive and neglectful
behaviors on the part of parents.

That American education has not
been involved in the eradication of
child abuse and neglect has been well
documented. Education, however, can
play an important role. Schools can
initiate appropriate agency services,
and they have a significant contribution
to make to treatment services through
agency coordination. Schools, if not
universally respected, are at last
accepted as a prime influence, perhaps
next only to the family, in the child's
life. Just as the role of the school in
educating children in not limited to the
teaching of textbook facts, the school's
role in the management of child abuse
and neglect is not limited to reporting.
Identification of the problem and the
reporting of suspected cases are, of
course, essential. But many schools
have the resources and the motivation to
go beyond these basic responsibilities.

It should be noted that the
involvement of schools in the
identification and referral of abused
children creates a need for more social
workers, counselors, psychologists, and
nurses. Given this perspective, one
must keep in mind that the main business
of the family and the school is to
influence directly the formation and
growth of attitudes and dispositions,
emotional, intellectual, and moral.

Taking into consideration the
historical conditions in which the
modern educational system developed,

70

this writer concludes that the role of the school in the area of child abuse and neglect will ultimately be determined by the educational philosophy of its administrator. Principals must decide whether it is the social function of the school to perpetuate existing conditions or to take part in their transformation.

---

[1]Gil, "What Schools Can Do About Child Abuse," pp. 2-5.

[2]J. Lebsack, Highlights of 1974 National Data (Denver, CO: National Clearinghouse on Child Abuse and Neglect, Children's Division,American Human Association, 1976).

[3]F. Ferro, "Combating Child Abuse and Neglect," Children Today 4 (1975); B. Shanas, "Child Abuse: A Killer Teachers Can Help Control," Phi Beta Kappa 61 (1975): 479-82; Education Commission of the States, Child Abuse and Neglect Project, "Educational Policies and Practices Regarding Child Abuse and Neglect and Recommendations for Policy Development," Report No. 85, Denver, CO, April 1976.

[4]C. Murdock, "The Abused Child and the School System," American and Public Health, 1970, pp. 106-09.

[5]D. Broadhurst, Project Protection: A School Program to Detect and Prevent Child Abuse and Neglect," Children Today, 1975, pp. 22-25.

[6]Education Commission of the States, "Educational Policies and Practices Regarding Child Abuse and

Neglect and Recommendations for Policy Development."
[7]Pennsylvania School Law, Section 1402, Health Services, 1976:
"Each child of school age shall be given by methods established by the Advisory Health Board, (1) a vision test, (2) a hearing test, (3) a measurement of height and weight, (4) tests for tuberculosis under medical supervision, and (5) such other tests as the Advisor Health Board may deem advisable to protect the health of the child.

All teachers shall report to the school nurse or school doctor any unusual behavior, changes in scholastic achievement, which may indicate impairment of a child's health. The nurse or doctor or school dentist may, upon referral by the teacher or on his own intiative, advise a child's parent or guardian of the apparent need for a special medical or dental examination. If a parent or guardian fails to report the results to the nurse or school doctor, the nurse or school doctor shall arrange a special medical examination for the child.

The school physician of each district or joint board shall make a medical examination and a comprehensive appraisal of the health of every child of school age upon entry into school in the Commonwealth, while in sixth grade, and while in eleventh grade."
[8]Lasch, The Culture of Narcissism,

pp.454-55.
[9]J. Dewey, Democracy and Education. (New York: Macmillan Publishing Co., 1944)
[10]D. Kline and M. Hopper, "Child Abuse: An Integration of the Literature and Concept Analysis with Recommendations for Educational Research," final report, Contract No. OEC-0-74-9052, U.S. Office of Education, Department of Health, Education, and Welfare, Washington, D.C., 1975.
[11]The states are Alabama, Alaska, Arkansas, California, Colorado, Connecticut, Delaware, Florida, Georgia, Hawaii, Idaho, Massachusetts, Michigan, Minnesota, Mississippi, Missouri, Montana, Nebraska, New Mexico, New York, North Carolina, North Dakota, Ohio, Oregon, Pennsylvania, South Dakota, Virginia, Washington, West Virginia, Wisconsin, and Wyoming.
[12]Education Commission of the States, "Educational Policies and Practices Regarding Child Abuse and Neglect and Recommendations for Policy Development."
[13]Ibid. p.9.
[14]M. Bechold, "That Battered Child Could Be Dead Tomorrow," Instructor 79, no. 8 (1974): 20 "Principal Problem: The Child Molested at Home," Instructor 79 no. 9 (1974): 35.
[15]M. Paulsen, "Child Abuse Reporting Laws: The Shape of the Legislation," Columbia Law Review 67 (1967): 1-49.
[16]B. Fraser, "Momma Used to Whip Her," Compact 8 (1974): 17.
[17]Kline and Christianson, "Educa-

tional and Psychological Problems of Abused Children."

[18] S. Smith and R. Hanson, "134 Battered Children: A Medical and Psychological Study," British Medical Journal 3 (1974): 666-70.

[19] R. Oates and J. Kent, The Spectrum of Failure to Thrive and Child Abuse: A Follow-Up Study (London: Pergamon Press, 1976).

[20] O. McAffee and S. Nedier, "Education for Parenthood: A Primary Prevention Strategy for Child Abuse and Neglect," Report No. 93, Education Commission of the States, Denver, CO, 1976.

[21] Ibid.

CHAPTER 3

CORPORAL PUNISHMENT AND THE SCHOOL

The U.S. Supreme Court recently decided that "paddling" of pupils by teachers cannot be prohibited by invoking precedent based upon the cruel and unusual punishment clause of the Eighth Amendment to the Constitution. [1] In this case, a young teenage child was extensively beaten on the buttocks with a wooden paddle. The resulting damage required medical treatment from wounds that prevented the child from sitting for an extended period of time. Any parent who exerted similar force on a child would be liable for reporting under the child-abuse legislation.

New Jersey, which has the oldest state law against the use of corporal

punishment in the schools, currently
shares this status with only
Massachusetts, Maine, and Maryland.2

It would appear that there is a
belief in the United States that the use
of corporal punishment in the schools is
either not a problem or a problem of
such low priority that it is not worth
considering.3 There seems to be a
general belief that either corporal
punishment is little used or that when
applied it is usually minor and
preferred by most children to other
forms of punishment. A substantial
percentage probably feel it should be
used more often. This latter belief is
related to the results of recent Gallup
polls which indicate that most citizens
feel that disciplining is the major
problem in schools.4

The general definition of the term
corporal punishment indicates it to be
the infliction of pain or confinement of
the human body as a penalty for some
offense. 5 The legal definition is
similar. **Black's Law Dictionary** defines
corporal punishment as "physical
punishment as distinguished from
pecuniary punishment or a fine; any kind
of punishment of or inflicted on the
body, such as whipping or the pillory.
the term may or may not include
imprisonment according to the individual
case."6 Educationally, corporal punishment has been generally defined as: the
inflicting of pain by a teacher or other
educational official upon the body of a
student as a penalty for doing something
which has been disapproved of by the
punisher. 7 The infliction of pain is

not limited to striking a child with a paddle or the hand. Any excessive discomfort such as forced standing for long periods of time, confinement in uncomfortable space, or forcing children to eat obnoxious substances fits the description. The intent of corporal punishment laws which forbid its use is to offer certain limitations. Therefore, corporal punishment is not implied when (1) the teacher used force to protect himself or herself, the pupil, or others from physical injury; (2) to obtain possession of a weapon or other dangerous objects; or (3) to protect property from damage.[8]

Implicit in any legal definition of punishment in American democratic society is the constitutional right of "due process." Also implied, is that without "due process" a penalty cannot be administered.

There are two main areas in which the constitutionality of corporal punishment is argued.[9] One focus, that corporal punishment is cruel and unusual, is based on the Eighth Amendment to the constitution. This rests on a number of grounds, most importantly the concept that the application of physical punishment to children violates democratic freedom and the dignity of the individual. The other argument, based on the Fifth and Fourteenth Amendments to the Constitution, is that corporal punishment violates due process of law. This is divided between substantive due process and procedural due process. Under the substantive issue it is argued that

corporal punishment is often done in an
arbitrary and capricious manner and does
not bear a reasonable relationship to a
societal purpose. Under the procedural
issue it is argued that before being
punished one is entitled certain
procedural safeguards, such as notice of
charge, right to a fair hearing, etc.

Irwin Hyman, director of the
National Center for the Study of
Corporal, Punishment and Alternatives in
the School, states that

the official sanctioning of
corporal punishment in our schools
constitutes an atavistic vestige of
a deep-rooted and long-lasting
current of the acceptance of
violence that runs through the
history of our country. The issue
transcends all political orienta-
tions, is not directly related to
the concept of permissiveness, and
had international implications when
we are viewed by others. It also
reveals underlying attitudes
concerning the worth of children in
our society. There is a final
concern about officially sanctioned
corporal punishment which had
disturbing implications when one
considers it within the
psychological framework of hitting
as a way of controlling children's
behavior. For in this context, it
is considered by some (i.e., the
American Psychological Association's Task Force on the Rights of
Children and Youth) as a form of
child abuse.10

Hyman says that the practice of corporal punishment in the schools poses the following problems:

1. It perpetuates attitudes that schools are places where children are denied rights granted to them in all other institutional settings and which are granted adults.
2. It perpetuates the belief that "Might makes Right" and that violence is an acceptable method of solving problems.
3. It presents the ever present danger of physical trauma.
4. It perpetuates the concept of America as a non-child oriented society given the abolition of the practice in many European countries, all, Communist bloc countries and many so called primitive societies.
5. The humiliation, shame and anger engendered as a result of corporal punishment has many possible consequences including counter violence upon the schools and teachers. [11]

The development of laws pertaining to the education of children has historically been relegated to state and local legislators. Because of the doctrine of the division of powers, federal courts do not like to interfere with local educational issues. It has always been the responsibility of the state government to legislate for the schools, and therefore to legislate for the permissibility of corporal

79

punishment.[12]

It is a basic principle that unless denied that right by statute, a teacher has the authority to make pupils obey by means of inflicting corporal punishment. Along with the principal, a teacher stands "in loco parentis" to the pupil. Other school employees or officials do not. But a teacher may make and enforce rules that he believes to be necessary in order to control pupils and maintain the efficiency of the school. His right to punish corporally is more limited that that of the parent. A teacher can do some of the things to correct the child that the parent can do, including the use of physical punishment. The courts agree, though, that a teacher's method must be reasonable and that there must be no injury to the person of the child.

The use of corporal punishment, as a sanctioned method of controlling children's behavior in American Schools, poses one of today's most complex and controversial issues for those concerned with the influence of education upon the development of children. In a paper presented at the Conference on the Social.(Costs of Maltreatment of children, Hyman suggested a paradox between what we teach in our schools and how we teach it:

> Our schools supposedly reflect the Constitution and Bill of Rights, including the eighth and fourteenth amendments which guarantee relief from cruel and unusual punishment and insure due process. However,

the courts are continually hearing cases involving the school's denial of basic civil liberties to children. Our schools have never really grasped the concept of helping children to internalize controls through learning the use of freedom with responsibility. We teach democracy as content but we have failed to teach it as process even though some of our most notable educational and psychological theorist have urged this for many decades.[13]

There is a growing literature in educational research that offers alternatives to corporal punishment based on empiracal findings. Jacob Kounin has discovered common mistakes made by poor classroom managers.[14] Hyman had developed Kounin's work into a system for training teacher to be better managers in order to avoid the need for paddling.[15] Further research by Schultz and Hyman suggests certain personality and teacher concepts which affect teachers' management style as measured by Kounin's system.[16] Marino completed a doctoral dissertation in which teachers received training in recognizing their ineffective management techniques.[17] He was able to demonstrate improved management and thereby less need to rely on the "last resort."

Research on the democratic classroom has demonstrated that teachers using clearly defined techniques help children to internalize controls in the classroom setting.[18] By sharing a goal

81

setting and accepting freedom with responsibility the need for corporal punishment is eliminated.

Gil believes that:

A teacher who uses physical force against a child teaches that child and all the children in the classroom that physical force in an appropriate means for human interaction. Education has developed constructive approaches to motivate children to create challenging, learning milieu and to assure the necessary discipline in the classroom and needs no longer to regress to the destructive approach which is symbolized by corporal punishment.[19]

He also feels that Congress ought to outlaw all forms of physical force used against children in the public domain, in schools, and in child-care facilities under the guise of disciplining them.

This form of discipline undermines the human dignity of children. It is nothing but an ancient, cruel ritual which never serves the real educational and developmental needs of children, but merely provides ventilation for the frustration of adults. Being exposed t corporal punishment teaches children that might is right. It results in resentment and fear of their attackers. At best it achieves short-range, externally enforced,

discipline based on fear, but not
steady, long-term, internalized
discipline based on positive
identification with caring adults.
One important by-product of
outlawing the use of physical force
in schools and institutions would
be an unambiguous signal to all
parents and educators that it is
the sense of Congress that
educators and parents should use
more constructive measures to bring
up and discipline children than
inflicting physical pain and
indignities upon them. Such a
message from Congress could
indicate a re-thinking of the
entire child rearing context in the
country. Without such re-thinking
and without an eventual
redefinition of the status and the
rights of children, child abuse can
simply not be prevented.20

In summary, it should be noted that
the doctrine of in loco parentis, long
an integral part of educational
practice, may no longer be viable.
Directly counter to in loco parentis is
te concept of due process of law for
students. There have been court
decisions establishing such civil
liberties for students as first amendment rights, freedom from unreasonable
search and seizure, the rights of
students to examine their records, equal
treatment for handicapped students, and
freedom from discrimination on the basis
of race or sex.21 In regard to student
right, the school administrator's

83

position is not an enviable one. The ambiguity surrounding the student right controversy makes hard and fast answers difficult to come by. This controversy will continue to plague the schools as long as the conflict in the society at large remains unresolved.

[1]Ingraham v. Wright, 430 U.S., 651 (1977).

[2]R. Friedman and I. Hyman, "An Analysis of State Legislation Regarding Corporal Punishment," paper presented at the Conference on Child Abuse, Children's Hospital National Center, Washington, D.C., 1977.

[3]I. Hyman, E. McDowell, and B. Raines, "Corporal Punishment and Alternatives in the Schools," paper presented at the Conference on Child Abuse, Washington, D.C., 1977.

4G. Gallup, "Eighth Annual Gallup Poll of the Public Attitudes Toward the Public Schools," **Phi Delta Kappa,** 1976, pp. 187-200.

5C. Barnhart, **American College Dictionary.** (New York: Random House, 1963.)

6H. Black, **Black's Law Dictionary,** 4th ed. (Minnesota: West Publishing Co., 1968).

7D. Wineman, "Policy Statement," Metropolitan Detroit Branch of the American Civil Liberties Union, 1967.

8National Education Association, **Report on the Task Force on Corporal Punishment** (Washington, D.C.: Library of Congress #22-85743, 1972).

9A. Reitman and J. Follman, "Corporal Punishment in the Schools: The

84

Use of Force in Controlling Student Behavior," American Civil Liberties Union, 1972.

[10]I. Hyman, "The Social Costs of the Maltreatment of Children," paper presented at the Conference of the Social Costs of Maltreatment of Children, Rutgers Medical School, March 25, 1977.

[11]Ibid.

[12]A detailed graphical analysis of state legislation regarding corporal punishment is presented in the Appendix.

[13]Hyman, "The Social Costs of the Maltreatment of Children."

[14]M. Schultz and I. Hyman, "Consistency of Classroom Climate of High School Teachers for Different Ability Groups," paper presented at the annual meeting of the New Jersey Education Association, 1971.

[15]I. Hyman, "Consultation in Classroom Management Based on Empirical Research," paper presented at the meeting of the American Psychological Association, Honolulu, 1972.

[16]Schultz and Hyman, "Consistency of Classroom Climate of High School Teachers for Different Ability Groups."

[17]M. Marino, "The Effectiveness of Teacher Centered Versus Case Centered Consultation in the Reduction of Classroom Management Errors and Negative Classroom Behaviors of Students" (Doctoral dissertation, Temple University, 1975).

[18]I. Hyman, "Some Effects of Teaching Style on Pupil Behavior" (Doctoral dissertation, Rutgers University, 1964).

[19]D. Gil, "Unraveling Child Abuse,"
American Journal ̄**of** **Orthopsychiatry,**
April 1975.
[20]Ibid.
[21]Kent v. U.S. 383 U.S. 451 (1966);
In re Gault, 387 U.S. 1 (1967); Madera
v. Board of Education, 386 F. 2d 778 (2d
cir. 1967); Tinker v. Des Moines School
District, 393 U.S. 503 (1969).

CHAPTER 4

SUMMARY AND CONCLUSIONS

Child abuse and neglect is characterized by a number of abusive or neglectful incidents over a period of time that becomes collectively more severe the longer the abusive or neglectful behaviors continue. It becomes readily apparent, therefore, that the school's resources ought to be used to identify and report any suspected case of abuse or neglect or any apparent inflicted injury to a child. Identification and reporting should be done at the earlist possible moment, not only to protect the child from further injury but also to avoid academic and personality deficits which may coexist with abuse and neglect.

The fact that we are witnessing a dramatic change in interest in the problem of child abuse and in the expansion of funding efforts and programs in this area does not necessarily represent a significant change in fundamental child-rearing value by either the family or society at large. Much of what has happened within our society has been a decrease in the responsibility of the parents for the children and of the family for itself. This change came from no single source, but rather as a consequence of a rapid social and cultural change that has taken place and the particular directions that have been set. To continue in this direction and to eliminate and prevent child abuse and neglect will require even more far-reaching changes in the family structure and the freedom of activity of the individual. For sometime now, there have been legal sanctions, community groups efforts, periodic expressions of professional concern, and broad social disapproval regarding the physical abuse of children. These various forces have now coalesced into a more integrated and potent movement to reduce the incidence and effects of child abuse. Given the past course of historical change in child-rearing methods, it seems reasonable to infer that the path of future change will be in the direction of a more compassionate caring for children.

This writer takes the position that child abuse and neglect is a problem for everyone, and therefore its alleviation also should concern everyone. There is a need for multiple intervention from medicine, the legal profession, education, social work, psychiatry, and the community.

States have a right to intervene into families' lives when there is a combination of life-threatening conditions and a child-rearing alternative offered by the state that is preferable to the child's present living condition.

There are two other levels of child abuse that are clearly more questionable and require careful judgment before intervention is coersively made. In fact, one could question the "right" of the state to intervene under these conditions.

The second level of child abuse concerns families with a combination of personal limitations and stressful events that shape their ability to take more initiative and to gain better control over their lives. This adaptive stress style can result in child abuse and requires intervention in order to change the network of family relations to provide better child-rearing practices. Typically, there are strengths within families under these conditions that surpass, in quality, alternatives offered by the state. It is a balanced judgment as to the appropriate mix between intervention and family integrity. The right to intervene coersively in these families is questionable and therefore depends on the interface between services and families' prerogatives and desires.

The third level of conditions that can result in child abuse involves culturally discrimination against children, regardless of race, income, or other factors. The rights of children to enhance their lives and insure protection is jeopardized by the very status they have within society. This can result in children abused, not only in their primary living setting, but also by institutions and policies that affect children's lives. Intervention at this level clearly requires the cooperation of families and institutions to bring a better quality of life.

As was mentioned earlier, the school has become more than a vehicle for cognitive improvement and development. The main business of the family and the school is to influence directly the formation and growth of attitudes and dispositions, emotional, intellectual, and moral. In order for this educative process to occur, however, parents and professionals must recognize and acknowledge the importance of their role as protectors of children. Given this perspective they demonstrate that they value the dignity of children.

Although legislation has been in effect for more than a decade, parents and professionals should be ombudsmen for children not because the law said so, but because it is right. The wide array of integrated services needed to initiate protective systems for abused, neglected, battered, injured, and molested individuals requires many disciplines, organizations, agencies, and professional people communicating and working together.

CHAPTER 5

DISCUSSION

Seen from only one perspective at a time, the picture of child abuse and neglect seems relatively simple to understand. The physician, for example, may perceive it as medical problems to be diagnosed and treated; the policeman, as criminal conduct to be punished. The psychiatrist may view the problem as one of parents in need of treatment, while the social worker may see it as children in need of protection.

Seen as a whole, child abuse appears as a tangled web of myths, half-understood relationships, contradictory approaches to management, suspicion, and unknowns. Fragmented perceptions and the divergent results they produce add to the inherent complexity of any attempt to define or deal with the problem.

Perceptions of what constitutes child abuse have differed with time and culture. Practices that we now consider abusive have been accepted in the past as the normal exercise of parental rights, as economic necessity, or as appropriate disciplinary measures.

Child abuse should not be considered only as a psychiatric disorder in the usual sense of the term. More accurately, it is a problem of deviant parenting behavior, a distorted and disordered pattern of child rearing. The origin, development, and expression of abusive and neglectful behavior have been described in this dissertation.

Psychological characteristics of the parents (immaturity, sense of personal incompetence, difficulty in experiencing pleasure, social isolation, misperceptions of the child) and the belief in the value of punishment have been discussed in terms of their impact on the problem of child abuse.

The motivations and forces which drive people to abuse their children vary greatly. In may cases, problems which the adults find difficult to cope with, marital difficulties, ill health, financial problems, or others -- frustrate them to the point where they lash out at their children without really wanting to do so. In a significant number of cases abusing parents were abused as children, establishing in their minds the idea that abuse is an acceptable way of relating to children.

Whatever their motivations or backgrounds, one fact about abusers stands out: the vast majority of abusing parents need help to become better parents, not prosecution or condemnation. They do not necessarily want to hurt their children; but they need help to break away from abusive behavior.

This dissertation examines the many problems that make the abuse and neglect of children so difficult to comprehend, including the problems of definition and incidence.

The problem of child abuse has often been compared to an iceberg: reported cases account for the visible tip, but estimates suggest a problem of staggering proportions yet to be revealed.

Estimates of actual incidence vary; in fact, most are inconsistent. But all suggest a far more massive problem that than which is reported. At least part of the reason for underreporting is that it is difficult to accept the fact that parents can non-accidentally mistreat their children. Child abuse violates the images of an ever-patient, always caring parent. Attempts to rationalize the problem of child abuse have surrounded it with myths, i.e., abuse and neglect are problems of the poor; abusive parents simply misjudge their own strength, the parents are psychotic.

Review of the available literature indicates complex patterns of child abuse. Children are abused and neglected in families from all socioeconomic levels, races, nationalities, and religious groups. The problem is not limited to racial minorities nor to the poor.

These facts, however, do not deny the profound effects of social and economic deprivation, housing problems, unemployment, and racial pressures on the lies and behaviors of parents who abuse their children.

No one would argue that child abuse is not a difficult and sensitive area for educators. it is. A teacher, principal, or other school worker bay be hesitant to act in any but the most flagrant cases of child abuse. Consequently, educators may view reporting with mistrust; they may hesitate to become involved. Knowledge about the often perplexing problem of child abuse and about the educator's responsibility to identify it can help dispel that mistrust and hesitation.

Most state laws mandate educators to report suspected child abuse. The laws recognize educators as trained professionals, caring people, and the largest single group that sees most of America's children regularly. Educators are frequently the first and sometimes the last line of defense for an abused child and his family. These laws are relatively new, however, and have caught many educators unprepared. This dissertation provides comprehensive, fundamental information that will help teachers better understand and deal with abuse and meet their new legal responsibilities.

Children are probably the single

most socially impotent group in this country today. Totally aside from their legal status and economic dependence on their parents, they may lack both the capacity to conceptualize and the ability to articulate their needs and concerns.

This social impotence tends to delay recognition not only of general, but also specific, problems. the latter is further compounded by our long-held respect for the integrity and sanctity of the family and for the privacy of its interrelationships.

Child abuse offers clear testament to both aspects of problem recognition regarding children, and it is likely to raise a serious value conflict in our efforts to eliminate it.

Against the traditional value of our reluctance to intervene directly into family life is emerging a sense of societal interest we all have in the growth and development of a national (i.e., federal) responsibility.

One may have serious misgivings about ever being about to formulate a national consensus that one or the other must take precedence, yet some intervention is necessary where abuse or neglect of a child occurs.

One may question whether it is appropriate for the school to intervene in the family even though there are mandatory reporting statutes. The right of parents to raise their children in a manner consistent with their attitudes, values, and beliefs has rarely been questioned in this country. While the majority of this nation's population will agree that all children should be protected against abusive treatment, the school's role as "watchdog" can become an emotional arena of debate. Therefore, it is very important that the school's role as a major resource for helping abused children and their families be viewed in the broader context that follows: That a social resource, education is second only to the family in its potential for sustained and thorough involvement in all children's lives; that because of the scope and complexity of the problem of child abuse, no single profession or discipline can effectively work alone; that education has an essential part in any multidisciplinary program to help abused children and their families.

The School is in a position to help deal with the problems of child abuse in ways no other resource or institution can.1 Perhaps most important, the schools are generally not viewed as punitive. School personnel can deal with many precrisis situations without threat or stigma to the parents and can advocate a nonpunitive and nonadversary relationship between families and service agencies.

The areas of education's greatest potential to help deal with the problem of child abuse are identification, precrisis intervention, and primary prevention.

Little progress seems to have been made in preventing the problem of child abuse and neglect. It is time that serious consideration be given to a possible way to enhance the quality of life for adults and children in families -- and to prevent child abuse and neglect. Many approaches have been used to help the abusing adults and abused children. These approaches include removal of the child from the home, provision of necessary social and psychological services, "parents anonymous," group and individual psychotherapy, and others. This writer recommends parent education as a strategey to prevent child abuse from occurring.[2]

This has important implications for education. Approaches can be developed to change knowledge, attitudes, and behaviors related to both specific and general factors of child abuse. An example of a specific factor would be unrealistic expectations of young children's behavior or lack of knowledge of discipline techniques other than physical punishment. General factors would involve such things as improving the quality of family life, coping mechanisms, and an understanding of interpersonal relations.[3]

Parent education can also be made available at a number of different points in human development -- to adolescents in and out of school, to pregnant women and their families, to foster and adoptive parents before placing children in their care, and to parents at critical points in the child's and the family's ongoing development.

Goals and objectives of a parent education program must clearly address techniques for strengthening the family.

Educational content must be determined
by professionals and by voluntary
representatives of the parents
themselves.

Implementing parent education
programs as a strategy for prevention of
child abuse will be difficult and
require long-range commitment, but the
effort has promise of equally long-range
social benefits.

---

[1]See Chapter II, "The Role of the
School and the Educator in Child Abuse
and Neglect."

[2]See Chapter II, "The Role of the
School and the Educator in Child Abuse
and Neglect: Primary Prevention."

3Ibid.

BIBLIOGRAPHY

Aries, P.
    Centries of Childhood. New York:
    Vintage Books, 1962.

Baken, D.
    Slaughter of the Innocents: A Study
    of the Battered Child Phenomenon.
    Boston: Beacon Press, 1972.

Barnhart, C.
    American College Dictionary. New
    York: Random House, 1963.

Bechold, M.
    "That Battered Child Could Be Dead
    Tomorrow." Instructor, 79, no. 8
    (1974): 20.

Black, H.

Black's Law Dictionary. 4th ed.
Minnesota: West Publishing Co.,
1968.

Brenton, M.
"Trouble Teachers Whose Behavior
Disturbs Our Kids." Today's
Health, 17 (1971).

"What Can Be Cone About Child
Abuse?" Today's Education, 66, no.
3, (1977): 51-53.

Broadhurst, D.
"More About Project Protection."
Childhood Education, 52, no. 2
(1975): 67-69.

"Policy Making: First Step for
School in the Fight Against Child
Abuse and Neglect." Elementary
School Guidance and Counsel, 10,
no. 3 (1976): 222-226.

"Policy Protection: A School
Program to Detect and Prevent Child
Abuse and Neglect." Children Today,
1975, pp. 22-25.

Bronfenbrenner, U.
Is Early Intervention Effective?
Washington D.C.: Office of Child
Development, 1966.

Caffey, J.
"Multiple Fractures in the Long
Bones of Infants Suffering from
Chronic Subdural, Hematoma." Ameri-
can Journal of Roentgenology, 56
(1946): 163-67.

Colucci, N.
"The Schools and the Problem of
Child Abuse and Neglect." Contemporary Education, 48, no.2 (1977):
98-100.

Commonwealth of Pennsylvania, Act 91,
August 14, 1967.

DeMause, L.
"Our Forebearers Made Childhood a
Nightmare." Psychology Today,
1975, pp. 85-88.

Dewey, J.
Democracy and Education. New York:
MacMillian Publishing Co., 1944.

Education Commission of the States
"Child Abuse and Neglect in the
States: A Digest of Critical
Elements of Reporting and Central
Registries."   Report No. 83,
Denver, Colorado, March 1976.

Child Abuse and Neglect Project.
"Educational Policies and Practices
Regarding Child Abuse and Neglect
and Recommendations for Policy
Development."   Report No. 85,
Denver, Colorado, April 1976.

Child Abuse and Neglect: The
Problem andIts Management. Vol. 1
Publ.   No.   (OHD)   75-20073.
Washington, D.C.: U.S. Department
of Health, Education, and Welfare,
1976.

101

"Teacher Education: An Active Participant in Solving the Problem of Child Abuse and Neglect." Report No. 99, Denver, Colorado, April 1977.

Elmer, E. "Abused Young Children Seen in Hospitals." Social Case Work. 4, (1960): 98-102.

"Emotional Neglect in Connecticut." Connecticut Law Review, 5 (1969): 100ff.

Ferro, F. "Combatting Child Abuse and Neglect." Children Today, 4 (1975).

Feshbach, N. "Punishment: Parents Rites vs. Children's Rights." Paper presented at the annual meeting of the American Psychological Association, September 1975.

Fontana, V. Somewhere a Child Is Crying: Maltreatment, Causes and Prevention. New York: MacMillian Publishing Co., 1973.

The Maltreated Child: The Maltreatment Syndrome in Children. 2nd ed. Springfield, IL: Charles C. Thomas Publisher, 1971.

Fraser, B. "Momma Used to Whip Her." Compact,

8 (1974): 17.

Friedman, D.
"Corporal, Punishment in the Schools: Discipline or Abuse?" Paper presented at the annual meeting of the American Psychological, Association, September 1976.

Friedman, R., and Hyman, I
"An Analysis of State Legislation Regarding Corporal Punishment." Paper presented at the Conference on child Abuse, Children's Hospital National, Center, Washington, D.C., 1977.

Gallup, G.
"Eighth Annual Gallup Poll on the Public Attitudes Toward the Public Schools." Phi Delta Kappa, 1976, pp. 187-200.

Garbarino, G.
Helping the Battered Child and His Family. Illinois: University of Chicago Press, 1968.

Gatti, D.
The Teacher and the Law. New York: Parker Publishing Co., 1972.

Gelles, R.
"The Social, Construction of Child Abuse." American Journal of Orthopsychiatry, 45, no. 3 (1975).

Gil, D.
Testimony of Gil. Hearings of the U.S. Senate Subcommittee on

Children and Young. "Child Abuse
Prevention Act." 8. 1191, 93rd
Congress, 1st session, March 1973.

"Unraveling Child Abuse." American
Journal of Orthopsychiatry, April
1975.

Violence Against Children.
Cambridge, MA: Harvard University
Press, 1970.

"Violence Against Children."
Journal of Marriage and the Family,
33 (1971): 637-48.

"What Can Schools Do About Child
Abuse?" American Education, 5, no.
4 (1969): 2-5.

Glick, H.
"The New York State Child
Protective Service Act: Its Impact
on School Systems and Children's
Education." Paper presented at the
annual International Convention,
the Council for Exceptional
Children, April 1977.

Gross, G., and Gross, R.
The Children's Rights Movement. New
York: Anchor/Doubleday, 1977.

Gsuerke, W.
Legal and Ethical Responsibilities
of School Personnel. Englewood
Cliffs, NJ: Prentice-Hall, 1959.

Gueringer, G.
"What About the Psychologically

Abused Children?" Journal of the
International Association of Pupil
Personnel, 20, no. 2 (1976): 95-97.

Harvard Educational Review. The Rights
of Children. Reprint Series No. 9.
Massachusetts: Harvard Educational
Review, 1974.

Heath, L.
The New Teacher. New York: Harper
and Row, 1973.

Helfer, R.
The Diagnostic Process and
Treatment Programs. Publ. No. (OHD)
75-79. Washington, D.C.: U.S.
Department of Health, Education and
Welfare, 1974.

"The Etiology of Child Abuse."
Pediatric Symposium on Child Abuse,
51, no. 2 (1973): 777-79.

Helfer, R., and Kemp, C. H., eds.
The Battered Child. Illinois:
University of Chicago Press, 1974.

Hyman, I.
"Consultation in Classroom Management Based on Empirical Research."
Paper presented at the meeting of
the American Psychological Association, Honolulu, 1972.

"Some Effects of Teaching Style on
Pupil Behavior." Doctoral dissertation, Rutgers University, 1964.

"The Social Costs of the

Maltreatment of Children.2 Paper presented at the Conference of the Social Costs of Maltreatment of Children, Rutgers Medical School, March 25, 1977.

Hyman, I., McDowell, E., and Raines, B. "Corporal Punishment and Alternatives in the Schools." Paper presented at the Conference on Child Abuse, Washington, D.C., 1977.

Ingraham v. Wright
430 (U.S.), 651 (1977).

Irving, S., ed.
Advances in Pediatrics. Illinois: Chicago Year Book Medical Publishers, 1974.

Kempe, Ch. H.
"Child Abuse: The Pediatrician's Role in Child Advocacy and Preventative Pediatrics." American Journal of Diseases of Children, 132 (1978): 105-260.

Kempe, C. H., and Helfer, R., eds.
Helping the Battered Child and His Family. Philadelphia: J. B. Lippincott, 1972.

Kempe, C. H., and Silverman, F.
"The Battered Child Syndrome." Journal of the American Medical Association, 181 (1962): 17-24.

Kline, D., and christianson, J.
"Educational and Psychological

Problems of Abused children."
Final report, Contract No., GOO-75-
00352, Utah State University,
Logan, 1975.

Kline, D., and Hopper, M.
"Child Abuse: An Integration of the
Literature and Concept Analysis
with Recommendations for for
Educatonal. Research." Final
report, Contract No. OEC-0-74-9052,
U.S. Office of Education,
Department of Health, Education,
and Welfare, Washington, D.C.,
1975.

Kristal, H.
The role of the Schools in Child
Abuse and Neglect. Washington,
D.C.: National Institute of
Education, Department of Health,
Education, and Welfare, 1977.

Lasch, C.
The Culture of Narcissism. New
York: W.W. Norton & Co., 1978.

Legsack, J.
Highlights of 1974 National Data.
Denver, Colorado: National
Clearinghouse on Child Abuse and
Neglect, Children's Division,
American Humane Association, 1976.

Levine, A., and Cary, E.
The Rights of Students: An A.C.L.U.
Handbook. New York: Dell Publishing
Co., 1977.

Light, R.

"Abused and Neglected Children in America." Harvard Educational Review, 43 (1973): 556-98

Marino, M.
"The Effectiveness of Teacher Centered Versus Case Centered Consultation in the Reduction of Classroom Management Errors and Negative Classroom Behaviors of Students." Doctoral dissertation, Temple University, 1975.

Martin, D.
"The Growing Horror of Child Abuse and the Undeniable Role of the School in Putting and End to It." American School Board Journal, 160, no. 11 (1973): 51-55.

McAffee, O., and Nedier, S.
"Education for Parenthood: A Primary Prevention Strategy for Child Abuse and Neglect." Report No. 93, Education Commission of the States, Denver, CO, 1976.

McRae, K., et al.
"The Battered Child Syndrome." Canadian Medical Association Journal, 108 (1973): 859-66.

Medinnus, G., ed.
Readings in the Psychology of Parent-Child Relations. New York: Wiley, 1967.

Melnick, B., And Jurley, J.
"Distinctive Personality Attributes of Child-Abusing Mothers." Journal

of Consulting and Clinical Psychology, 33 (1969)- 746-49.

Morgan, S.
"The Battered Child in the Classroom." Journal of Pediatric Psychology, 1, no. 2 (1976): 83-87.

Morse, C., et al.
"A Three Year Follow-Up Study of Abused and Neglected Children." American Journal of Diseases of Children, 120 (1970): 439-46.

Murdock, C.
"The Abused Child and the School System." American and Public Health, 1970, pp. 106-9.

National Education Association
Report on the Task Force on Corporal Punishment. Washington, D.C.: Library of Congress #22-85743, 1972.

Oates, R., and Kent, J.
The Spectrum of Failure to Thrive and Child Abuse: A Follow-Up Study. London: Pergamon Press, 1976.

Paulsen, M.
"Child Abuse Reporting Laws: The Shape of the Legislation." Columbia Law Review, 67 (1967): 1-49.

Pennsylvania Bulletin.
Vol. 6, no. 15, Title 55. Harrisburg: Public Welfare, 1976.

Pensylvania Department of Public
Welfare. "The Challenge," Vol. 19,
no.2 May-June 1976.

Pensylvania School Law. Section 1402,
Health Services, 1976.

"Principal Problem: The Child Molested
at Home." Instructor, 79, no. 9
(1974): 35.

Proceedings of the first National
Conference on Child Abuse and
Neglect. Publ. No. (OHD) 77030094.
Washington, D.C.: Department of
Health, Education, and Welfare,
1976.

Reitman, A., and Follman, J.
"Corporal Punishment in the
Schools: The Use of Force in
Controlling Student Behavior,"
American Civil Liberties Union.
1972.

Richards, L.
"Can the Schools Help Prevent Child
Abuse?" Illinois Teacher, 17, no. 1
(1973): 43-52.

Richette, L.
The Throwaway Children. New York:
Dell Publishing, 1973.

Riscalla, L.
"The Profession's Role and
Perspective on Child Abuse." Paper
presented at the annual meeting of
the American Psychological Association, September 1975.

Rubin, D.
The Rights of Teachers: An American
Civil Liberties Union Handbook. New
York: Avon Books, 1977.

Rubin, E., Simpson, C., and Betroen, M.
Emotionally Handicapped Children in
the Elementary School. Detroit:
Wayne State University Press, 1966.

Saunders, L.
"Child Abuse: Detection and Prevention." Young Children, 30, no.
5 (1975): 332-38.

Schmitt, B.
"What Teachers Need to Know About
Child Abuse and Neglect." Childhood Education, 42, no. 2 (1975):
58-62.

Schultz, M., and Hyman, I.
"Consistency of Classroom Climate
of High School Teachers for
Different Ability Groups." Paper
presented at the annual meeting of
the New Jersey Education
Association, 1971.

Sgroi, S.
"Sexual Molestation of Children:
The Last Frontier in Child Abuse."
Children Today, 4 (1975): 18-24.

Shanas, B.
"Child Abuse: A Killer Teachers Can
Help Control." Phi Delta Kappa, 61
(1975): 479-82.

Silverman, F.
"The Roentgen Manifestations of Unrecognized Skeletal Trauma in Infants." American Journal of Roentgenology, 69 (1953): 413-27.

Smith, S., and Hanson, R.
"134 Battered Children: A Medical and Psychological Study." British Medical Journal, 3 (1974): 666-70.

Solomon, T.
"History and Demography of Child Abuse." Pediatrics, 51, no. 2 (1973): 773-76.

Spinetta, J., and Rigler, D.
"The Child Abusing Parent: A Psychological Review." Psychological Bulletin, 77, no. 4 (1972): 296-304.

Steinmertz, S., and Strauss, M., eds.
Violence in the Family. New York: Dodd, Mead & Co., 1973.

Sussman, A.
The Rights of Young People: An American Civil Liberties Union Handbook. New York: Avon Books, 1977.

Thomas, M.
"Children Alone, What Can Be Done About Abuse and Neglect?" Bureau of Education for the Handicapped, Department of Health, Education, and Welfare, Washington, D.C., 1977.

U.S. Congress
An Act to Provide Financial
Assistance for a Demonstration
Program for the Prevention, Identi-
fication, and Treatment of Child
Abuse and Neglect to Establish A
National Center on Child Abuse and
Neglect. Pub. L. 93-247, 93rd
Cong., S. 1191, January 31, 1974.

Wald, M.
"State Intervention on Behalf of
Neglected Children." Stanford Law
Review, 28 (1976): 625-706.

Wall, C.
"Child Abuse: A Societal, Problem
with Educational Implications."
Peabody Journal of Education, 52,
no. 3 (1975): 222-25.

Webster's Seventh new Collegiate
Dictionary. Springfield, MA: G.&C.
Merriam Co., 1963.

Welsh, R.
"Violence, Permissiveness and the
Overpunished Child." Journal of
Pediatric Psychology, I, no. 2
(1976): 68-71.

Wilkerson, A.
The Rights of Children: Emergent
Concepts in Law and Society.
Philadelphia: Temple University
Press, 1974.

Wineman, D.
"Policy Statement," Metropolitan
Detroit Branch of the American

Civil Liberties Union, 1967.

Woolley, P., and Evans, W.
"Significance of Skeletal Lesions in Infants Resembling Those of Traumatic Origin." Journal of American Medical Association, 158 (1955): 539-43.

Young, L.
Wednesday's Children: A Study of Child Neglect and Abuse. New York: McGraw-Hill Book Co., 1964.

APPENDIX

CONTENT ANALYSIS OF STATE LEGISLATION

REGARDING CORPORAL PUNISHMENT

115

	AL*	AK	AZ	AR*	CA	CO	CT*	DE	FL	GA	HI*	ID*	IL	IN	IA*	KS	KY*	LA*	Category	Group
	×	×		×		×	×		×	×	×	×	×	×			×	×	permitted	LEGALITY if possible
			×		×										×	×			silent	
																			not permitted	
	×		×	×					×	×	×						×	×	administrator	WHO MAY INFLICT
	×	×		×		×	×		×	×	×						×	×	teacher	
									×	×	×								other certified employee	
																			noncertified employee	
									×										need approval of principal	RESTRICTIONS
					×				×	×			×						in the presence of another person	
																			without undo anger	
							×				×	×		×					reasonable	
																			not deadly force	
										×									approval from parents	
									×										provide parents with explanation	
																			not in head or face	
																			not in the presence of other students	
										×									restraint	JUSTIFICATIONS
										×	×								correction	
									×	×	×	×							to maintain discipline	
										×									promote welfare of child	
																			to quell misbehavior	
							×												to increase obedience	

116

Table — Legality, who may inflict, restrictions, and justifications of corporal punishment by state.

STATE	permitted	silent	not permitted	administrator	teacher	other certified employee	noncertified employee	need approval of principal	in the presence of another person	without undo anger	reasonable	not deadly force	approval from parents	provide parents with explanation	not in head or face	not in the presence of other students	restraint	correction	to maintain discipline	promote welfare of child	to quell misbehavior	to increase obedience
	LEGALITY if possible			WHO MAY INFLICT				RESTRICTIONS									JUSTIFICATIONS					
Maine	×			×	×						×								×	×		
Maryland	×			×	×						×								×			
Massachusetts	×			×	×						×											
Michigan	×			×	×												×	×	×	×		
Minnesota	×				×														×			
Mississippi*	×			×	×														×			
Missouri		×			×																	
Montana	×			×	×	×						×				×	×					
Nebraska*	×				×	×	×	×	×													
Nevada		×			×						×											
New Hampshire	×			×	×	×			×	×			×				×	×	×			
New Jersey	×				×								×									
New Mexico	×			×	×												×	×				
New York			×																×			
North Carolina*			×																			
North Dakota			×																			
Ohio																						
Oklahoma																						
Oregon																						

STATE	LEGALITY if possible			WHO MAY INFLICT				RESTRICTIONS									JUSTIFICATIONS					
	permitted	silent	not permitted	administrator	teacher	other certified employee	noncertified employee	need approval of principal	in the presence of another person	without undo anger	reasonable	not deadly force	approval from parents	provide parents with explanation	not in head or face	not in the presence of other students	restraint	correction	to maintain discipline	promote welfare of child	to quell misbehavior	to increase obedience
Pennsylvania*	X			X	X																	
Rhode Island		X																				
South Carolina	X			X	X						X								X			X
South Dakota		X															X					
Tennessee	X			X	X																	
Texas		X																	X			
Utah	X			X	X	X	X				X								X			
Vermont		X																				
Virginia*	X			X	X																	
Washington*	X			X	X																	
West Virginia	X			X	X																	
Wisconsin	X			X	X																	
Wyoming		X																				

*New Jersey Department of Education (unpublished survey, Rulings on Corporal Punishment in the United States, by State, 1976).

118